On the Highest Hill

Northwest Reprints

Northwest Reprints
Series Editor: Robert J. Frank

Other titles in the series:

On the Highest Hill

Roderick Haig-Brown

Introduction by Laurie Ricou

Oregon State University Press
Corvallis, Oregon

The paper in this book meets the guidelines for
permanence and durability of the Committee on
Production Guidelines for Book Longevity of the
Council on Library Resources and the minimum
requirements of the American National Standard for
Permanence of Paper for Printed Library
Materials Z39.48-1984.

Library of Congress Cataloging-in-Publication Data

Haig-Brown, Roderick Langmere, 1908-1976.
 On the highest hill / Roderick Haig-Brown : introduction by Laurence Ricou.
  p. cm. — (Northwest reprints)
 ISBN 0-87071-518-6 (cloth : alk. paper) — ISBN 0-
87071-519-4 (paper : alk. paper)
 1. Men—British Columbia—Vancouver Island—
Psychology—Fiction. 2. Mountain life—British Columbia—Vancouver Island—Fiction. 3. Loggers—British
Columbia—Vancouver Island—Fiction. I. Title. II. Series.
 PR9199.3.H2905 1994
 813'.52—dc20   94-29728
                                              CIP

PREFACE

People new to a region are especially interested in what things might set them apart from others. In works by Northwest writers, we get to know about the place where we live, about each other, about our history and culture, and about our flora and fauna. And with time, some things about ourselves start to come into focus out of the shadows of our history.

To give readers an opportunity to look into the place where Northwesterners live, the Oregon State University Press is making available again many books that are out of print. The Northwest Reprints Series will reissue a range of books, both fiction and nonfiction. Books will be selected for different reasons: some for their literary merit, some for their historical significance, some for provocative concerns, and some for these and other reasons together. Foremost, however, will be the book's potential to interest a range of readers who are curious about the region's voice and complexion. The Northwest Reprints Series will make works of well-known and lesser-known writers available for all.

RJF

Biographical Notes

Roderick Haig-Brown was born in Sussex in 1908. At age 18, he came to North America, where he worked in logging camps, first near Mount Vernon, Washington, and later on Vancouver Island. After a year in England, he returned to Canada in 1931. In 1934, he married Ann Elmore of Seattle, and they settled in a house on the bank of the Campbell River, which they called Above Tide. There he followed his productive and distinguished career as a judge, a conservationist, and especially as a writer, until his death in 1976. Glen Love, in his "Introduction" to the reprint of *Timber*, also in this series, provides considerable biographical information. Fuller details can be found in the studies of Anthony Robertson and E. Bennett Metcalfe.

Introduction

Things mean something. Places mean something.
It is people that are hard to understand. (205)

On the Highest Hill is a novel that reaches for the meaning of places—especially of the forests, the mountains and wilderness valleys of Vancouver Island—and then veers toward a tract on environmental politics. It is a novel that celebrates the meaning of things—especially (and somewhat ironically) of the hand-ax, and of the artifacts of the logging industry. But its people are more than a little difficult to understand. In the early stages of its writing, Roderick Haig-Brown (1908-1976) thought of *On the Highest Hill* as his "Wild Man novel."[1] As the Wild Man, Colin Ensley, should be more attuned to the violent forces of the mountains than to the satisfaction of logs hand-"hewn or adzed to smoothness" (227). Is he wild man or craftsman? The reader's puzzlement no doubt mirrors Colin's own "failure to understand the incoherence of the forces against him."[2] Yet in Colin's own incoherent differentness lies the central mystery of the novel—and a primary reason to read it again.

Colin's love of the wild dictates that he can never settle for the writer's life which his adolescent passion for words had promised. Haig-Brown's own passion for the wild speaks especially through the natural histories upon which his reputation as a writer ultimately rests. The reception of *On the Highest Hill* seems to have prompted his decision that the meaning of things and places is best expressed in the meditative essay, and that the novel, which depends upon an understanding of people in a story line, was not his strongest form. After writing it, and *Timber* (1942), his other adult novel, Haig-Brown opted for a more direct and sustained address to the colors of rivers and the sacredness of salmon in such works as his cycle of fishing books: *Fisherman's Spring* (1951), *Fisherman's Winter* (1954), *Fisherman's Summer* (1959) and *Fisherman's Fall* (1964). In the family of Haig-Brown's most loyal readers, there is no clear line between religion and fly fishing.

* * *

In Haig-Brown's correspondence with his publisher William Morrow and Company, the first reference to *On the Highest Hill* appears in May 1947. The novel was evidently written quickly—it is complete by November 1948—yet with a good measure of the attentiveness promised by the opening scene in which children try to "feel" their place through writing. Morrow's editor Thayer Hobson enthused that he and copy editor Frances Phillips "like Colin; we like all your characters; the family, and how extraordinarily well you do that country."[3] But his reaction to Haig-Brown's outline of the novel, sent a few months earlier, more accurately anticipates how reviewers and readers would respond:

> *If I didn't know you . . ., I think that I would be rather appalled by the bleak, unrelieved, defeatist atmo-sphere of your outline . . . . [T]here doesn't seem to be any high tragedy because high tragedy implies a real fight, and this seems to be pretty much flight rather than fight.*[4]

Thayer detects that preference for flight over fight which, for all the bust and boom of its adventure stories, shapes the Pacific Northwest narrative, from the amateur anthropologist James Swan to novelist Ivan Doig's rediscovery of Swan in *Winter Brothers* (1980) to the film "Sleepless in Seattle" (1993). Connected to the romance of getting away is a history of utopian experiment, from hundreds of ventures in founding imperfectly self-sustaining communities (such as the turn-of-the-century Finnish settlement called Sointula on Malcolm Island) to the dreams of environmentalist poet Gary Snyder, and to the send-up of the tradition crafted by Vancouver Island comic novelist Jack Hodgins in his *Invention of the World* (1977). But, as these writers surely show, flight runs out of West (if not North) on the Pacific Coast. On the continental edge the northwestern hero is stopped and forced to make sense of where he or she is, or to reach across the Pacific to find a misted aesthetic through which to imagine a different sense of home.

It is difficult to make fiction of endless flight or, ultimately, of submission to the avalanche: what I value in this novel has little to do with its convincingly plotting the lives of people. Undoubtedly, *On the Highest Hill* is sincerely trying to get somewhere. It wants to be a novel about social justice; it wants to present economic analysis; it could, with a small shift, have been a war novel; it certainly seeks the market of a romance. Introducing Colin as an adolescent, age thirteen, and following his life, uncertainly, until his late twenties, Haig-Brown depends on the lineaments of that most familiar novel, the story of growing up. A young man from a rurally isolated community goes off at age seventeen to the hostile hurried city (Vancouver) alone; he rides the rails, lives in poverty, suffers through a brief imprisonment, confronts police brutality, and as a hired hand to a prairie farmer learns the discipline of living off the land. He returns home to view his island idyll with fresh eyes but "growing impatience." (188) To a degree the pattern is repeated when Colin goes still further from Blenkinstown, serving as a stretcher-bearer with the Canadian troops in the Netherlands. Return from war, however, leaves him, more certain, if not wholly consciously, that "I'm no part of this any more." (264)

The will she/won't she pattern of Colin's consummated yet unconsummated love affair with his school teacher fits with Colin's not fitting in. Here is the essence of the love story frustrated: the older woman, the love for a *teacher*, the boy's dream of the perfect marriage never realized. But Haig-Brown also depends heavily on the story of macho adventure, deriving from an economy overwhelmingly dependent on resource extraction in isolated communities, where patterns of migration were so dominantly male. Whatever the traces of romance, the novel makes little space for women, and a reader in the 1990s can only think fondly of what Marilynne Robinson, author of *Housekeeping* (1980), or Seattle mystery writer Barbara Wilson, or the subtle Canadian story-teller Carol Windley might make of Mildred's largely untold story.

Colin Ensley has the promise of a "great man" (53) and the anarchic temperament of "a wild thing." (92) "He doesn't slip on rocks" (53): the mountain goat, Haig-Brown hints, is his spirit-guide (219-20). But civilization keeps challenging his sure-footedness: although he dreams of the all-encompassing vision, of literally rising above it all, Colin's chase to the highest hill is more psychological definition than physical achievement. As with so many a recluse and hermit, the mountain man, as he does in Earle Birney's poem, "Bushed," finds his home transformed, and can only run until "the great flint . . . come[s] singing into his heart" (Birney, "Bushed" 59). He is done in by thinking too much (296), by thinking he can preserve the forest as if it had no human presence, by dwelling on a hyper-idealized white and gold (8, 12) woman whom he naïvely forces into his own conception of the mountain spirit.

* * *

When the mountain-man hero of Oregon novelist Don Berry's *Trask* (1960) lights out for the territory, whatever his dream of escape, a goal and object give shape to his journey. At the moment he is truly "bushed," he is transformed through some mysterious, not quite fully assimilated spirit quest. Despite Colin's skill at trapping and tracking (and, somewhat paradoxically, at timber-cruising), the possible parallel with Berry's blinkered shamanism points up the sense in which *On the Highest Hill* is most obviously anomalous among Northwest fictions. In novels as different as H.L. Davis's encyclopedia of folk tales in *Honey in the Horn* (1935) and Sky Lee's neo-Chinese opera *Disappearing Moon Cafe* (1990), or in paintings as different as Morris Graves's visions of shore-birds and Jack Shadbolt's interpretations of blasted butterflies, the Northwest artist usually seeks, in some measure, however culturally limited, to translate and accommodate the mythologies and religions of the diverse First Nations of the North Pacific Coast. How odd it seems, then, that Colin, as Haig-Brown presents him, finds the forest and mountain completely empty of human presence. The context of Northwest writing suggests that had he discovered some of the ghosts and spirits of another tradition, as do poets Richard Hugo in the rivers of Washington State or Daphne Marlatt in the estuaries of British Columbia, he might have laid to rest some of his own ghosts.

In creating a character in such total flight from society, Haig-Brown creates an intriguing "study" for a character, but an almost insoluble dilemma for himself as novelist. How do you give definition to a character where "there was almost no history, no culture, and no class"?[5] Mildred and Marilyn, Colin's sister, his nominal teacher and nurse, adviser and friend, never get to tell their own stories. The meaning of places and things does not, by and large, give texture, nuance, and extension to character. But reintroducing this novel in a climate of post-modern cynicism, I take pleasure in reading these confusions. Haig-Brown (like his Colin, a bit of a nihilist) may have been tempted by the non-novel he could not understand. If so, he was probably content with the accumulation of unfinished narratives: love story, hill climb, logging excursion, aspiration to be a writer. When his friend Richard Erickson challenged him on the ultimate pointlessness of one chapter, Haig-Brown jots a marginal note which intones this uncompromising view of the dynamic of individual/society/ nature:

Nothing is resolved.

Nothing is resolved anywhere in the book until after his death.

The whole point is that it doesn't make sense. I told you the book was cumulative.[6]

XV

Haig-Brown's ideal reader will savor a narrative of "slow, unrealized retreat."[7] The novel becomes variations on a vague and existentialist theme: it doesn't make sense.

Colin struggles against the demands of society and loses. Haig-Brown undoubtedly set out to write a novel of social criticism, an agenda we sense as he extends the novel eastward, first to Vancouver, then to the foothills and prairies—traditionally in Canada the origin of so many west-coasters—and then to wartime Europe. While writing the novel, Haig-Brown, magistrate and committed citizen, was also writing letters discussing the need for probation systems in rural areas, fighting the state-supported anti-Japanese-Canadian prejudice of the time, and fearing the "coming of the Great God Hydroelectricity."[8] The historical scope of the novel, from 1933 to 1947, embraces the great twentieth-century upheavals of Depression and World War II (and the Holocaust). Haig-Brown perhaps harbors ambitions to make this a work in the tradition of Sinclair Lewis and Canadian novelist Irene Baird's *Waste Heritage* (1939), if not of Dickens.

Colin's instinct, however enmeshed in society he may be, is always to turn and flee. The novel gives telling details of xenophobia in the union movement, of the cultish importance of silence to the laborer, of the exploitation hidden in tie-cutting contracts, and of the power structures in a labor camp. These give substance and interest to the sentimental romance, but as Haig-Brown's social commitment contemplates where an expanding labor movement (and war and economic injustice) will lead, he joins his hero in turning his back on this most promising of subjects. Because he cannot trade the tyranny of the company for the tyranny of the union, Colin flees both. Another *it* which does not make sense, and one also connected to the conflict of union and company (at one point Colin is asked to participate in gangsterism) is institutional brutality. It is found in the behavior of small-town cops—and Haig-Brown may have been trying to raise a concern his office as magistrate would otherwise preclude his discussing—and, especially, in war, where Colin takes the pacifist, apparently dissenting, role of stretcher-bearer.

* * *

Haig-Brown's principal social message comes in addresses to the meaning of place and things, to the importance of wilderness, the mystique of mountains, the texture of rocks, the layers of geology, and the threat of the machine in the garden. But, despite the regional rightness of the phrase "skunk cabbage swamp" (18), or his eye for a "strong shoot of salmon berry" glazed with rainwater beside the black locomotive (50), this is not a novel keenly attentive to the markers of the bioregion. It does not show the sensitivity to slight shifts in place that H.L. Davis (by referring at key transition points to a triangulation of local vegetation) does in *Honey in the Horn*. Yet the theme of conservation which Haig-Brown pursues is of crucial interest to readers at the end of the twentieth century. The novel advocates a pragmatic environmentalism. Colin seems more bewildered than concerned about the hurrying disappearance of forest and river valley, of ecosystem and its intricate network of interdependencies. But the active conservationist Haig-Brown is also an intense admirer of the craft of hand-hewn wood, and of the religion of daily work accomplished with the hands and the body. Colin is a skilled hunter and must become so, but he hates to kill things. In a letter of the period, Haig-Brown identifies his own kinship with Colin: "I'm a fair naturalist, a keen fly fisherman and a keen hunter, though I've lost my enthusiasm for shooting and don't kill many fish anymore."[9]

Colin knows about the mink, its noises and smells and habits, just from his being solitary with nature: "It's quite easy to see things when you're alone and quiet, and there's plenty of time." (72). Colin is transformed in the woods; there he intuits the essential reciprocity of human and animal and vegetable worlds:

> He found no monotony in the great trees of the flat valley because to his eye no two of them seemed alike; each had its own particular way of surging upwards from its roots, each its own lean, its own color and texture of bark, its own climb to its lowest branches, its own marked position in relationship to its neighbors. (97-98)

This passage typifies the way the novel describes place. The writing is touched here and there by the rhapsodic strain often permeating nature writing. But, by and large, it delivers the taciturn environmental message essential to a culture of "hard work and spare living." (99) The message is to pay attention, to keep oneself open and receptive to the instruction of nature. But meanwhile, Haig-Brown provides less detail of "everything there is to know about trees" (41) and more specifics on the work of a skilled axeman. The influence of research and biological awareness which seems so evident in the nature writing of Aldo Leopold or of Portland's Kim Stafford, or in Haig-Brown's own *Measure of the Year*, is little in evidence. We are not told the particularity, the color and texture: we are to have faith that Colin knows these so that our attention settles on his psychology, his imperfect growing up, rather than on a place *per se*. Hence, too, the mythical map names with which Haig-Brown decorates his fiction (Annabis, Menzies). "Like the landscape painter who wishes to both describe and define," notes Anthony Robertson, "he is more concerned with meaning than precise, realistic description."[10]

* * *

Colin loves a teacher, and himself becomes, in his most socially successful role, a teacher of work. It is worth remembering as you begin to read this novel, or think back over it, that Colin begins as *writer*. *On the Highest Hill* is a novel about a writer who almost never writes. *On the Highest Hill* opens with the community—represented by Mildred's classroom—uniquely focussed on writing about mountains. In this family, it might be said, there was no clear line between religion and "living with mountains." (11) Before Colin had ever climbed above timberline, he finds "the swift words." (10)

> *He had written easily, planting his wind-stunted trees in the rocky clefts, treading heather and moss, skirting snow-slides, climbing rock-slides, drinking from the clear pools in the torrents, hearing the solemn roar of the long, misty falls.* (11)

Writing is a means for Mildred's pupils to "live with logs and lumber, with salmon and salt water," to touch the "closer things" in their lives. (9) But also, it is essentially "elation," a means to define ideals, and especially to sustain an aspiration to live with wilderness.

In the Roderick Haig-Brown papers, held at the University of British Columbia, is a remarkable parallel text to the novel itself, a confirmation of Haig-Brown's own deep commitment to the art of words, and its potential to provoke a reader (and writer) to reach for the ideal. During the writing of the novel, Haig-Brown corresponded almost weekly with Richard W. Erickson, a booklover who worked in the office of a Seattle ship-yard. Introduced to Haig-Brown in 1933 (his sister was a good friend of Ann Haig-Brown), Erickson was Haig-Brown's most important editorial adviser throughout the 1940s. The correspondence (Roderick Haig-Brown Collection, especially Boxes 8 and 21) is elaborated in carbon typescripts of Parts One and Two of the novel (124 typescript pages) interleaved with onion skin on which Erickson draws his deletions, and writes his comments, suggestions, and criticisms. Erickson de-scribes himself as "something of a smudge-pot, a showman";[11] exchanges between the two are usually blunt, combative, rich in elaborate bluster. Although the novel, like Colin's soaring paean to mountains, may have "poured from him," the exchange with Erickson shows Haig-Brown's seriousness of purpose, his appre-ciation of tough criticism, and his interest in language.

But the most vigorous persuasive language in the novel is, ultimately, the language of work, the lingo of the loggers, which has its own metaphysical zest and community definition. Maybe that's because *On the Highest Hill* is tempted to become a "windy," that tall tale of out-of-doors excitement which Nancy Pagh argues is a key Northwest form. And that may be why the more grandiose Whitman and the poets Stephen Benet, Edna St. Vincent Millay, and Archibald Macleish are writers called up as inspiration in an early draft of the novel.[12]

Erickson's comments emphasize dramatization: variations of the charge "Make it happen before our eyes"[13] are his continued caution. Relatively seldom does he query particulars of diction, and he never takes up the specifics of flora and fauna. Presumably Erickson finds, as does Suzanne Martin, reviewer for the Seattle *Post-Intelligencer*, that "He observes with the naturalist's eye for loving details. Then he puts it down like a poet."[14] At the beginning of Part Two, to take a typical example, Erickson objects to the phrase which begins the fourth paragraph: "That was how it happened that . . ." But Haig-Brown consistently rejects such advice. His decisions are a means, presumably, to sustain his sense of something inexplicable which governs his characters. Rather than try to search their motivations, he decides for a syntax that will emphasize some impersonal, manipulating force.

Two further examples of this exchange, both apparently minor, are yet very revealing. In the middle of Chapter Two, Haig-Brown describes Colin's sense of renewal and comfort in the alder grove (22). The typescript reads:

> *When Colin came back to the edge of the alder flat and saw the open pasture ahead of him, he felt a sudden disappointment, in spite of the fact that hunger had been hurrying him along towards supper through the whole way out.* (26 ts)

Erickson, noting "too many directional words for my taste," suggests four deletions. Only one, to delete "along," is fully accepted. Erickson changes "had been hurrying" to "had hurried" and pencils out "through." That Haig-Brown retained his original and (to most ears) more clumsy phrasing, may not make him a Northwest Thomas Hardy, but it does show that a certain ponderous, encumbered syntax is deliberately chosen to convey the slow unfolding of Colin's doomed journey. So, at the end of the paragraph, scribbling the sarcastic comment "stifling," Erickson deletes the phrase "that stifled good thoughts in the ordinary world."[15] Haig-Brown declines this advice. That he resists the editing of his cut-this-by-half adviser demonstrates his certainty that this story sometimes needs stifling sentences.

This specific, and in itself minor, instance of Haig-Brown's thoughts about revising, points to a determination, almost a stubbornness, to get at his characters. In this novel he may not frequently have discovered the unalterably and inevitably right phrase, but there can be no doubt that he deliberated carefully about how to find words to explain why and how people act. A primary example of this care is found in his comments to various correspondents regarding the elements of homosexuality in *On the Highest Hill*. "I see *absolutely no justification*," emphasized Richard Erickson, "for the hinting of the early sections."[16] As might be expected of a writer from Campbell River in the 1940s, Haig-Brown himself is not sure whether male or female homosexuality is normal or deviant. At one point he says, "It [homosexual interest] is a very natural point, almost inevitable."[17] But a few days later he worries, "You want me to say she was or was not a homosexual. She was not. But she had homosexual feelings and they scared her."[18] He resists Erickson's repeated entreaties to eliminate the suggestions of homosexuality; to editor Frances Phillips he explains both the importance and the indirectness:

Didn't you notice Carol Maxwell? And the mildly excessive interest in Margaret? And her [Mildred's] fear in chapter one of men who tried to push her too far? and attraction to Colin because of all this? . . . it's there for the reader to find or not, just as it usually is in life.[19]

In his analysis of the dream of the highest hill, Haig-Brown shows no willingness to simplify either his psychology or his syntax. "You want it sharp, clear," he told Erickson. "But I've got more to say than just that and I think I am saying it exactly in those points where you most doubt the validity of my approach."[20]

I suspect that Erickson, whatever his bluster, recognized what is going on: "Hardy you may not be, but it is also quite possible you almost are forced, like Hardy, to write clumsy prose."[21] This comment provides a key insight into what Haig-Brown tried to accomplish in this most Hardyesque of this writings. People may be hard to understand, but Haig-Brown is almost forced, and quite possibly forces himself, to face the difficulty to a degree I did not detect when I first read the novel. Awareness of Haig-Brown at work on his writing reveals a conviction that the difficulty of understanding people must be conveyed to the reader in sentences themselves sometimes hard to understand.

* * *

On the Highest Hill is a novel of first-stage regionalism. It begins to establish the mystique of mountains, the integrity of logging and working with wood, the terror of the clear-cut. While it might be read as a fable of "the brutal destruction of logging" (299), that approach confines its interest. Its full significance will emerge when it is re-read into the new Northwest culture which this reprint series represents. When it is reworked, as intertext, into the fabric of a more self-conscious and self-critical regionalism, as when Daphne Marlatt re-writes Martin Grainger's *Woodsmen of the West* (1908) in her *Anahistoric* (1988), or Ivan Doig rewrites James Swan, its "air-built moments" will be more completely realized. Listening for this potential in Haig-Brown's phrasing, your reading might begin.

Laurie Ricou

Notes

I am indebted to the author's daughter and literary executor, Valerie Haig-Brown for her generous assistance, and for sharing with me the typescript annotated by Richard Erickson, which will soon be added to the Roderick Haig-Brown Collection (RHB Collection) held by the University of British Columbia Library, Special Collections Division.

1. Roderick Haig-Brown to W.A.R. Collins 9 June 1947, RHB Collection, 21-16.
2. Roderick Haig-Brown to Mrs. Whitwell, 24 April 1950, RHB Collection, 22-6.
3. Thayer Hobson to Roderick Haig-Brown, 22 June 1948, RHB Collection, 13-1.
4. Thayer Hobson to Roderick Haig-Brown, 11 Feb 1948, RHB Collection, 13-1.
5. Robertson 10.
6. Marginal note on Richard W. Erickson to Roderick Haig-Brown, undated comments responding to the typescript (pp 138-354) of *On the Highest Hill*, RHB Collection, 8-5.
7. Roderick Haig-Brown to Thayer Hobson, 23 February 1948, RHB Collection, 21-19.
8. Roderick Haig-Brown to O.H. Borrodaile 8 October 1949 RHB Collection, 22-4.
9. Roderick Haig-Brown to Mike Crammond 4 August 1949, RHB Collection, 22-3.
10. Robertson (iii).
11. Richard W. Erickson to Roderick Haig-Brown, RHB Collection, 12 March 1948, 8-5.
12. Page 14 and carbon No. 1, ts. p. 13. *On the Highest Hill* RHB Collection uncatalogued.
13. Interleaf preceding ts. p. 65, RHB Collection uncatalogued.
14. RHB Collection, 70-7.
15. 22, ts. p. 27 RHB Collection uncatalogued.

16. Richard W. Erickson to Roderick Haig-Brown, 4 January 1949, RHB Collection, 8-6.

17. Roderick Haig-Brown to Richard W. Erickson, 26 June 1948, RHB Collection, 21-20.

18. Roderick Haig-Brown to Richard W. Erickson, 1 July 1948, RHB Collection, 21-21.

19. Roderick Haig-Brown to Frances Phillips, 28 December 1948, RHB Collection, 21-21.

20. Roderick Haig-Brown to Richard W. Erickson, 1 July 1948, RHB Collection, 21-21.

21. Richard W. Erickson to Roderick Haig-Brown, 17 June 1948, RHB Collection, 8-5.

Works Consulted

Birney, Earle *Ghost in the Wheels: Selected Poems.* Toronto: McClelland and Stewart, 1977.

Metcalfe, E. Bennett. *A Man of Some Importance: The Life of Roderick Langmere Haig-Brown.* Seattle/Vancouver: James W. Wood, 1985.

Robertson, Anthony. *Above Tide: Reflections on Roderick Haig-Brown.* Madeira Park, B.C.: Harbour, 1984.

ON THE HIGHEST HILL

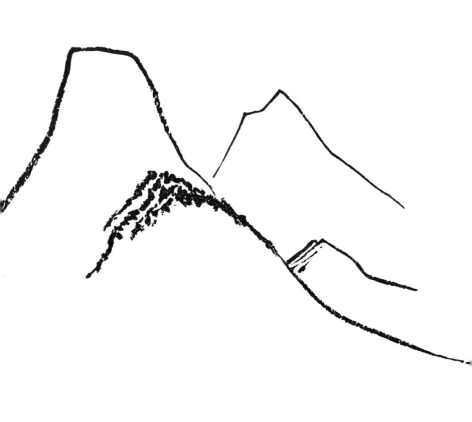

ON THE

HIGHEST HILL

RODERICK L. HAIG-BROWN

WILLIAM MORROW & CO., NEW YORK 1949

TO R. W. E.

For an idea and an unfaltering interest in it

PART ONE

THE ALDER FLAT

1

IT was very bright in the schoolroom. Fresh May sunshine washed down through the clear air and patterned the high windows across the desks and on the floor. Colin Ensley felt the brightness all through him, as he had felt it walking to school that morning and all day since then, clear in his eyes, fresh in his brain, vibrant in his body. Sitting awkwardly there, at the desk that was far too small for him, for once he did not feel awkward. Within an hour, his dreaming mind told him, he would be outside and with the brightness. But even that thought did not tear at him, as his thoughts so often did, and he was content to let it remain remote and vague. For the moment the intensity of the words he had set down on the page in front of him and the room's enclosing brilliance were enough.

In Colin's mind Mildred Hanson was part of the brightness, and the intensity of what he had written belonged closely to her. She was standing beside her desk, looking over her forty-odd pupils. She held an open book in her hand and had intended to switch the eighth grade section of the room away from the composition it was working on. But for once they were silent and busy, working not because they had to but because they wanted to. She had known she had reached them with her own enthusiasm earlier, when she had begun to talk of mountains; and they had followed her closely, clear around the world and back again, in search of mountains. She had spoken of the Rockies and the Andes, Himalayas, Urals, Caucasus, Alps, Pyrenees, then back over the Laurentian hills and the Rockies again to their own Pacific Coast Range, the tall snow peaks they could see from the schoolroom windows. For once even the dullest of them, even Tod Phalling and Jeff Burnside and Marge Elkhorn, had been stirred to reach into their own experience and find there an echo of the classroom words.

She wondered how long it would last. Colin Ensley was daydreaming already, she saw. But he had written steadily for fifteen or twenty minutes and what he had written would have life in it. There would be clumsy grammatical errors, the pages would be untidy with his spidery scrawl and certainly there would be at least one blot. But there would also be several sentences of sharpest imagination, acutely felt, clearly and freely expressed.

It was Mildred Hanson's third year of teaching and she was confident and successful in a profession that had once seemed beyond her reach. She had been born in a small coal mining town, the sixth child of a family that later grew to twelve. Her parents were immigrants, steady, hardworking, unimaginative people, and their children left school at the earliest possible moment to go out and earn money. Only Mildred had varied the pattern; she also had gone away from home to work, but she had stayed on in school and in due time had qualified as a teacher.

Now she lived a disciplined, almost a dedicated life. She was

8

finding all the satisfactions she had expected in the intensity of working with children and she was free of the fears that nagged at many teachers—inspectors' visits, criticism from the principal, the attacks of aggressive parents, all were part of her chosen profession, to be absorbed into fuller understanding of it. And she felt no fear of the dull, deep-voiced, overgrown fifteen- and sixteen-year-olds, indefinitely stalled in her grade; she was scarcely aware of how completely her calm competence had killed their early attempts to break her discipline.

The children working intently and silently in the sunlit room marked the measure of her success. She glanced over them once more, closed the book in her hand and went quietly back to sit behind her desk. This, today, she thought, reached all of them. But why? Because they live with mountains? They live with logs and lumber, with salmon and salt water, with a dozen other, closer things, but nothing before has reached all of them and held them all quiet for so long. It should mean something. If they can be stirred once, even the dullest of them, they can be stirred again. The bright ones are so few. In three years, how many? Not ten. Perhaps ten who handled the work surely and of those, five who added something of their own to it.

In the ten there had been more girls than boys, probably because the pattern of the country still turned boys early from books to tools; in the five, more boys than girls, but one girl who stood out from them all. Margaret, Colin Ensley's sister, was two years older than he, a dark, handsome, responsible girl. Mildred Hanson had felt her strength and maturity even when she was in Grade 8 and had begun then to treat her more nearly as friend and equal than as pupil. This friendship between them had grown in the two years since Margaret had passed into high school and Mildred had learned that her first judgment of her friend was solidly based. Colin had none of Margaret's strength and sureness and even his intelligence was of a different quality; he was instinctive, emotional, casual, where Margaret was logical and tidy. Margaret's qualities were clear and orthodox, Colin's elusive and unpredictable. Yet—and Mildred resisted the thought as she had resisted it many times before—there was a power of attraction in Colin that reached more deeply into her than the spoken, accepted affection of Margaret.

Mildred Hanson knew where this thought led her, because she had followed it before. It led by dangerous ways into a warm, safe haze of pleasure that was negation of every principle of her dedication. Today, because the sun was bright in the room, because the class was absorbed, because she was young and a woman, she disregarded the danger and let the dream take over her mind. His attraction was his awkwardness, his dependence, his simplicity. For all his clumsy size he was only a thirteen-year-old boy, a child still. Any woman might want to touch him, hold him in her arms, protect him. Then she felt her heart racing, felt the rush of blood through her body, speeding her breathing, parting her lips. It would be so safe—he wouldn't, couldn't possibly understand it. It could be done safely and stopped sharply at her own wish, short of his understanding. Safely, she thought, safely. The word held her by its repetition, twisted the dream and gave it shameful meaning. A boy who wouldn't understand, who was open to her because she was his teacher, who could be controlled because he was a boy, not a man. Safety! In the betrayal of her life's devotion for the pale echo of an experience. Now, with her blood quiet again and the haze drawn away from her dream, she knew there was no safety even in thought. The mood of the silent, sunlit room broke in her before it broke in the children, and she stood up.

While Mildred Hanson sat straight-backed behind her big desk, Colin sprawled at his small one. He was a very tall boy, big-boned, loose-jointed, with huge hands and feet. His face still had some boyish fullness and softness, but was fast becoming what the bones made it—high and narrow, with great dark eyes deeply shadowed between high cheekbones and the massive structure of his forehead. The nose was long and straight, though not excessively large, the mouth wide and easy, almost soft, the chin narrow and long.

Normally restless, Colin had moved little while Miss Hanson sat behind her desk. His mind was still with the brightness of day, inside and out, and with the elation of the swift words he had written on the page in front of him. He had never been in the mountains above timberline, but he had been born under the shadow of mountains, had lived his life within close sight of them and had listened often to the stories of hunters and woodsmen. He had only to close his eyes to have picture after picture vividly before him—gully and ridge and draw, shoulder and peak and face.

He had written easily, planting his wind-stunted trees in the rocky clefts, treading heather and moss, skirting snow-slides, climbing rock-slides, drinking from the clear pools in the torrents, hearing the solemn roar of the long, misty falls. No writing had ever poured from him so fast as these stored-up thoughts of the high mountains. He had stopped only when his imagination climbed beyond easy reach of words, and he scarcely knew that he had stopped; he had simply followed his thoughts into the mountains beyond reach or touch or need of pen and paper. Thought had climbed in him and with him, away from the room, from the valley, from the reality of the road home and suppertime and his father's return from work. It had become jumbled then, twisted and turned in upon itself, confused between its own brightness and the brilliance of the sunshine in the room.

Outside the window, the green of the alder leaves was so pale that it scarcely checked the sun; and the trunks of the trees were white instead of gray. Inside the room it was very quiet, and silver dust specks climbed in the light. Warm, safe, quiet, clean, yet exciting. Miss Hanson. Her eyes are very blue when she looks at you, bluer than the salt water on a day like this, and clearer blue; sometimes you can see them when you're only half awake in the morning, and see her pale white and gold behind them. It would be fine to do something for her, something big and important, and to kneel to give it to her. She would be cool and far away, but friendly, and she would smile. The sun is on her hair now, shining in the pale, clear gold of the thick braid around her head. Her neck is very white, like powder snow almost, but not cold. Her arms are the same, and you can see little blue veins in them, and when she moves in the sunlight a little gleam of gold hair. Would you feel that if you touched her, or only her smooth skin? Is it wrong to think like that? And to think about more of her than you can see? It's wrong to say it and laugh about it like some of the kids do, but not wrong to think about it yourself—it can't be, because it's warm and sweet and good all through you. A person could do anything she says to, because she is blue and white and gold and beautiful. Maybe not write tidily when she says to or spell words right or even speak right. But big things, like climbing a mountain to find her in the snow and bring her down. There wouldn't be sunlight then. But she would be warm and easy to hold and she would smile. It wouldn't be hard to lift her. I can lift a hundred pounds so I don't know I'm lifting. Or I could swim after her if she was drowning. If the old man'd let me use his gun next fall I could shoot a buck for her; maybe she'd like that, maybe it could really happen. . . .

Her voice reached him, then. He knew dimly that she had spoken two or three times, but now the room was full of his name and the other children were laughing.

"Colin," she said again. "Will you please come back to earth and pay attention? Stand up and tell me what I've just said."

He scrambled up and stood awkwardly, silent.

"Well, what did I say?"

"You said to pay attention, Miss Hanson."

The class laughed again.

"Before that?" Her voice was cold and patient.

He searched his mind hopelessly. "I don't know, Miss."

"I said we've just got time to read over the compositions before the end of school. You've wasted a lot of that time for us, so you can stay behind and read yours after school. Sit down."

Colin sat down. His feet tangled in the legs of the desk and his knees bumped heavily against the wood, so that ink jolted out of the well and trickled down the sloping face.

COLIN sat at his desk while the other children went noisily out of the room. It was not the first time he had had to stay after school and he sat straight and still, his hands on the desk in front of him.

Miss Hanson was writing the next day's work on the board and he knew it would be five or ten minutes before she said anything to him at all. Some of the kids didn't like that silent wait; they said they'd rather be sent along to old Siddons and get the strap and have it over with. Colin didn't mind. It was uncomfortable to have to sit straight and still for so long, but he liked being alone in the room with her and watching as she moved surely and smoothly in front of the blackboard.

She does send them up to Siddons once in a while, Colin thought, but not very often. She isn't mean, she's like Mother is and Johnny Harris and Johnny's old man, one of the warm people; you know how they're going to act, they don't get sore over nothing or tell you one thing one minute and another thing the next; if they do get sore there's a reason for it and you know it won't last.

He began to feel silly sitting there with his hands in front of him on the too small desk. He thought of coughing or moving his feet to make her notice him. But she spoke in time to keep him from that, without turning away from her writing.

"I suppose Margaret will be waiting for you?"

"I guess so, Miss Hanson."

She was writing on the board. "You know, Colin, you're just as smart as she is. Why don't you learn to be tidy and careful?"

Colin moved his feet uncomfortably. "Girls are different."

"No, they aren't." She turned around and he saw again how blue her eyes were. "There's nothing sissy about taking trouble. And keeping awake in class. It just takes determination." She sat down at her desk. "Bring your work up here."

He came up gladly and gave her the book, then stood beside her chair, a little behind her, his big hands hanging awkwardly in front of him. It was better not to have to read it aloud, he thought. Reading out loud from a book is not so bad, but when you've written it yourself the words sound silly and the other kids make cracks about it afterwards and you wish you hadn't put down so much.

Mildred Hanson read the untidy pages in front of her. She felt the wet moss underfoot, saw the fallen alder leaves at the edge of last year's snow-slide, heard the roar of the first fall storm across the peaks that closed the gully. "Why did you write of fall on a day like this?"

"I just thought of fall," he said. "Fall will come."

"Have you ever been in the mountains in the fall?"

"No," he said.

1 3

She turned a page and went on reading. He looked down at her and saw that her hair shone with the same pale gold even when the sun was not on it. He could see her shoulders clearly through her thin white blouse and the blouse was so clean and so fresh he wanted to touch it. His left hand moved a little, then she spoke again.

"Do you still think you'll be a bridgeman when you leave school, Colin?"

"I guess so," he said slowly.

She turned back to the beginning of the composition. Perhaps it's wrong to worry him about that again so soon, she thought. It's too much for him now. Yet he's got to stop and think about it. He's like all the others, rough and untidy and careless. He doesn't even keep his hands clean or brush his hair or look after his clothes properly. Yet he isn't like them. Things happen inside him and he can bring them out for the rest of us to see, like this composition.

What am I trying to do with him? Am I trying to kid myself that I'm the wise teacher who recognizes a Canadian Abe Lincoln or a beardless Walt Whitman in the little red schoolhouse? It isn't likely he'll ever be a statesman or a poet. The important thing is that he could be something and do something far bigger than the existing and job-serving and promoting that the best of these others will do. How do I know that? Just because he can be articulate on paper? Because something starts in him when I read good poetry? Woman's intuition—or a schoolmarm's hunch, maybe. It's a teacher's business to have hunches like that and do what she can about them.

Sometimes I feel about him as I suppose I'll feel about my own son. That's when I want to touch him and hold him, keep him near me as he is now. And that's why I may be wrong, why I may be lying to myself about him; because I let myself feel about him instead of thinking. If you give in to feeling it can grow and grow in you until those awful things happen, the things you read about between teachers and children. I've got to send him away, quickly, now.

"Colin," she said gently. "You must think hard about it. Try to want to go on and finish school."

1 4

"Yes, Miss Hanson." He was still watching her shoulders under the white blouse. His body was tense and his heart was pounding so that he could feel it all through his body. His hand moved again, towards her, just a little.

"Please try to want it, Colin. It's important—for me."

He touched her then. Just reached forward and set his big hand down on the white freshness of her blouse until he could feel the warmth of her shoulder against his palm. She felt the pressure, accepted it and held her body still under it. She moved her hand, as though to reach up and set it on his. Then all the intensity of her fear was with her again. He felt her body stiffen, then draw gently away from him. She turned slowly to face him and said only: "Why, Colin, you mustn't do that." But he saw the fear in her eyes and in the paleness of her face.

Colin's hand was at his side again and he looked away from her.

"You had better go now, Colin. We can talk about the rest of this tomorrow." She tried to hear her voice and thought it calm. "It's too nice an afternoon to waste indoors."

Colin heard the harshness of strain through the calm voice. He turned and found his clumsy way through the door, with tears of misery and confusion hot in his eyes.

Mildred sat on at her desk. She knew what she had done to him, but she knew also that it was useless to call him back, that there could be no explanation for him.

2

OUTSIDE the school building Colin did not hesitate. He crossed the yard and turned along the dusty road. As he walked he remembered the moment of fear he had seen in her eyes, tried to take the blame for it into himself and could not.

Surely it was a small thing, to touch her like that, even though she is a teacher. She even seemed to like it, just at first. Her shoulder felt warm where I touched it, smooth under her blouse and warm clear through me. I suppose that's sin, the sort of sin God might strike you dead for. A deadly sin. God and my father. God the Father. Father the God. My father is like God—Johnny Harris said so once, because my father has a big black beard. But my father isn't God. God is a spirit and couldn't have a beard.

Jeff Burnside and Tod Phalling were sitting at the side of the road, waiting for him. But he scarcely noticed them, even when they got up and began to walk with him, one on either side.

"How'd you make out?" Tod asked.

The question hardly reached Colin's mind, but he said: "O.K."

Jeff jostled into him from the other side. "Give us the angle, dope. What'd she keep you back for?"

"You heard her," Colin said. "For not paying attention."

"Yeah," Tod said. "What'd she do? Take your pants down and play with you?"

"Shut up," Colin said.

Tod stuck out a foot so that Colin tripped and stumbled. "Satchel-foot," Tod said. "What did she do?"

"Nothing," Colin said. He was scared but it was better to get beaten up than let them know anything.

"We know she's soft on you."

"That's right," Jeff said. "You may as well spill it."

"Nothing happened," Colin said. "You been kept back after school. You know nothing happens except more work."

"There's big sister," Jeff said. "Go tell her about it. We can wait."

Colin looked ahead along the road and saw Margaret standing there, waiting for him.

"Be seeing y', punk," Tod said.

They dropped behind as he walked on towards Margaret. They were scared of her, Colin knew, in much the same way and for much the same reasons as they were scared of Miss Hanson, but he hadn't expected them to give up that easily. Margaret had never backed down, even when she was much smaller; she never

16

ran away or hid or did any of the other things girls usually did when boys acted tough. She simply stood her ground and made them feel cheap. Tod and Jeff had had their share of it and weren't looking for any more.

She was waiting quite calmly, her books under her arm, as though she had known he would need her. "What happened?" she asked. "I'd almost given you up."

"We got kept back."

She glanced at him suspiciously. "I've seen just about everybody else in your room go by."

"It was only me," Colin said.

Margaret laughed. "I'm beginning to think Mildred Hanson likes keeping you after school."

Colin turned on her fiercely. "Don't say those things."

She looked up in quick surprise. "I'm sorry," she said. "I didn't mean anything."

"It's O.K.," Colin said. "Skip it."

They walked on in silence. Margaret watched the dusty road ahead. That's what those other kids must have been saying to him, she thought. But it's not like Colin to get sore. Mildred keeps him back too often. She says he's good in class and his work is good, so she must do it just to help him. But it's not fair to make him more different from the others than he is already.

"What are you going to do between now and supper?" she asked him.

"I'm going back in the alders a way."

"I've got to stop at the store and pick up a lot of stuff. But I'll have time to milk and do chores if you want."

"Thanks," Colin said. "I'd like to go back there quite a ways."

"Don't be late for supper, that's all." She left him at the store.

It was still over a mile and a half to the Ensley farm, but Colin walked the distance without a pause, his loose, big-footed awkward stride carrying him far more efficiently than it seemed to. He was in a hurry to get to the alders—he realized now that he had meant to go there from the moment he closed the door of the classroom. And he was glad that Margaret was not coming with him. Nearly always he would have wanted her. But today he wanted to consider only himself, to be guided only by his own

1 7

desires in where he went, how fast he went, where he stopped and what he thought about.

He turned off the road a hundred yards short of the gate by the house and swung round the edge of the pasture, keeping well clear of the barn in case his mother or father should be out there and see him. He came to the creek, cached his lunch bucket in a fire-blackened stump and turned into the alders.

He left the hot spring day behind him at once and felt the difference clearly as he had known he would. The light was still bright and clear, but filtered by the green leaves high overhead and reflected without harshness from the clean gray trunks of the trees. Underfoot there was no dust, only moist dark leaves and soft black earth. The creek was running strongly but quietly between the clay banks, broken into light only where a tiny sandbar forced a ripple or a sodden black tree branch, buried deep in the soft bottom, stood against the current. It looped in unpredictable ways across the wide flat, now lost in a salmonberry thicket, now spreading to a skunk cabbage swamp where the ground was low, now weaving under rotting windfalls. But Colin knew its direction and knew the cattle trails and deer trails that followed it.

He had come there for safety, safety from people—from Tod and Jeff, from Mildred Hanson, from his father and mother, even from Margaret; from all people and from the eyes and voices of all people. He had not known this when he came and he scarcely recognized it as he found it; he felt only a sense of wonder that any place, on such a day, could be cool and quiet, empty of human life, in tune and tone with his need.

He had meant to stop in the open place under the maples, near the line fence, but instead he went on, over the sagging wires of the fence and into a part of the flat that was unfamiliar to him. The ground was a little higher and the creek banks were clearer and easier to follow. He walked smoothly, little conscious of the change, for thought was quick and urgent in him. Along the known trails, through the known part of the flat, the old thoughts had been with him. He had been the trapper, following his line through the snow; a tie-cutter, searching timber for his trade; an explorer, venturing where other men had not been, through dangerous ways to high achievement. Well-loved

1 8

thoughts, these, tried companions of many days, kin to the thoughts of the Knights in the Round Table stories, men bold in quest and combat, gentle before their ladies, that had carried him again and again insensibly over the long morning miles to school.

Quite suddenly all these thoughts were dead and dull. They led nowhere, achieved nothing; they were part of evil. I must be bad all through, Colin told himself, if the best I can do is think fine things for myself. I'm bad in school, never the way Margaret is with all checks on her report card. I don't ever want to do the chores around home, except maybe split wood or go out and milk on a good morning. I tell lies. I think I hate my father sometimes and I talk back to Mother. I don't even know what I'm going to be when I grow up. The old man says I'm too awkward to be a bridgeman—he says I'd get killed inside of a week. But that's what he wants me to be. Miss Hanson thinks I ought to be something else, so does Margaret; but they don't say what except keep on with school and go to University. Fat Evans is going to be a telegrapher. Johnny Harris is going to drive truck. Jeff and Tod are going in the woods. I don't like Tod. I'd like to bust him one, right in the mush, every time he calls me punk or satchel-foot. Only I'm scared of him. He'd just hit me in the guts, like he did last time, and I'd crawl on the ground and be sick at my stomach again.

God could strike me dead for being no good, right here, by the creek where it's cool and soft. It would be quick, like a bullet in the heart, nothing a guy would feel at all. They'd all be sorry then because they wouldn't know what had happened. But then there wouldn't be any more sunlight and I couldn't see the creek again, or Margaret or Johnny Harris or Mother or Miss Hanson. I shouldn't even want to see her, but I do. It isn't bad, wanting to see her, not if you don't mean anything bad by it. I only wanted to touch her. There's nothing bad in that. I don't really mean those things I've thought about her—they're not like ordinary thinking, anyway; they're like the stories of the knights, not real but something that comes up in you so hard that it's all around you and close to you and seems real just for a little while. I won't let myself think those things any more. They're inside me right now, but I won't let them come forward. A person can't help what's inside him. He can't be watching all the time, either. Sometimes it comes up so fast nobody could shut it back, and once it's up there, with you, you want it too much to try to stop it any more. . . .

Colin noticed suddenly that he was near the end of the flat, and he stopped. For the first time since he had left the school he was fully aware of everything about him. The ground was dry and firm underfoot, even last year's leaves were dry. The creek was loud, rippling over a gravelly bed, and he could hear it in still louder sound as it poured down the mountainside. The alders were smaller, branched and more widely spaced, with a scattering of firs and hemlocks among them. Through gaps among the leaves ahead he could see the heavy dark green of the steep mountain slope climbing away from him. Because his eyes were fully at work again, seeing and feeling the brightness of the day that held on into the late afternoon, his mind felt free and healed. For the moment he was strong and sure.

There was a big maple tree beside the creek a little way ahead of him. He went to it and sat down on a root so that he could look into a deep pool below. Black water-striders moved across the surface from his shadow and he saw orange-tailed salmon fry holding in the current. A ruffed grouse drummed somewhere behind him. This must be a mile from the line fence, he thought. No, maybe half a mile. And it's a quarter of a mile from the barn to the line fence, less than a mile from our house to the mountains on this side. A man can climb up into Sales Gully in half a day from our place, Dad says, and that's four thousand feet, real mountain country, above timberline.

He tried to think seriously and calmly and usefully about himself, about being a logger or staying on in school to be something else. What did you get to be if you stayed on in school? A schoolteacher, maybe, or a doctor or a lawyer. He watched the swoop and flash of a kingfisher farther along the creek. A logger could turn himself into a prospector or a trapper or a timber cruiser like Mr. Grant. That's better than a teacher or a lawyer; you've got to use your head plenty in a job like that too. But there was something more to be found, something none of them had found yet. He searched again for it, deep in himself, felt it but did not find it and his mind turned back from the search.

A grouse drummed again and Colin leaned back against the trunk of the tree to watch a blue jay on a limb above him. You could make it to Sales Gully and back in a day, he thought. This creek comes right out of there and a guy'd only have to follow it. . . .

MARGARET was glad to come to the farm gate. She liked the walk from school well enough, but hated carrying clumsy packages from the store. She looked in the mail-box, found some papers and a letter, and added them to her load. As she opened the gate she saw her mother coming towards her along the rutted, grass-grown road that led between wire fences to the house.

"You were quick, dear," Mrs. Ensley said. "Where's Colin?"

Margaret evaded the question about Colin. "Did the radio batteries come?"

"Nobody's come up with the freight yet. Did Colin stay to play ball after school?"

They were walking side by side, quite slowly, towards the house. Margaret thought: why does she worry about him so? "He's gone back in the alders, along the creek."

"He'll be brooding again," Mrs. Ensley said. "Brooding and dreaming. I never saw such a boy for brooding on things."

"Colin doesn't really brood, Mother. He thinks a lot and he's got a good imagination. You ought to be glad. He'll amount to something when he grows up."

"It doesn't seem healthy in a boy, to be off by himself so much, and he seems worse lately. I don't remember that my brothers were like that."

"There were plenty of them to keep each other busy," Margaret said. "Colin'll grow out of it."

They went into the house through the back door, which opened straight into the big kitchen. Margaret dropped her packages thankfully and Mrs. Ensley sat down. She was a woman in her forties, with graying hair and a strong, pleasant face, almost youthful in animation, but deeply lined in repose. She had the same high cheekbones that Margaret and Colin had, but her eyes were a dark and vivid blue. Even in relaxation her face and body suggested a power of quick, efficient, purposeful movement, yet she did not seem physically strong and the lines in her face were a deep weariness.

Margaret crossed the room to the stove as soon as she was rid of her packages.

Mrs. Ensley watched for a moment, then she said: "Will Colin be back in time to milk and do the chores?"

"No. I told him I'd do it."

Mrs. Ensley nodded. "Don't let his father know."

"Did they move out to the new bridge today?"

"He said they were going to, but it shouldn't make much difference to when he gets home. He says they can walk over the hill to camp and get there the same time as the rest of the crew."

"I told Colin not to be late for supper," Margaret said.

WHEN Colin came back to the edge of the alder flat and saw the open pasture ahead of him, he felt a sudden disappointment, although hunger had been hurrying him towards supper through the whole way out. It had been safe and calm in the alders, not confused in any way. Everything he had thought while sitting on the alder root had been fresh and important and exciting, free from any of the limitations that stifled good thoughts in the ordinary world.

Crossing the pasture towards the barn, he thought: now it will all start again. Margaret will say I'm late. Mother will want to know why I didn't come home for a sandwich after school. The old man will be home from the woods. It's not fair to think all that though. Mother's swell and they're all swell and I'm glad I'm coming home to supper. Sure it was good back in the alders, close under the mountain like that. I'll go back there one day when it's raining hard. And I'll go back there next winter in the snow, when the creek's frozen maybe.

Margaret was still in the barn, but she had finished milking. She had not heard him coming and he stood silently in the doorway, watching her, until she looked up and saw him. Then he laughed at the surprise and annoyance in her face.

"It's not funny," she said. "I thought you were never coming

2 2

and Mother said not to let Dad know I had milked for you. You always make it difficult for anybody to help you."

"I've been here a long time, watching you."

"You can't fool me. Pick up these pails and let's get back to the house. Dad's home already. Did you have a good time?"

"I'll take you back there next time I go. It's nowheres near as thick as you'd think and the creek's real pretty farther back. I went right over to the foot of the mountain."

They had come to the house and Colin turned away to separate the milk. Margaret went in. "Don't be long," she said.

Colin hurried because he was hungry, and he washed his hands and face at the outside pump in case his father was still using the sink. The kitchen woodbox had to be filled, he knew, but the wood was split ready for it and there would be enough in the box until after supper. He went quietly into the kitchen and sat down in his place at the table. Margaret was bringing the dishes from the stove. He could hear his father moving in the bedroom. Mrs. Ensley was mixing something but she turned and looked at him without stopping the movement.

"You'll be hungry now, Colin," she said. "You wouldn't come and see your old mother, even to get something to eat after school."

"I wasn't hungry," Colin said. "I ate all my lunch."

"And didn't bring your lunch bucket in."

"It's outside. I'll go get it after supper."

Mrs. Ensley came over to the table, set down a loaded dish, then ran her hand gently over Colin's black hair. It was the confident movement of a mother who knows she is loved. "Did you have a good time, son?" she asked. "That's the main thing."

"It was swell. Much better than I ever thought it would be."

"I want to hear about it. Not now. Your father's worried about something. But don't forget any of it."

Colin smiled at her. "I won't."

William Ensley came into the room as his wife moved away from the table. He was a fairly tall man—probably an inch or two under six feet—but so broad he seemed squat. He wore a heavy jet-black beard, spade-shaped and trimmed very square. His eyes were black under eyebrows almost as thick and black as his beard. Thick black hair grew profusely on the backs of both hands. He seemed, and was, a man of great physical strength. Standing in the doorway of the kitchen, cleaned up after his day's work, wearing a good shirt of gray wool and heavy tweed pants, he seemed to have far more than mere physical power; he might have been John Brown or Daniel or Isaiah.

His wife said quietly: "Sit down, Will. Supper's all ready."

"So's Colin," Will Ensley said. "Ready and waiting." He turned his strong deep voice directly to Colin.

"You cleaned up, son?"

"Yes, Father," Colin said. "I did it outside after I was through separating."

"You don't have to remind him, Dad," Margaret said. "Colin never forgets that any more."

The four of them sat down at the table. Colin and Margaret sat straight-backed, their hands in their laps. Mrs. Ensley bent her head a little forward. Will Ensley held his head high, but his eyes were closed. "Almighty God," he said slowly, "Who hast seen fit to grant us of Thine abundance, bless this meal that is set before us. And of Thy mercy grant us strength to honor Thy Name through all adversity."

Colin listened, as he always did, to the rolling sound of his father's words rather than their sense. They were seldom exactly the same words—Will Ensley took pride in his power of extemporaneous prayer—but they usually carried the same implications of gratitude, humility and faith in bodily nourishment as a way to spiritual strength. Tonight there was a difference, not only in the words but in the solemn sound of them; they were spoken just a little more quietly than usual and with a shade of urgency beyond the normal duty of gratitude. Colin glanced towards his mother and saw that she had raised her eyes to her husband's face. She looked away again before Will Ensley opened his eyes, but Colin knew that she had noticed the difference too; it seemed to him that she had expected it.

They began to eat and Colin used his hunger. The Ensleys talked little at their meals—Will Ensley had made his growth on the silent meals of the New Brunswick logging camps, had brought the habit of silence west with him to the Pacific Coast camps and even in his own house had not grown away from it. But tonight he seemed to want to talk. He asked first Colin, then Margaret about the day in school. He asked about the cows and chickens, wanted to know if Colin had played ball after school, even teased Margaret about the new long dress she was to wear at the high school dance. Martha Ensley waited and said little. After nearly twenty years she knew all the weaknesses, all the needs that were so well hidden behind the front of physical strength. Because she was what she was they had made and built her love for him, they were her eternal care and her religion within the simple, undemonstrative Christianity she devoutly lived.

She said at last: "You were right about the new bridge, Will. You got home just as soon."

"We didn't go out there," he said, and she knew she had led him to his trouble as he wanted to be led. "We aren't going to build that trestle—not for a while, anyway."

"Where will you be going, then?"

"I don't know. Some say there's a long shutdown coming. Some say the outfit's finished—bankrupt. That talk's been going around for weeks, but I never thought much of it till today."

"But you worked today."

"Sure, we worked," he said heavily. "On the mainline. There's some sills need replacing in the framed trestles."

"They wouldn't do that if they were finished would they?"

"It's good maintenance ahead of a long shutdown." He reached over and cut himself a slice of bread. "It isn't as if it hadn't happened already other places. Half the mills are down and there's no price for logs."

"It won't last," Martha Ensley said. "If they do shut down it will only be through fire season and that's happened often enough."

"There'll be work," Will Ensley said. "There's always work for a man that knows his trade. But it may not come so easy as it has."

S I X days a week William Ensley got out of bed at five o'clock, put on his working clothes, then ate a solid breakfast that Martha Ensley cooked for him. Breakfast over, he took his coat and his lunch pail and went out to wait at the farm gate for Mike Varchuk's car to pick him up.

The wait was something Ensley liked well enough, even in the dark and cold of a winter's morning. It settled his breakfast, brought him to terms with the day ahead. On a clear summer morning such as this, it did more than that. He was genuinely fond of the two big broad-leaf maples that stood one on either side of the gate; their permanence and solidity, here at the entrance to what he thought of as his "property," gave him an increased awareness of ownership, a keen sense of being an established citizen. He was not, he liked to remind himself, an improvident, transient logger, but a solid man, a skilled craftsman, trusted by the company he worked for, the head of a family and the owner of a substantial property. Occasionally, as he did on this morning, he liked to turn and look towards the barn. It was a good barn, square and strong, standing well out in the pasture from the house. He had built it, with the help of neighbors, eleven years before, and it reminded him that there were cows and chickens on his property. These were another sign of providence and solidity, a background detail, quite properly the care of Martha and the children, yet a credit to his own substance.

The sound of Mike Varchuk's old car as it came over the crest of the hill destroyed Will Ensley's appreciation of himself. Without quite realizing it, Ensley did not like automobiles any more than he liked cows and chickens. He had never owned one or learned to drive one and they did not fit at all with his conception of himself or of his world. He was never at ease with a machine, nor could he consider a machine as a tool, in the way he thought of his axes and augers and saws. Though he had worked close beside machines all his life, he felt that they were in some way obscene, against the will and purpose of God, and he shut himself off from them as far as possible. That Mike Varchuk should own a car was in itself a faint condemnation of cars in general. Mike was a foreigner—Ensley would not use the term "bohunk" even to himself, because he considered it degrading and un-Christian—who still spoke broken English. He was a loudmouthed man and a radical, one of the few loggers who regretted the wane of the I.W.W. and the O.B.U. Will Ensley might have been able to forgive all these things, but he could never forget that Varchuk was also an atheist and an indifferent worker.

The car stopped and Varchuk shouted a cheerful good morning over the noise of the engine. Ensley answered civilly and climbed to his place in the back seat. Varchuk ground the old car into gear and they started off to pick up the others who rode to work in the same car—John Meldrum, the pile-driver engineer, Tony Soretto, the section foreman, Earl Mayhew, the rigger. They were all family men, except Varchuk, all in their forties, steady and hardworking men who had settled near the outskirts of Blenkinstown to raise their families within reach of a company they liked to work for.

Will Ensley sat squarely upright in the back of the car, nursing his coat and lunch pail on his knee. He always sat the same way, stiffly and tidily, as though the car were much too fragile for the weight of his great body and the roughness of his working clothes. This morning he was hoping Varchuk wouldn't talk about the shutdown, but he knew that this was expecting too much, so he modified the hope a little—he hoped that Mike wouldn't talk until the others were in the car.

But Mike began to talk as soon as he had the car bumping along in high gear. He took one hand off the jolting wheel and turned almost clear around. "Looks like hard times come pretty quick now. This outfit fold up. Lots of men laid off. Wages go way down. Some people be pretty hongry before she's all over."

"I'll believe it when I see it," Ensley said. "The world's got to have logs."

"She come," Mike told him. "You see. All over the world and the poor people will starve and die some places. Maybe here."

They were almost at Earl Mayhew's gate, where the other three were waiting. Will Ensley waited till Varchuk had put on his brakes before he said: "No man needs to starve in this country."

The car stopped and the three men climbed in, wedging themselves into their usual places. As Ensley had hoped, the stopping and loading and starting broke the conversation. Mike was busy with his gears again and the others were settling themselves, stowing lunch pails and coats. Will Ensley withdrew into himself, his eyes on the stumps and salal brush and second-growth that lined the road. It was all going to start again—shutdowns and lay-offs, argument and trouble and conflict, breaking into a man's life, making him less than he was, forcing decisions upon him that had nothing to do with his skill or strength. It would be a time for men like Mike Varchuk, the talkers, the weak ones, the improvident ones, the godless ones. They were all saying the same things now, even John and Earl, leaning forward to be heard in the front seat.

"It won't last," John Meldrum said. "It's just the big guys getting squared to freeze out the little guys and make a clean-up."

"Sure," said Mike Varchuk. "Sure it's the big guys. So the working stiff is going to starve if he don't get wise."

"Nothing new about an outfit going broke," Earl said. "Another set-up always comes in sooner or later."

"In good times maybe soon enough," Mike said. "In bad times, maybe not soon enough so your kids got full bellies."

The slow thoughts swung heavily across Will Ensley's mind, a procession of black, distorted shadows, the suffocating stuff of all terrible dreams. That Varchuk is happy, saying the things he's saying. He isn't a man to say honest things, yet he believes these things he is saying and they aren't the things he usually says, nor said the way he usually says them. When men talk that way it means trouble, bad trouble. There wasn't any work after the war. It was only like that for a while, but it was bad while it lasted and there was trouble and they told you "no" and "nothing" when you went to ask for work. That couldn't happen again. There hasn't been a war. And it would be different now. They know Will Ensley now—everybody knows Will Ensley.

Varchuk was still talking and the others were arguing with him, but Ensley could tell they were worried. Just over fire season, they were saying, open up again in September. We can last till then and forget all about it. A man could get work some place else anyway—good riggers and good engineers don't grow on bushes. Will Ensley tightened the muscles of his great shoulders and looked down at the broad palms and thick fingers of his hands. "They just don't make broad-axe men any more," he heard the superintendent say. "Will here is the last of them all and we're lucky to have him." And that piece in the Vancouver paper: "Ensley's axe can square a timber truer than any sawmill and leave the faces as smooth as though they had been planed. He can build a house and furnish it with no other tool than his axe." Will Ensley looked out again at the stumps and salal brush and second-growth, the normal things that were all about him every day, and would be. He was slowly searching his mind for a phrase he had heard, a phrase he had taken for himself as he heard it, that belonged to his present need if he could only find it again. "Work finds a man. . . ." No. "A good man doesn't have to. . . ." Then it was suddenly clear and sound in his mind: "A man that's good never has to look for work. Work looks for him." Let them talk.

COLIN never woke to the slight stirrings about the house caused by his father's breakfast and departure for work. Usually it was necessary for Martha Ensley to waken him in time to milk, do the other chores and eat breakfast before leaving for school. This morning he was half-awake when she called, trying to explain to himself his reluctance to face the sunlit day that reached in through the window of the little room. Doing the chores would be easy and pleasant, with the cows quiet and sunlight outside the open door of the barn—probably Margaret would come out to help before he was through milking, because she loved such mornings as well as he. Walking to school would be good—especially good for some reason. What reason? He remembered three—the meadowlark near Mayhew's gate, the red-winged blackbirds in the swamp, the yellowlegs along the edge of Craig's Bay; he and Margaret had seen them yesterday, had talked about them and been sure that they would be there to be seen again.

But he was fully awake now and knew why he had not wanted

to face this day. Facing the day meant facing Mildred Hanson and Tod Phalling. He knew what would come from Phalling, almost certainly, and as he dressed he tried to recognize what he feared from Mildred Hanson. It wasn't anything really, he told himself. She couldn't be sure it wasn't an accident, likely she's forgotten all about it. She didn't say so much when you stop and think about it. Then his memory was suddenly sharp and clear again and he knew she would not have forgotten.

He scarcely saw the sunlight as he milked in the barn, and Margaret found him silent and gloomy when she came out to meet him. After breakfast when they were on the way to school, she tried to solve his mood. "Did something go wrong yesterday? Something more than being kept back?"

"No," he said.

"There's something wrong. Is it Tod Phalling and Jeff Burnside again?"

"I'm not scared of them," he said. But he knew he was, so scared that he didn't want to think about them and wished she'd stop reminding him. It isn't what they do to you so much as the way they suddenly turn into strangers, two different people altogether. And Jeff gets hold of your arms and Tod stands in front of you with his face all white and his shoulders hunched up. Then he asks you a question and hits you before you can answer, then asks another and hits you again. Everything they do when they get you like that is slow and quiet, but hard and mean. It's not like when other kids get mad and fight. It's so slow there's no getting mad to it at all and it scares you so you think your insides are going to run out and it goes on and on. "No," he said again. "I'm not scared of them."

"They're mean and dirty," she said. "Tod especially. And they're older than you—bigger than you really even though you are taller."

Colin said nothing. They were coming near the Mayhew's gate and he looked for the meadowlark on the fence post where they had seen it yesterday. He didn't want to see it now as he had when .he was waking up, but he hoped it would be there because it would be something else to talk about. It was not there and Margaret said the thing he dreaded. "I'll wait and walk home with you."

"No," he said. "I'm playing in the ball game. You don't need to wait. They won't do anything." She doesn't know those guys. They don't give up that easy—Jeff might, but Tod wouldn't. He wouldn't care if he had to wait a week or till school closes or till it starts up again in the fall. She can't be around every place all the time. Once it's over they'll be O.K. and maybe I can make it tougher for them this time.

He heard the meadowlark then, in full song, as it flew up from the grass. They both stopped and watched its flight. Margaret said: "You told me we'd see it again today and you were right. You know, Colin, sometimes I'm proud of you." They started walking again and Colin said nothing; but something lifted inside him and he knew it would be there all day to help him. She hadn't meant to praise him because he had known the bird would be there.

MILDRED Hanson had faced the day with a concern at least as deep as Colin's, but she had at once a clearer understanding of what had happened and a more positive responsibility. In itself his touch had been nothing more than the lonely, yearning gesture of an adolescent boy. It had not been impertinent as Jeff Burnside's touch would have been or indecent as Tod Phalling's would have been. It would have been nothing and could have been passed as nothing had it not reached in upon her own dangerous thoughts and aroused all her fear of them. He saw that, she thought, and heard it in what I said. He will remember it for a long time and think that what he did was much more important than it was. I could have passed it off so easily—I didn't have to notice it at all. Anything would be better than what I did. There will be something between us now, something he doesn't understand, something to hurt him and make him suspicious. He's going to believe that he did something bad. He can never know that what happened came from inside me, not from him at all.

She was writing on the blackboard when Colin came into the room and did not see him go to his desk. Through the day Colin was silent and unresponsive, answering only when he had to. It has to be done slowly, she told herself, very slowly so that many, many little things are built up between him and that one thing I made so big.

Colin had been glad of the chance to get to his desk while her back was turned. He had anticipated the difficulty of looking into her face and wishing her good morning and had thought little beyond that. Now the difficulty was past and when she turned and looked over the class without singling him out he found himself wondering again whether she might not have forgotten.

At recess Tod Phalling spoke to him. "Going to play ball today, punk?"

"Sure," Colin said. "Why not?"

Tod laughed. "You're scared enough to wet your pants right now."

Back at his desk Colin knew what he should have done. Fighting in the school yard was always punished. But it would have been better to fight then, when Tod would have had to fight alone, even if it meant taking a licking from Tod first and the old man second. I haven't got the guts to think of anything like that until it's too late. Other guys do, but I haven't got the guts. . . . He felt the sweat hot all over his body and he was shaking.

The ball game was four innings only, but Colin played every minute of it with a concentration that let him forget what was ahead and even made him less clumsy than usual. He felt good at the end of it because his team had won, he had hit safely twice and fielded half a dozen chances well enough so that no one had yelled or laughed at him. Neither Tod nor Jeff had been playing and he lingered awhile over the break-up of the game. The security of the laughing, kidding, ball-throwing crowd made Tod Phalling seem unreal and distant. Why should he bother, Colin thought, he and Jeff have got more to do than waste an afternoon waiting for me. But the group of boys gradually broke up and he saw at last, as he had known all along, that there was no one there who would be going his way home. I should care, he told himself. They won't be waiting—not today; some other day perhaps, but not today. It's been too long.

He saw them as he came round the first bend beyond the school, waiting under the big maple tree beside the road. Jeff Burnside stood up when he saw Colin coming, but Tod stayed where he was. Colin made no move to turn aside, only walked on towards them, awkwardly, afraid, yet still not certain that what he dreaded would really happen. When he was still five or ten paces away Tod climbed lazily to his feet.

Tod hated Colin, but only with a tempered and intermittent hatred. He hated Colin because Colin was big and because he sensed in him a potential physical strength. He hated Colin for being untidy and awkward in appearance yet successful in school. He hated Colin because people who disliked Tod—which meant nearly every one in Blenkinstown—were fairly certain to like Colin. All these hatreds of Colin calmed into something approaching tolerance whenever he beat Colin, and he had learned years before that he could beat Colin into a crawling hulk with very little difficulty whenever he felt like it. Right now he felt like it. The multiple hatreds had been stirred into life by a precocious, muddled jealousy; Mildred Hanson's preference for Colin cut squarely into the cherished fantasy that made himself the recipient of her ultimate favors. So Tod now stood in Colin's way, legs apart and firmly planted, hands at his sides, fists clenched. Colin hesitated and stopped. Tod said: "So you weren't lying for once, punk."

Colin watched the pale eyes. The blood was throbbing in his body and his throat was tight. He tried to watch Jeff Burnside too, but knew he could not. He thought: why should this be me? I don't want to fight them, not even for what Tod did to me last time. Why should I be here, like this, and why should he hate me so his face goes pale like that?

Tod said: "You going to tell us now, punk?"

Colin looked down at his feet, then half-glanced over his shoulder at Jeff Burnside standing grinning behind him. "Tell you what?"

"Tell us what that chippy did with you yesterday."

The word reached into Colin's mind and slowly took on its full meaning. "You can't talk about her like that."

Tod thrust his pale face forward. "The hell I can't," he said. "Your mother's a chippy. So's your sister."

Colin jerked into awkward movement, felt Jeff grab his arms

3 3

from behind, felt Tod's fist in pain that shot up through his chest, half-choking him. But his slow strength responded, threw Burnside from him, crashed his own shoulder against Phalling, then let him stumble and fall full length in the gravel. They were on him in a moment, driving their knees into his back, twisting his arms. They rolled him over and Tod's hard fists hit him twice in the face. Tod laughed. "Quite the scrapper, ain't you, punk? Want to tell us about it now?"

"I've told you," Colin said. "I told you yesterday."

Tod climbed to his feet. "Let go his arm, Jeff," he said. "Let him up so's I can lick him good."

Colin rolled over, spat blood from his cut lips and began to get up. Tod kicked him.

Colin was crying. He heard himself say: "Let me alone, can't you?" But he got to his feet and lunged awkwardly at Tod. Tod sidestepped, hit him in the stomach, hit him in the face. Colin swung again, felt his right elbow smash solidly against something, saw Tod's startled face in front of him and struck at it with his left fist. Then he was held from behind again and Tod was standing in front of him, the red blood brilliant against his white face. "Why you awkward son of a bitch," Tod said slowly, and hit him. "You overgrown, under-balled bastard." Tod hit again, then brought his knee up hard into Colin's groin. Jeff Burnside let Colin slip to the ground.

Tod stood looking down at Colin. He raised his eyes and glanced up and down the deserted road. "I never did that to a guy before," he said. "Let's scram out of here."

4

COLIN was on his feet within two or three minutes of the time Tod left him. He felt sore and battered. His lips were cut and swollen, his cheeks were bruised and there was blood in his nostrils. His whole body ached and his head throbbed. But he was not as badly marked as he had been in previous encounters with Tod. When he came to a creek that crossed the road he turned into the brush and knelt beside a pool to wash the blood away from his face. Kneeling there he cried, because he had knelt in the same place before to do the same thing and it seemed to him suddenly that this could go on happening forever and he could do nothing to stop it and there was no one to help him. I haven't got any guts, he thought, I don't want to fight him and even if I did want to he's too quick and strong and there's always Jeff or somebody there to help him.

He rinsed the blood from his handkerchief, squeezed out the water and wiped his face again. A car passed on the road and he could see the dust from it, but it was quiet and cool where he was and he felt better. He remembered the surge of strength through him that had hurled Jeff away and jarred Tod. I did want to fight then, he thought. I might have got somewhere with it if there hadn't been two of them. Maybe I'll go on getting stronger until I can lick 'em both, easy. He held to the thought, keeping it hard in the front of his mind as he stood up and turned towards the road again. But deep in him he knew that he would never want to fight, that he would always be afraid of Tod's pale face and cold eyes. The old, often-used thought came back to him again, reducing his new strength but without renewing his unhappiness: if it could be quick, like a bullet in the heart, it would be good and quiet to die.

Tod Phalling kept away from Colin the next morning, but as they passed each other at noon he said almost kindly: "Feeling O.K., kid?"

Without looking at him, Colin said: "Sure." He wanted to say something more, something defiant, but he was afraid to.

"You sure caught me a dirty one in the mush," Tod said, and Colin looked at him then. He was smiling, his upper lip was swollen and a front tooth was broken. "No hard feelings," Tod said. "Jeff was sure scared when you passed out." He went away and Colin felt vaguely warmed and flattered. He fought against the feeling, remembering Tod's pale face thrust towards his and the hard, relentless fists, but he thought: it wouldn't be hard to like the guy, if he'd only stay that way.

THE problem of Tod resolved itself for Colin before the summer holidays. He disappeared suddenly, from the school and from Blenkinstown. For a week after his disappearance there were wild rumors of its reason—he had held up Joe's gas station, he had broken into the liquor store, he had tried to rape a girl, he had been caught stealing from mail-boxes. Whatever the crime, it exhausted the patience and influence of Tod's father; and Tod, it was learned much later, had been sent to the interior of the province to work under close supervision in an uncle's sawmill. It was several years before Colin saw him again.

Those early summer months seemed to solve other problems, too, for the Ensley family and for Colin. The Blenkin Lumber Company did not shut down, Will Ensley's crew moved out to the trestle on the new line and his job went on—at lowered wages, but it was still his job. Colin's school work improved and as the days went on he was less and less able to convince himself that he had ever seen the quick flash of fear in Mildred Hanson's wide, calm eyes. Mildred herself was largely responsible for this. She had tried at first to deny the problem by denying the attraction she felt for Colin. In time she convinced herself that this was unfair to him. He was different from the others, she admitted. He needed encouragement and affection as they did not and it was in her to give him these things. So she gave them, gradually, almost reluctantly, but with increasing conviction. She recognized his response and found a measure of absolution in it, though her dedication would not let her forget the moment of failure.

The school year had been a triumph for Margaret. Mr. Siddons, the principal, had driven out to explain to Will and Martha Ensley that she was the most brilliant pupil ever to pass through the school and that she must go on to the University in time. Will Ensley had been suspicious at first and reluctant to commit himself. Martha had seemed to agree with his doubts while cautiously and subtly resolving them. Mr. Siddons had said that he and Mildred Hanson would spend extra time with Margaret so that she would go to the University with every chance to get the most out of it. Will Ensley still did not commit himself, but he agreed to keep the matter in mind and see how things went in the next two years—a concession which meant, Martha well knew, that he would use the thing in bluster and argument and moralizing until he had grown used to it and fitted it to his own conceptions.

For Colin the end of the term was a release from the tension that was always on him when he had to come close to people outside his immediate family. He knew this tension only as a shadow that was over his days, growing stronger and darker when he had to speak in class or pass among the groups of boys in the schoolyard, deepening to utter confusion in the face of violence or intense competition or the jarring contempt of boys who found time to notice his physical clumsiness. He had learned that the shadow could often be made lighter by shutting himself away in his own thoughts, letting them carry him on and on until even the nearest and most jarring sounds were silent, and the pictures in his mind faded to a pleasant, quiet confusion of light. When he was with certain people, with his mother or Margaret, with a friend like Johnny Harris, the shadow withdrew altogether. When he was with his father the shadow was there; it could fade at times, almost to disappearance, or it could grow dark and heavy.

In spite of the shadow Colin was happy at school. His mind responded quickly to any phase of the work that went beyond the normal routines of learning. He had discovered already that there was pleasure and excitement and safety in reading. Mildred Hanson had been quick to notice this and lend him books that would lead him still farther beyond the narrow limits set by the Department of Education. She was opening up for him, as she had already for Margaret, the neglected splendors of Canadian history—the great journeys of McKenzie and Fraser and Hearne, the vision of men like Moberly, the westward thrust of settlement, slower, more orderly, more difficult but never less courageous than the same movement of the Americans. These were things to reach into a boy's soul and he was happy for them. He was happy also in things outside school hours. He liked to play ball, and he nearly always had a chance to because he had a strong throwing arm and was a good hitter; his lank awkwardness made him clumsy and slow as base runner and he was too erratic for the infield, but he could judge and handle long flies as safely as anyone in the school. The total of his virtues was far more than enough to carry him on any team he played for and adequately covered a lack of competitive spirit that would have betrayed him in a tougher league.

He liked also to be at the edge of a group of boys who were arguing or planning something, silent and unnoticed if possible, hoping that nothing would happen to turn attention upon him, but eager to listen and feel accepted. Nearly always he was accepted, and accepted on his own terms.

All these things lessened the shadow that was with Colin through his school days, but it had been too firmly planted at some earlier time to fade altogether, so the release of the summer holidays was something more for him than it was for most boys.

Summer meant many things to Colin. It meant fishing and swimming in the lake up beyond Mike Varchuk's place, with Johnny Harris and Dick Thompson. It meant picking blackberries in the old logging works with the blue grouse starting up from underfoot. It meant haymaking, when Earl Mayhew came to mow for them some early morning and later on to rake; Colin and Margaret would cock the hay from the windrows and Martha Ensley always came out to help when they had borrowed Earl's horse and wagon to haul to the barn. Summer meant hoeing the garden, which Colin did not mind because it let the long thoughts work in him. It meant going up to lie secretly in the hayloft with a book, it meant being alone when he wanted to, going alone to the big maples near the line fence in the alder flat, following the road to its end out beyond the lake, walking the other road out to the beach camp, to hide alone in the brush and watch the train come down with the logs.

It meant things Margaret would think of, books she would find for him, plans they would make together. He had an urgent plan of his own for this particular summer: he wanted to climb the mountain behind the alder flat. He had mentioned it once or twice since he had followed the creek back to the end of the flat, but he knew that Margaret had not really felt the idea with him— she had let it slide away out of their conversation very quickly and Margaret did not do that with any idea that really reached her.

Colin held to it, thought often of the ways it could be done and built pictures in his mind of what they would find as they worked far up from the valley.

There was one entirely new thing about this summer. Colin had known of it since the previous fall and had thought of it often because it meant for him a long advance towards manhood. Each year Will Ensley cut from the alder flat several cords of wood for the house. In previous years Colin had gone out to watch and had been allowed to help by cutting away limbs and brush and by piling the cordwood as his father cut it. He had helped again later in the year when they fed the cordwood to the circular saw that reduced it to stove-wood and when they piled the short lengths into the woodshed. From then on the daily chore of splitting and packing the wood to the kitchen had been entirely his care. In the previous fall, as they piled the last of the wood into the woodshed, Will Ensley had said: "Next year it's your job, son. You'll start it and you'll finish it. I'll help you with the gas saw, but that's all."

Colin said, "You mean I'll cut it in the bush, fall the trees and everything?"

"That's right," Will told him. "You're man enough to be learning now."

He did not mention the matter again until the evening of the third or fourth day after school closed. Then he called Colin out after supper, as he often did, to turn the grindstone for him. Tonight, Colin saw, he had only a double-bitted swamping axe instead of the great, heavy broad-axes he usually brought home.

"Turn slowly," Will said. "I only want to touch it a little." Colin took the handle and brought the even stone into smooth, easy movement. The axe sang against it in Will's huge hands, gathering a rippling film of water on the upper side of its edge. It was withdrawn, turned and it sang again. Colin had served a long, straining apprenticeship at this grindstone and he had learned to control it absolutely, to hold it always at the speed his father needed.

Will Ensley asked him: "How's your own axe?"

"Fine," Colin said. "I haven't used it since I last ground it."

3 9

Will straightened up and felt the edge of his axe with his thumb. "Bring it along. We're going out to the alders."

As they walked across the pasture together Will Ensley looked at Colin and smiled so that his strong teeth showed very white in the black of his beard. "Think you're going to be able to handle it, son?"

Colin thought he had never seen his father so happy about anything. "Sure," he said. "I'm a whole lot stronger than I was this time last year and I can chop better too."

"Think you can hit twice in the same place, maybe." Will Ensley was still smiling. In spite of his powerful conception of himself as head of the family, he seldom felt wholly at ease with his children. He had children because children made a family and because having a family was part of man's duty—he had accepted God's words to Noah: "Be fruitful, and multiply, and replenish the earth"; had Martha been a stronger woman the family would never have stopped at Colin and Margaret. But now that he had the children, they were a surprise to him. He found that he did not know quite what to expect from them or, usually, what to do with them. He worked steadily and brought home good wages so that they should be fed and clothed; he taught them the righteousness of God and was himself righteous before them and before God. He corrected them and disciplined them when it seemed necessary, he read their school reports carefully and approved their successes when he could understand them. But he had seldom been able to feel, as he felt now, wholly sure of the duty he was performing and of his ability to perform it. He had never before been able to feel, as he was feeling now, that in Colin was a repetition of his own boyhood.

As they came to the edge of the alders, he said: "I was a year younger than you when my father started me cutting cordwood."

"Was it alder?" Colin asked.

"No, mostly spruce. Some birch and poplar." They had stopped and Will Ensley was looking around him at the tall, gray-barked alders. "Nothing as big as these," he said. "Except the maples and a few pines, but the pine was mostly gone and we cut the maple into logs, not cordwood. This Pacific Coast is the greatest country in the world for growing trees, except nobody knows enough to take care of it. Log and burn, log and burn and move on, that's all they know."

Colin listened respectfully and with a strong sense of belonging where he was, with his father and in the woods. He looked at the huge, competent hands resting on the axe handle, at the wide black beard jutting forward as his father swung his head slowly to look at the trees. He's the finest axeman in B. C., my old man, Colin thought. Everybody knows that. And he knows everything there is to know about trees. I can't be the same as he is, I'll never be that strong, I'll never be able to learn like he did, from working in every province in Canada where they cut logs. But he can tell me and show me a lot of what he knows and I'm going to learn it.

Will Ensley slid the bright axe to his shoulder and walked across to a tree. He set one hand against the smooth trunk and looked at Colin. "Which way does this one go?" he asked.

Colin looked at the lean of the tree, looked along the ground, then back to the tree again. "Right here," he said and pointed along the line of the tree's lean.

Will Ensley shook his head. "No," he said. "Too many young trees along there. You'll want trees twenty years from now. No sense to breaking those down." He struck four short blows with his axe and there was an X on the side of the tree, clean-edged, deeply cut, perfectly proportioned. "Make your undercut on the mark. Drop her across the lean—there's nothing to hurt there and it'll let your tree down easier."

They went from tree to tree until Will had marked a dozen. "Those'll be enough," he said. "Till you see what you've got. And they'll square away this corner good."

They went back to the first tree and Will Ensley began to put in the undercut. He worked without a sign of effort, yet the bit of the axe drove deep and the hickory handle seemed to bend in the air and the heavy white chips flew out in bright arcs and fell fifteen or twenty feet away. It seemed to Colin that his father had struck not more than twenty or thirty times when the cut was finished—yet the tree was deeply notched, the lower side of the notch perfectly horizontal, the upper sloping to it at an angle of fifty or sixty degrees, the faces of both as smooth as though sliced by two cuts of a giant knife.

"Finish it off," Will said. And Colin went round to the back of the tree and tried to do as his father had done. The alder wood was soft and his sharp axe bit cleanly into it, but he hurried a little and drove his strokes harder than usual in the hope that the chips would fly far out as they had for his father.

"Not so fast," Will said. "And let the weight of the axe work for you." He thought: the boy's grown a lot and he's strong, going to be really strong. Takes after me. He'll have a weak back though—too tall for the big strength he'll have in his shoulders and chest. How does he come to be tall like that and with those great feet of his? I like to see a neat-built man, all in one piece and quick on his feet. The boy'd trip and break his neck on a bridge stringer, leave alone one of them little poles they spike between the bents. He don't get that from Martha nor me. Some say it's the coast climate, makes the kids grow tall and soft like the trees. I don't believe that, but it's a queer thing, just the same. Margaret's taller than her mother too, but she's neat on her feet, not like him.

He looked towards the top branches of the tree, saw them quiver to the axe stroke, and moved a little. The boy's strong, though, and he chops good, clean and good like a man that knows his trade, and he don't seem to tire none. The tree cracked sharply and the top began its slow swing in the line of the undercut. Colin had judged the cut well, leaving the tree strong on the side opposite its lean. The strength held it until it crashed forward and down, broke clear and lay perfectly at right angles to its lean.

"Good," said Will Ensley. "You showed that one who was boss. Could've drove a stake with it."

Colin felt a hot flush of pleasure in his face and for a moment he thought he was going to cry. Will Ensley reached forward and set a hand gently on Colin's shoulder. "You will be a strong man, son," he said. "And great strength is a gift of the Lord. You must learn to use it well."

PART TWO

THE FIRST VALLEY

5

IN spite of Colin's size and increasing strength, cutting the alder was a big job for a boy of his age and it ordered most of his summer holidays. He did not mind that at all. He was always happy when he was cutting it and when Johnny Harris came up to be with him and help he felt a vague resentment and tried to keep Johnny from doing very much. Johnny was a year older than Colin and his physical opposite—a short, thickly built boy, very neat and economical in his movements. He had a round, cheerful face with eyes that were strongly and inescapably blue and a rare, slow smile that showed short, even and very white teeth. Johnny talked little, at any time, but he always seemed at ease with himself and everyone around him. Probably because of this, Colin always felt at ease with him.

Johnny had already left school, to help out on his father's farm on the other side of Blenkinstown. He was used to working and liked working and whenever he came to see Colin and found him cutting alder, he would start in automatically to pile the cordwood or clear away limbs, anything that would keep his hands busy and speed the job along. After a very short while of this Colin would stop working himself and suggest that they do something else. Johnny would smile happily and agree, or else make a suggestion of his own, and they would go off to fish or swim or simply walk in search of anything at all. But once he said: "Look, Colin, why don't you let me help and get this darn job done with? Then we could go places any time."

The question embarrassed Colin. He had not admitted, even to himself, that cutting the alder was an ever-ready excuse to get away by himself and he did not want to admit to Johnny that he loved the work, the sharp, clean bite of the axe-strokes, the flight of white chips from the deepening cut, the scent of crushed leaves and stripped bark; or that he wanted the whole job to be his own achievement, from start to finish. He said: "You've got your own work to do at home. I don't have to hurry any with this job. Times like this, when you're free, we may as well go places and do things."

This was how it happened that Colin made his first attempt to climb the mountain with Johnny, not with Margaret. They started without plan or preparation, at about two o'clock one afternoon, simply turning away from the piles of cordwood and into the brush. They crossed the alder flat quickly and were climbing steeply as soon as they left it. Colin led the way, following the draw to which the creek had brought them.

Because he had seen the start of the slope from the flat and because he had made the climb so often in his mind, this first part seemed almost familiar to him. The draw was shallow at the start and they kept very close to the creek, crossing it from time to time to find easier going. The timber was mainly hemlock, but it was tall and straight and mature and little brush grew under it. The draw grew deeper as they climbed and they worked away from the creek, keeping it always on the right of them, to the south. Then they came to a bench, where the creek spread in swampy ground and salmonberry bushes and devil's clubs grew thickly. On the far side of the bench they came to the first rock bluffs.

So far they had not stopped at all, but Colin hesitated at the foot of the bluffs. Johnny was breathing hard and his face was flushed. "Don't you ever get tired?" he said. "Let's take a spell."

"We started out so late I thought we ought to step on it," Colin said. They sat down on a slab of rock just below the bluff.

"You're not figuring to make it to the top, are you?" Johnny asked.

"I suppose not," Colin said slowly. "I hadn't figured much about it—just that we'd see how far we could get."

"We couldn't make it under a whole day," Johnny said. "Maybe not then."

"We can learn something about how it is today. Then we can take a day out sometime and do it right."

"Where'd you get the idea from anyway?" Johnny asked. "What do you reckon to find up there?"

"Nothing. I just want to see what it looks like." Colin searched himself for words to tell Johnny what he wanted of the mountain and why he wanted it, but he could find none that made sense. It was easy to see the mountain from Blenkinstown and it was not in any way a spectacular mountain. No one had even bothered to give it a name, so far as Colin knew. Its top was a rounded height rather than a peak, separated only slightly from the range that climbed back to divide Strathmore Valley, where the Blenkin Logging company operated, from the larger valley of the Wind River, to the north. The mountain was heavily timbered to within about a thousand feet of its top and from there on the timber thinned rapidly to bare gray rock that was snow-covered only in winter and early spring. Colin knew he wanted to come out to the scattered timber and the bare rock, to see and touch the lonely wind-torn trees that Mildred Hanson said grew in such places, to search the rock for the alpine plants she had described and to find the freedom of looking far out over Blenkinstown to

45

other mountains and other valleys. There was nothing in all that you could tell anyone about and he said: "I've always wanted to get up there. I think it would be different from down here. The air'd be different and you'd see things differently. Heck, I don't know why I want to get up there. I just do."

"That's O.K.," Johnny said. "My dad always says a man don't have to account for everything he wants to do. I guess I know how you feel."

They found a way up between the bluffs along the creek, climbing the damp and slippery rock slabs easily enough. Colin was happy because this was different from anything he had done before and the steepness of the climb gave him a sense of achievement. They came to another bench at the top of the bluffs and Johnny said: "I get a kick out of that. Suppose we'll find more like it farther up?"

"Should do," Colin told him. "Some a whole lot tougher, I guess. Everybody says mountains get steeper near the top."

But they climbed for another hour, following the creek through its timbered draw, skirting occasional bluffs and crossing several benches without finding any real difficulty. They turned then and made their swift way back to the routine of chores and supper, but Colin knew the day had been made important to him forever, because now he would certainly climb the mountain. It was far forward in him now, a real purpose, no longer a dream that might fade beyond recall at a moment's notice.

THE logging company was still running when school started in September. There were rumors of bankruptcy and shutdown, but Will Ensley worked steadily until an early snow came in November, forcing a shutdown that seemed likely to last over Christmas. The camps were still closed at the end of January, though the weather had been good and there was little snow in the woods.

Most of the married men who lived near Blenkinstown clung to hope of some kind through the early spring months; there were rumors again—a bunch of big shots coming up from town to look the place over; ten sets of fallers due on the Wednesday boat; a scow-load of steel had come in for the new line. But when Will Ensley and Earl Mayhew went up to the beach camp they found only old McPherson, the bookkeeper; he told them he knew nothing, nothing except he was drawing ninety bucks a month as caretaker. Mike Varchuk laughed when Earl Mayhew told him that. "She won't roll a wheel up there or put fire under a boiler, not till they get good and ready. They starve you out first, make you good and hungry. Then you go back and work for any wages they say, just to get full belly again. You see. She all happen before."

Mike Varchuk talked more than ever. Will Ensley still did· not care for the things he said, but he found himself remembering them and trying to fit them in to what was happening. He could not make them fit, because he still believed in himself, believed in his strength and in his skill at his craft, and in the worth and importance of his craft. He believed that there was work to be done in the world; if a man could do the work he would be paid for it. The things Mike Varchuk said matched nothing in Will Ensley's experience and they were wicked, against God and against God's order. In spite of the easy laughter that Mike always found to go with them they were bitterness and weakness—the excuses, Will felt, of a man who was not a good worker.

Martha Ensley recognized the thing for what it was from the start. She was a child of a solid pioneer family and she had grown up to know her world as alternations of hardship and prosperity. The bitter periods were never far away, even in the highest prosperity; they could come suddenly, through fire or storm or sudden death, as well as by the slower, mysterious paralysis that crept periodically from the cities, out to farms and woods and even the salt water, cutting away the prices of logs and fish and beef cattle until there was no hire for men and no return for work. She was wise and experienced in meeting such times and she did her best to prepare for them when things were going well.

She warned Colin and Margaret of what might be ahead one day early in February. They had come in wet and cold from the walk from school and they were hungry and she had bread and jam and tea ready for them in the kitchen.

"You must be careful not to bother your father," she said. "He's worried and I'm afraid it's going to get worse."

4 7

"Some of the kids were saying the camps are going to open next week," Margaret said.

"They've been saying that since before Christmas," Colin told her.

"I don't suppose anyone really knows," Martha said. "But I've seen all this happen before and it's going to be very hard on your father. It's always hard on the men."

"What happens when nobody's working?" Margaret asked.

"Your father will find work," Martha said. "It won't be easy to find and there won't be the same steady wages he's been getting. All those things worry a man with a family."

Colin slumped a little farther down in his chair. There had been long shutdowns before, for fire season and for snow over Christmas, and he remembered his father's frowning silence and increasing irritability as the weeks wore on. They were stretched beyond that stage already and he was trying to picture what was ahead. "Won't we have enough money for things we have to have?" he asked. "Like food and clothes?" He felt a little ashamed because the idea seemed exciting, yet he knew his mother was worried.

"We'll manage," Martha said. "No one needs to starve in this country. But we'll have to make everything count."

"I could leave school and get a job," Margaret said.

Colin straightened in his chair. "So could I. Let me do it, Ma. She's much smarter in school than me."

Martha spoke sharply. "You can both of you put that sort of nonsense right out of your heads. As long as I have anything to do with it you'll stay in school and do your work properly. There may be a little more to do around here to keep things going, but the most important thing is to keep your father cheerful—do what he says and never complain in front of him." That's enough, she thought. They know him as well as I do. "Run along and do the chores. For all I know they'll be working again within a week and we shall have forgotten all about it."

"It's happening all over," Margaret said. "It can't be any worse for us than for other people." She stood up. "Come on, Colin."

Martha went to the window and watched them as they crossed the field towards the barn. They had taken the thing farther

4 8

than she had meant them to, realized more of it than she was ready to admit to herself yet. But she was not altogether sorry. Her defenses were good. The farm would mean a lot—cows, chickens, fruit trees, garden—and the children could do much of the work. Will was the one who would suffer—Will's pride and power and faith in himself, Will's black strength, his black and exacting God. As she had before, Martha measured Will's God against her own, though without recognizing that they were different Gods. He gives us different kinds of strength, she thought, and if another kind of strength is better than Will's kind for a little while, he mustn't know it. That must be part of the other strength, to keep him from knowing.

6

IT seemed at first that Will Ensley was right in his belief that a skilled workman need never be without work. His ability was well known around Blenkinstown and several people asked him to do small jobs of hewing and building. They apologized because the jobs were small and the pay was low, but Will had never learned to measure himself in terms of wages and so long as the jobs were worthy of his axe he was contented enough. He was helped, too, by his confidence that the company would start work again; the small jobs merely filled in until that time and the low wages were at once a subsistence for his family and a service to his neighbors.

But as the months went on the jobs became fewer and smaller and once or twice the wages were no more than a promise to pay. In June Will went along to Earl Mayhew's house.

"I'm going to walk up to the beach camp," he told Earl. "Want to come along?"

The two men said very little as they walked. There was little that needed to be said. Each knew what he was going to look for, and each knew what was in the other's mind.

They reached the camp between rain showers and found it silent and empty in the June sunshine. There was no smoke from the stove-pipe over McPherson's cabin and they found the door locked when they tried it.

They turned and walked out along the wharf. There were logs in the water, two or three sections made up and ready for the tug. "Side Two stuff," Earl said. "The last we put in. Can't be much call for logs or they'd have taken them out."

The cables on the dumping rig were red with rust and there was rust on the casing of the blocks. Will looked down at the piles under the wharf. "The worms will be in 'em good," he said. "It's four years since we put in any new piles."

They turned and walked back along the track to the car-shop and the roundhouse. The big Baldwin and two Shay locomotives were inside, black and silent.

"Reminds me of a graveyard," Earl said. "A locomotive without steam up is the deadest thing there is—deader than a dead person."

"Must figure to use 'em again some time," Will said. "They put paint and grease on before they tied 'em up. Where's Number Three?"

They walked along a short spur line and found Number Three, a small Climax locomotive, painted gleaming black and with fresh gilt on the figure 3. The track had been seldom used at any time and the brush grew thickly to the edge of it. A strong shoot of salmonberry, green in the sunlight and still wet from the shower, curved gracefully right across the front of the little locomotive. Earl turned away. "Looks like she's going to be a tough one," he said.

Will knew that he meant the winter ahead.

FOR Colin and Margaret life was little different. Their father was at home more often but he kept away from the house during working hours, coming back only just in time to clean up for the evening meal. Martha worked harder than usual in her garden and was sometimes tired to exhaustion when they came home from school; but she seemed happier than she had ever seemed, quicker in her movements, surer and more purposeful in her planning. It was a gradual, almost imperceptible adjustment to the new conditions, as Martha intended it should be. She had begun to build the farm steadily, yet without spending money. She had bartered cream for setting eggs and doubled her flock of chickens. Colin and Margaret were raising calves and hoeing root crops. The fuel supply was sure and cost nothing except Colin's work. Everything that could be canned or stored or preserved was harvested in its season and set away for the winter.

Colin found his life fuller and more real to him and he was happier for it. He did his work easily at school, finding new satisfactions in it, but he did not grow out of carelessness or away from the long daydreams that crept into his mind with every lapse of attention. Mildred Hanson's calm competence had almost effaced memory of that air-built moment between them; Colin remembered it, but it became less and less believable to him. Sometimes, looking at her cool and inaccessible loveliness, he tried deliberately to recall the moment of courage that had let him touch her. He became instantly afraid then, and awed and unbelieving. He tried to crush the desire away from him by assessing its presumption and wickedness. The memory of her warmth and firmness under his hand would become strong and stirring and for a moment he could believe again that she had responded to his touch. Then memory would fade in disbelief. His mind would deny it because Mildred herself so plainly denied it in everything she was and did.

Mildred also denied her clear memory of what had happened, forcing it away from her with a control Colin did not possess. But she remembered the loneliness into which she had sent him and which must have been in him when he touched her. She saw it in him again, often, as he sat in class or walked about the schoolyard and always there was something in her, far deeper than any teacher's obligation or simple human pity, that longed to reach out and lift it from him. Because she did neither more nor less than any teacher would have done, she believed herself secure from the attraction she still felt for him.

Mildred spent several hours each week with Margaret, drawing

51

her and rounding her beyond the narrow teaching limits of a small country school. Their friendship grew steadily and they often found themselves talking simply as friends rather than as pupil and teacher. Mildred welcomed this and worked quite deliberately towards it, not merely because she was fond of Margaret, but because she felt that Margaret could make more growth in it than she could in more orthodox study. They talked freely of music and painting and literature, drawing on Mildred's collection of books and the school's small library. They talked of religion, testing the differences between the Gods of Will and Martha and those of Mildred's Lutheran parents and friends. They talked of what was happening around them, of the broken stock markets, the innumerable remedies that innumerable prophets were proclaiming, of unemployment and strikes and misery, and of what was happening to Blenkinstown. Mildred's salary had been cut already, but she was not politically minded and she was not bitter. "It can't last here," she told Margaret. "Because the town depends on something essential. People have to have lumber. They can't live without stores and houses and bridges. They have to have new roofs and boxes to put things in, and paper to print news on."

Margaret laughed. "You talk like Father," she said. "He says over and over 'The world can't get by without logs and lumber.' I think maybe it can get by on a lot less than it's used to."

"What's happened to your father? I used to see him going past here every morning on his way to work."

"He and Mr. Mayhew have taken on some kind of contract," Margaret said. "They're cutting alder for a furniture factory. I don't think it's working out very well."

Mildred looked at her anxiously. "If it keeps on will you and Colin stop school?"

"Mother won't hear of it. Colin wants to go out and work, but that's silly—there isn't any work. And we both can help a lot at home, with the cows and chickens and garden."

"Colin might find a job somehow. He's growing very big and strong even though he is so dreamy and clumsy. You mustn't let him stop school."

"He isn't clumsy," Margaret said. "Not when you see him

5 2

working or in the woods. We tried to climb the mountain last week and he walks so much more quietly than I do that I'm ashamed. He doesn't slip on rocks like I do either. He seems to belong there."

Just for a moment Mildred hesitated, then she said: "He could be a great man. I don't know why I'm so sure, but I am. It's there in the way he speaks and looks, but much more in the way he thinks. He doesn't think like any other boy I've ever known."

"Colin?" Margaret spoke the name slowly. "He's so shy and gentle to be great. He's afraid of so many things and so many people. Great men are sure of themselves."

"Not always," Mildred said. "Great men have been weak and sick and blind, they've been half-mad by ordinary standards sometimes, shy and withdrawn and doubtful of themselves very often."

"They all wanted something very much though—to do something or be something. I don't think Colin does."

"A boy doesn't dream the way Colin does unless he wants something."

"Colin dreams all right," Margaret said. "But I don't think he dreams anything practical."

Mildred laughed. "Dreams aren't supposed to be practical, but practical things grow out of them."

"That takes something more than just being able to dream a dream," Margaret said. "Something Colin hasn't got."

"You're too close to him to see it. But I've seen it in some of the things he writes and in some of the things he does. It isn't anything you can name. It's a spark of some kind, it's being different in a special way."

Margaret tried again to think of greatness in Colin, but she could remember only slowness and untidiness and lack of purpose. She felt a sudden irritation because Mildred was so interested in him. "Everybody worries about Colin and makes allowances for him," she said. "I think it's time he did something for himself."

"He has to have a chance to grow into whatever he is," Mildred said. "That's what schools and teachers are for." She felt her deep conviction and it was in her quiet clear voice. "We have to watch them all and make them grow just as far as they can. It doesn't really matter whether I'm right or wrong about Colin. If

I think there's something special in him I have to help him find it."

"Won't he find it himself if it's there? Doesn't greatness always come out in the end?" Very gently her tone mocked Mildred's intensity.

Mildred hesitated. "No one can know that," she said at last. "I think most great men get help somewhere along the way. And we can't know about the ones who might have been great if they had had help at the right time. Think of the times when only rich people learned to read and write."

"If they had a bright boy in a poor family they made him a bishop's secretary or something. And he went on from there."

"A few maybe. But most of them used up their greatness herding pigs or dreaming dreams or in being good common soldiers for some baron." Mildred laughed. "At least that's what I like to think. I guess any teacher likes to think it. It's a long way from Colin, though. At least, he can read and write."

Margaret had been watching her closely as she spoke. She said: "You're terribly fond of him, aren't you? I mean more than just because he's bright in school?"

The direct simplicity of the question made Mildred flush. She knew that Margaret's mind had asked it, not her emotions, that it was simply a further shrewd point in her argument against Colin's potential greatness; but she knew also that anything she herself thought of Colin was colored by emotion, born of intuition even though nurtured on reason. "Yes," she admitted slowly. "I'm fond of him. He needs help so much. But I should still believe he could be great, even if I weren't fond of him. I get fond of lots of the children. No teacher can help that." That's the truth, she thought, looking into Margaret's dark eyes. It's the truth and it isn't the truth yet I don't really know why it shouldn't be. And I'm sure she can't know why it isn't. She can't know, she isn't old enough to know, and no sister could ever think it of her kid brother.

"I'm fond of him, too," Margaret said. "More than most sisters are of their brother, I think. Lots of people are fond of him. Perhaps that's part of what could make him a great man."

Mildred moved eagerly. "Yes," she said. "It is. It is part of it. All his gentleness is part of it. If you feel it too, it must be."

5 4

She hesitated a moment, then went on. "We aren't being fair though. He doesn't have to be great to make it important to help him. That's a stupid big word that doesn't mean much anyway. He just has to be what we both know he is."

7

B Y the end of July Will Ensley knew that he and Earl Mayhew were going to make no money out of the alder contract, but they worked on until the job was finished in mid-August. Will said as they loaded the last log: "We won't get taken that way again. We've got to find something that'll make a few dollars next time —if," he added hopefully, "they don't open up soon as the bad fire weather's over."

"There's nothing that says they will," Earl said. "I'm going to get me a fall buck or two for the old lady to put up. They'll start to move down pretty soon now."

Will Ensley had never been a hunter, but Martha had the same thought as Earl—it was less thought than a simple reaction to the season of the year, and the times. Deer hunting had been a routine in her family, intensely pursued in the early fall, fluctuating vaguely through the rest of the year, but always a part of normal living. Her father had hunted and her brothers had hunted; and, though they found sport in the hunting, the family's meat supply had depended upon their success or failure more often than not. Unlike most other Blenkinstown boys of his age, Colin had never hunted, and he felt a sharp surprise when Martha said: "You'll have to shoot some deer this fall, Colin. Your father won't, but that's no reason you shouldn't."

Colin hesitated. "Father won't like it," he said. "And anyway I don't know how to hunt."

"Circumstances alter cases," Martha said grimly in one of her

5 5

favorite phrases. "You can learn to hunt—Earl Mayhew will soon show you."

"He wouldn't want me along," Colin said.

"Nonsense," Martha said. "I've never yet seen the hunter who wasn't glad to help a boy out that way. When I was a girl every boy learned to hunt just as naturally as he learned to read and write—most of them learned it a good deal better. Your grandfather taught all my brothers to hunt as soon as they were old enough to hold a rifle—there weren't any butcher stores in those days."

Colin moved awkwardly from where he was sitting and crossed the room to the door. "I'll go ask Mr. Mayhew right now," he said. "I'd sure like to learn to hunt." He had thought past the learning and saw himself alone, a rifle over his arm, searching the timber, planning his hunt, finding his buck. It would not be hard. He knew that, because he had seen deer often and easily without thought of hunting them.

"You can use your father's rifle," Martha said and pointed to the Winchester hanging on the wall. "It shoots true even though it's never used."

EARL Mayhew was a good hunter but, like most loggers, a poor woodsman. Standing timber overawed him, even frightened him, and he kept as far as possible to the open logging slash, working the draws and swamps cleverly enough when he had to, but preferring the high grassy ridges even to these. He was pleased and flattered when Colin asked to go along with him.

"The boy'll be good company," he told his wife. "And he'll learn quick."

"I'm sorry for that boy," she said. "He might as well not have a father."

"Will's all right," Earl said uneasily. "Just different from the rest of us—kind of religious and set in his ideas, but he means well enough."

"He's a dark man," Joan Mayhew said. "And a hard man. I wouldn't want to be his child—or his wife. Not for a million dollars."

"He's a man you've got to respect. There's not a finer man at

5 6

his trade any place. He's got a good house and he's raising a good family."

"He scares me," Joan said. "Him and his beard and his Bible. He scares the boy too and he'd scare Martha if he could, only she's too strong for him. Think of that boy coming to you to learn to hunt. He must be all of fifteen. Any natural father would have started him out years ago. You would have."

"We can't all be the same. Will's a good father—there never was a straighter-living man. If Colin grows up as good he won't come to any harm."

Joan glanced at him impatiently. She was a tall, big-boned woman of about thirty, with a decisive, practical face and the calm assurance that comes to a woman in love with a man less strong than herself. "How you all stick together," she said. "It doesn't matter about Will Ensley—I know he's your partner and I know he's straight. But be kind to that boy. He needs kindness."

The warning was unnecessary, for Earl was naturally a kind and gentle man. Colin hunted with him regularly through the fall months and they killed several deer. Joan Mayhew followed Colin's development with interest that turned at least as much upon Will Ensley as upon Colin. Even in November, after a year of shutdown, the men still half believed that the camp would open up again within weeks; but Joan, like Martha, had recognized the difficulty of the times almost at once and was fully aware of their threat to the security of her family. She sensed the weakness that was hidden under Will Ensley's strength and was almost instinctively afraid of her husband's close association with him. She was genuinely fond of Colin, but she felt that through Earl's interest in him she could reach out against Will.

One Saturday, late in November, she heard Earl come in from hunting with Colin. It was already dark and she had supper on the stove, so she did not go out to him; but she heard him drop a buck from his shoulders in the woodshed and knew that the hunt had been successful. She knew his every action from the sound of it, knew that he had hung the buck on the gambrel, knew that he had slipped his blood-stained coat away from him, taken off his caulked boots, put on the slippers that were waiting there. She crossed the room and opened the door then. "It's good you got one," she said. "We need the meat. Supper's ready."

Earl came into the room, walking stiffly and blinking in the light of the gas-lamp. "We got two," he said. "I never saw anything like the way that kid can hunt." He took the kettle from the stove, went to the sink and began to wash.

"Where did you go?" Joan asked him.

"Up to the big burn and along the line of swamps to the Swan Meadow. It was a bad day to hunt too—frost every place in the shade. I wouldn't have bothered with it if it hadn't been the only day the kid's free to go out. Far as that goes I needn't have bothered—he shot them both."

"Colin did? He certainly learns fast. Did you hunt them up for him?"

Earl clamped a towel against his dripping face and laughed. "Let's eat," he said. He was still laughing when he sat down. "I can get my share of deer alongside most men," he said. "But that young Colin makes me look like a two-bit amateur."

Joan put their two plates on the table and sat down with him. "You rate pretty well in my book," she said. "It isn't often you come home without what you went for. But what's this wonderful thing Colin did?"

"I told you it was a tough day to hunt. Well, we didn't work at it much on the way out—just hiked on through to the meadow. Soon as we get there Colin stops and points down to a big buck track going away from the meadow. 'He ain't heading our way,' I told him. 'What we want is tracks going down towards the meadow.' 'You know,' Colin says, 'it's real warm in the sun when you get out of the wind.' Where we were standing was in shadow from that rocky hill on the south side of the meadow, so I said: 'If we keep right on the way we're going we'll come out into the sun again.' Colin didn't even seem to hear that. He said: 'You know, Earl, if I was that buck I'd go find me a sunny place out on the bluffs, sheltered from the wind, and lay there all day till feeding time in the evening.'"

Earl paused to eat, then went on with the story. "He told me he'd follow the track and for me to go round the other side of

5 8

the hill in case the buck heard him and tried to sneak off. I didn't think either of us'd stand much chance, but it seemed as good as anything else, so I started off round the hill like he said. I wasn't more than just round into the sun again when I heard him shoot. And when I got up to him, sure enough, there's a big four-point stretched out in the sun at the base of a bluff. He hadn't even got on to his feet when the kid shot him."

"I've heard you play hunches like that and have them pay off," Joan said.

"Sure I can get me a good hunch sometimes," Earl said. "But not follow a buck's track on a frosty day and shoot him when he still don't know I'm in the same country. Wait till you hear the other one though. It was down this end of the burn, where the big alder and willow thicket runs along the bottom of the draw. We'd gone up on the north side in the morning and were coming back along the south side, down wind from the thicket. Colin stops again for a buck track, going down towards the thicket this time. 'That was made last night,' he said. 'And we didn't cross any track coming out on the other side. I'm sure of that. Likely he's still in there.' So he starts down the trail to follow the track and I find a place up on this ridge where I can see both sides of the draw. Pretty soon there's a shot down in the thicket and I go down there and darned if he hasn't shot this buck too, right on his bed."

"How did he learn it all so fast? You haven't been out more than a dozen times all told."

"That's what gets me," Earl said. "I've noticed it in him before, but it seemed like today he just got his confidence to ask to do things his way. I asked him when we were cleaning the second buck how he learned to track like that. 'Track?' he says. 'It's just the same as hunting the cows when they go back in the alder bottom. Only easier. There's not so many tracks.' That's right enough, I guess, but it doesn't tell why an awkward-looking kid like that can go quiet enough to come up to a deer on its bed on a frosty day. Nor how he can shoot the way he does, just one clean shot in the neck each time. He's a natural hunter, that's all. But what I like about him, he hasn't got enough conceit even to know he's good."

"I'm glad," Joan said. "It ought to be good for him. He's a boy who needs something like that to bring him out."

Earl shook his head doubtfully. "It'll take more than that. Colin's the quiet kind. I never did see a kid take less pride in what he can do."

BECAUSE of the long shutdown, game seasons meant little that year in places like Blenkinstown. The coast country had gone back to hunting its meat and wise game wardens looked the other way, so long as the hunting was done in daylight and no one took more than his reasonable share. People needed meat and there was little money to buy it.

Colin hunted right through the winter, sometimes with Earl, sometimes alone. He liked hunting with Earl. Earl was kind and wise and always the same. Earl laughed easily at things that happened and talked of logging and the men he worked with as though life were all simple and pleasant and natural, as though no hard things really happened and people were never afraid of each other. He was never gloomy and depressed about the shutdown, as Will Ensley was, he was never distant and obsessed with things he would not share. When he was with Earl Colin felt that if he could only finish with school and go to work in the woods, life would have no more problems.

But though he liked being with Earl, Colin enjoyed the hunting most when he was alone, working through a thicket, following out a track, climbing along the open bluffs above the logging slash. And he never forgot that he wanted to hunt in the timber rather than in the open. Earl discouraged him at first. "There's far more deer in the logging works," he would say. "There's more feed for them there than there is in the green timber. Anyway, you'd just lose yourself in the timber." But as time went on and the effortless, unlearned quality of Colin's woodcraft became clear to him, Earl changed his mind. The next trip they made after the day at Swan Meadow he said: "I believe you're going to be one of those guys that really know how to hunt in the woods. Do you still want to try it?"

"Sure I do," Colin said. "It seems more natural that way, as though the deer'd be better up there."

60

"You could be right about that last," Earl said. "Most of the bucks down here are getting strong. They might be later up around the snow-line, especially if you pick out a spike or a real big one. Meet me back on the grade here by four o'clock, though. I don't want to have to worry about whether you're lost or not."

Colin turned and started on his way at once, half-afraid that Earl might change his mind. He crossed the half-mile of logging slash quickly and entered the timber without thought of hunting, climbing steadily until he could no longer see light through the trees behind him. He stopped then and stood still on the easy slope, looking about him. It was a day of cold rain, with a wind in the treetops that threatened to grow stronger. Everything, logs, moss, salal leaves, the fir and hemlock needles underfoot, was soaking wet. A creek rattled down a draw a few hundred feet away. The wind swept water in great drops from the crowns of the tall trees. But Colin thought only: it is quiet here. None of this is sound. It is part of the woods, part of being free and away from sounds; there is nothing here that I am afraid of.

He went on up the hill, hunting now, traveling in the swift silence that so amazed Earl Mayhew. Colin was not conscious that he traveled silently. Whether or not he was hunting he wanted to see without being seen, hear without being heard; this had grown in him from early childhood until he had strained his clumsiness into a wild animal's habit of breaking stride to avoid any stick or stone or hard object in his path. His eyes were quick about him as he walked and his ears were alert; in spite of his awkwardness he seemed able to pass among leaves without brushing against them, and the sum of his movement was smooth, swift, but little perceptible.

He came into scattered patches of thawing snow and saw fresh deer tracks. There were many tracks and he did not turn aside for them, but merely slowed his pace a little and began to watch more closely than ever. Earl had said it was difficult to see deer in the timber, but Colin had seen them there before and had a picture in his mind of what he was looking for. In a little while he had seen a two-point buck with a doe, then two more does, then another buck, and had passed them all without stirring them to flight. He was glad that Earl had said to wait for a spike or a big buck. This is pure and clean, he thought, and it means something. Perhaps no one has ever stepped right here, where I'm stepping, in the whole history of the world, perhaps no one has ever seen these trees before, no one ever touched this rock till now. If I swing over a little way I shall come to the creek. People have seen that, but not the water I shall see flowing down it and not the ferns that I shall see hanging over it. Mother couldn't come here and Father never would. Margaret would and could, but only if I brought her. This is my own place, this whole hillside under the timber. No one else uses it or wants to use it. There is no one on it to stop me or turn me or tell me, no one to hear me, no one to see me. And the woods go back along the valleys and the hillsides, along the lakes until they run out in rock and snow and ice beyond timberline.

The big buck was feeding on the top of a little fallen cedar. Colin saw him and stopped, but made no move to raise his rifle. I could shoot him, he thought, and still go on, then come back for him later. But it wouldn't be the same. It makes so much noise. And there is the blood and the smell of him would be on me through the rest of the day. It wouldn't be the same. I don't want to shoot him, I don't want to hurt the silence, I don't want to see him dead and see his blood. I hate the blood. But I ought to want to shoot him. We have to have meat and I'm yellow to be afraid of the blood and not to want to shoot. What am I afraid of? The brightness of the blood, or the hotness of it, steaming on the snow? Or his dead eyes and the sound he would make when I put the knife in his throat? I'm not afraid. I've done it all before. Why not today?

The buck looked up and saw Colin, but could not recognize his stillness. He raised his nostrils, tested the wind, bit at the cedar again, but was still uneasy. He moved away, along the little cedar, as though he still meant to feed, but not feeding. He disappeared behind a big fir and Colin saw him only once again, far up the hill, turning to look back.

Colin's mood was built, not broken. I am alone, no one has seen me, no one but me can ever know the buck was there. No one can ever know anything I do back here in the woods. He turned up the hill again and began climbing steadily into deepening snow. He climbed far beyond the last sign of deer, then turned along the hill and hunted the barrenness of the deep snow. The wind grew steadily in the trees and the rain had turned long ago to heavy snowflakes. It was late in the afternoon when fear and shame caught up with him again and turned him, strained and sweating, down the hill. He had to hunt now and find his deer and kill. He did not want to face Martha with the knowledge that he could have killed and had not. He did not want Earl to be able to tell him that it was better to hunt in the open logging works.

8

MARTHA Ensley worked at her garden in the cold rain of a day early in March. She was happy because she loved gardening and it was good to be getting such an early start. The last of the snow had disappeared soon after the end of January; February had been cold and sunny; now March brought rain, a cold rain still, not a growing rain, but there were many things to be done in the two or three weeks before it would be time to plant seeds.

The camps had opened up again and Will had been working at his old job for nearly three weeks. Wages were very low and the men were organizing and there was strike talk. Even Will, who had little use for unions, had shown some interest. "It's no better than starvation wages," he had told Martha. "Maybe they can't pay any more and keep running—that's for us to find out. But if there's something to spare the men should have it. The laborer is worthy of his hire."

Martha broke a clod of wet earth with her fork. There'll be fighting of some sort before it's all over, she thought; men always come to that. But if they work for a little while it'll be a help.

Will's got to get his pride back and he'll never find it in the way this last year has been. There's a lot to be thankful for, though. There's been plenty to eat and a good roof over our heads and the children are still in school. Perhaps it was wrong to make Colin start hunting; sometimes Will hates him when he brings in a deer. No one could have guessed he'd be so good at it; Earl says he's a natural hunter, the best he has ever seen. In some ways he's a lot like brother Jim was, the quiet kind; they always make good hunters. But Jim was a much neater man than Colin, he was never all feet and hands and loose joints like Colin is, not even when he was a boy. It must be in the way they think more than what they do, and in how good their eyes are. Colin has good eyes, like Jim's; he is always seeing something before anyone else —a hawk over the chickens or a deer in the pasture or the first robin that comes.

She lifted a forkload of the heavy, clinging earth, drew in her breath sharply, set the fork down and leaned against its handle. It's too wet, she told herself, too wet and heavy. She breathed carefully, to keep the pain away while she rested. In a little while her breathing was calm again and she went back to her digging.

She forced her thought straight on, as though there had been no interruption. It has been bad for Will to feel that Colin was the man of the family when he came in with a deer. He wouldn't ever have felt that in ordinary times, and he wouldn't have allowed Colin to go hunting in ordinary times. But there wasn't meat without that and the boy was doing it on his Saturdays, so there wasn't anything he could say. And it isn't as though Will could have taken to going out himself after all these years. He's not the kind to change easily, over anything, and that's a good thing most of the time; it makes for a steady man, a good worker and a good family man. But it's hardest of all on that kind when things go wrong.

Will is a good family man. He's always been good to the children; he believes in God in his old-fashioned way, really believes in God, and he's tried to pass that on to them. He never swears in front of them, they've never seen him drunk or careless with himself, the way so many men are. He earns good wages, comes home when his work's done and brings his money with him. He's a good husband and a good father. It's a lot to be thankful for.

I am thankful, truly thankful. I only wish . . . I only wish he could be closer to us, more part of us. I love Will. I would have liked to hold him close to me sometimes and to be held sometimes. I would like to sit with my hand in his sometimes, just for no reason except that we are close. But it doesn't happen, it can't happen now. I suppose I'm still afraid of him in a way, the same way I was before we were married. I used to think then that it would change. He's never done anything to make me afraid, but it hasn't really changed. Perhaps I should have tried harder—I know I should. Perhaps it can still happen, we can still come close. I'm an old woman to be thinking such thoughts; it's hardly respectable to think them at my age. But we poor weak humans need some other human close to us and I don't think any God would call that sin.

Martha knew she was crying, but there was no acuteness of grief or misery in her tears, only regret for what might have been and hope for what might still be. Her thoughts were prayer now, prayer offered silently in the spring rain and as naturally as thought, without even a lifting of her face to pray. Not for me, O God, not for me, but for Colin. Let him come closer to his father and his father closer to him. Give him cause to look up to his father and respect him and feel strength from him, as a boy should. He needs that help more even than most boys do. Colin's a strange boy, too strange and moody for the world to be easy on him. He needs some strength of his own, just as Will needs it and finds it in his work. Only Colin needs more than just strength in his body and skill in his hands. If he could be more like Margaret, sure of himself as she is, less of a dreamer; he will grow out of all that, I know, and find his place, but he needs help, the kind of help a boy gets from being close to his father. In some ways Will is more of a child than Colin ever will be again, but Will has his place in the world; he knows his work and his work gives him his place and lets him earn all that money he has been bringing home for so many years—just the work of his hands and his big muscles, and a way of thinking about caps and stringers and donkey-sleds.

Will is a good man and I should be content for Colin to grow into a man like him, except that Colin is not a man like Will; he is less like Will even than Margaret is and he has to find something more if he is ever to be a full man and a happy man. I don't believe it is wrong to ask that for my child. I ask it for his need, not just in a mother's pride and in the hope we all have that our children will grow up to be finer people than we are.

Martha stood quite still for a moment, her hands folded on the handle of her digging fork and her body bent forward over them. Her face was strained, but she was no longer crying. Her prayer worried her a little, as her prayers often did. She wondered if it might not be too direct and practical and personal. She knew she had to stop her gardening and go back to the house and sit down for a little while, and she knew that she had to make another prayer: Give me strength, Jesus, to go on doing all that I have to do. It happens so quickly now, I get tired so long before anything is finished and my heart beats so fast over little things even, that I'm afraid. They need me, especially in this time when things are so hard for Will and while Colin and Margaret are still growing up. Give me strength to go on until everything is right and safe again.

She walked slowly and carefully up towards the house, still stooping forward a little because that seemed to ease the pain in her chest, and with her hands thrust into the opposite sleeves of her coat, to shield them from the cold rain. If I make a cup of tea, she told herself, and sit down quietly with it for ten or fifteen minutes, I shall be strong and ready again when the children get home from school.

NEITHER the children nor Will Ensley suspected that Martha was sick. She had always worked hard, from the first thing in the morning until after supper, and she had always stopped several times during the day to sit down with a cup of tea. She allowed herself to move only a little less briskly now and she brewed an extra cup of tea and sat down with it only when the pain of her heart forced her to. After the first recognition of her trouble Martha herself was able to forget about it, almost to deny it. She told herself that it was natural to slow down a little at her age and she convinced herself that she could remember for years back the straining at her chest and the dizziness that came on her when she did too much.

The camps worked steadily through the spring and into the summer. Will Ensley's pay-checks were the smallest he had ever brought home, but he was working at his own job in the way that he knew and trusted and he found once again a sense of security and peace of mind in the routine of his working days and the clear headship of his family.

For Colin and Margaret the summer passed quietly and was little different from the previous summer except in the regularity of their father's comings and going. He was easier with them, less moody than in the previous year; but he had become active in the union and while he found a certain satisfaction in the authority and responsibility that this gave him, his conscience was never entirely calm under it; at one moment he gloried in the sense that he was serving his fellow workers, in the next he remembered the wordy violence of leaders like Mike Varchuk and the paid organizer, Miller, and felt that association with them was a betrayal of his whole life.

Martha made no concession at all to the fact that Will was working for regular wages again. She forced every part of the farm and garden exactly as she had the previous year and kept Colin and Margaret working as steadily at it.

Neither Colin nor Margaret was deeply conscious of any fundamental change in the way the family lived. Martha herself had anticipated the change, accepted it when it came and put her counter measures to work; but to her it was less a change than a part of life, a personal and family problem that could be solved within the family. She was aware that other families were facing similar problems and she helped when she could the Mayhews, the Meldrums, the Sorettos and others of her neighbors; and, just as naturally, she expected and accepted the occasional help they could offer. It was all done without organization, without sense of effort or obligation; it was a simple projection of the pioneer's reaction to adversity, no more than a phase of normality.

Margaret accepted a responsibility for the family that was only a little less than Martha's because it grew from her own wish to test and prove the strength and ability she felt within herself. At times she wished she had Martha's responsibility to the full—a family of her own and the need to plan and work for it. It seemed to her she would do it differently, with everything planned and organized instead of growing out of a mixture of experience and tradition. It irritated and worried her to see Martha doing so much herself; she seemed to go on and on through the days, always finding things to do and doing them because she found them rather than reminding someone else to do them. Like clearing out the chicken-house when Colin left it too long; and picking and canning all the cherries when Margaret herself should have done it over the previous week end.

Then, just for a moment, she saw her Mother's problem more clearly. It isn't so easy to organize a family like this, she thought. Dad's always so deep in his own affairs he doesn't notice what's going on; he never works around the place, the way Mr. Mayhew does at his place. And Colin's so absent-minded; nothing could change that. I'm just as bad, always going out somewhere or studying at home, studying with Mr. Siddons, studying with Mildred.

I think Mildred's sort of crazy about Colin; that sounds silly, but it's not; she looks quite different when she's talking about him, her voice goes very soft and you can see in her eyes that she's looking at him even though he isn't there. Colin won't talk about her. He doesn't blush every time he sees her, the way he used to, and he's not as awkward with her as he is with lots of people; but there's something tight and straining inside of him and sometimes, when he thinks no one is watching, he sits and looks at her as though he thought he would never see her again.

Perhaps I imagine some of that. Perhaps I'm jealous of Colin with Mildred because she talks about him so often and seems to bring him between us. I must be or I wouldn't feel this way when I know she wants to help him. Yet it makes me afraid for him, as though she was going to hurt him instead of help him.

COLIN lay on his back under a maple tree beside the creek in the alder flat. It was a very hot day in July and he had just come down from the mountain, after climbing to where he and Margaret had turned back the previous summer. Traveling by him-

6 8

self had been easy, much easier than with Margaret or Johnny Harris. He could have gone on farther, perhaps right to the top. But he had promised Margaret they would do it together and had turned back faithfully just beyond the place she had failed to cross.

He tried to understand the sudden fear that had broken her confidence on the narrow ledge, and could not. But tomorrow would be different. They would have the rope and she would know she was safe and cross easily. Tomorrow, his mind said, tomorrow, tomorrow. Before this time tomorrow. It's hard to believe that. It will be clear of timber up there, and we shall see over into Wind River and the big lake and all the way to the mountains at the head of the valley. And the little trees will be flat and twisted and there will be snow in the shady places and flowers where it's sunny. There will be wind and clear air and high clouds. And no one else near.

He felt his heart pounding at his chest and his breath short and his body hot, hotter than it had been when he was climbing. He moved restlessly, trying to break the strain of excitement and expectation. It seemed weakness to him, dangerously close to fear, and he remembered it had touched him just as fiercely when he had left Earl to hunt alone for the first time.

He lay back, feeling the moist earth against his shoulder blades, and gradually his heart slowed and his body relaxed. He could feel the strain of his climb now, pleasantly, in the muscles of his thighs and belly and buttocks. He was conscious of the day's achievement, of having earned this rest, this distant, pleasant awareness of his body. Looking up through the green of the maple leaves over him, he saw blue sky and white clouds. As he had half-known they would, these made him think of Mildred Hanson. He let himself think of her, with his body as well as his mind. His body had earned this right by its struggle with the hill, just as one of Arthur's knights might have earned a similar right in triumph over some darker, stronger opponent. Momentarily Colin tried to deny that the right was his, but his body told him plainly that it was and he yielded to it, remembering other such yieldings when he had lain in bed on winter nights. The strain was across his shoulders then, as well as in legs and thighs, from carrying his deer out of the woods, and his face was hot and stretched with burn of wind and cold rain. But the right was the same, irresistible and safer with each use, the body's reward for successful endeavor, the mind's delight in the setting of soft, imagined things against the fresh memory of harsh and challenging things.

9

THE day that Colin and Margaret started to climb the mountain was hot and dry and still. They milked very early, laughing at the surprise of the cows and their unaccustomed hesitation about coming into the barn.

"We shan't get as much milk," Margaret said. "But we'll make it up tonight so long as we get home on time."

"We won't. Not unless we quit again."

"We've got to be back for supper. Mr. Grant's coming in and he told Mother he wants to see you."

"There's always something to wreck it," Colin said. "I should have gone on yesterday, when I had the chance."

"I won't quit on you," she said. "I promise I won't."

The shadows were still very long and there were tiny pockets of mist here and there along the creek as they crossed the alder flat. The intense stillness of a hot day's dawn was everywhere about them and small birds flickered among the trees and brush near the creek, feeding actively ahead of the day's heat. Colin walked his own swift, awkward pace across the flat and Margaret followed in silence; she knew he was still irritated by the thought that they had to be back by supper time, not so much because it reduced their chances of reaching the top of the mountain as because it set a limit to the day's freedom; but she knew also that he would forget this in time, as they climbed away from the flat and he began to let his eyes and mind work upon the things of the hillside.

Colin in the woods and Colin at school are two quite different people, Margaret thought as she watched his angular back and shoulders under the faded blue shirt. Generally I think of him as a baby, weak and shy and almost helpless. You never know what he's going to do—stumble over something, break something, spill something; he is sure to stand wordless when he ought to say something, or blurt something out when he ought to keep quiet; his clothes and his hair are always untidy and he is afraid of people and things that couldn't possibly hurt him. In the woods you don't notice any of that. He isn't afraid of anything; he always knows what he is going to do. Walking behind him like this I feel as though he would do anything he could possibly have to do, solve any difficulty or danger that could come up. He still looks awkward, his clothes are still a mess, his hair is still untidy, but none of that seems to matter. When I see him like this I think Mildred's right about him; I believe he could *be* something. But he can't be something by running away from everything and that's what he's doing here, today, climbing the mountain, even though he is good at it.

They had crossed a bench and were climbing round the first easy bluffs when Colin turned round and asked: "Want a rest?"

"No," she said. "Not unless you do."

"We'll take one anyway. There's lots of time."

They sat side by side on moss-covered rock and Colin said: "There's a mink around, quite close."

She looked at him in mild surprise. "Did you see it?"

"No," he said. "Can't you smell anything?"

"That musty smell, you mean? Is that what it is?"

Colin nodded. "Sure. He's quite close, just a little way up the bluff from us. I heard him as we came up. That's why I stopped."

Margaret was silent for a moment, then she said: "Why did you stop? We might have seen him if we had gone on."

"I don't know," Colin said slowly. "Because he was scared, I suppose. He must have been or he wouldn't have made the noise and let out his scent. It isn't very nice to scare things. Anyway, you see things best when they don't know you're there, not by chasing them."

Margaret picked up a little stick and probed at the dry moss between her feet. "I don't see how you know all those things. I mean about the noise a mink makes and the way it smells and what it's doing just from hearing it."

"I've seen them."

"Where? I never have."

"Along the creek sometimes. And down near the beach. It's quite easy to see things when you're alone and quiet, and when there's plenty of time." He stood up and looked ahead, up the bluffs. "Only there never is plenty of time," he said. "Let's get going again. Once we've passed this bluff we can work back to the creek. It'll be cool along the creek."

When they found the creek it was an easy, slanting funnel in damp rock, steadily noisy in little cascades that fell into basins of clearest water. "It goes a long way like this," Colin said. "I didn't try it before yesterday because I thought it might run into a straight bluff somewhere. But it doesn't."

He turned away again and climbed on, making little sound even on the bare rock, his feet always sure, never slipping. Behind him Margaret climbed her best, stretching her legs to find the footholds he had found easily, using her hands and arms to help her. She was breathing hard and she felt very hot, in spite of the cool dampness around her and the cool sound of the water, but she said nothing and climbed on. There was wind in the trees now, summer wind, fresh and strong but without violence. Fire wind, she thought. That's why they are going to shut the camps down again. Dry weather and the steady westerlies, Dad said last night. They've got to do it, he said; even a cable running over a stump could set a fire and the wind would drive it out of control in no time. They had been working for two weeks now on the early shift, starting out at two in the morning to catch the night's humidity, but even that was not safe any more and this morning they had not gone out.

Margaret stopped thinking and gave her whole effort to climbing. Climb and climb and climb, her mind said, won't he ever stop and rest? I can't ask him to, after what I said in the barn this morning and after what happened last time. But in a little while Colin looked back and saw how far below him she was. He waited for her and as she came up to him she said: "Couldn't we stop for a minute?"

He pointed up. "Just a little farther. There's a flat place before the next climb."

So they went on and came out of the funnel of the creek to a broad sunny bench. Colin lay down and she lay beside him in the bright sunshine, watching the branches of the firs and hemlocks move in the wind against the blue sky while her lungs strained to fill themselves and calm her body.

After a little while, Colin said: "We're almost up to where we turned back last time. Do you want to try it again?"

Margaret lay quite still, her eyes closed, remembering the steep place that had stopped her, the six-inch ledge, and the straight face above it that had seemed to push her outwards until she dared not move along it either way. "We've got to, haven't we?" she asked quietly.

"There's a way round it," Colin said. "It'll take much longer."

"We've got lots of time, haven't we? It isn't noon yet and we're quite high."

"We don't know," Colin said patiently. "We don't know what we may run into."

He's going to make me decide, Margaret thought, and I wish he wouldn't. It's an awful feeling when you're afraid of falling and you can't move. It doesn't happen to him. I remember climbing trees with him and climbing on the roof of the barn and he never got scared or seemed to think anything of it at all. It's nice lying here, resting and feeling the wind and knowing I can see the blue water away down below there through the trees if I want to sit up and look. It's far enough really. Yet I want to go on, just as much as he does. No, not as much. I want to go on and see something I haven't seen before; it's much more than that with him, much more. I don't know exactly how or why, except that it's in him and part of him. But I can tell how important it is simply because he keeps so calm about it now we've started.

"Let's go the hard way," she said at last. "We've got the rope this time and I won't be stupid about it again."

"It won't be so hard," Colin said. "It never is the second time."

Margaret sat up. "Not for you maybe. I'm not so sure about me."

An experienced rock-climber would have found no difficulty at all in the bad place. It started easily, a long, steep rock-slide cutting into the face of a gray cliff. They climbed it cheerfully, stopping to look back over the treetops to the islands and water far below them and the high mountains of Vancouver Island beyond the smaller islands. Blenkinstown was tiny and far away under the smoke of its two sawmills; the slope of the hill below them still hid the farm, but Colin said: "We'll see it from a little higher up. I'll show you."

Margaret thought: I wish we could go on right to the top like this, just climbing over boulders, with nothing to worry about except getting out of breath. But they were at the source of the slide already and Colin had stopped. There was a rock face in front of them now, and on the left a wall of rock and on the right another face of rock with a slanting, narrow ledge across it. By crossing on the ledge, Colin had said, they could come to another funnel that made easy climbing to the top of the cliff. Margaret looked at the place and remembered. Last year she had stopped twenty feet out along the ledge, frozen by fear of falling, and Colin had come back to stand beside her, touching her, speaking gently and calmly until she was able to move back to safety, his voice guiding her at least as strongly as the grip of his hand on her arm.

He said now: "This is where we use the rope."

He lifted the loose coils over his head, freed an end and passed it to her. "Round your waist," he said. "I'll go across with the other end and take a couple of wraps around something solid." He bent down to fasten one of his shoes, then looked up at her, smiling. "You won't need it, you know. It's just to make you feel good."

"I know," Margaret said. "I'm going to be all right. I was just silly last time." She thought: I've never seen him smile like that before. He hardly ever smiles and when he does he sort of hesitates and looks down. But now I feel as if his smile had touched me and gone on inside me and made me better than I really am.

Colin stood up and turned away towards the ledge along the rock face. She noticed that the end of the rope was in his hand, not tied around him. "When you come," he said, "don't hurry. And don't think any more of it than when you walk those cross-braces in the barn. It's easier, really."

Margaret watched him step out on to the ledge. The first few feet were wide enough for him to walk easily, then he had to turn in towards the face and move sideways for fifteen or twenty feet until the rock footing widened again. He went without hesitation, keeping his body very straight, balanced on the balls of his feet, his hands easily at his sides. Margaret watched him, half-expecting him to trip or stumble, knowing that he would not. I should have made him tie the rope to himself, she thought. He can't be so sure as he seems up here when he's so different everywhere else. Yet he is, and I know he is. Everywhere else he is my little brother and I have to watch for him and worry for him; now he's suddenly like an older brother, much older, much surer, much stronger. He doesn't know anything about mountains; he can't know because he has hardly been in them any more than I have. Yet I believe in everything he says and does—he doesn't even give me a chance not to.

Colin had crossed the narrow part of the ledge and was walking easily where it widened again. She saw him lean forward for a moment with the rope in both hands, then he straightened and looked back to her. "All set," he said. "Take lots of time and don't think about anything except getting across."

Margaret stepped hesitantly on to the ledge, then forced herself into firm movement over the easy part. She turned to face into the bluff much sooner than Colin had and began to edge her way along, her arms stretched out and the palms of her hands against the rock face. She felt her legs quivering and the muscles of her thighs seemed soft and useless in spite of the effort she was forcing upon them. The rock seemed to lean towards her and force her outwards and she felt terror growing in her. It's because I'm a girl, she thought; he shouldn't expect me to do it; my breasts make all the difference, I can't get close to the rock like he can. But it's my head that's touching the rock, not my breasts. It's just that my legs aren't strong like his. I'm not going to quit

7 5

again, I'm not going to, I'd rather fall all that awful way down and break to pieces than quit.

Colin's voice reached her, calm and easy and soft. "Stand straight, Marge, don't lean in so much. Stand straight and balance. It's easy that way."

She stood quite still, listening to him, feeling the panic draw away from her. She forced herself to straighten back, slowly, outwards, away from the rock, until her weight was squarely on her feet again. Then, quite suddenly, it was easy. The balance of her body told her she was secure; secure, upright, relaxed as Colin had been when he crossed. She let her hands fall away almost to her sides, holding them out only a little, the palms turned inwards. Her eyes looked straight at the rock from a few inches away. She moved her feet, moved them again and confidence grew in her. The ledge widened and she was across.

She found Colin standing at the base of a deep cleft in the rock that climbed away between narrowing walls to a distant slit of light. They stood side by side for a moment, then Margaret pointed up the cleft and asked: "Is that the way we go?"

Colin nodded. "It's the only way there is from here. And it's easy, at least for the first part."

"Shall I take the rope off?"

"Yes," he said. "We'll put it on again if we need to."

For several hundred feet they were able to climb side by side. The floor of the cleft was a sloping mass of raw boulders, varying from a few inches up to twenty feet or more in diameter, angularly shaped, solidly wedged together. It was damp in the cleft and the sunlight seemed very far away; a few ferns grew palely here and there and there were mosses and lichens in the drier places, but otherwise there was nothing to shield the rawness of the rocks. Margaret felt awed by the place, by its silence and by the hugeness of everything in it—its boulders, its walls, its height, the gigantic forces implicit in the chaotic litter of thousands upon thousands of apparently immovable tons. She asked at last, as they climbed: "What made it? An earthquake?"

"I wouldn't know," Colin said. "I hadn't really thought about it. Must have been the rock was weak and broke away or washed away. It's just part of the mountain. It's the way mountains are."

Their voices seemed muffled, yet there was a hollow quality of echo in them. "It wasn't water or ice that did it," Margaret said. "Or the boulders wouldn't be sharp and square." She searched through the simple fragments of geology she had learned at school. "Maybe it happened when the mountains were first pushed up. Maybe it split here and the rocks broke away as they cooled."

Colin shook his head. "I don't think so. The rock is all too new. I think maybe there was a softer rock underneath and it washed away, then all the hard rock broke up and caved in. I guess a person'd have to be an expert to say."

The climbing was more difficult now and slowed them and kept them silent. The summit of the cleft was less than two hundred feet above them and the way to it was very steep. Looking up at it, Colin thought: it might stop us, just the last twenty or thirty feet might stop us. It can't do that, it wouldn't be fair after all this going so well. We wouldn't have time to come back down and go round the other way now, either. We've got to get up today, I've got to see how it is up there, how it feels to be at the top and see all around.

He heard Margaret stumble and slip behind him, heard the clatter of rocks rolling away from under her feet and on down the slope of the cleft. She was safe, he saw at once, her arms around a big boulder, but the slip had scared her. He moved back down and stood beside her. "We'd better put the rope on now," he said.

From there they climbed slowly and carefully. They had about sixty feet of rope and Colin would climb to the full length of it, then turn and take up the slack in his hands as Margaret began to climb towards him. After her slip, he had warned her: "Try out any place you are going to step before you put your full weight on it. Don't trust anything that doesn't feel solid. Keep trying until you know it's O.K." He had had to search his mind to find this to say; for him the climbing was still easy and natural and only Margaret's slip had made him realize that it was less easy for her. He had anticipated her difficulty on the ledge and had solved it a hundred times in his thoughts during the year since their previous failure; but in the tumbled slope of the cleft, with its infinity of crevices and footholds, he had supposed that she would be as

7 7

secure as himself. Now, standing with his feet apart, firmly planted, holding the rope so that it did not pull on her, yet could instantly check the least slip, he felt a power in himself that was unlike anything he had ever known before. He knew it instantly for a good feeling, strongly based, rightly earned; but he put it away from him in concern for what he knew was still above them, the narrow precipitous way out of the cleft.

They came to it at last and stood side by side on the pile of small, loose rocks that sloped from the sheer face. It was a true rock chimney, less than three feet wide, twisting only a little through some thirty feet of climb; there was no apparent slope to the three walls that formed it and from where they stood it was difficult to imagine a crevice for foot- or hand-hold anywhere in the smooth rock.

Margaret looked at Colin. Her face was flushed with the exertion of climbing and her body felt weary with disappointment, but she knew that he would feel it far more than she would. "That's the end," she said gently. "Isn't it? We can't go any farther."

Colin was still looking up and she knew as she spoke that there was no disappointment in his face. He shook his head slowly. "No," he said. "I've been thinking about it for a long time. It's just the way I was hoping it might be. We're going to make it."

"Don't be silly," she said. "You'd have to have wings."

He looked down at her and again he was smiling, with the same easy confidence that was so unlike him. "Sit down," he said. "I'll tell you about it. I'm sure we can make it—if you're game to try."

"I've got to be. I promised not to quit on you. But I still don't think there's any way except wings."

"Remember the hay chute in the barn?" Colin asked her. "You bet me I couldn't climb that once."

"Sure. And you put your feet against one side and pushed your back against the other and got slivers in your back. What's that got to do with it?"

"I got up into the loft didn't I? It's the same here, only no slivers."

Margaret glanced quickly over her shoulder at the cold, dim

light of the chimney. "You're not going to do that here," she said. "I won't let you."

"It's the same," he said. "Only easier. A little longer, but easier."

"It's not. There was hay underneath you in the barn. You'd be killed if anything went wrong here."

"It'll be easier," he repeated. "Rock is never smooth like boards. Nothing will go wrong."

His calm insistence was as strange to Margaret as his smile. She felt trapped and afraid and she resisted. "Maybe you can do it. I know I can't. You're not going to leave me here, are you?"

"You won't have to do it. We've got the rope. I'll make a sling you can sit in. I know how to."

"You can't pull me up there. I won't let you try, even."

"Yes I can, if you help a little the way I show you. Look, Marge," he said earnestly. "Do you want to know something?" He paused, but she said nothing and he went on: "All we've got to do is get through here and we're at the top. I'm sure of that."

In spite of herself Margaret felt an echo of his eagerness. I've got to stop him, she thought. I know so much better than he does, I've got more sense than he has—I always have had. But if we could get through there and find the sunlight and the wind again, suddenly; if we really were at the top and could see all around us, how good it would be. Nothing would seem silly then. I should know what it's like up there, really and truly know, and it would be part of me forever. He wants all that, too, and something even more than that. I can't be the one to keep him from it again, after he has waited for me all this time.

She stood up. "We can try it," she said. "But please, Colin, be careful. Come back if it's too difficult. Promise you will."

"Sure," he said. "I just want to try. I know I can make it."

IT was difficult getting into the chimney. Colin found a way up the left wall at last, using every smallest roughness or break in the rock to get him to the point where the two walls came close enough together to let him wedge his body between them. Once there he settled himself securely and rested. He looked down at Margaret. "It's going to be O.K.," he told her. "You'll be able to rest like this whenever you want. And there's quite a slope on the inside face a little way up. With the rope you'll almost be able to walk up it."

He began to climb then, forcing his body upward until his legs were almost straight, finding new footing on the opposite wall, forcing again. It was hard work and his body strained to it, but his mind worked freely and intensely ahead of him. His throat was dry and his heart was beating fast with excitement and he thought: what will it be like? Will there be grass or moss or heather or flowers or just rock? Will it be easy from there to the top? I think that's grass at the edge of the hole above me. Will the little twisted trees be there? Shall we see over into Wind Valley? All those things can go wrong so often; nothing is ever how you expect it to be, but this must be. Let it be, God, please God. Let it be real mountain, different from anything else, different to look at, different to feel, different to know. This isn't an ordinary day, this isn't an ordinary thing we are doing today. Something is going to happen from it, something big and important. Let it happen, God, and let it be big.

He reached the twist in the chimney and saw that from there on he could climb the inside wall without difficulty. He worked his body over, found footing and settled himself solidly. Looking down, he could still see Margaret. He called to her to start her climb and took a gentle strain on the rope as she moved in towards the base of the chimney.

Margaret trusted the rope and climbed boldly. Once or twice Colin lifted her almost bodily over a difficult place, but she found the roughnesses of the rock as he had found them and wedged her body as he had wedged his, and in a little while she was beside him. Ten or fifteen minutes later they were out in the sunlight again, standing on short dry grass, looking over the gleaming water and the tiny islands to the ranged peaks beyond and a distant haze beyond those that might have been the Pacific Ocean.

"We're above timber, anyway," Colin said at last. He turned and looked behind him. "But we still don't know how far we've got to go. It looks from here as though that next little hump might be the top, but I know darn well it isn't."

Margaret stood very straight, facing into the wind, letting it blow her hair back and flatten her skirt against her body. "It's nice here. Couldn't we stay for a few minutes?"

"Sure," Colin said, and sat down in the grass. He reached into his pockets and brought out some hardtack and a couple of battered candy bars. "Do you want to eat? I brought these for you."

Margaret laughed. "I didn't trust you," she said. "I brought some of my own."

Colin was thinking: it hasn't happened. We've made it, we've beaten all the bad places and come out above the timber, but it's not really so very different. Sure, you can see out for miles and miles and it feels good to be here, but it isn't so much really. He asked Margaret: "Are you tired?"

She shook her head. "Not now." Her eyes were bright and the wind had flushed her cheeks and her teeth showed strong and white between parted lips. "It's exciting. I love it. Why don't people live in places like this?"

"There's fifteen feet of snow here in the winter," Colin said.

Margaret laughed. "I shouldn't care. It'd be fun, living in a house almost buried in snow and looking out of the front door and seeing all the rest of the world 'way down below you."

"How'd you get to school? How'd you get grub and mail and all that stuff?"

"Don't be so practical," she told him. "I'm supposed to be the practical one. They could have a town up here if they wanted to. They do build towns on mountains. And they make tunnels under the snow to get from one house to another."

81

"That'd be just swell," Colin said. "To come all the way up here and bring the same old mess right along with you."

Margaret turned to look at him. "Isn't it what you wanted?" she asked. "You were so happy on the way up, but now you're sour. You ought to be proud. You planned it all and made it happen."

Colin rolled over on to his stomach and pulled impatiently at the grass. "It's O.K.," he said. "It's swell. Let's go on the rest of the way now we've seen it all from here."

IT took them over an hour to find the top of the mountain, though it was easy walking all the way, over gentle slopes, around great outcrops of rock, along dry creek beds. Colin's mood changed slowly as they traveled. There was sparse timber all over the face of the mountain, wind-torn and rock-hard in the exposed places, tall and slender where there was shelter. They found a tiny lakelet in a hollow and followed the creek that fed it through soft meadows. The creek bed climbed away from the meadows into the rocks again, and little flowers that were strange to them both bloomed everywhere. Once or twice they saw deer on the open slopes and Colin recognized a wolf track at the edge of the swamp that drained into the little lake. Once, in deep shade between two walls of rock, they came upon a stretch of deep snow; but through most of the journey the sunlight was brilliant all about them and the wind was fresh and strong against their bodies. Always, as they climbed, the earth widened below them, opening up new valleys, raising distant peaks above the nearer ones, uncovering lakes and river beds, the long white spray of falls on the mountainsides, the smooth, graceful sweep of distant glaciers.

The mountain top was bold rock, terraced by wind and driven snow, supporting a few dwarfed and twisted trees in the clefts of its sheltered side, but essentially a hump rather than a peak. A little pile of broken rock, built by some forgotten surveyor, marked its highest point. Colin saw it from a distance and pointed to it. Margaret uttered a little cry of pleasure and relief.

"Now we can really say we've been at the top, we can really know. I was so afraid there would be no way to be sure."

"I think we'd have known anyway," Colin said. "There doesn't seem to be anything else nearly so high. But it's good to be sure."

They went on to the cairn and stood in silence, one on either side of it, looking out over the tremendous stretch of country that opened away to the north and east, on the far side of the mountain. The whole world seemed blue and green and white before them—blue of water, green of timber, in infinity of shades, white of the glaciers and snow peaks, blue again in the sky and white again in the sailing summer clouds. Colin drew a deep breath of satisfaction. It had been better every minute since they had started away from the chimney, strangeness piled on strangeness, half-expected yet always unexpected and beyond expectation. He thought: this is of me and I am of it. Nothing here is evil, nothing is touched, nothing dirty or destroyed. The wind is strong and clean, the rock is strong, the little trees are strong; this is how I knew it would be, how I wanted it to be, why I came.

Margaret said at last: "We could have come here long ago. Why didn't we?" She sat down on the rock beside the cairn. "You always did want to come so badly. Why? Did you know it was going to be like this?" She swept her arm in a half-circle over the sweep of the valley, from the river's mouth to the high peaks. "Was that what you wanted to see?"

"Partly," Colin said. "But I wanted this, too." He moved his foot on the rock. "And this," he said, pointing to the slope in front of them. "All the things we've seen since we got up above the timber, the close things as well as the far things."

Margaret leaned forward and hugged her knees, half-closing her eyes to look up at him against the bright sky. "Don't you ever get tired?" she asked him. "Don't you ever want to sit down?"

"Sure I do," Colin said. "I was tired after we climbed that last bad place with the rope. But it's been easy since then. And right now I want to look at it all."

Margaret pointed down at the wide river mouth to the north of them. "Is that Wind River?"

"Sure it is. You know that. You can tell it from the map on the wall in the kitchen, easy." His finger traced the tiny gleam of the river back through the standing timber of the valley until it widened into a long, narrow lake. "That's Wind Lake," he said. "See that valley halfway up on the far side? That ought to be Carlson's

Valley. And the next big valley, just up beyond the head of the lake would be Amabilis Creek. And the other big lake in the main valley is Christina Lake."

He was completely absorbed in his own unfolding of the valley's secrets and Margaret watched him in surprise. "Well," she said at last, "you certainly have studied it. How much more do you know? What about the names of all the little lakes down there?"

"It's harder to figure those," Colin said. "See those three up the south fork of the main valley? I think those are Wolf and Loon and Beaver. Gem Lake is a little farther up, just out of sight." He sat down on the rock, still gazing out across the valley. "Something else I know. Everything beyond the divide on the far side of the lake is Menzies National Park. All those tallest, jagged mountains with the snow on them. They drain down into Menzies Lake, and that's in the park too."

He lay back with his hands behind his head, stretching his long body comfortably. "Boy," he said, "that's quite some valley. Earl Mayhew says it's the last big untouched valley on the coast."

Margaret still sat with her arms around her knees. but her eyes had turned to identify each thing as Colin named it. Now she turned her body a little so that she could watch him. "Why was Mr. Mayhew talking about it? Did you ask him?"

"No," Colin said without moving. "I don't think so. We often talk about places like that—places we'd like to go someday. Why? Is there something wrong with it?"

"Is that why you wanted to come here? To see the valley?"

"Only partly. I told you that before." He rolled over a little, on to his side, so that he could look at her. "Heck, what is this anyway? You ask a person more questions than a schoolteacher."

Margaret did not smile. "You're crazy about the woods, aren't you, Colin? That's all you think of, woods and mountains."

"What's the matter with that? Can't a guy think about things he likes? Woods and mountains never did anybody any harm."

Margaret moved awkwardly but her face had a determined look that Colin knew, both in her and in his mother. "No," she said. "But a person can be too single-track about anything. There's lots of other things that should be just as important for you."

"What for instance?"

8 4

"Oh, going to college. And knowing more people. And reading more. Those sort of things."

"What brought all that up?" he asked her. "Did Mother tell you to say it?"

"No."

"Mildred Hanson, then?"

Margaret flushed. "Sort of," she admitted. "But I think the same. Look, Colin, if you go to the woods for all your life you'll be running away. It isn't right for you to do it. You know it isn't."

"The woods is the only place I'm good for anything. They're the only place a guy's free to act like himself, without everybody watching and yammering at him."

"Nobody's bothered you at school since Tod Phalling went away. The kids all like you."

"That's what you think. It's O.K. for you. You're good-looking and the same size as everybody else. Nobody thinks you're queer or nags at you all the time to act different from what you really are."

"You're not queer," Margaret said. "You make yourself seem queer just because you're shy and you give in to it. That's what I mean about running away. Lots of people are shy, but they make themselves get over it and soon nobody knows the difference."

Colin lay flat on his back and watched the high white clouds across the wheeling sky. Let her talk, he thought, she doesn't know what it's like. Everything always did go right for her. She's better than me around home or in school or pretty near any place else you can think of, except maybe here on the mountain. Sure, she's going to college, but that's no reason she should expect everybody else to go too. She's neat and tidy and all pulled together. Anyone can tell right away, just from looking at her, that she's smart and things go right for her. I wish she wouldn't drag all that stuff up today, though, when we're away from it. She doesn't generally get on to it when we're out on a trip together—that's one reason why she's so good to go with. It's funny about people, you never can tell what they're thinking, not even when they're your sister or your mother or your old man. You don't even know what they're seeing. It could be something you see looks quite different to them. Take Margaret up here, for instance. She's so much smarter than me, so much quicker about things, it could be none of this looks the same to her. And even if it looks the same, that's no reason I should think she feels the same way about it.

Colin raised himself on one elbow and looked past the cairn at his sister. "Marge," he said. "What do you like best about all this?"

She was sitting with her clenched fists together under her chin, her elbows on her knees. "I like it all," she said slowly. "The whole thing. Just looking at it makes my heart beat fast and I feel as if I wanted to be every place at once and make it all mine. The high mountains are most exciting, I guess—those and the way the river is, all quicksilver where you can see it between the trees." She paused, then went on: "If it had to be just one thing, I think I'd say the lakes and most of all the little ones sitting up at all different levels on the sides of the mountains. They look so friendly."

Colin lay back again, satisfied, and for a little while neither of them spoke. Then she asked him: "Colin, don't we have to start back soon?"

He sat up again and looked at her with suspicion. "Why? Do you want to go? Are you sick of it already?"

"No, of course not. I'd like to stay here for days. But we have got to be back for supper. You haven't forgotten about Mr. Grant, have you?"

Colin turned and looked at the sun. "We've got a little while longer," he said. "Going down will be easy, but we'll go the long way, round all the bad places, so it'll take time."

"What are you going to say to Mr. Grant?"

He looked at her again, quickly, and again suspiciously. "How do I know? I don't even know what he's going to say to me."

"Yes, you do. You know what he said this spring—that maybe you could go in the woods with him and run compass next year. He'll ask if you still want to go."

"You could be right," Colin said. "But I guess I have to wait till he asks."

"You aren't going, are you? Not in March like he said and lose all that school-time?"

"Sure, I am if he wants me to. Why wouldn't I? He's the best timber cruiser on the coast. A guy'd learn more from him than he ever would in school."

"You could go later, just for the summer, and not miss any school."

"He didn't say so. He said he was going up Wind River in March and work there right through till fall. I wouldn't miss any more than three or four months of school."

"Mother doesn't want you to go."

"When did she say that? Father said it'd be O.K. to go. He wants me to go. Mother said it wouldn't be so bad if I was just out of school for the summer."

"You won't be. If you go you'll stay out. All the kids that go off early to a summer job say they'll come back in the fall, but they never do. Mildred Hanson says they get used to earning wages and can't give it up. Or their families can't."

"Might be something to that," Colin said. "If a man's got a chance to earn steady wages these days he's got to be crazy to give it up."

"It's not going to be like that any more. Things are getting started again and we won't have to worry so much."

"Oh yeah?" Colin looked at her almost angrily. "A person'd think you didn't know Dad stayed home today."

"That's just for fire season. They'll open up again as soon as the weather breaks, Dad said."

"That isn't what Earl Mayhew says. Earl says they'll stay closed just as long as it suits them, and that means till it's time to cut wages again."

"Dad says Earl shouldn't talk like that. He says the companies need to keep working just as much as the men do. More, because they've got all that machinery going to waste."

"I know," Colin's voice was calm again. "One says one thing and another says something else. And they change, and get sore at each other about it. Dad is always sore at Mike Varchuk, but when the camp's been closed for a while he gets to saying almost the same things as Mike."

"That's the union," Margaret said. "It's supposed to get them all together, but it never seems to. Mildred says it will one day, but they have to learn the hard way."

Colin stood up. "Well," he said, "if it's going to be as tough on Dad as it was last time I'd just as soon have a job waiting. At least it'll mean there's something Mother can count on."

"There's plenty to do around home," Margaret said. "And Dad always finds something that brings in a little money." But he doesn't, she thought. When the camp's shut down he's not God in Genesis any more. He's just a man, and even his strength seems to go away from him gradually until he looks lost and shrunken and untidy instead of upright and huge and powerful. Colin's right: it would mean a lot to Mother to have something she could depend on in times like that.

"I guess we can't really tell what's going to happen," Margaret said. "But if you do go with Mr. Grant, don't give up school altogether, will you?"

"It's almost a year before it happens," Colin said. "But I don't suppose I will."

"Promise?" she asked him. "On your heart?"

Colin looked at her in surprise. "That's kid stuff," he said. "A person can't do that for something like this. It's too serious."

"Of course you can. The more serious a thing is, the more reason there is to make a true promise. Please, Colin."

He looked down at her, half-smiling. "Oh, O.K., if you want, Marge. On my heart. But it won't ever come up. The job'll be over by fall and I'll just naturally go back to school." He glanced up at the sun again. "No more sitting around. We've got to be on our way if we're going to make it on time."

Margaret stood up and Colin said: "Give you a start to that little flat tree and race you to the first swamp."

"Following," she said. "No fair short-cutting behind a guy."

"Following," he said.

MARTHA Ensley did not go away from her home very often. She recognized certain occasions: every Sunday, without fail, she and Will and the children went to the church in Blenkinstown; she went to the town's small whist drives and dances, usually spending the greater part of the evening in the kitchen, preparing food or washing dishes; occasionally she went into the town during the daytime, to attend a meeting, visit at the hospital or do some shopping that seemed to call for her personal attention—though she infinitely preferred, from long habit, to do her important shopping through the mail-order catalogs. When she went to visit her friends it was either in full Sunday ceremony with Will and Colin and Margaret, or else to help out because of sickness or impending childbirth.

Essentially she continued the social habits of her mother's house and her childhood, when neighbors had been few and distant. Like her mother, she was a sociable and deeply affectionate woman, and like most pioneer women she was extravagantly and sincerely hospitable to any person, friend or stranger, who came to her house. But the daily work of looking after her house, her garden and her family amply filled her time and she would have considered casual daytime visiting little less than a sin. When she decided to go and talk to Joan Mayhew one afternoon in March she was uneasily conscious of the break in a lifetime routine and had to remind herself that her going was of importance to the family.

Before she left she piled wood in the stove, filled the kettle, closed all the drafts. That was routine. She wrote a note and propped it on the table, where Margaret and Colin would see it when they came home from school. That also was routine. Walking out to the gate, turning left along the road towards the village, was still routine. But her thoughts were not routine. In spite of her concern, she felt happy and excited. She liked Joan Mayhew and the thought of talking with the tall, strong girl was reassuring. She hasn't got a lazy bone in her body, Martha thought, nor a crooked one. She says what she thinks, straight out, and it's always good, sound common sense. I've heard them say she's too frank and it makes enemies for her, but I like it and I like the way her eyes look at you when she's talking; I like her broad white face and black hair, and the way she generally stands, so strongly, with her feet a little apart and her arms folded across her chest. Most of all, except her eyes, I like her voice. It's deep and natural, straight out like the things she says, yet simple and gentle; it's a voice that belongs to the women of this country, the real women who raise the families and keep them together.

Martha walked quickly, with short quick steps, her body bent forward a little, her head inclined against a fresh wind that she knew would soon bring rain. She turned in at the Mayhews' gate without looking up and hurried to the door of the house. It opened before she could knock and Joan was standing there.

"Why, Martha," she said. "How nice to see you." She felt the warmth of Martha's lake-blue eyes, met the dancing smile that was always near them. "Come in out of the cold," she said. "There's nobody in the whole wide world more welcome."

"I shouldn't be here in the middle of the day," Martha said, and turned to watch Joan close the door behind her. "But I thought it was time we talked."

Joan crossed to the stove and slid the kettle towards the holes immediately over the firebox. "We don't talk enough," she said. "The men do it all while we stay home."

Sliding her arms out of her old brown coat, Martha said: "I generally leave those things to Will, but it seems to mean more than usual this time." Joan moved a chair nearer the stove and Martha sat down in it. "Where is all your family?" she asked.

"Earl's up at the meeting," Joan said. "The kids are out in the yard—Earl made a sandpile for them last year and they never leave it alone."

"It's cold," Martha said.

"I bundled them up warm. They're both strong and healthy, praise be. It'll be different next year, I suppose, when little Earl starts school and the germs all follow him home. We haven't had a cold in the house all winter." She reached automatically under the table to touch the unpainted wood.

"It's always worst when they first start. That first year is too hard on them. But they get used to it after a while."

Joan poured boiling water from the kettle into the teapot. "How are you up your way? It's quite a while since Colin was around to see us."

"We keep well enough," Martha said. "We've got a lot to be thankful for in times like these. But it worries Will. He wants to take too much of the blame to himself. It's like an insult to his trade not to be working."

"It doesn't seem to matter any more whether they're good workers," Joan's voice was deliberately restrained, resisting any suggestion of special sympathy for Will Ensley. "It just goes on and on. There isn't work any more."

"Will still says it's going to pick up. He thinks the company may be bought out—that's why Mr. Grant was doing all that cruising up there last year."

"Earl talks the same old stuff," Joan said impatiently. "Shutdown for fire season, shutdown for snow. Open up soon as the rain comes. Or the snow melts. Or the sun shines. Or the heavens fall. Or hell freezes. What difference does it make what they say? It's always the same old story when it comes to buying groceries—no pay-check, no cash. It'll take two years of steady work to pay what we owe now."

"I know how you feel," Martha said. "This is the longest stretch of hard times I can remember. But it always does come out in the end—slowly, so you can't see it's happening, but it happens. Will's right about the signs. Little things, like Mr. Grant cruising timber, are what you notice first, and the rest comes later. He's going up Wind River next week—Colin's going with him."

"I'm glad," Joan said. "At least you'll have something you can count on. And I guess it must mean they plan on opening something up there, sooner or later. I'm glad for Colin too. It's just what he needs."

"I worry about it," Martha set her cup down gently in its saucer. "All my brothers were off in the woods long before they were his age and it seems natural to let him go. But Mr. Siddons and Miss Hanson think he ought to stay in school, and I guess young people nowadays need all the education they can get."

"Colin's made for the woods. He loves it and Earl says it all seems to come natural to him. Education may be all right for city folks, but there's a limit to it for people like us. Colin will make out all right."

"He'll go back to school in the fall. Mr. Siddons wants him to go right on through to the University, but it's early to talk about that yet. We can wait and see what happens to Margaret."

"You don't have to worry about Margaret. It'll be natural to her as breathing and talking. Colin's different. He's—he's like a wild thing. Pen him in and he's liable to go to pieces."

"I'm afraid you're right," Martha said. "That's why I worry about him. I can't help thinking that if he goes off in the woods with Andrew Grant he'll come back worse than ever."

Joan looked at her. "Why do you say 'worse'? There's good in being the way Colin is just the same as there's good in being the way Margaret is. People don't have to be good all the same way."

"I don't really know," Martha said slowly. "I don't know why I'm afraid for him, except that I feel it. I feel that there are things always waiting to hurt him. Things inside him and outside him, and it's very easy for Colin to be hurt." Watching her, Joan saw that her face was strained and lined and the smile had gone far back behind her eyes. "I haven't felt it so much lately. He's been happier this last year, more like a normal boy. But when there's a big change for him, like this going away on his own, I have to worry."

"Perhaps getting away into the woods has had something to do with making him happier. Perhaps he's finding what he really is when he's out there."

Martha's face brightened and the smile came to life in her eyes again. "Do you really think that? I've thought it sometimes, that perhaps he's going where he belongs instead of running away from it. If it's true he'd be certain to be happy, wouldn't he?"

"Yes," Joan said. "And I think it's true." She picked up the teapot and poured more tea. "Martha, do you ever stop worrying about Colin and worry about yourself?"

Martha looked at her in surprise. "Me? Why should I?"

"You're doing too much around that place of yours. You're working yourself to death. You should make them help you more."

Martha laughed. "Don't be silly. Work is nothing new to me —I've worked all my life. I'm not so quick as I used to be and I get a little tired sometimes, but it's easier now than when the children were small."

"No one can work the way you do without paying for it. I'm twice as big and twice as strong as you are, but I couldn't stand it, I know that. You ought to go to the doctor and have a good check-up."

"Nonsense," Martha said abruptly. "I'm spry as a cricket. And I didn't come here to talk about myself."

She stood up and held her hands towards the stove. "What are those men up to? Is it going to make things better or worse?"

Joan hesitated before answering. "I think they're right," she said. "I'm not sure they are. But it won't be easy. There hasn't been a loggers' union that amounted to anything for over ten years."

"There'll be trouble. Strikes when they need the work. Maybe fighting and violence. Do you think they're wise enough to understand all that?"

"They'll have to learn. Earl says the leaders know all about it and they expect to have a strong organization by the time they're ready to use it."

"Why are the leaders all foreigners?" Martha asked her. "Varchuk and Zobieski and this man Miller—he changed his name. Aren't there any Canadians who know what to do?"

"They aren't all foreigners—just up here. Earl says they're smart men. After all, half the men in the camps are foreigners; more than half."

"Then why do they need Will and Earl if they know so much?"

"Because the men trust them, Earl says. Johnny Meldrum and Mr. Sorretto and several others of the old timers are on the committee too. Earl says the company will have to pay attention to men like that and I think maybe he's right."

"Then you think it's a good thing?" Martha said.

"Yes," Joan told her. "I'm afraid sometimes, but I think it's good. It's got to be. Things can't go on the way they've been for so long. The men have got to have some say about what wages they'll work for and the only way they can have it is by getting together and all holding out for the same thing."

"That's all I wanted to know," Martha said. "I felt it was good, but I wanted to hear someone else say so. Will is so easily taken in."

Joan looked away from her. "He's a big influence. Earl says the men trust him." She looked back and met the smile in Martha's eyes.

"It'll take a lot more than Will to make this thing work out," Martha said. "I expect they know that as well as we do. It's not Will's kind of thing, nor mine either. But if he can help I'm not going to stop him."

Martha was standing with her small feet apart, her clenched fists on her hips. Her blue eyes shone with determination and her gentle mouth was firmly set. Suddenly they both laughed. "I think we'd be the ones," Joan said. "You and I. If only we could change places with them."

COLIN and Andrew Grant started for Wind River during the third week of March. It was a wet and windy day and the rain was cold, laced with snow streaks and fiercely driven. Grant had hired a small gas-boat to run their canoe and other equipment round from Blenkinstown to the mouth of the river. When he saw what the weather was he had said to Colin: "No use waiting for it. There's a cabin with a dry roof less than a mile above the salt water."

So now they were working the canoe up the easy tidal part of the river, with the flood following them. Colin was paddling at the bow, Grant at the stern and the gear was piled between them under the shelter of a tent fly. The wind was behind them, with the tide, but the river was appreciably strong against them, even at the mouth, and Grant used the river's bends and the eddies behind the little grassy islands to work against it. The river flowed to the sea across a treeless tidal flat fully half a mile wide, cut by a hundred deep channels and sloughs. Mallard and teal, pintail and mergansers flew from the water at their approach and passed and repassed overhead, sweeping down the wind or battering strongly against it. Colin heard the chatter of geese somewhere out on the flats and the lovely cry of the flocks in flight came down through the sound of the storm. He worked his paddle steadily, stroke after stroke without change or slackening, as Grant had told him to, and his heart was full of a hundred surging things that jumbled the endless flow of his thoughts in the wetness.

Mother was just the way she is when I go to school in the mornings, so busy and quick with everything; yet it wasn't quite the same and at the end she pulled my head down and kissed me and said: "Be good, Boy." That's the first time she's called me "Boy" since I was a little kid and it made me want to bawl. The old man didn't say much to me; he just kept talking to Mr. Grant about fir and hemlock and cedar and the prices of logs and how soon the camps'll open up. But he had sharpened my axe himself, the way he *can* sharp them, so the fine bit will cut a hair from just resting the hair on it. Gee, this sure is a great place for ducks and geese. I've heard them talk about it; but I never knew it would be like this. Mr. Grant doesn't talk much; he hasn't said a thing since we left the gas-boat. I wonder what he thinks about? He's such a little guy, but he's powerful; you can feel it right through the canoe every time his paddle goes into the water.

He's my boss now. But there can't be much bossing to a job like this, with just two of us in the bush, you wouldn't think. Just the same, he is the boss and Dad says to remember that and call him Mr. Grant and jump when he says anything. It sure feels good to be starting out like this. This canoe is a honey, so light and easy to paddle and we've got a real load in it too. The other kids are all in school right now. Algebra. I'm sure glad I'm missing that. Poor old Johnny, he'd sell his grandmother to be here doing this and he's sweating away at algebra.

Miss Hanson sure was nice when I said good-by to her yesterday. "Don't forget school," she said. "Come back in the fall. You'll learn a lot with Mr. Grant and maybe it will make you want to learn more in school." I wonder what she meant by that? She put her hand on my arm and her mouth was smiling and her face soft and her eyes the bluest I've ever seen them. I'm not going to let myself think about her any more the way I've been thinking. I know I'll want to, I want to now; I won't let myself, I'll stop it, I'll keep it down shut away inside me. I know I won't, it's too precious for that, too good and warm and rich when you're lonely, but I can worry about that when the time comes. Just for now I'll shut it out and keep it shut out, because it's good to be starting out like this, all clean and fresh; and I'll be strong and different and a man when I go back and see her again and she'll know that and treat me like a man.

They had come more than a mile from the salt water and the tall green timber was closing in to narrow the open meadow. A little ahead of them alder trees came right down to the banks of the river and Colin knew that they must be growing beyond reach of the tides. The river current was strong now but the wind was still helping and the canoe moved steadily under the paddles. There was a windowless farmhouse and a rotting barn on some higher ground near the alders and Colin thought: that would be where the guy lived that ran beef cattle here on the flats in the early days. He cut hay for them out of the slough and let them pick what they could off the flats, but he lost all his money at it in the end and had to pull out. Because he couldn't afford to get the beef to a market, they say it was. Seems a darn shame; it must have been a swell life in a place like this, with the cattle spread all over the flats and all the ducks and geese to see when you were looking for them and the mountains so close. He was married and had a whole lot of children. Mother remembers visiting there, by boat, when she was a little girl. And now they're all gone and the place has fallen apart.

Behind him he felt Grant slow the stroking of his paddle. "Ease up for a spell, laddie," Grant said. "The tide's away behind us."

Colin set his paddle across the gunwales and turned towards him. "We'll land at the old Underhill place," Grant said. "And have ourselves a bite to eat while she's coming up. The high tide is twenty-two feet and that'll save us near another mile of battling with the river."

ANDREW Duncan Grant was a short, spare gray little man. His eyes were a pale, hard blue, with bushy reddish eyebrows over them. His sandy hair was thin and graying, his nose was sharp, his mouth a thin line over a small but rocky chin. He was the son of a Hudson's Bay factor who had retired to Victoria from the prairies. Young Andrew grew up with sound mathematics, a hard integrity and a tireless body. At sixteen he was timekeeper in a logging camp. At eighteen he was camp foreman, at twenty a log-buyer. And then, being a bushman at heart, he turned to cruising and staking standing timber.

He was not a friendly man, nor a communicative one, and he rode Colin hard during the first two or three weeks they spent in the valley. They had made a base camp some miles up the river from tidal water and were working through the dark, heavy timber of the valley floor; the weather was consistently bad, cold and wet and windy, but Grant made no concessions to it and they lived in wet clothes and slept out in wet blankets night after night, returning to the comparative dryness of the base camp only when they had to. Colin was not unhappy. It did not occur to him that Grant was exacting and the cold wet gloom of the forest was what he had expected, almost what he had hoped for.

Grant made little effort to explain the work to Colin. He showed him how to mount the compass on the jacob staff, how to check it against the section line, how to sight it and how to pace off a tally of three hundred and thirty feet, allowing for broken ground and windfalls. Everything else he did himself, swiftly and easily, in a silence that seemed half-contemptuous, half-patient. But Colin was interested, and at home. He could not match the little man's quick, ferreting energy, but he had a power of endurance that let him handle his own work surely and easily and still left him free to watch everything about him. He found no monotony in the great trees of the flat valley because to his eye no two of them seemed alike; each had its own particular way of surging upward from its roots, each its own lean, its own color and texture of bark, its own climb to its lowest branches, its own marked position in relationship to its neighbors. Under the trees the ground, for all its riverbottom flatness, was as varied as the trees themselves; Colin's compass lines crossed swamps and creeks and larger streams, passed hummocks and hollows, led him over piled windfalls and rock outcrop; he walked on moss and on spruce needles, over gray gravel and red gravel, across sodden loam and on the spongy softness of rotted wood. From time to time they came upon the worn trail that was the valley's highway; lesser trails of deer and bear ran everywhere through the length and breadth of the flat and Colin's quick eyes always checked them to learn what had passed that way recently.

The original survey of the valley was so old that all the blazes were long grown over and the cedar corner posts were black and half-rotten, often covered with moss or lichen, blending almost perfectly into the forest. Colin gradually built himself a picture of that original survey and the men who had made it thirty or forty years earlier. Men much like himself and Grant, he supposed they were, probably more cheerful and more talkative, men who knew nothing of automobiles or airplanes, men who had known the Underhill farm in its prosperity and Blenkinstown when ox teams brought logs from the Ensley farm to the old booming ground in the corner of the bay. He learned to judge them by the shape and size of the blazes they had left, by the symmetry or roughness of the corner posts they had made, by the markings of their bearing trees, by the ancient score of a nicked axe blade, by the blackened stones of their fires, by the way one would hew bark from a leaning fir or another split dry kindling from a dead cedar.

By the end of his third week he could pace the sixteen tallies from section line to section line so accurately that he was rarely more than ten paces from the line when he finished. Grant gave up finding corner posts for himself because Colin was nearly always ahead of him; he slowed his impatience and he talked more often, but he worked as tirelessly as ever. They were up at dawn each day, breaking camp, cooking oatmeal and bacon and coffee. Through the day they traveled, stopping only to eat a

9 8

quick lunch around noon. While Colin ran his compass lines and blazed his tally-marks Grant checked the timber and made his notes. Grant had a way of his own of covering ground in the bush. He moved quickly and actively and silently, ranging like a little gray dog, often far out of Colin's sight, seeming to care nothing for brush or windfall or hard going of any kind, if there were trees he wanted to see beyond it. He seemed to pay attention to nothing but the timber, yet he always knew where he was from the compass line and he could return from his wandering to one of Colin's tally-marks as surely as though it were a blazing light on a city street. And at the end of each day he knew of a good camping spot within easy reach of wherever they were. When they came to it he would slip his pack away from his shoulders and settle with his notebooks and figures until Colin had supper ready.

Early in the fourth week the weather changed sharply to sunshine and a warm wind that sprang everything to life. They were back at the base camp, near the main river, and Grant had worked all afternoon at his figures while Colin cut wood and straightened up the camp. Towards evening Grant came out of the tent and walked slowly to where Colin was sharpening his axe. He watched him for a moment, then said: "You work too hard, boy. Don't you ever want to go off fishing, or take a rest?"

Colin looked up in surprise and Grant smiled at him. "I know, I know, laddie. You think I'm a hard driver and you've got to keep up. So I am. So you have." He walked over and sat down on a stump. Colin started to say something, but Grant held up a forefinger and silenced him. "We're 'way ahead of ourselves," he said. "And in weather not fit for seals and sea-otters. You're as good as any compass-man I ever had and if you can keep to it there's no reason we shouldn't ease up a wee and act more like humans. Ye may not think it from what ye've seen, but there's a human streak in me."

"It's O.K. with me, Mr. Grant," Colin said. "I like it in the woods."

"Oh aye, it's easy to see that. And you're not a great talker either, which is a virtue on its own. But we've a whole summer of hard work and spare living in front of us. Except old Robbie, up at the lake, there's nobody in the valley but the two of us, so we may as well get to know each other a little."

Colin laughed. "I guess you know all there is to know about me," he said. "You've known Mother ever since she was a little girl and Dad pretty near as long."

Grant shook his head quite solemnly. "There's a lot more to a man than his mother and father. But suppose we cook us up a bite of supper now. Afterwards we'll take the canoe and catch us some trout for breakfast."

AS the summer drew on and they worked their way farther and farther up the valley, a slow, unspoken friendship grew between Colin and Grant. Grant changed little. He still drove relentlessly through his work, he still held to moody, day-long silences, broken only by a contemptuous word or two when Colin overran a line or slipped into some careless error with the compass. But his easier moods became more and more frequent and lasted longer. Grant's occasional scolding, sharply and bitterly expressed as it always was, bit into Colin, confused him and hurt him momentarily; but he quickly lost the hurt in the silence that followed and in the crowding of other thoughts that came to him through the quick and ceaseless searching of his eyes. Each day he saw and learned new things and he treasured them all, piecing them into his own steadily clearer picture of the complex world of the forest.

Because of the difference in their ages and because Grant was immensely secure in his professional skill and his woodcraft, Colin was slow to understand him. That Grant was a shy man he learned only on one of their rare trips to Blenkinstown to pick up supplies. They had taken the canoe into the wharf and were walking up towards the general store when they met Mildred Hanson. She came across to them at once and held out her hand to Colin.

"Why, Colin," she said. "You look so well. The woods must agree with you."

It was a sunny day and she was without a hat, so that her pale gold braids caught the sunlight. A short gray skirt swung from her hips and a clear blue blouse, open at the throat, reflected the blue of her eyes. Colin thought he had never seen her look so beautiful and he felt strong from his height above her. But he knew his hand was clammy in hers and his own voice sounded rough and awkward to his ears after the soft, easy song of her words. He grinned and looked down and said only: "It's swell up there, Miss Hanson." He saw her quick eyes turn to Grant, ready to smile, and knew somehow that Grant would not respond. He fumbled to introduce them, but before the words were out Grant had nodded shortly, muttered something and gone towards the store.

"Are you out for long?" Mildred asked Colin.

"Just for today," Colin said. "I guess—I guess I'd better go along with Mr. Grant."

Mildred laughed. "He's not very friendly, is he, the great Mr. Grant? You must be a silent pair, back there in the woods."

"Oh, we talk," Colin said. "But I better go now."

"Good-by, Colin," Mildred said. "Take care of yourself up there and come and see me before school starts."

Colin left her and hurried after Grant. As they turned into the store Grant asked: "Who was she?"

"One of the schoolteachers," Colin said.

"Acted more like a schoolgirl. Too young for me. Paint for lips." There was something defensive in the clipped sentences that Colin dimly recognized. He searched his mind and remembered Grant meeting Joan Mayhew at the Ensley house and how Martha had said later: "Andrew never did learn to be easy with the girls. He hasn't changed any."

That was their last trip out to Blenkinstown and they took the loaded canoe clear up the river to Wind Lake, lining and poling their way through the twelve miles of rough water in a single day.

"We'll go on to Robbie's," Grant said. "His cabin's about half-way up the lake, on Cameron Creek, and we can leave most of the stuff there. It'll be safer than in a cache."

They made Robinson's their base camp for nearly three weeks while they worked over the timber along Cameron Creek and along the lake shore on both sides of the creek-mouth. It was a pleasant time because Grant worked shorter days so that they were able to get back to the cabin nearly every night. He and Robinson were old and close friends, though they were very different types of men. Robbie was in his sixties, a tall thin man with bent knees and a sliding walk. He talked easily, laughed freely and treated Colin with the respectful admiration that age quite often has for the bright future of youth.

"Enjoy it all while you're young," he would say to Colin. "Don't let it slip away from you. Don't let old Andrew here work you to death just because he's a dour Scot. Andrew takes everything hard and look where it's got him. You take the canoe and the pole and go fishing. Or just go using your eyes to see God's good sights all up and down this lake."

And Colin would go, traveling the lake in the calm peace of the summer evenings, finding the creeks from Robbie's directions, learning the mountains for himself from Grant's maps. It was a partial fulfillment, but far more truly an extension of what he had done in climbing the mountain with Margaret the previous year. From parts of the lake he could see the mountain and even recognize the thrust of rock where they had sat by the cairn, but his strongest interest was in the high mountains to the north, in the fierce precipices of Carlson's Valley, two or three miles beyond Cameron Creek, in the deep mysterious fold of Amabilis Creek just above the head of the lake, and in the high white peaks that marked the boundary of Menzies National Park. On some evenings, with the lake glass-still, he took the canoe and paddled out to where he could see the tallest mountains in all their height. Then he would let the canoe drift while the sun sank and the colors changed, watching the coming of night to the valleys and the linger of light on the peaks and ridges, feeling rather than thinking, recognizing little of what he felt, knowing only that he was happier than he had ever been in his life.

At other times he stayed in the cabin and listened through the evening to the talk of the two older men. They were very different, the one simple and cheerful and talkative, the other taut and sparing of words, withdrawn, often harsh and bitter in judgment. Yet they had one thing in common: a contempt for the outside world and the people who lived there. Robbie would say, half-joking, half in earnest: "You're bad news, Andrew. There'll be others come after you and tear the woods apart and burn the hills. In a few years there'll be nothing left for me in all this country."

"Aye, they'll come," Grant would agree. "There'll be a railroad past your door and a spur line up the creek. But they'll come in their own good time, when it's ripe for money-making and some jumping jack with a hold on the purse strings pulls the whistle."

"You should know, Andrew. You walk with them and talk with them down in Vancouver and Victoria. It's you that tells them where the good timber is and how it can best come away and leave the cash in their pockets."

"If it weren't me it would be someone else. I give them an honest cruise for my fee and have done ever since I first put calipers on a tree."

"They have to make money or they couldn't have their cities with the electric light and automobiles and the painted whores on the corners. I've been out to Vancouver twice since we came back from overseas in 1919 and I don't mind if I never see the place again."

They both laughed, then Grant was solemn. "You want to watch it a wee, Robbie. A man shouldn't shut himself away too far."

"That's fine talk from a man that's been forty years sneaking through the bush like a panther. At least I've God's good daylight to shine down on me and a little free space to look out on." Robbie waved a hand towards the windows of his cabin that fronted on the lake.

"I'm out to the city three or four months of every year, with a collar and tie and all the trimmings," Grant said defensively.

"And I go out. Down to Blenkinstown to sell my furs in the spring and down there again to buy grub in the fall. If it was any more than that I'd be hanging around the beer parlors like the rest of them and turning into a half-man that couldn't walk an honest mile to save his life."

And the friendly argument would go on, back and forth between them, getting nowhere but establishing each man in his belief that the life he had chosen was right and good, while life in the cities was a pale, vicious half-life, dangerous and contaminating.

Often they talked more seriously, searching over things that were really important to them. Colin learned then that they were

103

both lonely men, though Grant was by far the lonelier of the two. Robbie had run away from home in his teens and had learned years later that his mother had died soon after he left. He mentioned her often and it was clear that he blamed himself for her death. He had fought with the Canadian Mounted Rifles in the South African war and come back to work cattle ranches in Alberta until 1910. Then he had traveled west to the coast and somehow chosen his trapline on Cameron Creek. In 1914 he had volunteered again and gone overseas to fight in France. Between the wars and again after the second war he had been a heavy drinker and this, it seemed, was the source of his grievance against the outside world.

"Out there," he said, "you work a while and make a stake, then the job folds or you quit and there's nothing to do but hit town. So you hit town and all you can do there is drink to pass the time and blow your stake so it's decent to go back to work again. After a while it gets you and you don't even stay with a job long enough to make a stake. Up here there's always work to be done, trails to cut and cabins to build, and it's work you do for yourself without any boss to watch over you. I've got my trap-lines up the valley, I've got mining claims staked in the mountains—and good assays on them too, copper, and lead and silver and zinc." He paused to reach for his tobacco can and papers. "And when you don't want to work you can study." He waved his hand towards a shelf of books above his bunk. "Or you can just look around you and see what the millionaires pay thousands of dollars to see for a couple of weeks in the year."

"Nobody's arguing against ye," Grant said. "Not even Colin here. It might even be you'll wake up a rich man some day if that railroad comes and the claims are as good as you say."

"I've all I'll ever need right now, with the fur money to buy tea and coffee and beans and rifle shells. There's more deer and fish than I'll ever need right outside the door, more wood to burn, more berries to pick. There's ducks and geese in the winter, and bear fat for the rendering of it and grouse in the swamps."

"Aye, and huckleberries to make a brew of wine when you've a need for it. You're well provided for, Robbie, I'll grant ye all of that."

104

Robbie laughed and glanced towards the row of ten gallon crocks standing against the cabin wall. "Now, Andrew, you know I'm a moderate man. It's nothing more than a taste for friends like yourself that come visiting."

"You'll die of your moderation yet," Andrew told him.

Robbie nodded. "That day'll come," he said. "It has to."

1 3

WHEN the time came to leave Cameron Creek Grant had a full day's work to do on his maps, so Robbie and Colin took the canoe up to Amabilis Creek and set up the new camp there. It was an easy day and they had ample time to catch a mess of trout and cook an early supper on the beach before starting back down the lake.

While they were eating, Robbie said: "You're the first compass-man Andrew ever had could get along with him. Mostly he runs his own compass. He's a hard man to work for."

"I like him O.K.," Colin said. "He never bawls you out unless you're wrong. And he sure knows his work."

"Andrew's the best there is. Timber's his whole life, always has been, and if things had gone right he'd be up there with the biggest lumbermen in the province today."

"He likes what he's doing," Colin said. "He likes the woods."

"He does and he doesn't. Andrew's an ambitious man. I can remember the time when he thought nothing mattered in the world except starting his own logging show and building himself up to a real lumber baron. He made his start too—did real well at it." Robbie poked at the fire. "He'd be on top today if he hadn't got himself married."

"I never knew he was married," Colin said.

"There's a lot you don't know. Likely there's a lot I don't know, but I know some of it. I guess Andrew never was what you'd call a ladies' man, but when I first knew him he was always aiming to marry some girl and never getting up the nerve to ask her. Your mother was one and Will Ensley took her off while Andrew was still trying to scare up nerve to say 'Howdo' without stammering over it. The oldest Underhill girl was another—real pretty girl, too, and sensible. She'd have made a good wife for any man."

Robbie speared another trout from the frying pan and looked down the lake. Colin waited and said nothing. "The woman he did marry, well I guess she must have married him. Never saw her, but I heard all about her. One of these girls with so much mother you never thought to look around and see if she had a father as well. Good-looking, they say, and proud and mean as a weasel—take everything, give nothing. Of course, that's all from Andrew's friends and it might be there's two sides to it." Robbie paused to finish his trout and pour a cup of coffee. "This was just the time Andrew was going good with his logging show, building her up steady and making deals that would put him up where he wanted to be. Seems like she was just as ambitious as he was, only her ambitions was for spending, not making. She had to have a big house in Victoria and servants and clothes and friends in to afternoon tea. And they'd gab and think up more ways to spend money faster than Andrew could make it, until in the end there wasn't anything he could do that was good enough for her any more, so she up and took the baby and went off some place with Ma."

Colin listened closely, trying to fit what he knew of Grant into Robbie's picture. "Where are they now?"

"California. Hollywood, I guess. Last Andrew told me the mother was trying to get the kid into the movies. I guess she's still ambitious."

"Why did all that stop him going ahead?"

"Well," Robbie said slowly, "that's mighty hard to say. There's not many of us do the things we do for the reasons we say we do. Andrew's still married to that woman, he still sends her and the kid money—darn near all he makes. He says if he made more he'd have to send her more, so he just don't make it. To my way of thinking, Andy's not that small. He's a hard man, but I can't

106

figure him doing anything just for spite. Seems to me more likely he was just disgusted when he saw what having money did to people—that, and he wanted to keep away from people who knew what had happened. A man's self-respect is pretty important to him, and a good woodsman's always got it when he's in the woods."

Colin stood up and stirred the fire. "Robbie," he asked, "is there anything wrong with a fellow wanting to get back in the woods—to put in his life there, I mean, the way you and Mr. Grant do?"

Robbie looked at him sharply "A young fellow, you mean? That ain't no way for a young fellow to start out. Why, a young fellow's got the whole world ahead of him. There's nothing he can't do if he sets his mind to it, so long as he's sound in wind and limb and got a good head on his shoulders. Don't you listen too much to us old fellows. Most of us is here because we got disappointed with ourselves—we couldn't make the grade on the outside and got scared and come away where there was nobody to laugh when we messed it all up."

"That wasn't the way it happened to you. You like it here."

"I'm not so sure it ain't," Robbie said. "I never was any hell for success outside, that I could see. Sure I like it, or I wouldn't have come. But that don't mean I didn't run away to get here."

"You aren't sorry. I don't think Mr. Grant is sorry."

"Andrew hasn't quit the outside—you'll see, he'll get in there yet and come out on top. Him and me's different, and it's more than just education. We believe in different things. You won't see Andrew out looking at a lake in the sunset like us here. When he looks at a tree he's figuring what she'll cut out down at the mill and when he looks at a mountain he's wondering how much timber will come off without a switchback in the railroad. Andy's hard and he's practical. It's all figures to him." They were washing the supper dishes at the edge of the lake and Colin watched the colors of the sky touch the cheap tin plate in his hands. "I don't mean to make him sound all hard," Robbie said. "That'd be all wrong. Andy's got a heart big as a mountain. He's an honest man and a good friend—none better." He scooped sand into the frying pan, then glanced at Colin. "You might not think

107

it," he went on. "But I'm a religious man. Andy believes in a god —I've heard him talk—but the God he believes in ain't no stronger than a real good man; more strait-laced maybe, especially about liquor and women, but not much bigger and not much stronger. I don't see it that way. Never could see God with a beard on his face and a thundercloud behind his head. God's in everything— in this sand and in those mountains and in that sky. More'n anything else He's in the way a man feels." He straightened himself slowly. "You're a young fellow," he said. "It'd be hard for you to understand. But if it weren't for the feeling I get that God's in me I wouldn't be staying up here alone like this. It's never been so strong any other place I've been."

As Colin listened to the old man he knew that the words touched himself, touched things he had seen and known and felt. He reached behind the words and tried to make what he found there break through and fit his experience; for a moment he thought that he could, then it slipped away from him and was lost. But he nodded slowly: "I know what you mean, Robbie. I know how it must be. I don't think you're running away. You can't be running away if you've come towards something and found it."

"That's wise talk," Robbie said. "And you might be right. When a man gets to thinking out all the angles on why he's done a thing, he's sunk. Like as not he starts thinking up reasons with a little bit of truth in them and forgetting reasons with a whole lot more truth in them. I never was one to lie to myself if I could help it, so I go a whole lot by the way I feel. And I feel right in here. That don't mean it's good for a young fellow, though."

"Why not? If he feels the same way."

"A young fellow's got no business feeling that way. It ain't healthy. A young fellow's got the whole world in front of him and he ought to want to go out and rip her wide open. When he's seen what's inside maybe he's got some right to an old fellow's way of thinking. But not before."

Going down the lake Robbie was silent. Colin dipped his paddle in the silent water, dipped it again and watched the pale stars come out in the light sky. The smooth ripples of the canoe's passing moved like silver over the dark surface of the lake. I feel good, he thought, better than good. But feeling good isn't feeling God in you like Robbie says. Or is it?

THEY finished the cruise of Amabilis Valley in mid-August. "That's the purest stand of silver fir you're ever likely to see," Grant told Colin. "And it's the only one like it within hundreds of miles of here. Right now you couldn't give it away."

"Why did we cruise it, then?" Colin asked.

"Because it'll be worth good money long before they get the railroad in here."

"How long will that be?"

"Might be ten years," Grant said. "Might be twenty. It won't be five years before this valley's worth money."

"Why does it change like that?" Colin asked. "Seems as though a thing that's going to be worth money in five years ought to be worth money now."

Grant laughed. "Ye've got the makings of a business man," he said. "Sure it's worth money, if you've got the money to put up and the nerve to put it up. That silver fir is as fine a pulpwood as there is and pulp's the future of this whole coast—it's got to be, now the Douglas fir's running out. Log prices are down to nothing right now and money's tight, but that won't last."

"You mean you think the camps'll get working again like they used to? Steady, all the time?"

Grant nodded. "It's never failed yet and it never will. It's a bad one this time and the money's badly scared. But it'll be sticking its neck out again—the head's out of the hole right now, for anyone with eyes to see it."

"Then Dad'll get his job back and everything will be the way it used to be?"

Grant nodded again. "There'll be grief and trouble yet while it's all working out. But there'll be camps working this fall, lots of them, and Will Ensley will always get his job."

"That's what Dad used to say himself when the shutdowns started, but it hasn't seemed to work that way. He doesn't say it any more."

It was still early in the morning, but they had had breakfast and were breaking camp. They had used the camp for only a few days, but it was a good camp and Colin liked it. The timber around it was small and clean and scattered; Amabilis Creek was very clear and very cold, not more than twenty or thirty feet wide here, fast running and shallow. The elevation by Grant's aneroid was over two thousand feet; Amabilis Lake was three miles downstream and Wind Lake another five or six miles down from there. Even with their packs they would make it out to Wind Lake well before evening, and Colin knew suddenly that he was sorry, that he did not want to leave the valley so soon.

"What is there up farther?" he asked. "On up the creek, I mean."

Grant turned and looked upstream. "Well," he said, "I'll tell you. If you ever want some really rugged country, that's the place to find it. I was through there once, around twenty years ago, right over the divide and down the Milky River to Menzies Lake and it was the hardest trip I ever made. There were four of us and two died of it."

Grant's tone was grim and Colin sensed that he wanted to leave the subject alone, but he said: "What happened? Why was it so bad?"

"You ask too many questions," Grant said. "It's time we got started." He swung his pack on to his back, picked up his axe and turned down the stream.

Colin followed in silence. Every step had suddenly become a retreat from what he wanted and he thought: if he doesn't want to tell me about it, why don't I go on up there and see for myself? He couldn't stop me. The rate the valley climbs beyond that last camp I'd be out of the timber in two or three miles. I'd like to see that. We haven't been above timber all summer and I sure wish we could have been. I wonder what happened to the guys that died up there. He says not to ask questions, but he never tells you anything, never even where the next job's going to be or how long it will last or anything. I guess we'll go down to Robbie's tonight, but he hasn't said so and now I can't ask him.

It was a hot day and Grant stopped at the foot of Amabilis Lake, where they had camped a few days earlier. The creek ran deep and slow through meadows at the outlet and it had been a pleasant camp. They slid their packs from their shoulders and sat down, and Grant began to fill his pipe.

"You still want to hear about that trip?" he asked. "I guess there's no reason you shouldn't. I don't know why I shut you off like that just now, except that it's something I haven't talked about for years." He lit his pipe, drawing at it almost impatiently. "The whole thing was a mistake, and partly my fault. It was too late in the year for the trip and Tom Hughes made it worse by stopping to shoot a big goat. It all looked pretty easy then. When you get up beyond the timber this valley opens into a great wide gully and you feel safe as in a church—we did, anyway." The pipe had gone out, but he held it in his hand and made no move to relight it. "There's high mountains all round the gully and no pass out except what they call Windstorm Gap—that's over six thousand feet. Tom got his goat and we made it into the Gap. Then the bad weather caught us. There was snow on the ground already, lots of it, and we'd had some tough traveling. But the wind came at us right out of the north, driving snow so thick you couldn't see thirty feet. We got a tent pitched somehow and holed up in it for three days. The worst of the storm let up then, but we were short of grub and there was snow to our waists every place we looked." Grant looked at Colin. "Still interested?"

Colin nodded, but said nothing. His throat was dry and his body tense. Grant's short, abruptly spoken sentences made a strong, clear picture in his mind and his imagination built on it.

Grant went on: "We kept going instead of turning back. That was my idea and I guess it was wrong. Another storm caught us the next night and we were on an open ledge that time and never did get ourselves any kind of shelter. Tom was killed almost as soon as we started the next day—stepped on an overhang of new snow and fell a thousand feet with a hundred tons of snow going down after him. We couldn't even get down there and we wouldn't have found him if we had made it. John Lynch was in bad shape and Al Hughes and I weren't much better, so we had to keep going. We were down into the timber and clear of snow that night, but John was a sick man and he died less than a week after we got out—pneumonia."

Grant sat forward and put the pipe back in his mouth. "Not a very nice story, is it?"

"It was tough," Colin said. "But you did the best you could have."

"It cost two lives," Grant said. "And there wasn't any sense to it." He slipped into the shoulder straps of his pack and stood up. Colin stood up with him.

"You couldn't tell about the storm," he said. "If it hadn't been for that you'd have been O.K."

"We didn't have to go through that way at all," Grant said slowly. "It came out of boasting and kidding, no more than that. I was the one that knew better and ought to have stopped them." He looked at Colin. "I'm kind of glad I told you now. If you stay with the woods you'll be in a spot like that, sooner or later. When you are, you make them go back. Never mind the talk and kidding. You make them go back."

They came out to Wind Lake late in the afternoon and Grant said, as Colin had expected he would: "We can load the stuff and make Robbie's tonight, easy."

While they were loading the canoe, Colin asked: "Where do we go next?"

"There's two days' work near the foot of the lake," Grant said. "Then we'd better get you back to Blenkinstown. You won't have more than a week before school starts."

"I don't have to be there," Colin said. "If there's more work to do I'd sure like to stay with it."

Grant shook his head. "The job's done except for some bits and pieces I can do on my own. I wouldn't hold you out anyway. You've got all summer to make up for and the sooner you get working on it, the better."

Colin felt all the strength of the summer slipping away from him. He looked down at the loaded canoe, at the sweat-stained packsacks, the bright blade of his axe, the steel-shod jacob staff, the roped bulk of the tent. They had none of the meaning they had had a few moments ago. "Let me stay with it," he said desperately. "I'll catch up in school. Honest I will. Easy."

"I promised your mother," Grant said. "But it'd be the same if I hadn't. Listen, son, you've got a life in front of you. You're smart enough to make something of it. Don't make it tough for yourself by quitting halfway through school. Too many fool kids do that." Grant stepped into the stern of the canoe, reached for his paddle and swung the bow back in for Colin. As they started down the lake, Grant said: "Don't let it get you down, son. You knew it had to end sometime."

Colin drove his paddle for half-a-dozen strokes without speaking. He was looking ahead at the light ripple where Carlson's Creek ran out into the quiet lake.

"It'll be O.K.," he said at last, his voice flat and gloomy. He was remembering Robbie's words as they had looked down the lake from the mouth of Amabilis Creek. 'In the way a man feels,' he thought, that's what he said; well, it's all gone now. I don't feel any more.

PART THREE

THE BIG LAKE

1 4

MILDRED Hanson had stayed at the school to correct some papers and she hurried the quarter of a mile up the hill to the cottage she shared with Carol Maxwell. It had been cold in the schoolroom and the rain was cold as she walked, but it would be warm in the cottage.

She pushed open the door into the small living room and stood for a moment while her eyes got used to the light. There was a bright fire in the little fireplace and the room was warm and full of cigarette smoke. Carol was lying on the couch, an open book face down on her stomach, a cigarette in one long-fingered hand.

On a low stool beside her there was an empty coffee cup, a piled ashtray and several more books, all open and face down. Carol had turned her head as the door opened and lay watching Mildred.

Mildred slipped her coat away from her shoulders. "Did you hear about it?" she asked. "They're going back to work."

Carol nodded. "Yes, I heard. And they haven't got as much as they would have had a couple of weeks ago. I told you that man Miller was pushing it too far. He's single-track, like all the professional organizers."

"I know you did. But they've gained an awful lot, haven't they?"

"If they hold the union together, sure. But if too many of them lose faith and drift away because of Miller it won't be much good. This strike should be just the start."

"I'm glad they're going back, though," Mildred said. "Glad for all of them."

Carol smiled at her affectionately. "We should have a mirror right by the door," she said. "So that you can see what the wind and the rain do for your cheeks. Wheat-gold, sea-blue, rose-red, snow-white, all the trite words for lovely things. And so conscientious too."

Mildred laughed. "I just wanted to get those papers out of the way. I hate bringing them home. Did you start supper? I'm hungry."

"I peeled potatoes," Carol said. "And they're probably boiling by now. I made a salad with my own little hands. There are lamb chops in the ice-box. And all for you, my pet. I'm eating out."

She stood up, stretching her arms above her head. She was a girl of about thirty, very tall and slender, black-haired and dark-skinned. Her face was strong and sharp and keen and her eyes were very dark; with a little effort she could have been remarkably handsome, but it was quite evident that she had not made the effort and didn't intend to. Her hair was stringy and untidy, her black dress hung shapelessly about her and cigarette ashes marked the front of it; she wore no make-up and there was no ornament of any kind to relieve the dullness of her dress.

Mildred hung her coat up and smoothed the front of her skirt. "Where are you going?" she asked.

"To the Vickers'. A new policeman has just arrived and old Dan's got some kind of a promotion. He's a captain or a corporal or something all of a sudden instead of just a constable. June Vickers asked me. She's all tickled about it."

Mildred sat down on the edge of a chair and stretched her fingers out to the fire. "I'm glad," she said. "They don't have much fun, and Mr. Vickers has been here a long time."

Carol glanced lazily around the room. "I suppose I'd better go and wash my face," she said. "I'm due there at six and I ought to be hiking right now. Will you miss me, darling? What will you do? Go to bed with a good book?"

"No," Mildred said, without looking away from the fire. "I'll be up when you get back and the coffeepot will be on the stove."

Carol turned to go out of the room, then stopped suddenly, looking at Mildred's back. "That boy's not coming tonight, is he?"

"Of course," Mildred said. "He always comes on Thursdays."

"I should have thought of that," Carol said. "Maybe I'd better stay home after all."

Mildred turned slowly to look at her. "What *are* you talking about, Carol? Hurry up and change your dress."

"Sixteen," Carol said slowly. "Six-foot-two and big, even if he is gawky still. People in small towns do talk, you know, darling. Especially about schoolteachers."

Mildred flushed. "I wish you wouldn't say things like that, Carol. Even in fun."

Carol came a little way back into the room. "I'm sorry, darling. I'm always teasing when I shouldn't. But there's some truth in it, you know. The old cats would love to get hold of something like that. It's only once and they won't know anything about it, but I think you ought to send him away, just the same. He can come tomorrow night instead."

Mildred laughed. "I thought I was the fussy one. Go and change that dress. You've given them more to talk about than I ever will."

"Could be," Carol said. "But they don't talk. They never do about plain girls."

Mildred went into the kitchen and began to cook her supper while Carol was changing. Carol came out, kissed her and disappeared with a bang of the outside door. Mildred ate supper, changed her own dress, then tidied the living room and sat down to read. Colin was due at seven and he usually stayed till eight-thirty or nine. He was taking two grades in one year, to make up for the time he had missed the previous summer. Actually he was handling the work very easily and required little help beyond mild supervision, but Mildred had encouraged him to come as often as possible because she knew he would do little on his own, especially now that Margaret was no longer at home.

Through supper she had shut the implication of Carol's half-serious warning away from her. But now, sitting with a book open in front of her and the firelight warm on her face, she could no longer do so. Of course Carol's right, she thought, much more right than she thinks she is. She doesn't think there's anything attractive about Colin. What was it she said about him the other day? 'The primitive type, with the smell of the woods on him while the smell of his mother's pap still lingers; he doesn't just know whether to be a shy fawn or a roaring bull-elk and he never will know.' Then: 'He's like that father of his, not enough drive to be anything at all; that kind just lets things happen to it.' But she isn't right, Mildred thought calmly; nearly always she is right about people and she's kind about people even though she says such hard things; but not about Colin. There is something more in Colin than most people can see very easily, and it is something positive, something that he is, not something that happens to him. Perhaps it's only gentleness and kindness, but those are positive things and they can be very powerful. In Colin they will be; I used to feel that years ago, when he was only small, and I felt it again when I saw him down from the woods last summer. The same thing is in Margaret, but she uses it and makes it different; Colin doesn't use it, it's what he is and stronger for that, though not so easy to see. Carol doesn't look for things like that; she sees so many things so quickly that she expects everything to be plain, where you can see it and explain it. But people will feel that from Colin and respond to it; I think they do already.

She heard Colin at the door and went over to let him in. He

came in shyly, as always, and a little awkwardly, knowing that his hands and feet and body were too big for the room. He glanced around, as though expecting to see Carol Maxwell, then put his books down on the table. Mildred thought he was relieved that Carol was not there, but his deep voice sounded almost disappointed when he asked: "Miss Maxwell go out?"

"Yes," Mildred said. "I don't think she'll be back till after you've gone." She went back to her chair and sat down. "That Geometry again tonight," she told him. "You know where to start."

He settled himself with his books, then looked up and said: "Miss Maxwell is a swell teacher."

"It's good you like her," Mildred said. "She's very clever. She could have her Ph.D. if she wanted—she's done all the studying for it."

"She makes everything so interesting," Colin said. "Seems like you don't ever come near the end of what she knows and it's all there waiting, any time. Much more than is in the books."

"You're lucky to have her," Mildred said. "She could be teaching in university or anywhere she wanted, but she says she likes country schools."

"Seems funny," Colin said. "They must pay more in the big places."

"They do. But Carol—Miss Maxwell says country schools need good teachers just as much as the big places and she likes to live in the country. I expect she'll move on one day, though."

Colin turned to his work and said no more. The relationship between them was easy now, but his shyness never quite left him and Mildred had done nothing to draw him away from it since the day he touched her in the schoolroom. Deep in her teacher's soul, she knew she was wrong, knew that she should have found ways to build strength and confidence in him; but for a long while she had deliberately held the image of her own fault sharp and clear in her mind, using it to strengthen still further her familiar, calm control. The thoughts that had shocked her that bright spring day while the children wrote of mountains had come back many times, but she had learned to explain them to herself and she thought she understood them, though they still shamed her. Colin's power of attraction for her still waited in him and at times reached strongly out to her, but that, too, she had explained and thought she understood.

Sitting in the room while he worked, remembering the sharp thrust of joy in her heart when she had found him suddenly on the village street with Grant, she was able to tell herself that it was natural to have felt that, that any woman whose care was for children must feel it. Some girl will love him terribly one day, she thought; he's so helpless and yet so strong, and there's so much gentleness in him. Carol's wrong about him every way; the strength he has is not what she means by bull-elk strength, and the gentleness is not a fawn's gentleness; he's simple, but he's not primitive simple nor stupid simple; it is something in him that will keep him from hating or hurting anybody or anything and it can be made more than that, into something that will make him help people and do things for them.

She got up from her chair and stood behind him, looking over his shoulder. He drew away from the page in front of him and looked up at her. "O.K.?" he asked.

"It's good," she said. "You hadn't asked any questions for so long I was getting worried about you."

"It's so quiet in here it's easy to work."

She went back to her chair and sat down. I've been silly about it all, she told herself, so worried about being wicked and evil, always afraid for myself. Yet I'm strong about most other things, and sure, not hesitating or doubtful or afraid. I'm six years older than he is, a woman while he's still a boy. I'm not afraid of other men; there's never been one I couldn't keep in his place. I'm not afraid of Colin, I never have been afraid of him, only of my thoughts of him. And because of that I've held him away from me, cheated him of things I should have done for him, left him lonely when I knew he needed help.

"Colin," she said. "You aren't going off with Mr. Grant again this summer, are you?"

He looked up from his work. "No, I don't think so. He hasn't said anything about it. I'm not sure he's going himself."

"Don't go. You would never make it up again if you did."

"I might have to go if the camps don't keep working. They're

119

starting up again the first of the week, but that doesn't mean there won't be a shutdown or another strike or something."

"Is your father glad they're going back?"

"Dad? He sure is. He figured they should have gone the first time the company offered. They had the wages then and that was the big thing, he said. He's awful sore at Miller, the organizer."

"Why should they strike again so soon?" she asked.

"I don't think they will," Colin said. "There's only a few of them want to. It's been tough for a long time."

"You liked it with Mr. Grant last summer, didn't you? I was afraid you weren't going to come back in the fall."

Colin smiled. "He didn't give me any chance not to come back. I tried to talk him into letting me go on with him, but it seemed like his mind was made up before I started. Mr. Grant is a hard man to talk around."

"I'm glad there's someone you'll listen to. He seemed nice when I saw you that day, but he certainly wasn't very talkative."

Colin flushed. "He's no talker, except sometimes with Robbie Robinson. But he's sure a swell guy to be in the woods with. There isn't anything he doesn't know about timber."

"Come and sit by the fire," Mildred said. "You've done enough work for tonight and you can tell me what it was you liked back there so much. You can talk a composition instead of writing one, for a change. It's good practice for speaking out in school."

Colin got up from the table and came hesitantly towards the fire. She pushed the stool over for him and he sat awkwardly on it for a moment, then moved to the floor. His body was tense and suspicious from the strangeness of the thing she had asked of him and for nearly a minute he sat staring into the fire. Then he said: "What do you want me to tell you?"

"Whatever you like," she said. "Try to make me understand what it was you liked so much and about your Mr. Grant and this Robbie Robinson. Start anywhere you like and just talk."

Colin leaned back against the stool and stared into the fire. He thought of the great trees on the flat of the valley below the lake, of the wet darkness under them, of the clear water and clean gravel up the little creeks. It was good there because it was new, he told himself; I didn't know anything there. It was better

120

later on when I knew the score and Grant got friendly. Why does she want me to talk anyway? Why couldn't I just be here like this, near her, and both of us quiet? But I'd like to tell her, I'd like her to know, except that in talk things always sound foolish; you always forget things and the things that matter won't really go into words. If I could just lie here and think it and she could see it at the same time it would be different. That is how people ought to be able to talk, so they could both mean the same things at the same time.

"There's an old ranch," he said. "Down near the mouth of the river, just above the tide flats. It's falling apart now and nobody lives there, but it's a swell place; and in the old days some people named Underhill raised a big family there and had a school and everything." His body relaxed and he talked on steadily, describing the Underhill family and its life as Grant had described it to him. The rotting farm buildings, the overgrown garden, the landing on the river, the wagon roads into the brush, all came to life for him as he spoke; he saw the cattle on the flats, heard the clatter of the mower, the noise of the children in the orchard, smelled the sweat of the horses and the sweetness of fresh hay.

"People used to stop in there a lot," he said. "Mr. Grant did and all my mother's family when she was a child, anyone who was going up or down the coast and put in near the river. And the Underhills always fed them and looked after them and often if there were enough of them they'd put on a dance and people would come up from the camp that was here, where Blenkinstown is."

He hesitated and looked up at her face to see if she was listening. Their eyes met for a moment and he felt a softness in hers that made his pulses throb and forced him to look away. He began to talk again, of the big timber along the river, of the lake and then of Amabilis Valley. He tried to tell of the faith he felt from Robbie, but could not find easy words and turned away from it to tell her how the lake had looked from the mouth of the creek that night, how the shadows had fallen across the timbered valleys, how the sun had touched the tall snow peaks and the great rock faces. He forgot himself in the telling, forgot Mildred, became only a voice, distant to himself, and eyes that distantly watched the red light of the fire. The stool slipped away from him and he moved slightly to set his back against the arm of her chair.

Listening to him, feeling the warmth of the room, and its remoteness from all the rest of life, she let cold control slip away from her body and her mind. This is what I want of him, she thought, this is what he sees and feels and is. His mind has met these things and made something of them; he can bring them back and give them meaning for me, meaning and under-meaning, because that is there in the things he chooses to tell me and in the way the words come from him. I know now that he is one of the live people and I can make him grow; I have to because there is no one else who will.

Colin had stopped talking, but neither of them stirred. I should say something, Mildred thought, but not yet, not for a little while. He must go quite soon, but this will not happen again so naturally and so easily unless I leave the whole memory of it secure in him. She moved her left hand a little on the arm of the chair, towards Colin, but otherwise she did not move until she heard Carol's footsteps outside the door.

Carol came in quickly and stopped sharply, her hand still on the door. "Well," she said emphatically, then seemed to check herself. "You folks certainly look cozy. Know what time it is?"

Colin scrambled awkwardly to his feet, went over to the table and began to pick up his books. "I'd better start home," he said. "It must be pretty late."

"Don't hurry," Mildred said easily. "I'm going to make some coffee and we've got a cake out there."

"It's after ten o'clock," Carol said pointedly.

Colin moved towards the door. "The folks'll be waiting up," he said. "I better step on it. Thanks for everything, Miss Hanson."

Carol watched the door close behind him. "Thanks for everything," she repeated. "It's nice to know he appreciates it." She turned to Mildred and saw that she was angry. "Suppose," she said, "Old Siddons had walked in. Or the preacher. Or Mrs. Davidson. Instead of me?"

"I knew it was you," Mildred said. "And suppose it hadn't been. Can't he even sit near the fire?"

Carol slipped her coat off and flung it over a chair. "Don't be cross with your old aunt, darling. She's only looking out for your own good."

"You've frightened him," Mildred said. "He'll shut himself away again and I never shall be able to help him."

Carol looked at her. "You mean you're really serious about it? You really think you've found the streak of pure gold that's going to make him the Father of his Country or the Singer of its Songs?"

"There's something in him that isn't in most of us. I'm not sure what it is, but I'm good and sure it's a teacher's business to find out if she can."

Carol crossed the room and stood beside her. "My conscientious darling," she said. "I'll have to look at him again." The tips of her long fingers touched Mildred's pale hair, drew gently across the gold sheen and returned again. "If there's anything there you shall have your chance to wake it." She sat down on the arm of the chair beside Mildred. "Don't build too many hopes for him to live up to. There's nothing harder on a child than that."

"I won't." Mildred looked up and smiled. "But I've always felt someone owed Colin a break."

"You'd much better spend your time on the new cop."

"Another primitive?" Mildred asked. "Fawn or elk?"

"A craggy lion, darling. Tall, broad and magnificent. Granite jaw, hawk nose, steel-gray eyes, everything a girl could ask. He doesn't talk much more than your friend, but I've got a feeling he could make his words count."

MARTHA worked in her kitchen on a June afternoon and counted her blessings. Will had been working steadily since the strike and there was no suggestion so far of a shutdown unless a spell of dry weather made it essential. The strike itself had been a bitter and worrying time, but Martha had accepted it with a grim and almost glad determination; from the first she had held Will to his part in it, strengthening his resolve again and again when he showed signs of wavering or of reluctance in forcing a point. For her the issues had been simple: higher wages and no Sunday work. Because the strike won both points she was satisfied and her conscience was clear—the companies had been holding back something that it was in their power to grant.

Margaret had come back from Vancouver after her second year at the University and she was doing fully as well as Mr. Siddons and Mildred Hanson had said she would. She's changed a lot, Martha thought, much more a city girl than she used to be, quicker and busier and she talks differently and has more ideas and dresses differently. Perhaps all that would have happened if she had stayed right here, but you notice it more when she's been away. She's the same Margaret at the bottom, of course; she hasn't grown away from her family the way some girls do when they go to the city and she settles right in as soon as she gets back here. I'm glad she wants to be a nurse now instead of a teacher; all that about going on to be a lady-doctor later might come to something and it might not, but it's good for a girl to have ideas like that when you know she's smart enough to be able to go through with them.

Martha opened the oven door and took out a batch of bread. She turned the loaves upside down in the pans and set a clean dish-towel over them to hold in the moisture while they cooled. I don't suppose it's been easy for Margaret, she thought; Sister Edith never was an easy one to get along with and I can tell from the way she writes she thinks she's doing a lot for Margaret. She is, too; if Edith and Arthur didn't board her, Margaret couldn't go to school down there at all. But I don't doubt they get their money's worth back and a little more besides. If there's anything Margaret doesn't do in that house, from making beds to cooking fancy suppers, I'd like to know what it is.

It makes me proud of Margaret that she has never complained; if it weren't for Edith's letters and if I didn't know her so well I don't suppose I'd be able to guess what goes on down there. But Margaret is the determined kind, and that Miss Hanson has taught her a lot of things besides school work. She's got a big influence with Colin, too, making him study night after night the way he does to finish up those two grades. I didn't think Colin would ever settle to anything like that. Will says he can probably go up on the bridge-crew for a while this summer and next year he'll finish high school.

Martha lifted the lid of the potato pot and saw that the water was boiling. She heard footsteps outside and knew that Colin and Margaret were back from the barn with the milk. Will's late, she thought, and remembered, as she always did when he was late, the time the speeder carrying the bridge-crew had jumped the track. Two men had been killed then and all the others more or less seriously injured; Will had been lucky, with only a broken leg. His work's as safe as most, though, she reminded herself; a whole lot safer than the rigging crews.

Margaret came in then and Martha told her to set the supper table. "Your father's late," she said. "But he'll be here any minute and supper's all ready."

"We got nearly seventy pounds of milk tonight," Margaret said. "Colin says the rain has brought the pasture right up again." She took a pile of plates from the cupboard and Martha heard her quick, efficient steps go back to the table again. "You don't know how a person misses that, Mother, living in town. You almost forget that rain makes things grow."

Martha laughed happily. "So that's what we send you to college for." She looked up from the stove, listening. "That's them now. One thing about Mr. Varchuk's car; you can never mistake it."

Will Ensley's evening routine was fully restored. They heard him pause outside the door to loosen his laces and kick off his caulked boots, heard him murmur something to Colin at the separator. Margaret opened the door and he handed her his lunch pail without a word. Then he crossed the kitchen silently and hurriedly in his stockinged feet, as though ashamed of his working clothes, muttered an embarrassed greeting to Martha as he passed the stove, and went on into the bedroom beyond. In a little while he came back into the room, his working clothes changed for the bulky tweed pants and a thick dark-gray shirt. He spoke easily now and moved in a more relaxed way, but Margaret thought: he doesn't seem as huge as he used to. His shirt looks almost loose on him, but I remember when the largest shirts he could buy were always tight across his chest, so it seemed that the buttons would break away. His beard is just as square as ever, but it doesn't seem as black as it used to and his eyes don't seem as brightly black behind it.

She bowed her head and listened to the familiar intonations of his grace. "Bless this house, O Lord, and this family gathered beneath its roof. Bless the food that is before us and by its nourishment grant us strength to do Thy will." In the bad times, she remembered, the grace had sometimes faltered, sometimes wavered towards disillusion, sometimes shrunk into despair, sometimes forced out in hope and courage. It's almost like a diary, she thought, a daily part of him, so strongly a part of him that he lets it tell what he is thinking as nothing else ever does. Perhaps he feels it is secret to himself, that no one else will notice how much of him it gives away. But we do notice, all of us, me and Colin and especially Mother. Sometimes Mother waits so hard for it that she puts her head a little on one side to listen before he even starts to speak.

Mother's tired tonight. She's happy, but she's tired. Those long lines that run down past the corners of her mouth, from her nose almost to her jaw, don't fade out the way they used to. They're deeper and more tired when she's sitting quietly like this than when she's working. She doesn't seem old enough to have lines like that; she does everything so quickly and well and her eyes are so bright and young and laughing that I never think of her as old at all. Anyone who does as much as she does, who moves about so fast all day, takes so many steps, lifts so many things, uses her hands so much, is bound to get tired. When you get tired there are lines in your face, little lines at first, then deeper lines. And if you go on getting tired every day the lines get so deep they are there all the time, even when you're not tired. I suppose that's what getting old is. But I don't want Mother to get old. I don't want anything to happen to her ever so that she can't move about quickly and seem young and full of life; if that happened she wouldn't be Mother any more, if her eyes changed she wouldn't be.

For a moment, and for the first time in her life, Margaret saw and recognized death. Sharply, death forced itself upon her; people grow old, their bodies wear out from living and doing, they die. But not Mother, her mind said, not for years and years and years. She will change slowly and gently, her eyes will always laugh and burn blue, her hands will always move swiftly and surely, her feet will always be quick and light. I shall grow older myself, and change with her, and because of that we shall always be the same to each other.

Will Ensley said: "We moved out to the new trestle on the spur line today. Seems like the turn has come."

"That does look more hopeful," Martha said. "Things seem a little better everywhere."

"Not in the cities," Margaret said. "There are thousands of unemployed in Vancouver."

Will Ensley looked at her and frowned. "That will be changing. It can't all happen overnight. They'll get their chance—some of them will be getting it right here in Blenkinstown now the mills are running again and they're starting a new side up at camp."

"Some of the boys I know in town don't think so," Margaret said. "They're talking about organizing a big march on the government in Victoria."

Her father looked at her in astonishment and irritation. "Foolish talk," he said, and Margaret caught her mother's anxious glance and knew that she must say no more. "Child's talk and wickedness. If they get out of the cities and look for it they will find work."

"It's a hard time for young people, Will," Martha said gently.

"You can't altogether blame them for thinking there must be something wrong."

"They'll gain nothing by setting themselves up against authority, and I'm sorry that a child of mine should have any dealings with such people. If they were older they would know there's nothing new in all this and nothing that can be changed by threats and violence."

"They just want a chance to work, Will. And perhaps the government will do something when they see how many of them there are. People do get things by going out after them."

"There's some truth in that," Will said. "We gained something by the strike. But I hope there'll be no more of them."

Margaret watched him turn back to his food again, as though the subject were entirely forgotten. He's changed a lot, she thought, and Mother has too. I'm sure he wouldn't have given in to her like that a few years ago, and he would have been much angrier with me. We've all changed, I suppose, even Colin, though I think he's still scared of Father. In a way I am, but it's different because I can see through the being scared; I know that he isn't God after all, that he's quite a simple man and not nearly so wise as he used to sound. I wish I knew what Colin thinks. I must ask him sometime, except that it's a hard thing to ask exactly the way I mean it, and he probably wouldn't tell me anyway.

The meal was finished and Margaret was washing the dishes when Dave Vickers and the new policeman came to the door. Dave said cheerfully: "Hope we're not disturbing supper, folks."

"No," Martha said. "Everyone's finished."

Will was standing up and came across the room. "Come on in and sit down," he said. "It isn't often we get to see you." Will liked Dave Vickers. "Glad to see you've got those stripes at last," he added.

Dave laughed. "They're like old age and false teeth—you always get 'em if you wait around long enough. But I want you to know Constable Munro. I've been telling him that's a policeman's first duty—to get to know all the old-timers in his district."

Margaret turned away from the dishes and watched. Both Vickers and Munro were tall men, so tall that they stood in the low-ceilinged kitchen with slightly stooped heads, and both were in uniform. Vickers was a man of fifty or fifty-five, red-faced and heavy featured. He was cheerful and sure of his welcome, an easy-going man, used to liking people and being liked. Munro was much younger, about twenty-five Margaret thought, with a pale, hard-cut face and quiet gray eyes. He was wearing breeches and high boots and carried a police stetson in his hand; everything about him, boots, breeches, tunic, belt and holster seemed fitted and polished and in place, in sharp contrast to Dave Vickers' slightly sagging appearance. Dave introduced the whole family, then dropped his flat uniform cap beside a chair, loosened his belt a little and sat down. Munro sat stiffly in another chair Will had brought up for him, Martha sat in her own chair talking easily to him and Will settled to talk with Dave Vickers. Margaret and Colin went back to the dishes.

Colin reached past Margaret for a dish, so that his head was close to hers. "Gee," he said. "That's a lot of man, that new cop."

"Beautiful, but dumb," Margaret whispered back.

"How do you know?"

"He hasn't said much, has he?"

"Girls," Colin said. "You're always critical. He probably knows a whole lot more than you ever will."

"I'll believe it when I see it."

When they had put away the dishes they started out of the room, but Dave Vickers stopped them.

"Don't run away," he said. "I want to hear about college and the big city. I see by the papers you came through with flying colors again, Margie."

Margaret smiled at him. "That's only the second year, Mr. Vickers. I've got a long way to go yet."

"And you'll come through at the top of them all, my dear. It's an honor to the town to see your name where it is on those lists." Vickers shifted in his chair and looked at Colin. "You going to follow in your sister's footsteps, young fellow?"

Colin looked over at his father, then back to Vickers. "I don't know, Mr. Vickers," he said. "I guess I wouldn't make much of college."

"Nonsense," Vickers said. "I hear you're every bit as smart as

Margie was at your age." He turned to Munro. "Smartest family in this town," he said. "You ought to be proud of them, Will."

"Colin's coming up on the bridge-crew with me as soon as school lets out," Will said.

"Think they'll keep running for a while?" Vickers asked. The question was one that Margaret had heard asked a thousand times, and Vickers asked it casually; but something in his tone made her glance quickly at him, and she knew that Martha had noticed too.

Will had not. "Nothing to stop them," he said. "Unless bad fire weather and there's certainly no sign of that yet."

"Wettest spring in years," Vickers agreed. "If I were new to the coast like Clyde Munro here I believe I'd be applying for a transfer to the Interior right now."

"No logger minds a wet shirt in June and July," Will said. "I'll take the coast climate ahead of anything I ever saw east of the mountains."

"I guess there's no fear of another strike coming along to break things up?" The question was almost elaborately casual this time and Margaret felt again that there was purpose in it. She watched Clyde Munro's face, but saw nothing there beyond a polite, unsmiling interest. He's a cold one, she thought, hard and cold and I don't think I like him. But she watched him closely as Will answered.

"We don't want any more of that for a while. There was good in the last one, up to a point. But what we need now is a spell of steady work."

Margaret saw that Martha was looking hard at Will, trying to catch his eye. He must have looked towards her, because Martha shook her head twice, very slightly, very cautiously. Margaret recognized the warning.

"I heard Miller was up around these parts again," Vickers said.

Will moved sharply in his chair. "An empty vessel," he said sharply. "Sounding brass and a tinkling cymbal. He's wasting his time if he hopes to stir up anything among sane men."

"Have you seen anything of him since he got back?" Again Martha was signaling, almost frantically this time. Will started to speak, saw her, hesitated and blundered into clumsy denial.

130

"No," he said. "No, Miller hasn't shown up around any place I know of. He could be around, mind you, and I wouldn't know about it. But I don't think that's so."

Watching Munro, Margaret saw the muscles at the corners of his mouth relax ever so slightly. There, she thought, you almost trapped him but not quite. You haven't got anything, it didn't do you any good, you can go away now. Poor Father, he's miserable, he doesn't know whether he has done right or wrong. He's truly fond of Dave Vickers, he always likes policemen and he's said a hundred times that it is the duty of a good citizen to help them uphold the law. Now he's had to betray that, to put himself on the other side, the wrong side, the side of the unrighteous and the ungodly, the men without dignity or worth.

Vickers said easily: "It's not important, Will. I was just curious for myself. I don't suppose he is around or we'd have heard of it. I think you're right anyway, he wouldn't get to first base with the boys this time." He turned to Colin. "So you're going to work with your dad this year, Colin? You couldn't learn from a better man."

"That's right," Colin said simply.

"Colin would sooner be back in the woods with Andrew Grant, like he was last summer," Will said. "But Andrew's not going out this year, so he'll be learning to use his arms instead of his legs."

"It's a fine trade, the broad-axe," Dave Vickers said. "But it's dying out, like a lot of other good things. They're using pretty near all sawn ties now and more bridge timbers from the sawmills all the time."

"A sawn stringer will never have the strength of a hewn stringer," Will said. "And sawmill ties may be good enough for a mainline, but on a spur line where you want to take them up and use them again, nothing will ever beat hewn hemlock."

"True enough," Dave said. "I guess it's not so much they don't want the goods as they can't get the men to make them."

"The sawmill stuff is cheaper, too," Munro said. "At least at the start."

"That's all you can say for it," Will told him. "A trestle built of sawn timbers is no better than a house built upon the sand."

The tension had dropped away and the four adults talked

comfortably. Colin whispered to Margaret and they both went quietly out of the room. "Let's go to the hayloft," Margaret said, and Colin knew she wanted to talk.

As they walked towards the barn Colin said: "Do you still figure the new cop is dumb?"

"No," Margaret said. "He's plenty smart, I guess. But he's a cold sort of fish; figures he's a hard guy, I suppose."

"You sure don't give him any breaks, do you? I like him. I like the way he looks at you and the way he sits listening to other people talk instead of gabbing away all the time himself."

They came to the barn and sat down on the ledge of the wide doorway instead of climbing to the hayloft.

"Sure he listens," Margaret said. "Sometimes you make me tired, Colin. Couldn't you see what they were trying to do, trying to trap Dad into telling them where Miller is? Dave Vickers was doing the talking, but that Munro is the smart one. I'll bet he's been sent up here specially for that kind of stuff." She thought: why did I say that? I hadn't thought it until just as I spoke and I'm not sure it's right anyway. I knew I didn't like him long before Mr. Vickers said anything about Miller; I don't like him because he's cold and stiff and conceited, that's all.

Colin said: "Mr. Vickers said it wasn't important about Miller. What could they do about it if they did know where he was? It's none of their business."

"They'd probably put him in jail. They do put labor leaders in jail."

"They couldn't," Colin said. "There's no law against having a union."

"They do though. They put them in jail for something else. Pretty nearly everybody's done something he could be put in jail for."

Colin shrugged his shoulders. "Sounds crazy to me. I think Mr. Vickers just wanted to know if there's another strike coming up."

They heard the screen door slam and looked towards the house. "It's Munro," Colin said. "I wonder where he's going?"

"Looks as though he's coming over here," Margaret said, and

they watched the tall policeman walking towards them across the pasture.

When he came near Colin stood up, but Munro smiled and said: "Don't move. I just wanted to look around a farm again. You've got a nice place here."

Margaret looked at him suspiciously. "Did you ever work on a farm?"

"I was raised on one, Miss Ensley," he said. "I used to think sometimes I wouldn't mind if I never saw a cow-barn again, but I guess it gets in your blood. I can't pass one up now."

Colin met Munro's slow smile and liked him in spite of what Margaret had said. "I know what you mean," he said. "It must be quite something when you have a big bunch of cows to milk every day, night and morning. The most we've ever had is four."

"With us it was anywhere from twenty-four to thirty and generally three of us to milk. Most of the time I liked it fine, but once in a while it'd seem to get you down."

"Would you like to see the cows?" Margaret asked Munro. "They're Jerseys."

"I sure would," Munro said. "We had Holsteins."

"Can you find them, Colin?"

Colin nodded. "They'll be in the edge of the alders, near the creek."

He started across the pasture and Margaret followed him closely without another word to Munro. Farm-boy, indeed, she thought; he likes cows and barns. He does like heck. Next thing we know he'll be asking us about Miller. I'll have to watch he doesn't get Colin alone. Colin wouldn't tell now I've talked to him, but he's like Dad; he can't tell a lie and make it sound like anything except a lie.

She held herself very straight as she walked, and moved gracefully, in spite of Colin's swift pace. She knew that she looked trim and well-made, knew that her skirt swung handsomely about her knees and hoped that Munro was watching. At least he can see that we aren't all simple country people who'll fall for any soft line he wants to put out. Chances are he'll trip over his big boots before we find the cows, anyway; I hope he does.

They were in the alders and there was a big log across the way

Colin had gone. Suddenly Margaret realized that Munro was ahead of her, over the log, offering her his hand. "Thanks," she said. "I can manage."

They found the cows and Colin showed them off proudly. They were very tame with him, swinging their heads to his voice, standing for his touch, their eyes brown and calm and incurious. But when Munro moved closer they stirred nervously, watching him awkwardly, ready to swing away and plow off through the breast-high brush. He went on toward Brownie, the nearest of them, speaking gently to her, passing smoothly and quietly through the brush. She'll fool him, Margaret thought, old Brownie'll never stand for him and he'll look silly turning away to try it out on another one. But Brownie stood and he laid a big quiet hand on her back, near the shoulders and slid it along to her rump and she only watched him curiously. He stooped and Margaret knew he was feeling the milk veins and the udder; and she knew at the same time that he was really interested in the cow, that he hadn't been simply trying to make them like him there at the barn.

Munro looked up at Colin. "She's a good one," he said. "A four-gallon cow anyway."

"Four and a half when she's fresh," Colin said. "Brownie's the best of the lot. But I've never seen her stand like that for a stranger."

"Those neat-built Jerseys are often nervous, especially when they've got little feet like she has. They seem more like a deer than a cow if you're used to Holsteins. But they're wise too, if they've been treated right. Seem to know who means well by them."

Margaret watched his face. The big dope's happy, she thought; I believe he really was homesick for his old farm. Now he's up with Colin looking at Fern and she's standing for him too. That's all black mud in where they're standing and I didn't think he'd ever take a chance on getting those shiny boots dirty.

The three of them walked abreast back towards the house. Munro was as tall as Colin but seemed taller because he carried himself so well, and Margaret felt very small beside them. Colin asked: "Will you be staying here, Mr. Munro?"

"That's something they never let us know for sure," Munro said.

"But I hope so. I've never been on the coast before and I like this part."

"Will Mr. Vickers be leaving, then?" Margaret asked him.

"No, Miss Ensley. They've made Blenkinstown a two-man station and we're going to have a boat here when they get around to it."

"Who is 'they'?" Margaret asked aggressively. She was still trying not to like him.

Munro laughed apologetically. "The Commissioner, I guess, when you come right down to it. He's the one who decides. But it goes through a lot of people on the way up to him—sergeants and inspectors and different departments. I guess that's why we always say 'they.'"

Something in the simple explanation conveyed to Margaret the respect and affection he had for his force. That's why he holds himself so proudly and carefully, she thought, and why his uniform is so clean and pressed and polished.

"You like being a policeman, don't you?" She asked.

"Yes," he said simply. "A good policeman can do a lot for people."

16

COLIN swung the scoring axe in an easy rhythm, stroke after stroke so that the bright blade drove always the same depth into the soft wood. As he scored the face of the stringer he moved along the log, feeling his caulks bite crisply into the sapwood. He had been working on the bridge-crew for nearly three weeks now, scoring for his father's broad-axe most of the time, and the muscles of his shoulders and wrists had learned a control that brought him a deep satisfaction. At first he had been inaccurate and slow, although the axe was a familiar tool, and his father had drawn his attention to every error. But now Will Ensley worked in satisfied silence, swinging his own huge axe with the full power of his great arms and body, flattening the faces of his caps and stringers to plane smoothness in which it was almost impossible to find even a hairline where one of Colin's strokes had gone too deep or the slightest break where the scoring had been too light.

The bridge-crew was building a trestle on the spur line and it was a good show. It was a fair-sized trestle for a spur line, sixteen bents, the highest about forty feet to the cut-off, but there was new rigging on the driver, the piles were good, the driving was good and things had gone smoothly. Old George Smith, the foreman, who rarely spoke above a whisper and never took his hands out of his pockets, even to bend down and sight a cut-off, was less in evidence even than usual. He spent a good part of every day roaming the side-hill above the trestle, marking down deer that he claimed he would shoot in the fall. The crew was happy about it; George hadn't treated life that way since the first long shutdown.

Will Ensley's work was well ahead. For once there had been plenty of logs for caps and stringers and they were good stuff—the right size and really clean. He had a perfectly flat landing to work on right at the approach to the trestle and it was already ankle-deep in chips and shavings and full of the clean cedar smell that he loved. He hadn't faced such an abundance of straightforward broad-axe work for years and he shut himself away into it with the intentness he always used on the job, speaking scarcely a word to Colin or the rest of the crew even when they gathered to brew coffee and eat their lunches each noon.

The noon break was two hours behind them now and it was a hot July afternoon. George Smith had just come back from a short trip up the hill and was moving quietly about near the pile driver, smiling absentmindedly and seeming to care nothing at all about how the work was going. He stopped and spoke to Sam Boulder, the oldest of the regular bridgemen and George's best friend, squinted ahead at the bent the driver was working on, then climbed on to the driver to stand by Johnny Meldrum at the levers.

Colin finished the face he was working on and stood back to

look along the evenly spaced marks of his scoring. He had seen George Smith come over the hill and down the slope, had watched him walk the slim poles that were spiked to the caps of the completed bents, stop to speak to Sam and go on to climb on to the pile driver and stand beside Johnny Meldrum, as he often did when he was not on the hill. Vaguely Colin envied George his freedom. He knew he would be talking lazily with Johnny, almost knew what they would be saying. "Four-pointer, in the velvet, down under the blackberry vines" or "A whole brood of blue grouse, must of been ten anyway, so that wet weather in June didn't drown 'em all." That was George's talk, always, or something much like it. Occasionally something had to be said about the trestle, but it was always said as off-handedly as possible, and the bridge-crew liked that and worked better for it because it recognized that they were all skilled men. Once George had overheard Will checking Colin on the accuracy of his chopping. "Kid's doing pretty good, Will," he had said. "You won't get many take to it like he does."

"A boy'll never learn without telling," Will had said. But, like the rest of the crew, he respected George Smith and he said less to Colin from then on.

Colin walked over to the next timber and sized it up against the line his father had already stretched along it. He thought: it's easy work, this swinging an axe all day, easier than school-work and you hardly have to worry about it at all after the first little while; you can just go along with it, thinking your own thoughts, not even thinking really, just letting pictures go on and on through your mind any way they want to go. You do that in school and it always catches up with you—some teacher asks a question and you don't even know what he has asked. I like working with Mr. Grant better than this job. You've got to pay attention to that, but you've got time to think and new things to think about all the time because you're moving all the time. Here you can find new things to think about because things move and you see them, people move and talk and do things, or the pile driver chunks out the bridge-site and turns up old logs that haven't been moved for a hundred years. You can think about those and the moss growing on them and the dirt underneath and the insects inside. But it still isn't as good as moving yourself. And this job isn't as good as the other. It's like Miss Hanson says, a man needs something that makes his brain work, not just something that stretches his shoulders. Dad has to think a bit, but he's so used to the job it's hardly thinking any more. George Smith uses his head; he has to, a whole lot more than he ever lets on; the boys say he can figure out anything, better than the best engineer, by just using a steel-square; they argue about that—some of the boys say he bluffs a lot and he's really no more than a darn good carpenter. But the older ones say he can figure out any kind of trestle there is; Sam Boulder says he built one once with a horizontal and a vertical curve and there wasn't an engineer came near it from the time they chunked out until they put the ties on. But even George Smith is doing the same thing over and over until it gets so easy for him he doesn't really have to worry.

He watched the bright arc of his axe and for a moment was conscious of the rhythm of his work—the lift of the blade and the slide of his right hand along the handle, the timed drive of shoulders and wrists, the clean soft shock as the blade swept into the wood, repeated and repeated. His body felt powerful and sure. He was still thinking of Mildred Hanson, but his mind called her Mildred now, instead of Miss Hanson, and he wished she could be there with him at the moment of his power and certainty. If they were alone he could touch her, perhaps even hold her and feel her, small and cool and beautiful against him. If I could go straight to her from work I might feel like this and say what I want to say. Only it wouldn't really happen that way; I wouldn't be able to say it and she would smile a little or perhaps be angry, and send me away. She'd have to.

Colin heard the rattle of the speeder along the tracks before anyone else noticed it. He was well started on the new log, but he drove his axe firmly into the cut and turned to watch the speeder come into sight round the curve. He saw that his father had stopped work and was watching too.

Colin recognized Gordon Holman, the woods superintendent, and Red Peterson, the speeder-man. The others were obviously city men, but he could not remember that he had seen any of them before.

138

"The little one is Mr. Blenkin," Will said. "Don't stand staring at them. Get on with the job." He spat on his hands, picked up the broad-axe and swung it down in a great smooth stroke on the face Colin had scored. Colin swung his own axe, but as it fell he saw George Smith walk out on to the rear of the pile driver and shade his eyes to look towards the speeder.

Five men came up from the speeder, Mr. Blenkin with Holman, a little in the lead, the other three trailing behind. Red Peterson waited beside his speeder.

Mr. Blenkin walked straight up to Will and held out his hand.

"Glad to see you again, Will," he said. They shook hands and Blenkin looked around at the hewn timbers on the landing. "It's easy enough to see you haven't lost your touch." He turned and introduced the other men who shook hands with Will in turn. "These gentlemen have never seen real broad-axe work, Will," he said. "I was telling them about you on the way up here on the boat and I don't think they believed half of it. Have you got any-thing fancy around here to show us?"

Will set the head of his axe down on a log and crossed his huge hands on the handle. "There isn't much around a pile-bent trestle, Mr. Blenkin," he said. "You know that. Just straight hewing—caps and stringers and a mud sill or two."

"You framed the first bent the way you always do," Gordon Holman said. "And that's one of your sleds, under the pile driver."

They moved away to look at Will's work and Colin watched them. He felt proud of his father, yet ashamed for him too. There had been something patronizing in the way Mr. Blenkin spoke to him, in spite of his friendliness; it had seemed as though he were showing off a good work-horse or a hunting dog. But Will had accepted the attention proudly, stretching his great chest and holding his bearded head high as he went off with them. There's none of them can do what the old man can, Colin thought; that little Mr. Blenkin couldn't even lift Dad's big axe, let alone hew with it all day. Let them watch him and look over what he can do. He may not be as smart as they are most ways, but this is one place he's the smartest man there is.

He saw that Gordon Holman and Will Ensley were walking

back towards the landing. Holman was talking but Will was saying nothing and his face was set. As they came closer Colin heard Holman say: "We know you old-timers don't want any more of it, but that guy's around this neck of the woods again and he's going to make more trouble—so's that other one, Zobieski."

They were standing close to Colin now, Will with his feet firmly planted and his thumbs hitched into the belt band of his pants, Holman small beside him, hands pushed down into the pockets of his light cruiser coat, his lean face intent.

"It's nothing to us who's around," Will said at last. "We aren't going out again."

"You maybe think you aren't, but if they pull the rest of the crew you'll be out too, whether you want it or not."

"They can't do much, hiding out in the bush."

"They're holding regular meetings—we know that too. Look, Will, I'm just telling you for your own good. A bunch of you could get together and run 'em out in jig-time—just rough 'em up enough so they won't come back in a hurry. Show 'em they're not welcome."

Will turned away sharply and picked up his axe. "It's bad, Gordon," he said. "Have you talked this way to anyone else?"

"A few. You could have a bunch together in no time."

"Earl Mayhew?"

"No, not yet."

"George Smith? Leo? Tony?"

"No."

Will stepped up on to the log he was hewing and looked down at Gordon Holman. "Those men helped us when we needed help," he said deliberately. "My hand will never be upon them." He picked up his axe and swung it and Holman turned away to meet Blenkin and the others coming up from the trestle.

When the speeder had clattered out of sight around the curve, Colin asked his father: "Was he talking about Miller?"

Will nodded slowly and Colin saw that strength had gone out of his face and the lift of his shoulders was proud no longer. "What's the man to me, that they should plague me about him?" Will asked, and he seemed not to be speaking to Colin at all. "Our ways are different. He had his part and it is done. I have

140

my part." He held his axe so that the handle rested across his short thick thighs and somehow his body indicated the bridge timbers and the trestle and the woods all about him. "Let them leave me to it."

IT was two or three days later that Colin heard Don Williams' voice as he came down towards the shelter where the bridge-crew was eating lunch. Will had stayed up on the landing to eat. "Him and his goddamned beard and his Bible-punching play-acting," Williams said. "All he is is a company stooge."

Sam Boulder's voice asked quietly: "What's Will ever done to you?"

"Nothing. Nor ever will. But I sure hate a company man. It made me sick to my stomach to see the act he put on for the big shots the other day. More like a performing dog than a man."

Colin felt his face hot and his breath short. He half turned away, thought better of it and went on into the awkward silence of the shelter. For a moment he stood there, his big hands hanging at his sides, his head down, his eyes on the ground. Sam said something, but Colin forced himself to look across at Williams and said: "I heard you."

Williams laughed. He was a sandy-haired, blue-eyed man, two or three years older than Colin, heavily and strongly built. "Ain't that just too bad," he said. "What are you going to do about it?"

"It isn't true," Colin said, and Williams laughed again.

"Aw, shut it off," Sam Boulder told him. "You'll spend years trying to be as good a man as Will Ensley and like as not you'll never make it." He looked at Colin and nodded towards the little stove. "There's your old man's coffee, kid," he said. "Take it up to him."

Colin took the blackened can without a word and went away with it.

THE camps shut down for fire weather early in August that year and Colin was glad. Although he had learned the work quickly and well, he had felt always that his father was ashamed of his awkward appearance and expecting him to make mistakes. His father was nearly always silent on the way to and from work and mixed little with the crew on the job or even during the noon hour; he seemed tightly shut within himself by his age and his dignity and his craftsmanship, both unable and unwilling to become a part of the good-natured friendship that George Smith stimulated so easily in the rest of the crew. Most of the men had known Will for years and had accepted his aloofness and granted him the right to it long ago. Because Colin worked with Will and talked little, they let Will's aloofness include him and made little effort to draw him into their fellowship.

Colin had felt this isolation of himself and his father and at first his shyness had welcomed it. But in time he had come to hate it. George Smith, Johnny Meldrum, Sam Boulder and the half-dozen younger bridgemen who made up the crew seemed like free men and heroes, playing mightily in the sunlight while he and his father toiled like slaves in the shadow. To work as he did and to be in silent shadow was part of his father's dim, bearded godhead; but Colin had no godhead; he was condemned to silence and shadow and isolation by his own frailties, by his awkward body, his uneasy mind, his fear.

For one positive reason Colin had been hoping that the shutdown would come. Johnny Harris wanted to go up to Wind Lake to see Robbie Robinson. "I want to ask him about getting a trapline up around there," Johnny had said. "The old man says it's O.K. and I can take his gas-boat to run around to the mouth of the river. Want to come along if we get a shutdown?" Johnny was working for Blenkin Logging too, blowing whistles over on Side one. So the shutdown meant they were both free to go.

Johnny's "gas-boat" was a fourteen-foot rowboat with a small single-cylinder motor in it, so they ran right up to the old Underhill farm and dragged it up on the beach above tide level. They were in no hurry so they left their packs by the boat and wandered up to the old buildings. "It sure was a big enough house," Johnny said. "You wouldn't think a man would go to all that trouble in a place like this."

Colin had thought so often about the Underhills that he felt an immediate need to defend them. "He raised a big family on the place," he said.

"And went broke at it. Wouldn't do for a guy like you or me that hasn't got two nickels to rub together. We've got to find some other way to raise a family."

"I've got a hunch a man could make it stick," Colin said. "If he went at it right."

As they walked back to get their packs, Johnny said: "You wouldn't be thinking of trying it, would you?"

Colin looked at him in surprise. "Who? Me? Of course not. That would be for an old married guy, like Underhill was. A guy that wanted to raise a family."

"You seem to have done a lot of thinking about it," Johnny told him. "A person'd almost think you'd seen the place when they lived here."

"It's just what I've heard from Mother and from old Robbie," Colin said. But even as they shouldered their packs he was looking at the rickety legs of an old landing. And he knew the Underhill children had once lain at full length on its deck in the summer sun, dangling fishing lines as the tide came up.

THE weather was good and they took their time in traveling up the valley. They camped the first night about six miles up the river, where the trail passed near the edge of a big pool. After supper they went fishing and caught big cutthroat trout on caddis grubs and surprised a bear that was looking for salmon. To Colin it was like a return to the life he had lived with Grant, only better because of their freedom and because he liked Johnny Harris so well. Johnny was an easy friend; you could tell him things because he was a friend and know that he would treat them gently and understandingly, that he would answer with things of his own

143

that enriched your things and bound him to you, as you were bound to him. Johnny was not shy or awkward or afraid; he was of the world, the fullest possible world of school and the village and people. Yet he could stand away from all that world if you asked him to and be with you and for you; yet, being of the world, he knew its thoughts and its answers, and being with you and for you he could explain the thoughts and quote the answers without impatience or contempt. Without realizing it Colin had learned long ago to depend upon Johnny's simple and direct wisdom to answer many questions that he would never have dared ask anyone else except possibly Margaret or Mildred Hanson. He asked him now, as they knelt by the edge of the river to clean the trout they had caught: "Johnny, what's a 'company man'?"

Johnny carefully slit the belly of the trout he was holding. "Depends who says it, I guess," he said. "But mostly it means a guy who's for the company—who thinks the company's O.K. and doesn't mind putting in overtime or anything else they want him to do. Why?"

"Is my old man one?"

Johnny picked up another fish and slowly considered the point. "No," he said at last. "Your dad's an old-timer and I guess he figures the company's O.K. But he was on the strike committee and he hasn't got the kind of job that makes for a real company man. A company man mostly is a side-push or a bookkeeper or some guy that's going to get a better job with the company if he keeps his nose clean."

"Just the same," Colin said. "Some people say Dad's a company man."

"What do you care?"

"They hate him for it. They talk like he was a scab or something. Like he wasn't a man at all."

Colin tried to make himself repeat what he had heard Don Williams say, but could not. "It's not something a guy can just forget about once he's heard it."

"Likely it was people that didn't know your old man. There's a difference between an old-timer who works steady for the same company and a real company man. Some guys just talk to hear themselves, anyway—don't mean nothing by it."

144

"He meant it," Colin said. "He said it like he hated Dad, like he'd just as soon do him real dirt or even kill him. You couldn't hate a guy like that if you didn't know him."

Johnny washed his hands off in the river and picked up the string of trout. "My dad says you can't hate a person you really know. You just hate what you think you know about a guy; soon as you find out a little more about him you stop hating him. I've tried that out on kids at school and it sure works."

"Did you try it out on Tod Phalling?" Colin asked.

Johnny looked at him and grinned: "I hadn't heard about it when he was around," but he added seriously, "I kind of think it'd work even with Tod. At least you wouldn't hate him quite so bad."

They had walked up from the river and Colin stirred up the small camp-fire. Johnny sat on his blankets, rolling a cigarette. Colin said: "I can't see hating guys and fighting and all that stuff. It makes me sick at my stomach. Maybe I'm yellow or something."

"A man can't crawl," Johnny said. "There's times when he has to fight. But he don't have to like it. Not liking it isn't being yellow." He lay back and drew happily on his cigarette. "You going to school again next year?" he asked.

Colin nodded. "No sense to quitting now. I don't mind it."

"My old man wants me to go back and finish. But I couldn't take it. I guess it's not so bad if you've been going right along, but going back to it seems like going back to short pants."

"Mother wants me to go to a university, like Margaret. So does Hanson."

"You can't lose," Johnny said. "You always were smart in school."

"I don't see what it gets you, unless you want to be a doctor or a teacher or an engineer maybe."

"What's wrong with being an engineer? You're a darn good woodsman and that's a fair start on it."

"I'm no good at figures," Colin said. "Even Hanson admits that."

"You ought to go, anyway. A guy who's been to college has got a chance at a whole different set-up of jobs. It means something."

"You've got to get some kind of job to pay your way through, to start with. I couldn't even do that."

"Guys do it all the time."

"Not guys like me. I wouldn't know where to start in. I've only been in Vancouver once in my life."

Johnny was silent, looking into the fire. After a while he said, "It's no use a guy trying something he doesn't believe in. You've got to believe in a thing to make it work."

"I know," Colin said. "The only time I believe in it is when Mildred talks about it. Other times I can't even remember how she made me believe in it."

Johnny had glanced up sharply when Colin used Mildred Hanson's first name, but he only said: "I know how it is with her. Seems like a person could do anything she said to do."

Colin was lying back on his blankets, looking up at the night sky through the trees. "I believe I could make it if she was down there. That's the only time I feel good for anything, when I'm with her or when I'm in the woods."

Johnny moved uncomfortably. "Sounds like you're crazy about her or something," he said.

Colin didn't answer. The words as Johnny spoke them hardly reached him, but he thought: I could do anything she said to do, but she'd have to be there or it wouldn't make sense. She'd have to be there and wanting me to do it. I guess that's what being crazy about a person really is. That's the way people feel about each other when they want to get married. But I'm only a kid and she's a grown woman. Maybe if I went through college and came back it would be different. People don't have to be the same age to get married. You get married and you live together and you know each other all through, you're never alone, you don't hide from each other, you don't lose each other, you have all of each other, you sleep together, you lie in bed naked together, you are for each other, together in everything. But it's only me that needs all those things, not her, and I'm a kid. I've no business even thinking about it like that. Seems like all I'm good for is dreaming about things that can't happen; I've always done it, ever since I can remember, and I've got to cut it out and do something for a change. Maybe if I worked and worked, this would happen; then

146

it wouldn't be just a crazy dream and I'd be right to be thinking it and wanting it.

He sat up on his blankets and looked across at Johnny. Oh hell, he thought, now I'm back where I started. I don't want to think about it any more. "Johnny," he said. "Johnny. Wake up and get inside your blankets."

But Johnny was sleeping soundly and he had to go across and touch his shoulder to wake him.

THEY camped at the foot of the lake the next night and laughed at themselves for making such a slow trip. But it had been a good day. They had turned aside from the trail a hundred times, to go down and look at the river, to search for a giant spruce tree or a corner post that Colin remembered from the previous summer, to follow a bear track or trace out a creek to its fall from the hillside. Johnny said: "If Robbie was white enough to leave a canoe at the foot of the lake for his visitors we could go on to his place tonight. But I'm too darn tired to hike all that way around."

Colin asked: "Does he know you're coming?"

"Sure, but he doesn't know when. I was talking to him when he was out last spring and he said to come in any time I could make it."

"Does he want you to trap with him?"

"No," Johnny said. "He promised he'd show me how to go about it, but he wants me to make my own line—up one of the other valleys and maybe along the lake shore for a piece."

Colin went over to the fire and swung the boiling pot away from it, threw in some coffee and swung it back to boil up again. "Do you think you'll go through with it? I didn't know you liked being in the woods that much."

"I like it O.K., but it's not that so much. If you've got a trapline you've got a job and nobody can take it away from you. You may not make a hell of a lot out of it, but you'll eat."

"I hadn't thought of it that way," Colin said. "But I guess it makes sense, the way things are. Or the way they have been."

"The way they are," Johnny insisted, emphasizing the last word. "There's going to be more trouble of one kind and another for quite a while yet, lay-offs and strikes and so on. They've run Miller and Zobieski and those others out of town, but that's as likely to make trouble as get rid of it."

"You mean they found Miller? I didn't hear that."

"Couple of nights before we left," Johnny said. "Earl Mayhew was in and I heard him telling Dad about it."

"Earl wasn't there."

"No, but he knew about it. It wasn't the police—just a bunch of guys the company got together. Earl says they beat 'em up pretty bad and put 'em on the boat and told 'em never to show up around Blenkinstown again or they'd get more of the same. Earl said Miller never lifted a hand to fight back, just let them go ahead and beat him till he fell down. Some of the guys that were there were kind of sick about it."

Colin felt a physical shock from the words. He said: "I didn't think those kinds of things happened any more."

Johnny laughed. "They sure as hell do. In the cities it goes on all the time—you can tell that from the papers. We don't see much of it because we live out in the sticks."

"But what's the sense in it? Why couldn't they just tell 'em to get out of town if that's what they wanted?"

"Scared I guess. My dad says people are always scared when they act like that—scared for their jobs, scared of another strike, scared because they don't understand. It doesn't have to make sense."

"Miller wasn't scared."

"Miller knows what he's doing. Earl doesn't like him and Dad doesn't like him, but they both say he believes in what he's doing, whether it's right or wrong."

"My old man doesn't like him either," Colin said. "But I guess he must feel the same way. I heard Gord Holman try to talk him into going out after Miller, up at the trestle one day, but Dad turned him down cold."

Johnny laughed again and Colin looked at him in surprise. "That sure lets your dad out of being a company man," Johnny said. "He'll be lucky if he isn't looking for another job."

"You mean they could fire him for that?"

"They wouldn't have to say it was for that."

For a short while they sat without talking, looking out over the quiet surface of the lake. Colin's thoughts strained at him but he could not lead them anywhere. He wanted to talk more and to hear Johnny explain more, but he couldn't find what he wanted to say and for once he wasn't sure that Johnny would be able to explain. Why do people hate each other? he wanted to say. Because they're scared, Johnny says. Maybe he's right about the guys that chased Miller out; they were scared the company would fire them if they didn't go along or scared Miller would start another strike; all except Gord Holman—it's hard to think of him being scared of anything, yet I suppose it's his job too, perhaps he's even scaredest of them all because he's got the biggest job. Don Williams hates Dad—I could tell that from the way he spoke—but he isn't scared of him and I don't see what else he could be scared of to make him hate Dad like that. And he called him a company man, but Dad isn't that because he wouldn't go along when Gord Holman said to and now Johnny says maybe they'll fire him for not going. He wouldn't know about that though; they couldn't fire Dad when he's the only broad-axe man they've got around there, one of the only ones left in B. C.

It doesn't make sense, any of it, the hating and beating and fighting and firing people. It's supposed to be a free country. Why can't a man just go and do his job and be left alone without all this other stuff coming into it at all? Why do Johnny and I have to talk about it up here, why do I have to think about it? It doesn't belong up here. It wasn't here at the lake last summer, not when I used to go out in the canoe or when Robbie and I were up at the mouth of the creek that evening or with Mr. Grant or any time. Why can't a person stay up here forever and keep away from it? That's what Robbie does, but he says it isn't right for a young fellow and so does Margaret and so does Mildred. And I kind of know what they mean; there's a part of me that wants to see it all happening and try to understand like Johnny does, only more. Part of me wants that, yet when I do see it I hate it. Sometimes I just wish it would all end, very quickly and suddenly, like a bullet in the heart. That's because I'm yellow. I used to wish that when I was a little kid and got in some kind of trouble. Now I wish it about big things, things I ought to try to understand.

"Johnny," he said. "Suppose Robbie isn't home tomorrow?"

"We could look for him. You'd know where to look, wouldn't you?"

"Up at his claims, I guess, is where he'd be. Sure, I could find those—some of them anyway."

"I hope we don't have to, just the same. We can have a whole lot more fun just fooling around the lake in a canoe than climbing mountains looking for mining claims."

Colin leaned forward, then pointed up the lake. "He's home," he said. "There's his light just went on."

1 8

WILL Ensley didn't get fired. But when the camps opened up again with the first rains in September, he wasn't called. Earl Mayhew was working and John Meldrum and Tony Soretto. Mike Varchuk had gone away, leaving his shack padlocked, but he had sold his car to Tony, so they still went to work the same way. After a few days Will rode up to the beach camp with them and tried to see Gordon Holman, but Holman was up in the woods somewhere and there was only old McPherson in the office.

"They'll be sending for you soon as there's work," McPherson told him. "You finished hewing for the trestle on the spur line before the shutdown."

"There's the new sled for the unit on Side One," Will said. "And there's work to be done on the water tower at Camp 5."

McPherson shrugged his shoulders. "I've heard him say nothing about it. He did say there was ties to be cut ahead on the new spur line. Contract."

"Contract?" Will said. "Did he say for me to work contract?"

"It could be he had you in mind. He didna say. But if he wants you he'll let ye know."

Will kept away from the camp for the rest of September and all of October, but early in November he shook off his pride and went up there again. Holman offered him a contract to cut ties on the spur line. It was a bad show and the price was bad, but he took it and forced it to pay him a wretched wage. It was sometime in the new year that he learned the bridge-crew was working on a new trestle, using sawed timbers; and sometime later than that the company hired a man from town to work on the donkey-sleds. It was nearly a month before Will told Martha about those things.

"I'd take Colin out of school to help on the ties," he said. "But there'll be an end of that soon enough anyway. There's hardly any timber left along there that'll make ties."

"There's something behind it all," Martha said. "There must be. It seems they don't want you to work for them any more. Why don't you go and ask Mr. Holman right out?"

"Maybe I'll do that," Will said.

But there was at least a measure of self-respect in the work he was doing. He could go to it daily with a quiet mind and drive his strength in the familiar way, breathing security from the scent of sapwood and crushed branches all about him, feeling it in the smooth shock of his sharp axes, the bite of his caulks into wood, the wetness of rain and snow against his face and body. It'll work out, he told himself. They'll need me for something else when this job's done. In times like these we've been through a man gets to imagining things for no reason at all, listening to women's talk, getting himself all het up when he only has to wait his time.

In the end he had to say something, and he did. Gordon Holman wasn't an easy man to see, but Will found him at the beach camp one day when he came in from work. "I'm pretty near through up there, Gordon," he said. "There's no more than a week's tie timber left and I have to go a long ways from the grade to get that."

"Got enough ties?"

"No. You'll have to bring some in to finish it out."

"There was enough timber up there when we checked it. You'll just have to reach out a bit farther, that's all."

"It's not there," Will said. "A man can't go back any farther at that price even if it was there, not and make a living wage."

"Seems like you've slowed up a lot, Will," Holman said. "Time was when you'd have made good money up there. I figured we were giving you a pretty good thing when we handed out that contract."

Will looked at him for a moment without speaking. Then he said: "I'm not slowed up so I don't know what kind of show I'm working on."

"Nobody's holding you to the contract," Holman said. "But if you can't handle that kind of a show any more it's going to be tough to find anything else for you."

Will turned sharply away from him and walked to Tony's car without looking back. He held his body stiffly, feeling the heavy squareness of his shoulders and the tautness of anger in the heavy muscles of his arms.

At suppertime he told Martha: "I saw Holman today."

"What did he say?" Martha asked.

"They think I'm getting old. They think I can't work the way I used to."

"Nonsense, Will. They couldn't think that. You're just as strong as you were twenty years ago." She checked herself and looked at him anxiously. "You *are* all right, aren't you, Will? The work's not getting harder for you, is it?"

Will laughed shortly. "Ask Colin here. He's young and strong. Did it look like I was getting old last summer? Did Mr. Blenkin say anything about it when he was up? Was the bridge-crew ever held up for timbers?"

"No, Dad," Colin said. "It didn't look to me like there was anyone else there could work the way you can."

"Then what do they mean?" Martha asked. "Why did he say that?"

Will shrugged his shoulders. "They want to make out I can't handle the contract. Holman says there's enough tie timber to finish out the spur line. Maybe there is if a man goes five or six hundred feet back in the bush. Not otherwise."

"What are you going to do?" Martha asked him.

"Finish it out," Will said. He turned to Colin again. "You'll have to come up there with me for two or three weeks."

Martha caught her breath sharply. "Oh no, Will. The boy's got to stay in school and graduate now that he's this close."

"A couple of weeks won't stop him. Will it, son?"

There was a look in his father's face Colin had never seen there before. The urgency of fear was in it, and pleading; but there was affection too, and pride, the same pride Colin had seen when Will listened to George Smith praise Colin's work on the bridge-crew. "No," Colin said. "Two or three weeks is nothing."

So Will finished out the spur line and when the last tie was on the grade they told him, as he had known in his heart they would: "There's nothing else right now. We'll send for you as soon as anything comes up."

He told Martha as soon as he got home. "They're holding that strike committee against you," she said. "Can't the union help?"

Will shook his head. "Not without another strike. I wouldn't ask that."

"Earl's working. He was on the committee. Why should they pick on you?"

"I don't know," Will said. "Unless it's because I wouldn't go out and look for Miller."

"Earl didn't go."

"Holman never asked him." Will walked across the kitchen and looked out of the window. "They'll need me again. I can go to town and hire out some place else until they do. Work's not that scarce now."

"Did you hear where Mr. Varchuk's working?"

"No," Will said. "It might be kind of tough for him to get on any place. He's quite a trouble-maker and . . ." Will stopped suddenly and looked at Martha.

"It might be just as good to pick up what work you can around here for the next little while," she said. "They might call sooner than you expect."

COLIN went to Mildred Hanson's cottage to pick up some books the evening before school closed. Mildred opened the door to his knock.

"Come on in," she said. "Carol's out. I thought Margaret would be with you."

"She had a date," Colin said.

Mildred smiled. "Not with the police force again?"

Colin nodded.

"I made some coffee," Mildred said. "Sit down while I get it."

Colin picked up a magazine from a chair and sat down. The room was very familiar now and he was easy in it. He was glad Carol Maxwell was out. He tried to like Carol because she was Mildred's friend and he admired the breadth and depth of knowledge that seemed always so ready in her quick mind; but he could never be easy with her.

Mildred came back with the coffee. "I made a cake," she said. "It was supposed to be a celebration—for Margaret as well."

"Did Marge tell you she won't be going back this fall?" Colin asked. "She's going into a hospital."

"I know. It's a pity. But I think she'll get the other year in sooner or later. I suppose that means you won't go to University either."

"I'm going to look for a job down there. I might make it that way." For a moment Colin was very conscious that he was no longer a schoolboy.

"Lots of people go through that way," Mildred said. "But it's much harder to find jobs than it used to be. I wish that aunt and uncle would give you the same chance they gave Margaret."

Colin laughed. "Margaret could work for them to pay her board, and the family could send her enough to buy clothes and books."

"Is your father still not working?"

"He's cutting cordwood," Colin said. "But there's nothing to spare from that. There's no work up at camp. I tried for myself."

He glanced at Mildred and looked quickly away again. "Dad'll get work though," he said defensively. "There's not many men can do what he can."

Mildred said nothing. She knew the town's story that Will Ensley was on the company's blacklist and knew that Colin must know it too. She wondered if Colin or Will knew that the blacklist was supposed to cover all the big companies. They ought to

154

understand about it, she thought; they could fight about it better if they did—unless understanding would kill the last of Will Ensley's pride.

"What will you do if you don't go to University?" she asked.

"I don't know. Try to get work, I guess."

"Promise me something," she said quickly.

He looked up, surprised by the sudden intensity of her quiet voice.

"What?"

"That you won't come straight back up here, whatever happens. Stay away for at least a while. Go out and see something of Canada."

"Johnny Harris's got a trap-line up on Wind Lake. I thought . . ."

"Don't do it. Please Colin. You've got to grow. You've go to see what the world is and what you could be in it before you shut yourself away. What's right for Johnny Harris isn't right for you."

"I don't see why not. Johnny's my best friend."

"I know he is. Johnny's a nice boy and I like him too, but he hasn't got as much to waste as you have. You can go on growing and learning even if you don't go to University. You can be something. You can learn to help people."

"What do you want me to do then? Get a job in the city?"

Mildred thought for a moment before answering. "I don't think it matters, so long as you don't come back here or go to some other little logging town just like this. I want you to give yourself a chance. Whatever you do will lead you on to something else."

"How long do I have to stay away?"

"You'll know. A year anyway, then you'll know. Will you try it?"

Colin laughed nervously. "Sure I will. I'll take any job I can get. But a year's a long time."

"Not too long," she said, and they were silent again.

Colin tried to think of the meaning of his promise, but everything ahead of him was confused and suddenly strange beyond his imagination. He remembered the muddled, crowded streets of Vancouver and tried to see himself a part of them, looking for

155

a job, working in a job. What kind of a job? In a drug-store, driving a truck, in a bank, how do people work in town? They have sawmills there, but maybe she doesn't mean that, maybe that's too much like the woods. They work in offices and factories and run street cars and load ships. How do you get jobs like that? Who do you ask? How do you know they want anyone?

"I think I'd sooner work some place outside the city," he said.

"It doesn't matter," Mildred told him. "Go as far as you like. I want you to see something else, so that you'll know all Canada isn't just mountains and logging camps."

"I know that now," he said seriously.

"You mean you've been told about it. Wheat and mining, railroads and shipping, fishing and furs and manufacturing. You've been told that in every grade from one to twelve, but I want you to see some of it for yourself, make it your own." The late sun was flaming through the west window of the room and across to Colin's face. Mildred went to the window and pulled the shade part way down, then came back and sat down again. Her movement had drawn him out of his thoughts and he was suddenly and strongly aware of her. The chair he was sitting in was too low and he stood up. She looked up at him and smiled. "I'm always nagging at you, Colin. I'm sorry. We may not see each other again very soon."

The words hurt him sharply, left him lonely in what she had asked him to do. He stooped and picked up the magazine that had dropped to the floor from the arm of his chair. "I'm not going right away," he said.

"Colin," her voice was afraid, though she tried to keep it strong. "Do you remember when I talked to you like this one day years ago. After school?"

"Yes," he said.

"I scolded you and sent you away. I shouldn't have done that. I've been sorry ever since."

"It wasn't your fault. I scared you." He looked down at her from his great height and saw her small and frail and young, as he had never seen her before. Quickly, almost gracefully, he knelt beside her. "I wouldn't ever hurt you," his voice was strained,

156

almost fierce with strain. "I love you so much, more than anyone in the world. I can do anything you tell me to."

One of her hands moved and touched his hair. "You mustn't say that, Colin. Not now."

"When I come back?"

"You won't want to say it then. I'm an old woman, darling, compared to you. I'm like your woods and mountains—you haven't seen anything else. But now you're going out to look."

"I won't change," he said.

"Of course you will. That's why you're going. You'll change and grow and learn to think bigger and stronger things. That's what men have to do. That's what it's all about, Colin. Don't you see? There are so few who can be more than just job-fillers and time-servers, so few who can take and feel and understand and use what they see, turn it into something with meaning and life and growth. You can do all that. It's in you. You must stop being afraid, stop being shy and humble and easily hurt." She stood up and Colin stood up with her. Her face was unsmiling, near tears, full of the effort of her pleading; she was so beautiful to him, so far beyond any other beautiful thing the world had shown him that everything he was seemed to leave his body and become part of her. He wanted only to answer her pleading and let her eyes and her lips smile again.

"I haven't spoken just words to you, Colin," she said. "I've spoken your life and your happiness and the happiness of many other people. You have to believe in it. You have to try."

He took her in his arms then. She struggled and she said: "Please, Colin, please not now." But her body yielded and she lifted her face and he kissed her lips with a hard searching strength. He felt her body quiet against his strength, but the softness of her mouth forced against his and he knew only that until she wrenched her head sharply away. "Please, Colin," she said again and he released her and stood uncertainly, with his arms at his sides.

They heard footsteps in the gravel of the roadway, then the click of the gate latch and knew that Carol Maxwell was coming in.

Mildred's eyes were shining and her face was flushed. Her lips smiled to him. "You've grown up, Colin," she said, and the urgency of her voice strained at him. "You weren't afraid then. You did what you wanted." She reached out her hand and gripped his arm. "Write to me, darling. You're terribly important to me." Then she turned quickly away as the door opened.

PART FOUR

THE NARROW VALLEY

19

COLIN had found the place in the park during his first summer in Vancouver. It was a few square feet of rough grass, sloping down to the edge of a low bluff that looked out over the sweep of salt water between the Mainland and Vancouver Island; behind it the tapering, fluted trunks of three or four half-dead cedars, backed by heavy brush, shut away all sign of the footpath that passed almost within sound. No one else seemed to use the place and Colin came there whenever he could, to hate or forget the city in security.

It was easy to hate the city. The used, anonymous houses, the blank, eventful, hostile buildings, the hurrying concentration of its people in which the outsider had no part, the staring faces that never smiled and never questioned, all were easy to hate. But only when not seen too closely. When one looked closely the faces had meaning, each its own. The drab, staring woman on the street car, enclosed in her own concerns, had things to be concerned with—a home, a family, the things she must buy for them and do for them; the gray-faced old man, shakily gripping a pipe between porcelain teeth as though he would never again release it to talk, had his tenuous life still and his deep concerns—grandchildren, some precious hobby, some bitter fight that warmed his days; the laughing people in the big cars had flooded, stirring lives beyond the imagination; the young man hurrying had something to hurry for, a life to build, a woman to love, a family to raise. But seeing their deep concerns beyond the blankness only made the blankness more hostile, as the unshared bustle of the great buildings was hostile, as the closed hospitality of the houses was hostile, as the self-absorption of the hurrying crowds was hostile. To know that the city had sympathy and kindness and a shared life for its own brought full meaning to loneliness.

In the year since he had first come to it, Colin had never felt himself a part of the city's life. He had searched hopefully at first for a job that would take him through University. In a little while he was looking for a job, any job, that would feed him. Within two months he had worked at half-a-dozen places, always filling in for someone who was away on vacation. Then vacations were over and there were no more jobs, only the blank, defensive refusals, the hopelessness of searching, the sharp, helpless fear of hunger. He had left the city then, to milk cows for his board in the Fraser Valley. When the spring work came along there was a small wage as well as board and lodging, then nothing at all, then day-work in the hay harvest. Now he was back in the city again.

Colin lay in the grass and watched the water. He could find no pleasure in the quiet place today; only a sense of empty repetition that he hated, a sense of urgency that he forced away from him, a sense of failure that he accepted without protest. A tug was taking its raft of saw-logs slowly towards the mouth of the

Fraser, a flight of black scoters took heavy wing at the coming of a small powerboat, two murrelets disappeared in flickering dives a little way out from shore, a blue jay scolded in the brush behind him. A year ago all these things would have been consolation and renewal; now they were bitter things because they reached at his heart and told him he had no place or part in the city. They told him to go home and find them there, where they belonged, part of life, not secrets of a stolen hiding place.

Margaret had place and part in the city, had it as naturally as she milked the cows or climbed the mountain or did well in school. Colin had seen her two days ago and had drawn strength from her because she was confident, calm, efficient as she had always been. But the strength had died in him as the warmth of alcohol dies, quickly and leaving him weaker than before. "There's nothing at home," she had said. "Father's still not working and they're having a hard time."

"I could help out."

But she had shaken her head. "It wouldn't do any good. You wouldn't get work up there, any more than Dad. Mother wants to see you, but she said to tell you not to come."

"It's no good here," he had said. But she had given him two more names, two more people to go and face, to beg from without hope. When she told him about them the hope had been there, clear in her own confidence, but the next day it was faded and he had not gone. She had brought the message from Mildred Hanson, too, a calm and friendly message that recognized no failure or shift in purpose and carried no reproach for half a year of unanswered letters. "Don't be afraid to try anything in the world; whatever you do will be important one day, however it seems now." Those were the words, as nearly as he could remember them, and they renewed what she had said the evening before the last day of school. She had said then "a year anyway" and a year was gone and there was nothing to show for it, but she had not said "come back." Because, as Margaret had said, there was nothing to come back to? Or because nothing had come from the long, drab, muddled year? How could a person tell? Whatever you do will be important one day. Do hateful things, like asking again and again for a job that no one will give you, like living in

161

the city with no friend to talk to, no house to go to, nothing that belongs to you or means anything to you. Do drudging things, like delivering packages from a store and getting bawled out for being slow, like getting up at five all winter and milking cows for a grouch who never figured anything was right.

It's easy for her to talk, Colin thought. What does she know about it? Everything has gone right for her, all her life. She's had it easy, then she wishes all this on to me when I could just as well be up on the lake with Robbie and Johnny Harris, learning things and getting some place. But the thought shamed him and its denial of her made a surge of loneliness that left him defenseless and almost in tears. The words he had found and once read to her came back to him: "So that my vigor, wedded to thy blood, shall strike within thy pulses like a god's, to push thee forward through a life of shocks, dangers and deeds . . ." He had watched her as he read them and, though she made no sign, had known that she accepted them. Many times he had used them to give meaning to the year's dull, hopeless striving; now he accepted them again and made amends for the denial, but he was still ashamed.

Out on the water the tug with its tow was passing out of sight round a point, and a big freighter, flying a flag he did not know, was setting across the Gulf for the Straits of Juan da Fuca. Colin looked down at the worn boot on his left foot. It was still a good boot and he still had some money; only a few dollars, but more than he had had when he pulled out of town the previous fall. So far there had always been something in time to keep him off the relief rolls, but that didn't mean there always would be. Plenty of people did come right up against it, and not because they didn't want to work; people who could do more than just score for a broad-axe or run a compass line, people who had had jobs and were used to working in town. Yet thousands upon thousands more people were working and eating and sleeping regularly, sure of themselves, sure of their lives and their jobs. And other thousands wanted work done for them. Somewhere in the city was the thing he was looking for, the one exactly right thing; one could look for it through newspaper advertisements, through employment agencies, by going out and asking. But the chance of finding it was infinitely small compared to the certainty that it existed.

There should be some way, he thought, of climbing to a great height above the city and looking down upon it, so that everything and everyone in it would be open to understanding. Merely wanting the thing so strongly and being so completely sure that it existed should be power enough to reach through and summon the thing. Faith, they said, faith can move mountains. But could you claim to have faith in the existence of something you could not name? They said also: you've got to know what you want in this world. Mildred had never said that; she had said only to go and look, that anything would be important. But how can you look when you don't know what you are looking for? The simple truth is that you can't, so you start dreaming impossibilities, like looking down on the city from a mountain and knowing everything in it.

Someone had turned into the brush from the footpath. Colin listened as the movement came on towards him, and turned his head slowly as the policeman came out by one of the cedars at the edge of the clearing. The policeman stopped, put his hands on his hips and stood looking down at Colin. He was a young man, strongly built and good-looking, but his brown face held no expression that Colin could interpret.

"Come here pretty often, don't you?" the policeman said.

Colin climbed slowly to his feet, smiling nervously and feeling foolish. "I guess so," he said. "Quite often."

"Last year, too. Work in town?"

Colin shook his head. "Looking for it. I was up the Valley all winter."

"Got friends in town?"

"No. My sister works at a hospital. That's all. My folks live up the coast."

"If I were you, I'd go back to them," the policeman said. "Town's no place for a young fellow these days." His tone was friendly, almost fatherly, warning.

Colin shifted his feet and smiled. "I was thinking something close to that when you came."

"Well, I wouldn't be too long thinking about it. Outside the city a man that's got his health can always find something to keep him eating. In town when you're broke, you're broke."

He turned away and Colin watched until he disappeared into the undergrowth, then listened until the slow footsteps passed beyond hearing along the footpath.

It wasn't the first time Colin had been questioned by a policeman on duty, but he was not by any means hardened to it and he could not settle back into his thoughts. The hidden place was no longer hidden, no longer his own; it had become a part of the city, open as any part of it and no more friendly. After a little while he got up and went away. He went out of the park and, almost from habit, followed the long hot street to the little square near the offices of the big newspapers. As always, there were men in the square, young men like himself, wearing blue jeans and work shirts, sitting on the benches or lying sprawled out on the narrow plots of grass. Colin skirted the square and crossed the street to look at the newspaper pages pasted up in the windows.

There was a freedom in the square, half-suspicious, half-friendly, that extended over to the windows where the newspapers were posted. Men spoke to each other, listened to each other, believed or disbelieved each other, became friends or enemies of the moment, moved on and forgot they had ever spoken together. Colin was not surprised to feel an elbow in his ribs, drawing his attention to a thick, square thumb that jerked out towards a two-column headline. Colin read: "POLICE TO ROUND UP VAGRANTS. Closer check of undesirables from now on, says Police Chief."

"Hanging out the old 'git' sign," a voice said beside him. "Time to hit the ties again, I guess."

Colin turned towards the voice and looked down into a cheerful, sun-reddened face. The eyes were blue and small, but widely separated by a twisted nose above a thick, humorous mouth. The hair was very light brown, almost blond, and tightly curled in a short thick mat. "They'd have to have something on you," Colin asked. "Wouldn't they?"

"You never been vagged?" The small eyes measured Colin sharply, but the mouth was friendly.

"No."

"They don't need anything you'd notice. Pick you up for breathing good city air when there's a drive on."

Colin thought of the policeman in the park. He nodded to-

164

wards the newspaper in the window. "Do you think they really mean that?"

"Bet your life they do. It won't last, maybe, but while it does they sure as hell mean it."

"What can they do to you?" Colin asked.

"Likely a floater the first time. Maybe thirty days if the city's been twisting the beak's tail." The blue eyes looked sharply into Colin's. "Say, I wouldn't be talking to the wrong guy, would I?" The head cocked on one side and the mouth laughed. "No, I guess you just ain't been around much, have you? Name's Blake," he held out a hand and Colin took it. "James Warner Blake. Curly's more natural, though."

"Colin Ensley," Colin acknowledged in the words all the quick attraction he felt from Blake's easy good nature. "Just Colin."

"O.K., Colin. I'm hitting the road tonight." They had walked away from the newspaper building and crossed the street to the square. "I got around twenty bucks and a blanket roll. How's about throwing in together?" Blake found an empty space in a corner of one of the grass plots and flopped down in it. Colin sat down more slowly beside him.

"I'm short of that," Colin. "Five or six bucks is all I've got."

"Don't mean a thing. I hit her lucky. Done thirty days in the can and come right out and got me a job painting a boat for a guy. Just finished her up yesterday. He figured I done good, too, and give me ten bucks more'n I had coming."

"Where are we going?" Colin asked.

Curly lay back in the grass and looked at the sky. "Well," he said. "They'll be starting harvest work on the prairies. That's good as any place, I guess, unless we find something better on the way."

"You mean ride the rods?" Colin asked.

Curly laughed. "I never done that yet and I've had me free rides from here clear back to Quebec Province a couple of times. You don't want to listen to all the guff you hear. There's lots of places to ride freights besides the rods. And most of them brakies ain't near the tough guys you hear about, neither." He sat up and looked at Colin again. "Where you from anyway? Not right here in Vancouver?"

Colin shook his head. "Up the coast. Place called Blenkinstown."

"Jesus," Curly said. "You had me scared for a minute. I didn't figure you for no city kid and I kinda take a pride in how I can size a guy up first time I see him. You ain't as old as you look neither. You ain't twenty yet."

"Nineteen."

"Me, too. Shake on it." They shook hands again solemnly, in the bright sunlight of the open square. "Looks like we was meant to get together," Curly said. "You're kind of long and awkward, like you wasn't growed to size yet. But you're strong and you done some work some place or other. And you ain't one of these kids gabs his head off all the time. Only thing you're short on is you ain't been around much. You ain't seen Canada. Your uncle Curly'll soon fix that."

Colin laughed. He felt enthusiasm and excitement he had not felt since he had first left home. "When do we start?" he asked.

Curly leaned over and looked at a street clock. "I got to see a man," he said. "Meet me down around Hastings and Main about six o'clock. O.K.?"

"O.K.," Colin said, and wondered if they would shake on it again.

2 0

CURLY Blake knew the railroads and knew the prairies. He and Colin traveled eastward, through the mountains, across Alberta and into Saskatchewan with little less comfort than they would have found if they had paid their way. Colin's depression had left him as soon as they were well away from the city. Curly was unfailingly talkative and confident, full of plans and enthusiasms.

"Wait till you see them mountains," he told Colin. "There ain't nothing like them. The rich guys go and stay up there all summer long in fancy hotels with fancy women. I'd sure like to take time out and stick around there for a summer myself. I'll do it one day, too, and take a doll along with me."

They were put off a train and spent a night in the mountains, swimming in a rough, ice-cold river, making camp among poplars on a gravel bar. Colin's efficiency impressed Curly. "Makes it all easy," he said. "You do it like you been on the road all your life, only more neat and quick. And me figuring to myself I was going to have to look out for you. All I have to do is lie back and light me a seegar, except I ain't got one. I thought you was crazy when you said to drag our stuff all this way down from the track, but you sure as hell knew what you were at."

Colin listened and felt fully alive for the first time in many months. He let Curly's friendly talk merge with the friendly roar of the swift little river and turned on his side to watch the high mountains against the evening sky. After a long while he asked: "How do we make out from here on?"

"Easy," Curly said. "There's a water tank up the track a piece and they never look for nobody to get aboard there—too far out in the sticks. You don't need to worry about nothing, not when you travel with Curly Blake. We'll be dossing down in good prairie hay inside of three or four days."

He was right. Within four days they had joined the threshing crew on a farm where Curly had worked the previous summer. Curly was welcomed; it seemed that he had a way of his own with aging machinery. Colin fitted easily into the work of pitching the sheaves, using his height and his strength tirelessly through the long days. He saw little of Curly, who was always around the machines during working hours and pursued complicated affairs among the girls of the nearby village each evening; but the sense of partnership between them was never lost.

By mid-September the outfit had finished its work and they moved on. Curly had a new packsack, three good silk shirts and a pair of dress pants; otherwise he was broke. Colin had fifty dollars.

"We done good," Curly said. "But I wouldn't want to winter

167

around that dump. We better head back west again and see if we can get us a late season job on the way. Seen any place you think'd make good wintering?"

"I liked the look of it after we first got through the mountains," Colin said.

"O.K. by me. Any place so long as it's off the bald prairie. There's cow farms around there and they're good places to look for winter work."

They put in two or three weeks with another threshing outfit a little way east of Marwell City, still in Saskatchewan, and when that was over Curly said: "We better make time or we're liable to wake up froze to death some morning. Happened to an old partner of mine last winter. This here Marwell's got a reputation for tough cops, but we'll make it aboard something soon as she's good and dark. The big freight hauls always do a pile of bull-cooking around there."

They went down to the yards at dusk and Curly sized up the situation quickly. "That's ours," he said. "Two tracks over. We better duck under and load from the other side." They saw a brakeman's light coming along the train and Curly said: "Checking her over. We got lots of time." But Colin sensed his tension and felt a growing excitement in himself. It was always exciting, but Curly usually made it a joke. Tonight he was not joking about it and the coldness of the still air was a warning. The cinders were hard and slippery with frost underfoot and the lights of the town were very bright in the clear air.

The brakeman passed them and went on his way down the long train. Curly said: "Now," and they crossed quickly to the train, ducked between two box-cars and came out on the other side. There was a flat car with a load of machinery about ten cars back and Curly began to run silently towards it. Colin followed more slowly, a little way behind. Curly stopped suddenly and Colin came up to him.

"We got a break," Curly said and pointed at the open door of one of the box-cars. "Want to take a chance on it?"

"Sure. Why not?"

"One of us'll have to keep awake to make sure they don't close it up on us. That's how guys get froze to death."

168

"Fair enough," Colin said. "We can watch it. We could wedge the door anyway, so they'd have a time closing it." He saw the quick flash of approval on Curly's face in the dim light.

"Let's go then," Curly said and climbed aboard. Colin moved to follow and the voice stopped him.

"Just a minute," the voice said. "Hold it right where you are." Colin felt a hand on his arm and stood dead still. Another voice said from behind them: "Where's the other one? There was two of 'em." Curly came back to the open door of the car and dropped down to the track. "O.K., copper," he said. "You don't have to come after me."

Very little was said. The hand was still on Colin's arm as they went through the lighted station house and Colin saw that the other policeman was holding Curly. The station-agent looked up as they passed through and said: "Only two tonight?"

The policeman holding Curly grinned. "Most of them's wise to this place now. There's just a few still have to learn the hard way."

When they got outside and started up the street Curly said: "Where you taking us? We'll scram out of town quick enough if you let us go. We ain't done nothing."

"No?" asked the policeman. "Lodging in a freight car. Trespassing on railway property. No visible means of support. And we ain't even searched you yet."

The four of them had stopped, but Colin saw him tighten his grip on Curly's arm to force him forward. Curly moved, then suddenly dropped his head and butted it into the blue-coated stomach. The big policeman grunted sharply, but he brought his left hand forward and down and Curly sprawled on the sidewalk. The other policeman was still holding Colin, who had not moved. "O.K., Don?" he asked.

"Little bastard pretty near winded me," he kicked Curly in the ribs. "On your feet, tough guy. You ain't hurt."

Curly got slowly to his feet and they moved on again. Colin said: "You O.K., Curly?"

"Can the talk," said the policeman holding him.

The city police station was just off the main street. They were booked and searched. Curly gave his name as James Baker. Colin heard him, searched his mind frantically, found nothing and gave his own name. Curly's policeman unlocked a door and they all went into a small room with three or four cells made of metal bars. Curly's policeman slipped off his coat.

"Want to get fresh again, kid?" he asked and smashed the back of his open hand against Curly's mouth. Curly stood with his hands at his sides and a trickle of blood ran down his chin. Colin felt his whole body stiffen with fear and anger. The figures under the naked yellow light were dim and wavering before his eyes; his voice would not come and his body could not stir.

"Watch the big guy, Joe," Don said, and hit Curly again with his other hand. "Looks like the punk's yellow after all." He lifted his hand again.

Colin moved then. He said: "Leave him alone, can't you?" and stepped forward. He felt a blow from behind, hard on the back of his head, jarring him clear down to his knees. He swung round and suddenly was fighting Tod Phalling again, a bigger, silent Tod with a club in his hand. Jeff Burnside was behind, not waiting this time but beating heavy blows on his back and his arms and his shoulders, and he also had a club. Colin went to his knees, struggled to his feet again and was hauled forward into one of the cells. The door rang shut behind him. Another door slammed and he knew that Curly was in another cell beside his. The light snapped off and he knew the policemen had gone.

Colin tasted blood in his mouth, put a hand to the side of his head and felt more blood. "Curly," he whispered. "You O.K.?"

He heard Curly laugh, a nervous muffled laugh, but the voice was calmer than his own. "I bin worse. I bin lots worse."

"What made the bastards do that?"

Curly laughed again. "Lesson Number One, pal. Never talk back to a cop. Never, never take a sock at one. You can't win. Jesus Christ, you'd think I'd know that by now."

Colin could feel anger still strong in him. "They didn't have to do it. It was like they did it for sport. The dirty yellow bastards."

"Listen," Curly said. "Forget that stuff. Dry it off, throw it away, bury it. It never happened, see, none of it. Unless you want a winter in the can. If them guys want to crucify us tomorrow morning, they sure as hell can do it."

"They can't get by with that kind of racket," Colin said.

"Aw, get yourself a lawyer," Curly said. "Go to sleep. You've had worse bunks. All kinds of 'em."

COLIN slept little. Every time his mind quietened he saw Curly standing in front of the big policeman, his hands at his sides, the bright trickle of blood running down from his mouth. He felt again his own slowness, the utter failure of his strength until moments after he had called upon it, but he knew that this had lost them little; that was what made the other violence so strong and so evil. There had been no possibility of escape from it, no smallest possibility of effective resistance to it, in spite of his own move to resist. The thought made his stomach knot and his body sweat in the cell's coldness. Curly had been less than a man to them when they hit him, less than an animal even; he had been something to hurt, something to make bleed and cry and crawl, a helplessness to punish with strength, because the head had once lifted, the eyes once brightened. Colin fought with fear and hunted reason through the long night.

Soon after daylight another policeman brought them breakfast and unlocked the cell doors. He pointed to a basin and a bucket of water in one corner of the cell room. "Better clean up," he said. "You'll be up inside of an hour. You're the only ones this morning."

"What's the charge?" Curly asked him.

"Vagrancy. Going to make an argument about it?"

"Hell, no," Curly said.

"That's good. The boys wouldn't thank you for bringing them down after night duty."

Curly went over to the basin, washed his face and rinsed his swollen mouth. "Looks kinda good," he told Colin cheerfully. "Might get by with thirty days."

"Is that good?" Colin asked.

"Sure as hell is. They could throw the book at us. Resisting arrest, assaulting a peace officer. I didn't tell you, but I bin picked up once before in this lousy town—that's why I give a phony name. That big lug that had ahold of you was there, but

171

I guess he mustn't have remembered it. Christ, we're getting all the breaks."

The trial was very short. They entered their pleas of guilty and waited for sentence.

"These men been here before?" the magistrate asked.

"No record, Your Worship."

"They been working?"

"They claim to. Out at the Kronstadt place. Finished yesterday morning. They've got money."

The magistrate nodded. "They'll need it before the winter's over. We'll leave it with them. Six months hard labor." He paused, then added: "I'll hold the warrant for twenty-four hours." He looked hard at Colin. "Understand what that means?"

"We've got twenty-four hours to get out of town?"

"That's right. If the police can find you this time tomorrow you'll be arrested and serve your sentence."

"We'll be on our way, Your Honor," Curly said. "We sure appreciate the chance."

As they passed beyond the edge of the city and out into the prairie again, Curly said: "That's one time your uncle Curly pretty near balled it up for fair. Just goes to show you coppers can act white part of the time."

No part of Colin's depression had left him and he said nothing. Curly said: "You sure as hell scared 'em when you started in. You shoulda seen how quick that Don quit poking at me to go and help his side-kick. I believe you coulda took the bastard if he hadn't." He kicked at a rock in the road. "I reckon it helped too; they was set to give us a good working over, but you coming in made 'em forget it. Don't you never do that again though. You take it and don't do nothing, same as I did."

Colin still walked with his muddled thoughts. He felt stripped and ashamed, and Curly's cheerful acceptance of it all seemed more shameful than anything else. "Christ," Curly said at last. "What's eating you. Don't you know a break when you get one?"

Colin turned on him sharply. "Break," he said harshly. "What kind of a break is it when they beat you across the face and you're supposed to stand there and take it? What's white about it? It isn't even human."

"I had it coming," Curly said mildly. "That was a fool trick, butting that son of a bitch and trying to twist away from him. Cops is scared of that kind of stuff. They'll always beat you up for it."

"Scared! What have they got to be scared of, with you half the size of either of them and them with clubs and guns?"

"Oh sure," Curly said placatingly. "Them hick town cops is ignorant bastards. They scare easy and they ain't got no judgment. Just the same, they got to watch it. Size ain't everything and they don't know I'm scared they'll get wise they seen me before. Looks to them like I figure I'm tough or else I've done something worse than just try to beat a ride on a freight. You got to see it their way, too."

"My sister's going to marry a cop," Colin said. "I used to think he was quite a guy."

"Christ," Curly told him. "You don't have to change your mind because of how you seen a couple of small town harness bulls act. All cops is tough—they gotta be. But any of 'em I've seen has got a human side too, like those guys not coming down to crucify us this morning." Colin said nothing and Curly glanced at him anxiously. "Don't let it get you down, pal," he said. "I know how you feel, like you wasn't worth a pinch of cow-dirt. It's always like that the first time they pull you in. I was the same myself, but it don't mean nothing. One night in the can ain't going to change the way a guy looks to other people."

Colin smiled and felt some of the bitterness leave him.

"That's more like it," Curly said. "We'll hitch a ride and buy us a goddamn big steak dinner next town we come to. Ain't nothing like paying for a big meal in a real fancy eating joint to get a man to feeling good again."

CURLY said: "There was a guy I traveled with in Manitoba two summers back. Name of Fred Symes. Claimed his folks had a place up around Hedley, fifty or sixty miles west of Edmonton. Seems like he lit out from home to get a change of scenery more'n anything else and he said any time I was up against it to go see his folks. The way he told it there's all kinds of work up around the ranch and they can always use extra help."

"They wouldn't want to feed two," Colin said.

"There's farm folks all around there, Fred says. Cow-farmers mostly and that kind will always use help if it's cheap enough. They raise kids to do the work, but the kids gets soured on cleaning out barns and nurse-maiding cows. So they busts the old man one in the mush and pulls out for the bright lights. Happens regular as clockwork. I run into all kinds of 'em."

They found the Symes farm easily enough. Fred Symes was home and Curly was as welcome as he expected to be. Within a day or two the Symes family found work for Colin at another farm three or four miles away. The owner, Joe Pauluk, was a tiny, brown-faced Ukrainian, barely five feet tall and probably in his fifties. His wife was a dark handsome woman of forty-five, only an inch or two taller than her husband but generously built and as quiet and reasonable as he was excitable and enthusiastic. There were four daughters, one already married at eighteen, the others still at school.

Colin quickly learned to like and respect Joe Pauluk. The little man was simple, almost childish at times, but in less than twenty years he had made a soundly producing farm of a hundred and fifty acres from Alberta bush; if it was clear that Mrs. Pauluk had been the calm, reasoning power behind the achievement, it was equally clear that Joe had supplied the driving enthusiasm and the full wiry strength of his little body.

"The farm she's big," he told Colin a few days after he arrived. "She's not big enough. Six hundred and forty acres I got, only a hundred and fifty I clear. No sons to work. Is bad. But the country she's good."

"Better than the prairies?" Colin asked.

"All Canada is good country. Most Ukrainians like the prairies; to be same as old country—tall wheat, tall sky. Too much like old country is not the best. My girls, they marry good Canadian fellows, come back to finish clear the old man's place. Everybody Canadians then."

"You have wheat," Colin said. "Tall wheat and tall hills."

"Sure," Pauluk agreed. "Sure. Seventy acres of wheat. But rye and oats too, and cows and pigs and chickens and the old lady's geese. In the good years the prairies are rich. In the bad years they are nothing. Here there is always something. The hills lean over a man and make him small. But they hold the rain and the snow, and that is good."

From Hedley Colin wrote Mildred: "I think I have seen some of the things you told me to go out and look for. This Mr. Pauluk I am working for is a Ukrainian, but I think in some ways he is more Canadian than any of us. Both he and his wife were born in the Ukraine and raised there, but they haven't spoken a word of anything but English—Canadian he calls it—since the children were old enough to talk. He tells me so often why Canada is a good country (mostly, he keeps saying, because there is lots of land for everyone) and how his children will grow up to be good Canadians. Yet they don't have an easy life. They work terribly hard, much harder than most people do out on the coast."

He wrote a great deal more, about the Pauluk family and the farm and his work there, about Curly, about Saskatchewan and their journey from the coast. He wanted to tell her about the arrest and the night in Marwell City jail; it was important to him, he knew, but somehow it was a vicious, unclean thing, in which she must have no part. The other things belonged to her as he told them, brought her close to him, built upon the feeling that had been between them that last evening in her cottage.

She answered at once and as he read her letter he knew that she had written in memory as clear as his own. "I knew you would find the sort of things you wrote about, and recognize them for what they are. I've wondered so many times since you left

175

just how you would find them and what exactly they would be when you did find them; it is wonderful to know. . . ." She wrote also of Blenkinstown and the Ensley family: "Things are still not good here. Quite a number of families are on relief and the mill is shut down a lot of the time. It makes me very happy to see Margaret again and know she will be living here. It seems funny to have to think of her as a married woman, but Clyde Munro is a wonderful man and I know you will like him a lot when you come home again and get to know him. It has been good for your mother to have Margaret back in Blenkinstown. She misses both of you a great deal and things haven't been easy for her, but now she can be sure of Margaret's happiness and see it with her own eyes."

Mildred's letters, and others from his mother and Margaret, seemed to restore substance to Colin's life and set a sanction on what he was doing. He was happy with the Pauluk family. The girls were wild, undisciplined little creatures, full of easy laughter, but they liked Colin and respected him for his size and quietness. Joe and his wife seemed never to stop working. Mrs. Pauluk reminded Colin of his mother in her determination to make use of every least thing on the farm and in the country around it. Before Colin had been in the house two or three days she discovered he was a hunter. "Now," she said. "We shall have plenty meat. Because the old man is afraid of the woods we have no meat unless it walks into the fields. That is not a way to live in a country where there are deers all around." Colin killed a deer for her and when she mentioned bear-fat he remembered he had crossed the track of a small bear near the edge of the bush; he went back next day and killed again, and from then on her faith in him was unlimited.

Joe Pauluk was not a patient man. He had persuaded himself long ago that only a driving quickness could make up for the smallness of his body, so he was always in a hurry, always anxious, always scolding. But, like his daughters, he respected Colin. "For you the cows are quiet," he told Colin in the barn one night. "For you they stand still and give more milk. With me they are crazy things, always to stamp and move and toss their heads.

Many of them I have raised since they were born, but you are a stranger. Why is that?"

Colin smiled slowly and said nothing. He thought of Joe Pauluk clattering milk cans, of Joe scolding and slapping, often shouting with anger as he milked.

"Why is that?" Joe insisted. "If I keep out of the barn altogether, you get more milk. Tell me why is that?"

"They like you to move slow," Colin said. "All animals are afraid. Cows are very slow and very quiet and very easily afraid."

Joe nodded. "I think that is truth. When I come the chickens fly away. When the old lady come she can catch them and pick them up. She is slow and quiet. I am quick and noisy. You must tell me to keep quiet in the barn. Perhaps I shall learn."

It was the same with the other work. Joe was adding to his barn, hoping to make room in it for twelve more cows, all his hay crop and all the farm machinery. Like the house and the other farm buildings the barn was built of logs. Every day Joe and Colin went in to the bush behind Joe's cleared fields to cut logs and haul them down across the snow with the team. Joe used his axe with a quick fierce strength that completed a cut almost as quickly as Colin's slow and easy rhythm; but the work often went badly for him—a notch would not fit or a tree would swing away from the line of fall he wanted.

"The logs, they are like cows too?" Joe asked. "They want I should go at them quietly? They are afraid of Joe?"

Colin laughed. He liked the bright day and the crisp snow and Joe's company. "The team works for you, Joe," he said. "You shout and they pull."

Joe looked towards his team and his face lighted. "They understand Joe. They know he is always in a hurry, always shout and scream and don't mean nothing by it. The team work good for me. But the axe, no. She is fool me all the time."

Colin tried to show him Will Ensley's powerful, accurate way with an axe, tried to describe the full-arm, overhead swing of the great broad-axe, the downward arc of the blade and its clean, smooth bite along the grain of the wood. Joe listened and watched and shook his head. "Not for Joe," he said. "Joe is too old to change. To be quiet with cows, yes, I learn that. But with the

177

axe, no; with the team, no; with the plow, no. Joe must shout and hurry."

Joe had gone well back to take up his land and the Pauluk farm still had no near neighbors. The school that the girls went to each day was three miles away in a tiny settlement around which the Symes' and other farms were grouped, and the town of Hedley was two or three miles beyond that again. But the Pauluks were friendly and sociable people and they visited and were visited by several local farm families; and Mrs. Pauluk was a tireless worker at every possible community affair. At first Colin stayed at home when the family went out and sat silently in the cheerful kitchen when other families came to visit. But both Joe and Mrs. Pauluk worked to draw him out and gradually, because he was comfortable with them, he responded. The Symes family were as active socially as the Pauluks and Colin began to see a good deal of them and Curly. Curly wore his handsome shirts and made the most of the local girls. He was having a good time and didn't hesitate to say so.

"Softest winter I ever put in," he told Colin one day when he had walked over to the Pauluks. "They treat me just like one of the family. Fred's old man is a swell guy and so is the old lady. Sure feels different when you come up against real people like that. How're you making out over there?"

"They're fine people too," Colin said. "Couldn't want better."

"The old lady looks like she'd be a swell cook. He's a queer little guy though—jumps around like a cricket. How're you making out with the girls? The oldest one looks just about ready for it."

"Cathie?" Colin leaned on the handle of his axe and looked at him in mild surprise. "She's just a kid in school."

"Don't mean she ain't ready for it," Curly said. "You're right though, at that. There's plenty dames in this neck of the woods without taking chances on jail-bait. You ought to snag yourself one. It ain't natural for a young guy to be the way you are."

Colin moved his feet in the snow and picked up his axe again. Curly had urged him this way many times before and it made him feel uneasy and deficient. He had never told him about Mildred and did not intend to. "It's all right for you," he said. "But girls don't go for a guy like me."

"You ain't all that bad," Curly said. "All you got to do is work up a good line. Act like you're deep, maybe, or lonely. There just ain't no telling what a girl's going to fall for. You want to figure it the way I do. They all want what you got, but there's some won't admit it right off."

Colin remembered Curly's occasional admissions of failure during the previous summer. "Seems to me I remember times when they just plain wouldn't admit it at all for you."

They were walking towards the house now. "Time," Curly said. "That's all it takes. Only a guy ain't always got time. And there's some would take more time than they're worth, if a guy was to waste it on them." He stopped to kick snow from one of his boots. "Like Fred's sister, for instance, that was here around Christmas. She's a looker and you'd think she'd be easy-going like Fred and the rest of the family. But I knew to lay off soon as I seen her."

COLIN met Jean Symes about a week later. Since Christmas he had been hunting back from the Symes farm quite regularly, following the Vale River into the hills and working the open places along it, where the sun had melted the snow away from the brown grass. He was used to the country now and knew how to hunt it, but it still held a strange excitement for him, quite different from anything he had known in the coast country. The birch and poplar and little spruce trees were all strange to him, the sweep of the rivers was different and strange, the game was strange—he had killed a moose once, and seen others; twice he had seen caribou and held his shot because they seemed too beautiful to kill; even the deer were different, larger and prouder creatures than the coast blacktails. From all this he had a sense of being a foreigner and hunted the more keenly for it, constantly watching for tracks or signs that were strange to him. Every part of him was keyed to a pitch beyond normal keenness, and the hunting became a purification that stripped normal values away from him.

On the day he met Jean Symes he had killed easily and dressed his buck only a little way back in the woods. He was coming out to the farm to get Fred or Curly to bring back a horse for the buck and he found her suddenly, at the upper edge of the long field that sloped down towards the house. She was on skis, standing across the slope, hatless and with her head thrown back so that her pale hair caught the early morning sun. He stopped sharply as he saw her and stood perfectly still against the trunk of a tree. After several seconds he moved, stepping so that she would hear him. She turned to the sound and he came up to her; she was smiling and he saw that her face was beautiful.

"You must be the great hunter the boys talk about," she glanced at his hands on the rifle. "And a successful hunter, too, I see. I'm glad. It's so dull when the great reputations fail."

Colin had forgotten the kill, but the exaltation of the woods was still in him. He appraised her calmly, almost insolently, her blue eyes and scarlet mouth, the smooth throat framed by the open collar of her white shirt, the swell of her breasts, the curve of her hips.

"Well," she said. "Am I presentable?"

"You're like someone I used to know."

"Oh," she said. "How very nice. I suppose I should be flattered." She moved her skis so that the snow creaked under them and her neat body was more open to him; her mouth still smiled but her eyes were not friendly. "Where are you going now?"

The question reached through his mood. He became conscious of himself again and looked away from her. "I was going down to get the horse," he said.

"I can go for you. And much faster." But she stood quite still, her eyes willing him to look back to her again. "Well," she said. "Do you want me to go?"

"Don't bother. I can go. It won't take very long."

She laughed then and he did look towards her, but she had turned her skis and was already on her swift way down the slope, her slim body light and easy, the full sleeves of her blouse fluttering against the smooth air. Colin watched for a moment, then followed her.

Later, walking the road back to the Pauluks, he could not free his mind of her. He knew she was not like Mildred, yet he had spoken exact truth in the moment he told her she was. Like her, yet unlike her; younger and closer to him, yet unapproachable as Mildred had never been. He tried, in his loyalty to Mildred, to deny the attraction he had felt from her; but he knew that this was a loyalty Mildred had not asked of him, did not want of him. She had sent him out to look for just this, had told him that he would find it. "I am like your woods and mountains," she had said. "You haven't seen anything else." Loyalty became turned upon itself. He could deny the sudden power of this new woman only by denying the mission that Mildred Hanson had set for him.

Through the rest of the day, in the routine of his work, she became more remote; the exaltation of the woods had left him and he felt himself Colin Ensley again, an awkward, clumsy man, unproved, concerned with barns and cattle and heavy tools. He tried to fit her into it all and could not; her way was the swift way, over the bright surface of the snow; his way was slower, heavier, the weight of footsteps breaking through the crust.

In the evening Joe Pauluk came into the barn while Colin was milking. He had been to Hedley and Colin knew he had had a few drinks, as he usually did when he went into town alone; but in spite of that he was quite quiet. For several minutes he stood at the back of the stall, watching. Then, when Colin moved to another cow, he said: "That Curly Blake. I see him in town. He say in a little time, when spring come good, you move out."

"I guess that's right," Colin said. "Curly likes to keep moving."

"You don't want to move," Joe said. "I pay for spring work, same as prairies. Mr. Symes pay."

"I hadn't thought of it that way. Curly always did say we'd move on in the spring, and I figured to go with him. But maybe he'd change his mind if there was work to do."

Joe shook his head. "Not that Curly. I see other boys like him, lots of boys like him. They must be all the time go, go, go. Never stay any place. You are not the same as them."

"I guess not," Colin said. "But I kind of like to travel with Curly, just the same. He's been pretty good to me."

"Look," Joe said quickly. "I got no boys. You can have Cathie. She's a good girl, Cathie. She's make a good wife for a man. Then we build a house for you and you stay here."

181

Colin finished stripping the cow and stood up with the pail. "How about Cathie?" he asked.

"She's like you fine. She's do what me and her Ma say."

Colin said, very gently. "I haven't ever thought of anything like that, Joe. It would take time to think about it, quite a lot of time."

"You think," Joe said. "This place good for you. You think and we talk about it some more, yes?"

Colin said slowly: "It'd take a lot of thinking, Joe. I guess I'll go along when Curly goes. But don't ever think I don't like it here. You folks have all been swell to me."

"But you think," Joe said eagerly. "You think. And maybe you change your mind and stay."

At supper Colin watched Cathie and Mrs. Pauluk and was sure that neither of them knew of Joe's plan. Cathie played and giggled with her sisters, as always; was scolded, kept quiet for a little while, then began her play again. She was child, not woman. The Pauluks were arguing, as they often did, over their memories of the old country. Mrs. Pauluk liked to remember the good things, Joe hated to admit that anything had been good. Mrs. Pauluk remembered singing and dancing, gay and handsome colors in the dresses of her girlhood, the sound of a bell across the fields.

"Those things we have brought with us. It is only the bad things we leave behind," Joe said. "The wars and the fighting and the hunger."

"The children forget," she told him. "They grow up lazy and laughing, like Cathie. They are better here, but they forget many things, and some things they have never seen."

"It is good they forget. This is another country, here there is peace and a full belly."

"Very often we were happy there. I would not go back, but there was happiness and it is not right to forget."

"There was the fighting," Joe insisted. "Poles and Russians and Germans, always the fighting and killing."

"We were safe in the woods, down under the ground, with the sods piled over the door. The fighting would pass and there would be peace again."

"They were over our heads," Joe told Colin. "Running and killing and screaming. And afterwards we find them in the blood. This country is not like that. There is land for all."

"It was not only for land they fought."

"For land," Joe said. "For Ukrainians' land. Killing and screaming and fighting. The Russians were the worst."

"The Germans were the worst."

"All were bad. It was a bad place."

She agreed with him at last. "It is better here," she said simply. "But it is good to remember a little."

In bed that night Colin let his mind attempt to sort the day's happenings, but Jean Symes' smiling face and sharp words were over them all. He tried to think of Cathie, to find from her some trace of the excitement Jean Symes had stirred in him, and could not. He knew how to measure the thing that Joe Pauluk had offered him and felt the urge of his powerful liking for the little man. He knew with a clear mind that the farm and the Pauluks had given him happiness, a rest from himself, a new conception of his own strength and value. But he knew as clearly that Cathie was not for him and, ultimately, that the farm was not for him, however Joe offered it. Because he had a true affection for Joe and this was a rejection of everything most precious in Joe's life, the clear knowledge hurt him. Because Jean Symes, standing on her skis, her hair bright in the sun, seemed a creature from a different world than round, happy, good-natured Cathie, he felt ashamed. But he was still thinking of Jean when he fell asleep.

He saw her again three or four days later. She stopped her car as he was mending a fence near the road, pushed open the door and swung her feet to the running board.

"Hullo," she said. "So that's what you do when you aren't hunting?"

Colin lifted his hat and walked slowly towards the car. "I don't hunt so very often," he said. "Only when we need meat."

She looked at him, a little amused smile on her lips. "You don't look much like a woodsman. Or maybe you do. Where did you learn so much about it?"

There was a patronizing directness in her look and her words that confused him, but in spite of this he felt the warming flattery of her interest. "On the coast," he said. He was standing beside the car now and she was still sitting there, looking up at him, her feet on the running board beside the open door.

"The boys say you can do wonderful things with an axe, too. I should like to see that sometime."

"I'm not so hot," Colin said. "My dad is the man that can use an axe."

"I don't want to see your dad. I want to see you." Again her tone was impatient, yet flattering. She was commanding and expecting obedience.

"I put in a lot of time at it. I'll be cutting cordwood over at your place next week."

"And I suppose I may come and watch you then," she swung her legs back into the car and started the motor. "Well, I can wait."

Colin watched the car until it disappeared around a curve in the road, then went slowly back to his work. He knew she had been annoyed, almost angry, and he felt in himself a slow resistance to her impatience and arrogance; yet he had wanted to please her, had been planning ways to please her ever since he had first seen her.

It was the same when she came up to where he was cutting cordwood on the Symes farm; she seemed able to draw him and repulse him in a single sentence, to offer herself and withdraw herself in a floating movement of her body. She came up during each of the first three days he worked there, and on the third day she said, quite suddenly: "Who do I remind you of?"

Colin's mind fumbled with the question, vaguely sensed its danger, but he said: "A girl I know. Not a girl really, a woman."

"Out on the coast?"

"Yes."

"Were you fond of her?" Her voice was gentle now and Colin lost his sense of danger.

"I still am," he said. "Very fond of her."

"In love with her?"

Colin hesitated. "She's older than I am," he said.

She turned on him then and her body shook with anger. "You and your old women," she said. "Go back to your old women.

Why did you ever come away from them if you love them so much?"

Colin stood quite still. He felt his face flush as though she had struck him, but he looked straight into her anger and he asked quietly: "Why do you hate me?"

"Because you haven't got the guts of a louse," she told him fiercely. "Because you're big and strong and you're supposed to be good at things and there's nothing in you, nothing at all. You never have been anything and you never will be anything. I don't hate you. You just aren't that interesting."

She turned quickly then and ran away down the wood road. Colin picked up his axe and drove it with all his strength into the tree in front of him.

2 2

COLIN and Curly left the foothills in the spring, as Curly had planned, and traveled the prairies through the summer. One warm September evening they made camp at the top of a high, steep bank above a small river. Colin had wanted to camp in the bush right beside the river, but Curly had talked him out of it. Colin was sitting with his back against a mound of dirt and dry grass, watching one of the big prairie hawks as it circled high in the evening air. "I'm for the coast," he said. "It's time I went up home to see the folks again. I haven't even seen my sister since she got married."

"Suits me," Curly swung the coffee pot off the fire. "It's time I hunted up my old lady again, too."

Colin looked at him in quick surprise. Curly had been born in Winnipeg and his parents had gone their separate ways while he was still in school; until now, he had mentioned them only as belonging to the distant past. "Do you know where she is?"

"Somewhere around Vancouver," Curly said. "I'll find her. It was her I went to see just before we pulled out. She ain't much good, but I feel kind of sorry for the old bat and she's helped me out a time or two."

Colin knew Curly too well to be shocked by the hard assessment. "Have you heard from her lately?"

"Letters, you mean? Christ no. Give her a pencil and she might lick it, but that's as far as she could go. I wrote her when I was at Fred's place last winter, but the letter came back. She keeps moving, but she's O.K. Got the old man's pension. Drinks it mostly, but she picks up enough on the side to keep eating and sleeping. Seems like that's the way she wants it."

The prairie evening was still and the mosquito hawks hunted high. A mallard flapped its wings and called from the reeds in a marsh nearby and terns were busy in swift graceful flight over the marsh. Colin watched it all gratefully. There had been a dozen, perhaps two or three dozen such evenings in the past two years; evenings when they had been camped like this, alone and beyond sound or hearing of other human beings, knowing little or nothing of where they were going or what they would be doing in twenty-four hours' time. Always there had been the high arching sky over them and the distances of the flat land around them, usually a bird-filled marsh and something, a barn or machinery or a belt of trees, to break the endless roll of swaying wheat or dusty stubble. Tonight there was the river behind them in its deep cut; and the land in front of them, to the west, was pasture, broken by patches of rough bush; but it was still prairie.

"Must have been quite a country in the old days," Colin said at last. "With buffalos and Indians and everybody riding horses. I'd sure like to have seen it."

"I'd as soon have her the way she is. A guy can go further and quicker with the freights or hitch-hiking than he ever could with a horse. And it ain't so goddamn far between towns any more. I guess them buffalo was worth seeing though. What made you think of them all of a sudden?"

"I don't know," Colin said. He was rolling a cigarette, very slowly, looking down at the tobacco against the white paper. "Because it's more natural here than most places we go, I guess.

I get to feeling that way quite often—a man must have had a better chance in the old days, when things were more natural."

"There was bums them days, same as there is now. I guess there was work too maybe, but a guy could stay poor all his life doing it. Seems to me we got it easier all around than they had it then. Take these winter camps them kids was talking about the other day. I'll bet the government didn't have nothing like them in the old buffalo days."

"Those forestry camps, you mean?" Colin asked. "Sounded like relief camps to me."

"Sure, that's what they are if you want to call 'em that. But those kids figured they was O.K., just the same—good grub and a good place to stay and they don't work the arse off you. That ain't much maybe, but I've seen times it would sure as hell have looked like plenty to me. You have too. You'd have been better in a set-up like that than the winter you put in up the Fraser Valley."

"What kind of work do they do?"

"Most anything. Fixing up parks, mostly; building trails and roads and fancy entrances, clearing brush, planting trees. Nothing dirty. Straight eight hours, too."

"It'd be a hell of a lot better than stalling around town," Colin said. "You're right about that. And I guess it's the kind of a job a guy wouldn't have to worry in. Just do a day's work and let it go at that."

Curly laughed. "It's working for the government, ain't it? You never seen anybody kill himself working for the government yet, have you?" He looked over at Colin sprawled against the hummock, and affection momentarily softened his sharp little face. "You long-geared old son of a bitch," he said. "You'll never get fired from any place for the kind of day's work you put in."

Colin watched the mosquito hawks against the reddening sky and thought of getting back to the coast. Rain, he thought, and big trees, and the creeks down the sides of the mountains. The creek in the alders, the creek where I used to stop after Tod Phalling had cleaned up on me, all those creeks running into the Wind River below the lake. Cameron Creek, by Robbie's cabin, the creek out of Carlson's Valley, Amabilis Creek. Wonder how Johnny's making out up there on the lake with Robbie? And

187

Margaret married; that's hard to think about. No more prairies, he thought, no more wheat dust, no more evenings like this one, with Curly always knowing what to do next.

"Curly," he said suddenly. "How'll we get together again?"

Curly was lying flat on his back, looking up at the sky, but he rolled over on to his side. "What's that?" he asked. "When it's time to start out again, you mean?"

"Yes," Colin said slowly. "I guess that's what I was thinking."

"It'll work out somehow. Maybe we'll both get us good jobs and won't want to hit the road next year. A person can't tell what's liable to happen."

Colin felt loneliness again, cold, gray, empty. "We better keep in touch," he said

"Sure," Curly agreed. "Sure, we'll do that."

IT was early in November when Colin got home, and after the first few days he felt he had never been away. The prairies, Joe Pauluk, the whole time with Curly, were immeasurably far from him, removed by the long journey through the mountains, by the other journey up the coast, but most of all by the close familiarity of everything about him—the smell of winter apples in the store-room, the piled woodshed, Martha's quiet, happy acceptance of his return, the sodden maple leaves under the big trees out by the gate, the drip of rain from the barn roof. He had left Curly in Vancouver and they had promised again to keep touch; Colin had written already, but he knew that with Curly only the near things counted, the things in sight, the things one tripped over or ran into, and he did not really expect an answer.

Colin was busy from the moment he got home. He looked at the farm with Joe Pauluk's eyes and saw at once many things to be done; the fences were in bad shape, the pastures were run down, the chicken-house leaked rain, the barn needed repair, even the house itself sagged at one corner where a support had rotted away. He accepted these things almost gladly at first, using them to fit himself easily back into the life; but as he worked at them he felt a growing impatience and with it a sense of loss and despair that he did not fully admit or account for. Will was away, building a donkey-sled for some small outfit a little farther up the coast, but Colin knew that he had worked only occasionally during the past two years and there had been little money. There was only one cow on the place now, which Martha milked and looked after. He thought of Joe Pauluk and what Joe's little strength and his driving energy would have made of the Ensley farm.

Will came back when Colin had been at home for nearly three weeks, and the change in him shocked and hurt Colin far more deeply than the broken fences and dilapidated buildings. The square black beard was heavily streaked with gray, the bold face was thin, the great shoulders stooped, no longer forcing his thick chest proudly forward against the beard. These things Colin noticed and accepted. But the eyes were no longer proud, nor the voice, nor the words that the voice used. Will Ensley was tired, not in his arms or his shoulders or his chest, but in his mind and his heart. He looked searchingly at Colin when he first saw him, as though hoping to find some of his lost strength in his son, and he asked many questions about the prairies and about Colin's time away, old man's questions that seemed to listen for echoes of his own vigor in the answers. Colin answered him and talked with him, and they both searched with a fumbling awkwardness for some bond of understanding that they felt should have been between them. They did not find it.

Margaret was confident and happy as she had always been. Back on the prairies Colin had found it difficult to imagine her married to Clyde Munro, away from the family and mistress of her own house; but once he had seen her it was almost equally difficult to remember that she had once gone daily to school with him. He tried to tell her what he thought about Will and she said: "It's almost as though he had given up. He found out there was a new broad-axe man up at camp, so he went to town and tried to hire out from the agency—anywhere. They told him there wasn't anything, to look in again later."

"Did he?" Colin asked.

"Yes, he went down again. And they told him the same thing. He understood then and it just seemed to stop everything that had kept him going."

Colin thought for a moment, "Being blacklisted isn't anything to be ashamed of," he said.

"It's much deeper than that," Margaret said. She looked across at her husband. "He tried to tell Clyde about it once. What was it he said, Clyde?"

"It's his pride that's gone," Clyde said. "He's not a sure man any more. The things he believes in haven't worked out for him. He was telling me he believes in law and order, telling me over and over again—that's because he doesn't feel right about being tied in with those organizers."

"But he knows he was right," Margaret said. "Mother says he's told her over and over again that he couldn't have done anything else. And he couldn't have. But it's left him grouped with something he really despises—with people he calls agitators and troublemakers."

"He could have broken right away from the whole set-up," Colin said. "He could have worked the farm and made some sort of living at it."

"You know he couldn't," Margaret said.

"He could keep the buildings in shape."

"He's discouraged," Clyde Munro said. "It's not easy for a man as old as Mr. Ensley to change his whole way of life. Especially when he's been one of the top men in his trade."

Because Clyde was so obviously strong and sure in himself, his words had full force for Colin; for the moment he understood his father, felt as he had felt, thought almost as he had thought. But it was still difficult to accept that there was weakness in the great square body and the blackbearded godhead. He thought again of Joe Pauluk.

"They've been through some tough times," he said. "What are they going to do now?"

"Go on the way they are," Margaret said. "You can't change them. We can help out a little, and you can too, if you get a job."

"They'll take him back sooner or later," Clyde said. "It's not as though he was active in the union. I don't know why they've held out this long, except Gordon Holman seems to have it in for him."

"I guess it's time for me to pull out again," Colin said. "I've fixed what I can around the place and I'm not earning my keep there."

He saw Margaret look quickly at Clyde. "You could get on up at the forestry camp," Clyde said. "They're looking for a straw-boss that could teach the kids up there something about axe-work. Has to be a single man."

"I guess I'll pull out," Colin said. "If they don't want Ensleys around this neck of the woods they don't have to have them."

Margaret stood up and crossed the room to the fireplace. "Don't go off again so soon, Colin. It isn't fair to Mother. She'll never tell you, but she's been worried sick all this time you've been away."

"I write her as often as I can."

"I know, but she can't help worrying. It'd be a whole lot easier for her if she knew where you were."

Colin looked at Clyde again. "What is it?" he asked. "Relief work?"

"The camp is. But you'd be more like on the staff. They might even give you a chance to stay on with the Forestry Department all year around. I think you'd like it."

"Sounds like it might be O.K.," Colin said slowly. He thought of Curly—still in Vancouver, probably, making out somehow, planning without anxiety, watching for the break that he was always sure would turn up.

"Think it over," Margaret said. "I know it would help Mother a lot if you were near home."

Later, as he was leaving, she came to the door with him. As he started down the steps she called him back. "Colin," she said. "You haven't been to see Mildred. She was asking about you."

Colin felt his face flush in the darkness and a hard pulse in his throat. "I know," he said. "I haven't been visiting around much."

"She thinks a lot of you. You ought to go and see her."

"I guess I will," he said. "Soon as I get a free evening."

But when he went up to the forestry camp on Strathmore River a week later, he still had not seen her.

COLIN liked the camp and the work. They were develop
ing a small park near the low, slanting falls across the Strathmore
River, building roads and trails, flights of steps down awkward
places, bridges across the tributary creeks, signs to guide the
summer visitors. He had charge of about a dozen men who were
supposed to cut and peel poles and split or hew cedar slabs for
steps and tables and benches. The work was easy and familiar to
Colin and he went at it with a quiet concentration. The men on
his crew did little at first except stand off and watch him, helping
occasionally to lift a pole or roll a log or cut away some brush,
showing rather more activity when one of the regular foremen
was nearby, setting their tools down again as soon as he disappeared, talking among themselves and rolling cigarettes.

It did not occur to Colin to attempt to drive them to work; he
had been told to show them how to use tools, so he showed them
in the only way he knew, by doing the job himself. When he
needed help he asked for it. Otherwise he left them alone, to
watch and learn if they wanted. Within a day or two they were
working almost enthusiastically. They were the "single unemployed" of the province, most of them young and city-bred.
Something in Colin's competence attracted them; the smooth
shearing of bark away from polished poles over the blade of his
axe, the flaking of chips, the shredding of grain from grain into
clear, heavy slabs of wood; all the facets of a craft completely new
to them reached in and touched some unused impulse to craftsmanship. Above all there was Colin's unconcern with them and
concern with the work of his hands. He was a straw-boss, a symbol
of authority to be resisted or at least evaded. But the symbol
was without substance; resistance passed through, evasion evaded
nothing, idleness without challenge became boredom. There was
challenge in the bright blade of the axe, in the weight of the

sledges, in the way the wood yielded to blade and wedge and saw. They responded to this.

While he worked in the camp Colin's feeling for wood and his skill and ingenuity in working with it developed steadily. The foreman, Dan Settler, recognized his ability at once and used him fully, constantly setting him new problems and broader projects. Colin was absorbed and happy. He worked steadily through each week, often spending the evenings drawing plans or working out designs; but at week ends he went home, cutting over the easy divide between the Strathmore River and his own valley to the road that ran down past Mike Varchuk's empty shack.

During this time he was closer to his mother than he had ever been. Martha had known an intense loneliness after her children had left home, the more intense because their leaving had seemed to complete the disintegration of the world she had planned and worked to hold together. She had known that they must go sooner or later, but she had believed always that their going would be part of the plan, an extension of the world she had built and a renewal of it through grandchildren in houses nearby. For nearly two years it had seemed that the plan had failed her. But now Margaret was near, in a home of her own, and it seemed that Colin might stay within reach until he also settled down.

When he came at the week ends Colin simply dropped his small pack in the woodshed and turned to the work of the place as though he was living there all the time. Occasionally he went out to kill a buck, but more often he worked on the fences or the buildings or in the fields. For the most part Will was away—the small camps along the coast and out among the islands were calling on him more and more frequently—so the two of them were often alone when Colin came in from his work. Martha found Colin even more silent and withdrawn than he had seemed before he left home, but she worked steadily and gently to bring him back to her and she felt a measure of slow success as the winter drew on. She said once, when they were at supper on a Saturday evening: "You're fond of this place, aren't you, Colin? Of the farm, I mean?"

"Sure," he said simply. "It's home."

"It could be quite a good farm."

"There isn't much clear land," Colin said. "There's heavy soil back in the alder bottom, but a person'd have to drain it as well as clear it. And you'd need bigger buildings, and machinery. It'd take a lot of time and money. I'm not sure I like farming that well."

"You were telling me about your friend Joe Pauluk," Martha said. "It must have been even harder where he started."

"I'm not sure," Colin reached forward and cut himself a slice of bread. "That's farming country back there—this isn't. And he wanted land so much. I don't think I want anything so much as Joe wants his land."

He had spoken evenly and calmly, not at all intensely, but the words made Martha afraid for him again. "You do want things," she told him. "I remember how you wanted to climb the mountain. And you've always wanted to go in the woods. Of course you want things."

"I know," Colin said. "But they're the wrong kind of things." I want Mildred, he thought, the way she was when I went away; and things like that night with Robbie at the mouth of Amabilis Creek, and the night on the prairie when Curly and I made up our minds to come back to the coast. And the time on the mountain with Margaret. Those things don't come back. They are people and places, not things you can use like Joe's land. "Farming is a pretty good life," he said. "But it isn't so much on the coast. There's darn few make a go of it."

"It's hard work. They give up for something that looks easier and pays big wages. But a farmer ends up with something. The others don't."

"It might work out." Colin thought of a herd of Jerseys and a big barn, pasture land cleared from the alder flat. "But a man'd have to be able to sell to the Company. They wouldn't buy from us."

Martha stood up and began to clear the table. "That won't last forever," she said. "Things like that never do." Let it rest there for now, her wisdom told her. At least he's thinking of it, he's not planning to go away again just yet. With a good wife to help him someday he could make this place into what Will and I should have made it. I'm not even sure that's what I want for him, except that I want something that will protect him and I can't think of anything else. "Do you have to get back to camp tomorrow night?" she asked. "Margaret and Clyde will be over for supper."

"I can walk through in the dark," Colin said. "I blazed a few trees when I came down this afternoon."

EARLY in January a fresh crew of men came into camp. Colin worked as he always had, hewing and shaping and splitting, asking for help when he had to, using a man who was willing, leaving the unwilling to their own devices. But the temper of the new men was different and several of them were a good deal older than Colin. His interest in what he was doing and his easy skill with his tools had no appeal for them and they were careful to do no more than the barest minimum of work.

Colin noticed the change at first simply as a vague surliness in the men, which depressed and sometimes embarrassed him. A small group of older men, Mel Ross, Olaf Knudson, Charlie Merck and three or four others, usually sat or leaned through most of the day, talking and smoking; the rest of the crew did enough work to make some showing, but only one or two had anything approaching the interest of his former crew. The first clear break came when he asked Ross to help him roll a log. Ross was talking at the time and paid no attention. Colin asked him again and he said: "What's the matter, kid? Scared the push'll be riding your tail?"

The full implication of the question and its tone did not reach Colin. He shook his head and smiled good-naturedly. "Just trying to earn my keep."

"Go ahead," Ross told him. "You're the one that's getting paid to work, not us."

Colin understood then and felt a sharp stir of irritation. "You got a break when they quit charging for standing room," he said, and turned back to the log. Olaf Knudson, another of the older men, came up and helped him with it. Ross laughed and turned away.

Two or three days later Dan Settler called Colin aside as he was starting out to work in the morning. He asked one or two simple questions about the work, then: "How's the new crew working out?"

"O.K., I guess," Colin said.

"They aren't putting out the work," Settler said. "You had any trouble?"

"No. They don't get interested the way the others did, but there's no trouble."

Settler moved his feet and looked past Colin at a group of men walking slowly out of camp with tools over their shoulders. "This bunch is different from the last lot," he said. "Every second one's a sorehead. They'll take different handling."

"They'll settle down," Colin said. "When they see there's nothing else to do."

Settler shook his head vigorously. "They're shaping up for trouble. We got warning they're going to pull a strike." He was a nervous man and moved constantly as he talked, kicking at stones, putting his hands in his pockets, taking them out again. "Look, Ensley," he said. "You're a good workman, but you got to handle that crew so you get some work out of them. So long as you do all the work they'll take advantage of it, just standing around watching and trying to look like they was learning something. You've got to do the standing around and make the other guys work. That's what a straw-boss is for."

"You got to show them," Colin said. "There's not more than one or two of them know the difference between an axe and a peavey."

"Never mind that," Settler said. "Get them working. Don't leave 'em stand around and talk."

Over the next week or so the thing progressed steadily. In spite of Settler's warning Colin made little effort to change his handling of his crew. He knew that Settler was right and that most of the men watched him work and did nothing themselves, but he could not feel concerned about it. He was interested in the work and liked doing it; from time to time he had to have help and would ask for it; apart from that it seemed to him foolish to try to persuade unwilling men to do work that he could do faster and better alone.

Actually, in that last week before the strike, the men on Colin's

196

crew worked better and more willingly than they had before. When Colin came up to them the morning Settler had spoken to him, Mel Ross asked: "What did the big push want?"

Colin grinned. "He told me to make you guys work harder."

"You going to try it?"

"I haven't bothered you yet, have I?" Colin asked. "You can set on your fannies till your pants rot so long as you don't get in my way."

"We might do just that," Ross said.

The rest of the crew was standing around, listening to them. Olaf Knudson said: "Lay off the kid, Mel. He's treated us good enough."

"I ain't bothering him none, just so he don't bother us."

"Might be just as good to help out a little," Knudson said. "If we don't he's liable to get fired and some proper son of a bitch take his place."

Ross picked up an axe and put it down again. He was thinking. But Charlie Merck said: "What do we care? We're going out on strike, ain't we?" He was a thin, hungry-looking man, with a long nose, a long jaw and sunken blue eyes. Ross turned on him fiercely.

"Shut up, Merck," he said. "You're so goddamned ignorant you got no business being alive, never mind talking. I think Olaf's got something. We can just as easy pitch in and make the kid look good."

Colin had picked up his axe some moments before and was scoring a fresh log, but he heard Merck say in a hurt whine: "That ain't no way to talk to anyone."

"Shut up," Ross told him again. Then: "O.K., you guys. Pick up some tools and get to work."

Colin laughed. "Don't anybody bust a gut," he said.

The strike came off in due course. There was a union of a sort and a measure of leadership from men like Mel Ross, but in spite of talk and preparations they seemed to drift into it rather than anything else. Colin was never very sure of the issues. They wanted a higher rate of pay, without the planned hold-back that was supposed to help them out when they left, and a promise that the camps would be continued through the year instead of closing

197

down in early spring, when work became more plentiful. The plan seemed to be to carry on all the domestic routine of the camp, but to do no work beyond this.

During the first two days there was a good deal of activity. Committees were formed and met. There were speeches. Dan Settler addressed the strikers and asked them to go back to work. A more senior official arrived from outside and addressed them more firmly, threatening to close the camp. Colin watched and listened with a growing sense of hopelessness. He belonged fully to neither side and neither side had need of him. He liked the camp, liked Dan Settler, liked the work he had been doing and the men he had been working with. He wondered what Curly would say about it or Joe Pauluk or some of the prairie farmers he had worked for. Here was food and a comfortable place to sleep, easy work, short hours, some pay. They want more, he thought; most of all they want to be sure of something, not to go back to town at the end of a couple of months and start looking again with only a few dollars between them and hunger. That's what they are striking about really, not about this camp or this park they are working on or Dan Settler or me. They are one little part of hundreds and thousands and hundreds of thousands of people, all across North America, who aren't sure they can do enough and get enough to keep them alive. Curly and I always knew we'd get by somehow, Joe Pauluk knows, but these guys don't know and they want to know. That's what they are saying now. They hardly know they are saying it and they have to say other things instead, but that is what they feel. If I felt the same I guess I'd be in it with them.

On the third day of the strike some trucks came in and loaded all the food that was stored in the cookhouse. The strikers had been warned that this would happen, but it seemed to take them completely by surprise and they made no move to stop the loading. During the afternoon the permanent staff of the camp, including the cooks, moved out.

Colin had said he would walk home over the hill and he went into his tent to pack his stuff. Olaf Knudson came in and watched him. Colin liked Olaf. He was a quiet, sensible man of thirty-five or forty, a commercial fisherman who owned his own gill-net boat and used the camp to help him through the winter. He watched

Colin in silence for a minute or two, then shifted the big curved pipe in his mouth and coughed.

"Looks like she's finished," he said. "Where'll you go now?"

Colin rolled up a shirt and stowed it down into his packsack. "Have to look for some place, I guess. I was just hired for this camp. You think the strike can't win?"

Olaf shrugged. "No money, no grub. They called our bluff. Tomorrow the police come in and we walk out. That's all there is to it."

Colin had finished his packing. He sat down on his bunk and looked up at Olaf. "Why did it happen?" he asked.

Olaf shrugged again. "Trouble," he said. "Trouble every place. There's right in it, too. Most of these kids got no place to go but hang around town when they finish up their time in camp. But this won't help it any. They should wait and get a good plan."

"What about you?" Colin asked.

"I'll make out. I can live on the boat and pick up a few dollars for grub between now and the start of the season. But most of them got nothing."

"I'm going down home right away," Colin said. "Want to come along?"

Olaf shook his head. "I'll stay with the boys. Till they hit town, anyway."

It was almost dusk and raining a little when Colin started over the hill. He had talked more with Olaf before leaving, but he still felt confused and helpless in the face of what had happened. Only two or three weeks ago the camp had been a happy place. It had seemed to him useful, sensible, hopeful. There were things to be done, problems to be worked out; the results of the work showed plainly and they were good; the men he was working with liked the job, liked their food, and their own lively entertainments in the evenings and over week ends, even ran off a small newspaper of their own in the camp. Nothing had changed; it was the same park, the same camp, the same job and bosses, the same food, the same weather; yet now the camp no longer existed except as a street of tents that would be taken down within the next few days, and a few groups of men who stood around and talked. These men weren't essentially different from the men who had liked the camp, yet Olaf had said they were right to strike. Curly would have said the same thing, Colin thought; he'd have been mad about it, but that's what he would have said. And so would Joe Pauluk.

Near the summit of the divide Colin slipped his pack under a log and turned back. It was dark when he came in sight of the camp again, but three or four big fires were burning down the center of the roadway between the tents, throwing red light on the tents, on the straight clean trunks of the trees, against the bowed dark figures of the men. Colin thought of a picture he had once seen of Valley Forge. A ragged army huddled around its fires, but without the stacked rifles, with the soft, insidiously cold rain instead of snow.

He went down into the camp and stood near one of the fires. He did not know any of the men around it, but one of them turned and said to him: "You were one of the straw-bosses, weren't you? What are you doing here?"

Colin hesitated, started to say something, but the man had already turned away. There was strong heat from the fires and the woolen clothing of the men steamed. They were talking of what was going to happen, whether the police would come in, whether they should go out quietly or make a stand.

Colin went on to the next fire. Again he knew none of the men except by sight and again one of them turned and questioned him. "Christ, I thought you guys had all pulled out. You was one of the pushes, wasn't you?"

Colin wanted to say that he was only a broad-axe man, not a push, but again the man wasn't really interested and turned quickly back to the group about the fire.

At the third fire he recognized several men of his own crew. Mel Ross was there and Olaf and Charlie Merck. They seemed better organized than the other groups. Mel Ross was controlling the talk and they were planning almost carefully what they would do. Ross said: "We got to have a fund if we're going to get any place. Most everybody's got a few bucks. We ought to be able to collect enough so as we can at least hang together when we hit town."

He noticed Colin then. "Where in hell did you come from, Ensley? Thought you pulled out hours ago."

"I came back," Colin said simply.

"Better pull out again," Ross said. "A job's a job these days. If the higher-ups ever get wise to you being with us guys you won't last long."

Charlie Merck waved his arms foolishly. "The guy's a stool-pigeon," he said. "Throw him out."

Without looking at him or raising his voice Ross said: "Shut up, Charlie."

Colin felt a hand on his arm, looked round and saw Olaf. Olaf drew him quietly a little way away from the group. "Mel's right," he said. "You've got a job and you may as well hang on to it."

"I haven't got any job," Colin said. "Not that I know of, except in this camp."

"They'll put you on somewhere else if you keep your nose clean. Why did you come back?"

"I figured I might be able to help out."

"Forget it," Olaf said. "There ain't nothing to help. Never was much and she's balled up for fair now."

"Then why don't you pull out?"

"That's different. I been in on it from the start. There's nothing you could do but tag along and likely they wouldn't even let you do that."

Colin looked towards the fire again. "Doesn't make much sense," he said. "Not any of it. Seems like every time you get started on something it runs right out on you."

"You'll be O.K.," Olaf said. He held out his hand. "So long, kid. Be seeing you some place."

Colin climbed the hill very slowly. When he reached the last place from which he could see the fires below him he stopped and sat watching for a long while. It was still raining and he could feel wetness spreading through the worn place in the shoulder of his mackinaw, but he paid no attention to it. The little dark figures moved about below and kept the fires burning brightly. Alone on the hill, Colin knew that Olaf was right. He didn't belong there and there was nothing he could have done.

LATE in the afternoon of the day after he left camp Colin saw a man walking down the road past the farm. The man's walk was queer and awkward, almost staggering, and Colin walked out towards the road to meet him. As the hunched, shambling figure came closer he recognized Charlie Merck and called to him. Merck stopped, stared blankly for a moment, then started jerkily forward. Colin saw that his clothes were torn and wet; he had no hat and his wavy blond hair was dankly tangled and full of fir and hemlock needles. He began talking excitedly when he was still several yards away.

"Christ," he said. "I'm all in. Jesus, I've had a terrible trip. Been in the brush all night and all day. There's wild animals up there. Jesus, I might've been lost and never come out."

"You better come in and get something to eat," Colin said.

"Food? Christ I ain't eaten since noon yesterday." He peered behind him, back along the road, moving his head sharply from side to side. "They come down yet? They gone by here?"

"Who?" Colin asked him.

"The boys. The boys from camp. They gone by yet?" There was a look of terror in the blue eyes that shifted from the road to Colin's face and back to the road again. There was terror, violence, fear of violence in the hunched body and the jerking arms.

"They went down by the main road two or three hours ago. They'll be out to the wharf by now."

Merck's body relaxed instantly and the fear died away from his face. "Let me at that grub," he said. "Christ, what I been through." Following Colin along the roadway to the house, he still talked. "I got ten bucks. I'm O.K. Got it out of the collection we took up last night. They'll never miss it."

Colin turned on him sharply. "You what?"

"Grabbed off ten bucks from the collection. It won't do them no good. A guy's got to look after himself, ain't he?" Suddenly he stared hard at Colin. "Christ, you was up there, wasn't you?

Sure you was. I seen you. Don't you tell them guys nothing. Christ, they'd kill me." The terror was back on him, jerking his neck and his arms to violent movement again. "Christ, I'd better get out of here."

Colin felt a revulsion that turned him sick, but he said: "Come on, you eat fast, then get the hell out."

Martha was in the kitchen and Colin told her only that Merck had been lost on his way down from camp. She cooked bacon and eggs and coffee and Merck swallowed them hungrily and nervously. He got up from the table immediately he was finished and went quickly to the door. Colin followed him. Outside he stopped and suddenly thrust his face towards Colin, drawing his lips back from his teeth.

"Can you see I been eating? I got to get back with them guys. I wouldn't want them to know I been eating."

"You're O.K.," Colin said. "Nobody could tell anything. You'd do better to worry about the money you stole."

"That's why I got to get back. They'll never know the difference just so I keep with them till they hit town. I gotta be going."

Colin watched the hunched form stumble down the wagon road and finally disappear from sight in the direction of Blenkinstown. When he went back into the kitchen Martha looked anxiously at his face.

"What did he say to you? He was a horrible man. Was he threatening you about something?"

"No," Colin said. "Nothing like that. But he wasn't much good."

"Sit down," Martha said. "I'll make more coffee. You look as if you need it."

LATER the same evening Colin went to see Mildred Hanson. His mind was a confusion of thought and sensation so oppressive that he wanted the calmness of Mildred's voice and face and body as he had never wanted anything before. It seemed to him completely natural to go to her and he wondered only for a moment why he had not gone long before, when he first came back from the prairies.

There was a light in the cottage and she came to the door as soon as he knocked. She was as beautiful as he remembered her, as cool and golden and clear as he had known she would be. She recognized him without surprise, but her face softened instantly in a smile that reached out to him as plainly as the little gesture of her hands. "Why, Colin," she said. "How nice."

He knew as he followed her in that she was alone. The room was little changed and for a moment he felt himself a schoolboy again. There was pleasure in the feeling, so intense that he felt sudden tears in his eyes. He sat down and Mildred said gently: "It's been a long time, Colin. It's terribly good to see you again."

"I didn't come before," he said. "I know I should have. I'm sorry."

"I wanted you to come," she was standing beside the chair, looking down at him. "I told Margaret."

Colin looked straight in front of him at the fire. "I was afraid you would have changed," he said. "I didn't think it could ever be the way it was before I left."

Her right hand moved quickly towards him, but did not touch him. "I know. It was my fault. But I couldn't tell you—I had to leave you free. And I was afraid, too." Her hand moved again and touched his shoulder. "But it is the same, darling. It is the same if you still want it to be."

Colin stood up and they looked at each other and smiled. He saw that she was almost crying and drew her to him and kissed her, very gently because he was still afraid and unbelieving. But she held her body hard against him and forced her lips against his. In a little while she said: "We aren't easy people, are we, darling?"

"I'm not," he said. "Not even for myself. I came to tell you I'm going away again."

He felt her fingers grip his arm, but she nodded calmly. "I think I knew that," she said and drew gently away from him.

For a while they talked easily. Colin felt the strained confusion of his mind yielding to her calmness, but all the while a new tension was growing in him, of blood and muscle and feeling. She went into the kitchen to make coffee and he got up to pile wood on the fire. When she came back he sat on the floor beside her

204

chair as he had the last time he was there, and after a little while she reached up and switched out the single light.

"Go on talking," she said softly. "Tell me everything that has happened. More about the prairies and Curly and Joe Pauluk. Tell me what you thought, as well as what you did."

Colin told her. She prompted him occasionally with questions and whenever she did so he knew that her soft full-throated voice stirred his body even while it calmed his mind and freed his words.

She said at last: "You've seen so many of the things I hoped you would. Don't they all begin to mean something to you?"

"Yes," Colin said slowly. "Things mean something. Places mean something. It's people that are hard to understand. You can't ever be safe with them."

"You've been with some fine people," she said. But she thought: that's what he's been telling me over and over again, not in plain words but in the things he has told most intensely. People are afraid, people are violent, people hurt you, people mean to hurt you; they like hurting you and there is no shelter from them except in being alone or in finding just one person that you know and love. He has learned so much, yet he has learned almost nothing because he still doesn't know how to protect himself from the Tod Phallings, from stupid policemen, from the hard, mean things that happen to everyone.

"I don't belong anywhere," Colin said. "Most people have their own way of living and it fits them. Even Curly has his way and it works."

"You're still very young," Mildred said. "No one's life comes ready-made. You'll find yours and be happy in it." Why do I tell him that? Am I afraid of what I've done to him, afraid that I've taught him to want something big without showing him how to find it? I've tried to show him and a teacher can only do so much; the rest has to come in other ways.

"I'm not unhappy," Colin said. He turned round and took her hand in his. "When I'm with you I know what I have to do and how I have to do it. When I go away I sometimes forget, but if you've once known you can't really forget, can you? It's always there, just lost for a little while."

"Yes," she said. "It's always there, in you and through you and part of you. It can only die if you make it die."

She bent her head a little towards him as she spoke and the light of the fire shone on her pale hair. He reached up and touched the shine. "I love you," he said. "I can't make that die. I tried once and only made it more alive."

Mildred saw the words like sun on morning mist, moving and beautiful before her, veiling everything except themselves. *You've tried.* Oh, my darling, who was she and what did she do to you, what has she made you? Colin stood up and raised her to him. She kissed him with the straining desire that her calm mind had held back through the years. She felt the hardness of his body and the power of his arms and then, while she still sought him, her mind took charge again. He is full man now, she thought, and I am a woman, not a teacher. He needs me, not for always, but now, tonight. My body can give him a strength that my mind has never given him.

He held her away from him and looked down at her, as he had the night before he went away. "You're like a stream in the mountains," he said. "Everything about you is beautiful. You mustn't send me away again."

She moved towards him, her head thrown back, her wide eyes at once bold and afraid. Her heart longed to hold his head to her breast, to cry tears over him and whisper: "Poor Colin." But her body moved to him as to a lover, freely and boldly. It was her mind's decision and her body's choice: not to mother, not to teach, but to love.

IT was very dark and Colin knew he had not slept. Something like sleep had held his body still and rested it while his mind raced with thought and wonder. He could still feel the straining arch of his stomach muscles and the clean emptiness of his body. So much was washed away, so many days and nights of throttled desire and starved fantasy. The unexplained things seemed suddenly clear, so many of the hard things seemed small and unimportant.

Her quiet hand was in his and he could hear her even breathing beside him; he thought she was asleep. There was no hurt or confusion for him even in remembering that she had cried. She had said: "Will you believe in me now? Does this tell you how I love you?" and the urgency of her voice had made her tears not sorrow but triumph. Even while she was speaking she held him close to her, so that he could feel her love's rejection of every fear and restraint that had ever come between them.

Later, more calmly, she had said: "It's still true that I'm not right for you, darling. I mustn't ever try to hold you." And he had taken her to him again then, more boldly and surely than before, to bury the meaning of the words beyond reach or remembrance.

Colin freed his hand from hers and sat up very quietly in the darkness. She stirred beside him, instantly, and he sat without breathing, hoping she would not wake. But she said: "Are you going away now, Colin?"

"Yes," he said and the finality of the word kept them both very still in the darkness.

Mildred's head was turned towards him and her eyes strained to find some shadow of him against the blackness. I must let him go freely, she thought; I must not cling or cry or do anything to weaken what has happened. I must be generous with him and honest with myself. Whatever I have given him is no more than I have taken from him. I have no more right to hold him now than I had a few hours ago—or a few years ago, when he was still a schoolboy. But this time I must not turn him away. He told me that. He said: You mustn't send me away again.

"Colin," she said.

"Yes."

"You're going to the lake?"

"Yes," he said again.

"You'll have to come out quite often, won't you?"

"Every two or three months, maybe."

He heard her body move and felt her head on his arm. "You know now it can't change," she said. "I can't take myself away from you. So you must come, always, whenever it is."

He leaned back and kissed her and their bodies touched; but he did not hold her. He felt her draw away and he stood up.

She said quietly: "I can make breakfast for you. I can be very quick."

"No," he said. "I don't need anything." He wanted to hurry, to be away from her sharply and clearly, with only this quiet darkness coming after his memory of her.

She came to the door with him when he was ready to go and stopped him there and kissed him and said quietly: "Good-by, Colin." But still there was only darkness. Even the faint gray of the rainy dawn to come was not yet visible over the mountains in the east.

PART FIVE

THE GULLY

2 5

THE whole of July had been very hot, with strong north-westerly winds, and the sky had been full of the smoke of big fires though there was no fire in the green timber around the lake. Robbie had come down from his mineral claims in the hills and Johnny Harris, seeing smoke at Robbie's cabin, had come up the lake to fetch Colin. Now they were all three together at Robbie's and it was a quiet evening under the smoke haze, so they sat on Robbie's new front porch to watch the strange red sun burn its way out of sight in the west.

They were used to each other now, very sure of each other, and they did not talk much. It was over eighteen months since Colin had come into the lake and in that time he had been outside about half-a-dozen times, never for more than a day or two. He had built himself a good cabin at Amabilis Creek and two shelter cabins farther up the valley, along his lines; and he had added the long porch to the front of Robbie's cabin.

Robbie moved in his chair and reached behind him for his tobacco can. "We'd be fighting fire right now if we was outside," he said. "Pushing shovels and axes on some goddamned fire trail."

"No ranger will ever come back here to pick us up," Johnny said.

"No," Robbie agreed. Then his tone changed to the protective, fatherly reproof he liked to use towards the two younger men. "But we could have a fire of our own some day. We'd be out fighting then."

Colin listened idly. Under the smoke the lake was less beautiful than usual, but it was quiet; and smoke haze lay along the· deep valleys and the red light of the sun came along the lake to where their three canoes were pulled up on Robbie's beach. The lake had been good to him, as he had known it would be, and now Amabilis Valley was his and he was making the high mountains along both sides of it and at the head his own also. He claimed to be prospecting when he went into the mountains, but the claim deceived no one and Robbie and Johnny often kidded him about it. He laughed and said little when they did so. He had never explained, even to himself, what it was that he looked for in the mountains. Not just Tom Hughes, though Tom Hughes was part of it and had been ever since Andrew Grant had described his death in Windstorm Gap. The absorbing effort of climbing, power of lungs, power of legs and back and arms, utter confidence in the whole working of his body; the clean, windy space of the high country. And sense of possession. Perhaps that above all.

Colin was conscious of the radio only when Robbie reached over and shut it off. A man talking. The news. Robbie always listened to the news.

"They're going to have another war," Robbie said. "It's a worse mess over there every time you listen to it."

"They'll work it out some way," Johnny said. "They learned enough last time not to try it again."

"Don't you think it," Robbie told him. "The only way they'll ever stop that Hitler guy is with guns."

"What does he want now?" Colin asked.

"Just one more country is all," Robbie said. "And then another after that."

"Only part of it," Johnny said. "And he's got some claim on that."

"Part now and the rest later," Robbie said. "Them Huns ain't changed a damn bit."

Colin had heard Robbie talk that way before and had discounted it as the bitterness of an old soldier. Tonight, for the first time, some urgency of conviction in Robbie's words impressed him.

"Will Canada be in it?" he asked.

Robbie got up and walked to the railing of the porch. Colin watched his sharp-boned body, dark against the light surface of the lake. "The whole world'll be in it," Robbie said. "It'll be like the last one only worse. You boys'll see it, that's sure. I don't know but what I'm pretty near young enough myself."

"I'll believe it when I do see it," Johnny said and they sat in silence again. Colin tried to think of war, of wearing a uniform, carrying a rifle to kill men, going overseas to fight. It was not easy; he realized he had never seen a soldier. They wouldn't want us guys from back in the sticks anyway, he thought. They wouldn't even know about us. Poor old Robbie, it's just that he can't ever forget about that last war.

Later in the evening, when Johnny had gone out of the cabin for a little while, Robbie told Colin casually: "I saw your sister when I was outside last week."

"How was she?" Colin asked. "O.K.?"

"Sure. She said to tell you to go see your mother next time you're out."

"Marge said that?" Colin's shoes rasped against the floor as he moved in his chair.

"You ain't been going," Robbie said calmly. "She said that too. I was to tell you from me, not her. Only I figured you'd know who was back of it anyways."

Colin felt anger hot in his face. They could mind their own

business, he thought, both of them. But his anger was weak, not strong; ashamed, not proud. "I guess I should have gone more often," he said. "But I don't stay out there long. You know that."

Robbie's voice was still casual. "There's nobody driving you back." Then his tone changed. "Listen, son. A man's only got one mother and he don't have her here as long as he figures he's going to. You'll be sorry all your life if you let some slip of a girl come between you and her."

Johnny came back into the cabin then and Robbie asked Colin: "You seen any big old billy goats up in the hills lately?"

Colin steadied his voice with an effort. "Sure," he said. "There's two or three dandies up in the Gully. Why?"

"I'd like to get me some cooking fat against the winter."

"What's the matter with bear fat?"

"I'd sooner have goat, for a change. Ain't had goat fat around for years."

"I heard you say that once before," Johnny said. "Thought you were kidding."

"You shoot yourself an old billy in September and you'll see what I mean," Robbie said. "Pick out a big one, Colin, and you'll have yourself a dandy rug for that cabin of yours."

"O.K.," Colin said. "I'll look around next time I get up to the Gully."

COLIN had been camped in the Gully for two days. It was September and he had come to hunt Robbie's goat, but he had done no hunting yet. On the first day he had climbed up to Windstorm Gap, sure of it now that he had searched and rejected half-a-dozen other high passes out of the Gully. He had been there before but had never been far enough through. This time he went on and found the exposed ledge on which Andrew Grant and the Hughes brothers had waited out the night all those years ago. There was a faint powdering of snow on the ledge already and a hard cold wind was blowing through the gap, in spite of the clear blue sky above and the warm fall sunshine that lay along the Gully behind him and against many of the bare rock faces around him.

The ledge was a dank place that the sun touched only for a short while each day. Rock towered above it on one side in almost sheer climb to a mountain peak; on the other side it sloped gently for fifty or a hundred feet to an overhanging edge that cut away for a thousand feet or more to the start of the Milk River. It wasn't hard to picture that night on the ledge, waist-deep in powdery snow with a fury of wind hurling more and more snow at them through the gap; or the cold, stiff start at the earliest glimmer of the next day's dawn. Colin remembered Grant's words: "Tom was killed almost as soon as we started next day." They would have spent the night close against the rock wall. And gone on from there, wading the soft snow against the driving wind. Colin followed the ledge and found that it tapered in to within ten or fifteen feet of the wall, then straightened out almost suddenly and ran narrowly along it. In the corner, he thought, would have been the overhang. Looking down he could see the drop, almost straight for several hundred feet, then flowing away towards the creek bed through a massive snow-slide.

Lying in his camp near the head of the Gully's two miles of flat green meadow, Colin remembered all this and looked at the rifle that lay near him. It had been a good rifle, the tool of a man who had taken pride in his gear. It was in extraordinarily good shape; the stock was bleached and the barrel was rusted, but it was little more than surface rust and the mechanism still worked. There was a small gold plate let into the butt and the initials T. H. were still clear on it. Colin thought it must have been buried until this year, then exposed by the hot weather of July and August. Falling away from the man, it would have driven deeper into the snow bank than his body. For there had been no sign of the body.

The climb down to the slide had been enormously difficult, so difficult that Colin had slept the previous night still a hundred feet or more above it and had not attempted the climb back after finding the rifle, but had worked down the valley and found an easier way. There had been no sign of the body, not even a bone to show that the animals had found it, nor a knife or a waterproof match box to show it had been there. Yet Colin had been quite sure and before starting back he had built a cairn of rocks in a sheltered place near the edge of the slide and had slipped his own metal match box into the heart of the cairn, with Tom Hughes name in it. He had tried to remember whether Grant or Robbie had ever told him the date, but could not so he wrote only: "In September, about 1920."

Sometime this month, around eighteen years ago. Until Tom Hughes fell there no one had ever reached that slide. And from the time he fell until today no one else had been there. Grant said that. Al Hughes wouldn't let them go back; he had said that Tom couldn't be in a better place and wouldn't want to be.

Colin looked about him at the Gully. The level green meadow flowed away from him to the narrow entrance between the high bluffs of the canyon. It was late afternoon and the deer had already come down to feed. The mountains rose sharply and steeply from the meadow, climbing five or six thousand feet to hard, broken peaks. The shoulders of the peaks held high along both sides of the Gully and across the head of it. He could pick out the pass through Windstorm Gap only because he knew where to look for it and even so it looked less like a pass than a high ridge between two peaks. The floor of the Gully was already in shadow, but the sunlight was strong and clear on the face of the mountains beyond the meadow, where the slopes were more gradual and multiplied the Gully's width. They were hard rock slopes, Colin knew, rising in bluffs and benches and ledges, endlessly and massively broken, never easy for long; yet walking country rather than climbing country, with plenty of browse for goats and deer, and berry-grown slides for the bears. He could see the goats, far above him, tiny white dots that moved. There were two almost on the route he had followed down and he wondered what they would make of his scent.

He got up from his blankets and began to build a small fire to cook supper. Walking down to the creek for water he saw that a mist was starting up out in the meadow and he stood a moment to watch the brown shapes of the deer in it and against it. She would like this, he thought. I tell her about the mountains and about places I've seen and she listens and listens as though I were saying the most important things in the world. But I don't think she's even been into the mountains, not really into them like this is. I must bring her here and show it to her instead of talking about it.

HE began to hunt early the next morning, working far up towards the head of the Gully, then swinging back along the west side to look for the big goat he had seen there earlier in the year. There was no sun on this day and a sharp wind drew down from the head of the valley, steadily cold on the left side of his face now, and growing stronger.

After nearly two hours of walking and climbing he knew he was in the big goat's country and stopped. His camp at the head of the meadow was almost directly below him; perhaps a thousand, perhaps two thousand feet down. A long way, Colin thought, because these on this side are the high mountains, higher than the mountains at the head of the Gully. He felt the clear, sharp excitement that high places always brought to him, excitement without fear or blame or anxiety. It was living and strong in him today, not because he was hunting but because of Tom Hughes' rifle down there in the camp below him. Colin did not try to understand it or explain it to himself. It seemed to him that he had always known he must find where Tom Hughes had died and that now, having found the place and marked it, the Gully was his and the whole valley was his in a way it never had been before. It was as though some shadowy restraint had dropped away from his mind and he was free to think clearly for the first time in his life.

Possession of the valley had become intensely important to him. It was important that his trap-line was formally registered, with boundary lines that took in the whole watershed from the highest peaks to the edge of the lake. It was important that Robbie and Johnny called it his—"Colin's valley," they said or "Colin's country." But most important of all were the marks he himself had set upon the valley; the big log cabin on the shore of the lake near the mouth of the creek, the two shelter cabins, the occasional blazes along his trap-lines; and beyond even these, the claim he set upon it and constantly renewed, with his feet and the effort of his body as he followed out the creeks and climbed the mountains and hunted the ridges.

He stood up, still looking down at the meadow. He could find his camp-site by the little tongue of timber that ran down a draw and spread out a short way into the meadow, and he knew that he would build another cabin there. Next year, as soon as the melting snow drew back from the meadow.

As he turned away and started up the hill he noticed that the wind was stronger, and gusty. The mountain tops were in the clouds now and snow-squalls swirled here and there about the high slopes. He climbed easily, always across or into the wind, following dry creek beds and narrow rock draws, turning occasionally along the benches. He came into snow and wondered for the first time if he would be able to find the goat. He thought of Robbie's continual warnings about the mountains: "You'll die in them hills if you keep going out there alone. Die of a broken leg, maybe, and take weeks doing it. We won't be able to find you. No one'll know you're missing until it's too late to look, anyway." Even today, in the snow and wind and on the bad slopes the warning did not touch him. He could not feel that he would ever die in the mountains; in the water, perhaps; or among men, riding a freight train, crossing a city street, in Robbie's war. But in the mountains he felt no fear of death. Often one had to travel slowly and carefully and it was hard work. Sometimes one turned back, because a place was impossible, not because it was dangerous. Storms could close in swiftly, shutting out sight with snow and cloud, driving wind and ice against one's body, but they had never seemed unfriendly; one found shelter behind a rock or under an overhang and waited them out.

When he came to the edge of the rock-slide the storm had lessened. The clouds were higher and the snow seemed to drive in narrow belts across the face of the mountain, though the wind was stronger than ever and broken by sudden fierce gusts that tore at his body and lifted the fallen snow to lash it past him like spindrift. The goat would be in shelter, Colin thought, and there was no hope of finding him unless the storm broke up later in the day. But he still worked his way upwards, along the edge of the rock-slide, because it would be better to hunt from above than below if the storm did clear away.

Then he saw the goat. It was straight above him, standing broadside, head towards the wind. The head swung and the short black horns turned directly towards Colin. Colin threw a shell into the breech of his rifle, chose his spot behind the shoulder and fired in the moment the gust came. He saw the goat swing sharply to the shock of the bullet, then driving snow hid everything that was more than fifty feet away.

Colin started up the hill, traveled ten or fifteen feet, then stopped. He knew the goat had not gone down. The bullet had hit him too far back, well behind the heart. It would kill him in the end, but he could carry it, perhaps for many hours and many miles. Colin moved under the sheltered side of a great boulder and waited there. The sudden wind had spoiled the shot, he knew, either by carrying the bullet or by its unexpected pressure on the barrel of his rifle. He saw again the moment before the shot; the bold powerful shape of the goat's great body, long white hair swept by the wind; then the confident turn of the heavy head. He was calm and sure, Colin thought, not afraid. He was living his life and I didn't have to bother him. Now it's all changed because Robbie said half-a-dozen words down at his cabin over a month ago. He's weak and dying and hurt, probably afraid.

In fifteen or twenty minutes Colin went on. The storm had lifted again and the clouds were very high, shredding against the mountain peaks, leaving the lower gaps fully exposed. He found the place where the goat had been standing, saw where the turn of his strong feet had flurried the snow, saw blood there, powdered over with driven snow, but heavy and deep red when he scraped the snow away. He was sure now that the wound was a bad one. The hunt became an obligation, short of the impossibility of atonement, touched with the humility of penance, but touched also by his close share in the life of the valley.

The goat had traveled steadily and easily at first, along the face of the mountain, towards the big lake. There was no blood, but Colin followed the track easily in the light new snow. Then the track turned sharply up a square-sided funnel, a bold narrow crack in the breast of the mountain. It was vigorous flight still, with great leaps; there was no blood and no faltering. Colin moved cautiously and quietly, watching constantly above him, but he had seen no sign of the goat when he came up to the ledge where it had rested. There was blood on the ledge, a heavy clot in the snow, and white hairs on the blood. Colin put his hand down and felt warmth. The track led on up the funnel, but it was less sure now, less bold; and once Colin found the snow sharply stirred and recognized the print of broad knees where the goat had stumbled.

The funnel ended in a short, steep slide of rock little more than a thousand feet below the peak of the mountain. The wind had dropped and the clouds had broken. Colin saw the big lake, still under clouds, far ahead of him and far below him. The meadow was hidden from sight by the slope and jut of the rock he had climbed, but the mountains at the head of the Gully were clear against blue sky.

The track had turned along the face of the mountain again, angling a little down. Colin followed it past the gap, across a deep draw and out on to the slope of the next mountain. The sunlight was bright and warm about him now and the clouds over the lake were breaking up. The track was easy to follow; too easy, Colin thought. He's heading for some place where he knows he'll be safe, where he's been safe before, likely, and knows he can shake off anything that's following him.

He was past the second peak and the next gap was coming into sight around the slope of the mountain. He saw the goat at once and clearly, less than a mile away, close under the rim of the gap. It disappeared as he watched, reappeared almost on the sky-line, then disappeared again. Out of the valley, Colin thought, and into what? Johnny's valley isn't that close down here, it can't be. Into more mountains? He left the track and began to pick his own way to the rim of the gap. An hour later he was in the gap, close under the rim, climbing with his rifle slung over his back.

The climb ended suddenly and Colin found himself in a narrow pass formed between the shoulder of the mountain he had just passed and a long ridge that ran down from the next mountain. The pass angled northward and was so narrow and had such steep sides that it seemed at first almost a tunnel. The goat track led along the floor of the pass, following a clear trail worn into the rock by generations of passing game. Colin glanced upward at the strip of blue sky, then back to the twisting crevice ahead of him. It seemed to him that the floor was as nearly level as anything could be.

He came out suddenly, so suddenly that it seemed that the

2 1 8

world had dropped away from him. The pass ended, broke off altogether, and there was nothing between the few feet of rock in front of him and a great broken mountain peak two or three miles away. He moved forward cautiously and could see the lower slopes of the mountain. Then he was at the edge and could look straight down, thousands of feet to a blue-green lake. Colin forgot the goat, forgot that he was hunting. He was aware of nothing except the tremendous hollow below him and the details that made it. Straight across from him the great mountain stood proudly out from all the other peaks. Along its north shoulder lay a sweep of ice and snow and from this there fell away a heavy stream of water, through fall after fall until it disappeared in the narrow belt of timber around the lake, then reappeared in a clouded semi-circle that spread out from the lake's edge into the blue-green. The lake itself was nearly two miles long, roughly oval in shape, filling most of the length and breadth of the floor of the hollow. There were tall mountains again on either side of the main peak, and tall cliffs barred the foot of the lake except where a thin dark line showed a high-walled canyon outlet. The roar of the falls opposite came clearly across to Colin and he could hear behind it the roar of other falls still hidden from him. He thought: no one ever told me about this place. Then: how could they tell me? No one knows except me. It's a lost place, hidden between Johnny's valley and mine. Yet it's part of my valley. This is the creek that runs in just below Amabilis Lake, the one I followed out to the high falls in the smooth rock I couldn't climb.

He thought of the goat again and looked quickly down at the trail to make sure he had passed that way. The track was clear right out to the break-off. Colin went forward and saw at once a broad ledge trail angling steeply down into the hollow. It was clear and smooth for as far as he could see, evenly covered with fresh snow; but its start was still hidden by the sloping rock shoulder to the left of him. He lay down at full length and slid his head and shoulders forward over the break-off, rifle ready in his left hand. There was a rock ledge four or five feet below him, then a gap of six or eight feet, then the start of the ledge trail. The goat's tracks were plain on the first little ledge, and the snow was torn and tossed on the other side of the gap, where the trail

219

started. That was all. Colin looked down into the sheer drop under the gap in the ledge. Tiny and far down, a square of white against a gigantic wall of black rock, he could see the goat. How it was lodged he couldn't tell, but the wall of rock seemed to run on far past it, perpendicularly and smoothly, until it eased into a broken slope a few hundred feet back from the edge of the lake.

Colin stood up and dusted the snow from his clothing. He knew the goat was dead and knew almost certainly that he could never reach it. But the hollow in the mountains and the hidden lake were his, more surely his than any other part of Amabilis Valley. He stepped forward and dropped down to the little ledge under the break-off. There he turned, balanced a moment, and jumped where the goat had failed. By nightfall he was camped in the timber at the edge of the hidden lake.

2 6

COLIN lived very simply in his valley, buying only essentials like flour and oatmeal and salt, hunting all his meat, growing a garden in the summer time, constantly learning new ways of preserving and storing food. But fur prices were low in those years and he had to work steadily on his traps through the season to make the money he needed.

He usually spent at least five nights of each week up the valley, working out over his lines from the shelter cabins, but he tried always, as did Robbie and Johnny Harris, to get down to his main cabin on Saturday night and stay there until Monday morning. The three of them had agreed on this mainly as a safety precaution; it meant that they had a rough weekly check of each other's whereabouts and could leave messages with a fair certainty of when they would be found. Colin found that he liked the arrangement and seldom failed in it.

Although he was little conscious of his body's discomfort when he was in the shelters or out along the lines, he liked the warmth and space and solidity of the big cabin, and he liked also the company of his few possessions—some books, the canoe paddles and the fish-pole standing in the corner, the photograph of Mildred he kept hidden behind the books on their shelf, spare packboards and snowshoes that he had made at different times, Tom Hughes' rifle resting on a special shelf he had built for it under the books.

He came down to the cabin one Saturday night in January of the year after he had found the hidden lake. It was dark when he arrived and it was a bad night, with a gale of wind from the south and cold heavy rain down at the lake, though it had been snowing farther up the valley. He built a fire in the stove and lit his two lamps and the cabin seemed immediately warm and friendly. He set one of the lamps in the window that faced on the lake, more from habit than anything else, because there was no chance that it would be visible from Johnny's place through the storm, and there wasn't the least reason to suppose that either Johnny or Robbie would come up the lake until the next day—and only then if the storm had died down during the night.

After he had eaten supper Colin lay down on the bed to read, but in a little while he put the book aside and simply lay there, watching the red-gold light of his lamps on the ceiling and listening to the drive of the storm outside. He had built the cabin very solidly and very carefully, and he could feel the strength of his craftsmanship in the way it stood against the storm, without creak or tremor, without the slightest draught or any feeling of dampness inside it. The walls were of clear cedar logs, peeled and carefully matched, faced on the inside and with a lining of cedar panels split from fine-grained old-growth trees. The floor was a double thickness of two-inch planks, closely laid and perfectly smooth. The whole building was twenty feet square, divided into three rooms, but Colin used only the big main room that ran along the full length of the side towards the lake.

Colin had taken most of his first summer on the lake to build the cabin and it seemed to him now that he had always known exactly where and how he would build it. It was in the small curving bay just below the mouth of Amabilis Creek, where he and Robbie had eaten supper and looked down the lake that evening during his summer with Grant. But it was well inside the bay, set fifteen or twenty feet above the lake on an easy slope under the trees. It was within sound of the creek, yet in less than ten minutes from it he could climb to four or five hundred feet and find his way back into the mountains without ever touching the valley floor again.

All through the careful building of the cabin he had thought of Mildred. He planned and built not as though she were going to live in it but as though she were watching, approving or disapproving. Often it seemed to him that he lived his whole life on that basis; not as though she shared it or were ever likely to share it, but as though it were dedicated to her, and received in return her spiritual presence. There was satisfaction in the dedication, live, positive, almost physical satisfaction that gave a sense of purpose to everything he did.

Now, lying on the bed, isolated by the sound of the storm, he used her again, imagining her in the room, moving about in it, noticing things, changing things, talking to him, making him talk as she did at the cottage. The picture was clear and convincing, easy to accept until he turned his mind fully upon it. Then it became blocked and clouded by problems and difficulties.

He remembered how happily she had gone down to stay with Carol Maxwell in California during the summer. "I have to go," she had said. "I have to study down there." But he had known she wanted to go and had felt again his old dislike for the hold that Carol had on her. Yet he knew how weak was his own claim to her. It existed only in loving her and in what she would concede to his love. She still said sometimes: "I'm too old for you, Colin." And the last time he was with her she had said: "I'm not good for you, darling. Some of it is right and good, but it isn't really right—for either of us." After they had been together for a few hours she would nearly always say something of this sort, something that broke in upon their closeness and held him away from her.

For a moment he became conscious again of the lamplight on the ceiling and the sound of the storm outside the cabin. It had been more difficult, he thought, since Margaret had come into it all. First there had been the message through Robbie. Then Colin had seen her in Blenkinstown. She had asked at once: "Where have you been this time?"

"I saw Mother yesterday," he said defensively.

"For an hour or two. You wouldn't even stay for supper. I know—I was out there today."

"I had to see Earl Mayhew," he said. "And get my stuff down to the wharf."

"Of course," she said. "You have so many important things to do. But you might show Mother a little consideration. And the rest of the family, for that matter. You haven't been near Clyde and me since you first went up to the lake. And it isn't very nice for us to have the whole town talking about you."

"There isn't anything to talk about."

"There'll be plenty, if you keep on the way you are now. You ought to think of Mildred's side, too. No schoolteacher can stand that sort of thing."

He had known then that she was saying much more than she knew and had sensed a dishonesty in her purpose. But she was still the stronger and there was little he could find to say.

Later, she had gone to see Mildred and they had quarreled. Mildred would not talk freely about it, but Colin knew it had hurt her and made her miserable.

Lying on the bunk, Colin let himself feel the bitterness of the quarrel with Margaret and searched faithfully through all the thoughts that came to spoil and break the dream. Yet the dream persisted, warm, enfolding, comforting; more like religion, Colin thought, than like being in love; a light and a refuge that he could find again and again as he needed it, here in the cabin, out along the trap-lines, up in the mountains.

He reached a hand towards his book again, checked it as he heard the footsteps on the porch of the cabin. He swung his legs over the side of the bed and crossed the room, to open the outside door. Johnny Harris stood there a moment, shaking water from his clothes, blinking in the light.

"For God's sake, Johnny," Colin said. "I never thought you'd be up on a night like this."

Johnny came in without smiling. "I took a chance you'd be down tonight. It got so I just couldn't wait till tomorrow."

"You're crazy," Colin said. "You'll drown yourself if you take chances like that."

Johnny began stripping off his wet clothes. "It wasn't so bad as I thought it would be. Not so dark and not so rough, and the wind was mostly back of me."

Colin opened a cupboard and brought out a rum bottle. "This ought to help a little. I'll make some coffee to go with it."

Johnny stood holding his hands out over the stove. "I quarreled with Robbie," he said.

Colin checked a spoonful of coffee over the open pot. "With Robbie? What in hell over?"

"Over his goddamned war. He's gone bugs about it. Can't ever seem to talk about anything else."

Colin laughed. "That's not so new it ought to bring you up the lake in this weather. Robbie'll get over it. So'll you."

"It's not that," Johnny said. "I'm just not built for this kind of life. I've got to pull out. Go somewhere else, get a job where I see some people. I don't see how you stand it away up here on your own. At least Robbie and I are close enough to keep some track of each other. You never see anybody at all."

"It just means I've got no one to fight with," Colin said.

Johnny laughed, a little ashamed. "We didn't fight. Just got kind of sore at each other and said things we didn't mean."

"What does Robbie want you to do? Go off and join the army so you'll be all ready if his war comes?"

"You'd think so, to hear him talk. He'll say: 'Young fellows like you and Colin ain't got no business burying yourselves away up here. You should be out where things are happening.' On and on like that, generally because I don't pay attention to his goddamned radio."

"Why don't you stay out of his way for a while?" Colin filled two cups with coffee and poured a good shot of rum into each.

"I guess I could do that," Johnny said. "Trouble is I think old Robbie's got something. That's why I get sore at him, I guess. All that stuff that's going on over there, killing Jews and taking over countries that don't want to be taken over. Seems like a

224

person ought to do something more than just sit back and listen to the radio."

"It's a long way away," Colin said. "They've always had troubles over there. It isn't right, but they always have. I don't see you can help any by going outside."

Johnny drained his cup and refilled it. "What do we do up here, anyway, except kill a few little animals and skin them? What sense does it make, any of it?"

"Buys our grub," Colin said. "And there's nobody riding us."

"You stay up all summer too. You cut trails and build cabins and go off in the mountains by yourself. What does it get you?"

"What does any job get you?" You find the hills, Colin thought, you find the hidden lake. You see things and think things and learn things. He knows all that as well as I do. And the things that happen outside and make you sick at your stomach don't happen in here. You don't even have to think about them. He said: "I guess it depends some on what you want. If you want something different from this you have to go out and get it."

"Sure I want something different. I want to get married some-time and raise a family, like ordinary people. You couldn't do that in here. Hell, you never even see a woman in here."

"No," Colin said slowly. "I guess it wouldn't be easy. I guess people have got married and raised families on trap-lines. But I never heard of any."

"I wouldn't try it. Nor would you. You don't give a damn about women though. Don't you ever figure you'll want a family some day?"

"Sure," Colin said. "I think about it." It seemed strange to realize that Johnny knew nothing of Mildred. "I'll get me a farm some day and raise a family. There's not all that much of a hurry." He filled a plate with food he had been cooking and set it in front of Johnny, then sat down opposite him. "What's the real trouble, Johnny? Something's got you all het up. You didn't come all this way up the lake on such a lousy night just to tell me you want to get married."

Johnny put down the fork he had just picked up. "No," he said. "That's right I didn't. I came up because I darn near

225

killed poor old Robbie tonight. If I hadn't got out of there I would have."

Colin felt a shock that was like pain through his body. He stood up sharply. "Is he O.K.? What did you do? Hit him?"

"No. Nothing like that. I didn't touch him. I just wanted to kill him, wanted to so darn hard I had to get away so I wouldn't do it. That's how I know I'm no good for this kind of life."

Colin sat down again. Johnny wouldn't ever kill anybody, he thought; he wouldn't even hurt anybody. But I guess it's pretty near as bad for some people to think anything that hard. "Listen, Johnny," he said. "You wouldn't ever hurt him. You might think you would, but you wouldn't."

"Yes, I would, if I got to feeling the way I felt tonight. That's what happens to guys back in the bush like this. They go bugs and kill each other."

"Not guys like you and me and Robbie. We might think it just for a minute, but we'd never do it. All you need is a change. Stick around here for a couple of days, then go down and pick up your traps and get the hell outside for a while. You can take a look around and get to feeling better and likely as not you'll be all set to go again by next fall."

Johnny leaned back in his chair and looked down at the table. "I believe I'll do that. It might help a whole lot. I'd hate to quit the lake for keeps, but I could take a while out. I could even miss a season or two and still come back."

"If you don't get married," Colin said and laughed.

COLIN had finished his cabin in the Gully and was carving carefully on the smooth face of the log over the doorway: "Colin Ensley. 23rd September 1939."

Although it had been hard to find materials at the high elevation, this was the best finished of all his cabins, smaller than the one at the beach, but of yellow cedar logs instead of red, the logs flattened on three sides and so closely fitted that he had not needed to chink them anywhere. He had pitched the roof very steeply and built a vertical shaft down to the doorway so that it would be open to him in any depth of snow. Two windows looked down the length of the meadow, a third at the back opened towards the peaks above Windstorm Gap; floor and ceiling and the insides of the walls were patterned with different woods, pine and yew, yellow and red cedar, hemlock and maple, all hewn or adzed to smoothness.

Colin wondered what Will Ensley would think of it. He would scoff at the frills, Colin thought, quote a text on vanity, perhaps be really angry at the wasted effort; Colin remembered his contempt for some of the more intricate work they had done in the forestry camp. But he would recognize the craftsmanship, the planning and fitting and careful use of the different woods, and probably admit it, however grudgingly. He would be right to be grudging because nothing in his conception of things would justify the cabin. It did not fit in with the trap-lines or with essential hunting or any clearly practical activity. It could have been as warmly and solidly built of far simpler materials in a fraction of the time. There was not even the justification of craftsmanship, because that could have been as sure and finished with any plan and any materials.

Yet Colin knew he had found complete absorption in the work, as he found now a lively satisfaction in setting his signature upon it by the careful carving of the inscription. And he knew also that there was reason and logic in building it here and building it with the care he had used. Whether there was need to or not he expected to travel and hunt the slopes and peaks of the Gully, to the last slide, the last draw, the last creek bed, the smallest cleft in the rocks. From this cabin the Gully was his, in spring or summer or fall or winter, whenever he chose to come up to it. The cabin marked his possession, would be there to mark it beyond his lifetime; it extended the meaning of the cabin he had built at the lake through the whole length of the valley and with that it extended his dedication.

He left the cabin the day after he had completed the carving, turning at the foot of the meadows to look back and see it dwarfed by the great peaks, a tiny human sign at the point of the long tongue of dark timber that sloped down the draw and touched the head of the meadow. He looked up the broken slope above the timber, searched among the peaks and found the gap through which he had followed the goat into his hidden lake. He had climbed through the gap and down to the lake three times now and each time had learned a little more of the valley. Little stunted deer lived in its shelter, goats came down into it and the bear had found it. There were fish in the deep lake and berries on the slopes and it was very hot there in the summer when the sun climbed high over the peaks and blazed down into it. Even in winter, he judged, it would be windless and almost warm, though the snow would pile deeply over the meadows around the lake. So far he had never climbed to the Gap in winter and he knew that the way down the ledge trail would be hard and dangerous in deep snow. Standing now at the foot of the meadow in the Gully, looking back at his new cabin, he knew he would build again sooner or later by the hidden lake. And he would find a winter way into the lake, either by the Gap or over the smooth rock that had turned him back at the falls.

At the beach cabin Colin found Robbie's note. "The war's on," it read. "Better come down the lake soon as you get out. Johnny's gone down to enlist." Colin read the words and tried to place them in his life. The thought of war, of his own country in war, was not so strange and remote as it had seemed a year ago. He knew the broad issues and understood them; the war was still a long way away, but the shadow of it was a dark and menacing thing from which there was no safe withdrawal. Robbie had been right after all, Colin thought: they would want men, every man would have a place, even men like himself and Curly and Johnny Harris. Johnny had gone already.

He looked around at the cabin and thought of the valley behind it. They would never come here. He tried to think of war, of men being shot as deer are shot, of bombs and planes and great guns, of men dying and struggling and dying. That part seemed remote, so far beyond imagination that he could see no place in it for himself. One went with other men, in crowds and masses, and was little noticed. But he could not find himself in the crowds. Robbie will know, he thought; he's been through it once. He crumpled the note in his hand and went out of the cabin to launch his canoe.

COLIN stood in front of the desk and listened to the officer. Slowly he realized that he was being rejected, as Johnny Harris had been, thanked for offering his services, something about medical category, not your fault, just a tough break.

"You mean I'm not fit?" he asked.

"The medicals say you've got flat feet," the officer told him. "They won't take any chances on those things. It's too bad. I'm sorry."

"I can walk all day," Colin said.

The officer smiled and shrugged his shoulders, then stood up and held out his hand. Colin took it, turned away and went out.

It was September of 1940, nearly a year after he had come down the valley to find Robbie's note. He had not tried to enlist then. When he got to Robbie's cabin he found Johnny Harris already back there, rejected because the arm he had broken playing ball had been badly set. That had tempered Robbie's advice to Colin. "No hurry," he had said. "It must be they don't want men. But they will, you see. This thing won't be over in a few months. You'll get your chance and so will Johnny."

Johnny had been upset at being turned down. He wanted no more of the outside world and was glad to go back to his trap-line in Carlson's Valley. Colin went back to his own valley and stayed there as he had before. But through the summer of 1940 the valley seemed to lose its power over him and he found it more and more difficult to stay away from Robbie and the news that poured in over the old battery radio. In the end he had gone down to enlist. It had not occurred to him that he would be rejected and Robbie had never suggested the possibility. Now there was nothing to do but go back, as Johnny had.

He stayed a night at the farm on his way through Blenkinstown. When he told Martha what had happened, she said: "I'm sorry, if that was what you wanted. But I'm glad you don't have to go."

"It doesn't seem to make any sense," Colin said. "Getting turned down for bad feet when you can walk all day and all night." But he knew now that he hadn't wanted to go, that he was glad to be back, on his way to the lake, instead of being taken up into the life he had seen about him at the recruiting center.

"What are you going to do now?" Martha asked.

"Go back to the valley," he said. "It's pretty nearly time to get the lines ready again."

"You're happy there, aren't you?"

Colin noticed, as he had so many times, how warmly blue and intensely alive her eyes were. But it seemed to him that her voice was strained and tired, slower and softer than usual. He wondered if she knew about Mildred and thought she did not, in spite of what Margaret had said. And if she did know she would feel about it as she felt about the valley, would say in her heart almost the same thing.

He remembered her question. "Yes," he said. "I like it fine up there. There's room to fall all over myself and nobody knows the difference."

He went down to the village early next morning to buy supplies and load his canoe. As he came out of the store he noticed a man in uniform standing by the wharf. The man turned towards him and he recognized Tod Phalling. Tod held out a hand and smiled. Looking into the pale eyes Colin felt an echo of the old fear, but Tod was friendly.

"Sure is good to see an old-timer around," he said. "I was beginning to think there was none left."

"Johnny Harris is up at the lake with us," Colin said.

"There's a guy in the unit knows you—Curly Blake."

"Sure," Colin said eagerly. "I traveled with Curly pretty near two years. How's he making out?"

"Curly's a good soldier. He's doing O.K." Tod looked at Colin's clothes, the stagged raintest pants and the woods coat. "You coming in?" he asked.

"I just got back," Colin said. "They turned me down."

"The hell. What was the trouble?"

Colin looked away from the pale eyes. "Medical. They didn't say what." He was remembering Tod's endless taunting of his clumsiness at school.

"That's tough," Tod said. "But they'll ease up. A guy'll have a chance to make it if he really wants to."

Colin looked back to his face again, expecting to find the faintly contemptuous doubt he thought he had heard in his words.

It was not there. "I'd like to get in," Colin said, and in that moment he did want to get in.

"You'll make it, sooner or later. We're due for overseas any time now."

They were still talking when Clyde Munro drove up in the police car. "Your mother's sick," he told Colin. "I was afraid I wouldn't catch up to you. The doctor's there. You'd better let me drive you back."

Martha was in the big bed she had shared all her life with Will Ensley. She was unconscious and her eyes were closed.

"She's had a stroke," the doctor told Colin.

Colin nodded and watched his mother's face. It was peaceful and unmarked and she looked very young. He wanted desperately to see her eyes again, to feel the warmth he always felt from their deep blueness. "Will she be conscious again?" he asked.

The doctor picked up one of the thin wrists and held it in his hand. "We don't know," he said. "She might even get over it. It's hard to tell with these things."

With Margaret, Colin watched Martha through that night and through the next day until Will Ensley came back from his work farther up the coast. Will came silently and hesitantly into the room, stopped at the foot of the bed and stood there with his great head bent a little to look down at Martha's face. He said nothing. There was no text, no word, no prayer, only the sag of the heavy shoulders, the deep lines in the broad face above the graying beard, the tenseness of the huge hands on the rail at the foot of the bed.

Will looked up at last and saw Colin and Margaret. "Has she spoken at all?" His strong voice whispered in the small room and Colin shook his head. "Which is the bad side?" Will asked.

Colin pointed to Martha's left hand and arm. "There," he said. "She can move this arm."

Will came round and stood at the right side of the bed. Colin expected him to kneel or at least speak a prayer, but he only took Martha's hand in his own and bent towards her. She moved then and her eyes opened for a moment and Colin saw the blueness. He felt Margaret move beside him and put out an arm to hold her back.

"Is that you, Will?" Martha said. "I'm glad you're here."

"Yes," Will said. "It's me. Don't try to talk. We're all here with you." He knelt then, still holding her hand, his big body awkward in its grief and fear.

Martha moved her head as though to look for the others, but her eyes did not open again. "Stay with me, Will," she said. "Like this. For a little while."

Colin watched his mother's face and saw the tired lines relax still further until her lips were half-smiling. He knew then that Will's coming had brought the deep peace to her face, that the smile was for him and all the little of her that was left was for him. He turned to Margaret and saw that she too had seen and understood. Without speaking, they went out of the room together.

2 7

SHORTLY after Martha's death, while Colin was still down at the farm, Will got word that his old job was open up at camp.

"Well," he told Colin and Margaret. "They learned it at last."

"Learned what?" Margaret asked him.

"That a buzz-saw won't do the same work as a broad-axe."

"You'll go, won't you?"

Will hesitated, but Colin knew that the pull of the old, known work far outweighed any remnant of pride. Will saw himself again as he had been for so many years, silent, sure, respected in his craft, secure in the scent of cedar and the rustle of chips under his feet. "Well," he said at last. "They've gone to the trouble to send for me. I guess I'll go up there and help out."

Later, when they were alone, Colin asked Margaret: "What about the place?"

"He'll stay here. He told me he would because he knows Mother would want him to."

"He can't stay alone. He'd be better in camp."

"Clyde and I can look after him for a while. What will you do?"

"I'm going back to the lake. I'm late there now."

"Will you try to enlist again? If the war goes on, I mean?"

Colin felt a surge of irritation at the question. "Why should I?" he said. "They've told me once I'm not good enough for them."

WHEN he got back to Amabilis Valley again Colin felt, as he always did, a sense of freedom from everything that had happened outside. It was already late and he had a lot to do to get ready for the season. Through the season he was always busy, traveling his lines swiftly and regularly, running trial lines along ridges and draws in different parts of the valley, checking the movements of game against his experience in other seasons. But in spite of almost steady activity, he could not find the complete absorption and strong happiness he had found in other years.

He had seen Mildred only once since Martha's funeral and they had both been strained and withdrawn, realizing that Martha in death was more decisively between them than she had ever been in life. As he was leaving, Mildred asked: "How soon will you be out again, Colin?"

"I'm not sure," he said and knew instantly that this was what she wanted him to say. "I guess I'd better plan to stay back there for quite a stretch."

"I know." She had lowered her head a little and something in the movement and the flat calm of her voice made him draw her to him. "I'm sorry it had to be like this, darling."

"It wasn't your fault," he said. And then, with wisdom she had not dared to use: "It will change again."

But it had not changed. Always before it had seemed to Colin that Mildred was with him as he traveled or rested, ready to share what he was doing, what he saw, what he felt. Now it seemed often that Martha was with him, more distantly, more purely, a little reproachfully, but so strongly that thought of Mildred could not come alive for thought of Martha. At other times he thought of the officer in the recruiting center, denying and rejecting the strength that his body seemed daily to prove against snow and hills and harsh weather. Or of Tod Phalling, in uniform, accepting the fact of Colin's rejection without question, as something normal and expected.

In the spring, when his traps were all up and the snow had begun to melt from the hills, he took to going down to Robbie's again, to talk and listen to the radio. Johnny Harris had gone out, to work at Blenkin Logging for the summer, and once or twice Robbie tried to persuade Colin to do the same.

"You do too much thinking," he said. "You want to get out and see some people for a change."

"Why don't you go yourself?" Colin asked him.

"I go out more than you do. I've been for grub and mail three times since spring. Besides, I'm an old man. I've learned to stand being alone."

Colin was sitting on the steps in front of the cabin, carving a little figure from a piece of driftwood. He said slowly: "Do you ever feel you're alone? Really alone, I mean, with no one else but yourself?"

Robbie glanced quickly at him. "Sure, why wouldn't I? I'm alone plenty. But that's different to feeling lonely. I don't often get to feeling that any more."

"I guess that's what I mean," Colin said. "I don't ever get to feeling lonely. Seems like most of the time I'm not even alone."

"That don't make any sense," Robbie said. "If a man's by himself, he's alone. Hell, you ain't even got a dog up there, like I've got old Bonnie here." He reached down and pulled the bitch's ear. "If that ain't being alone I wouldn't know what is."

Colin nodded. He decided to let it go at that. For a moment he had wanted to tell Robbie that people you know very well, like Mildred and now Martha, seem to be with you when you are alone. He had half-hoped that Robbie would admit something of the sort himself, but now he knew he wouldn't. "I'm not going out," he said. "I want to make the trip through Windstorm Gap and down Milk River to Menzies Lake. I've never been through there yet."

"Sure," Robbie said. "That's O.K. Just so you're doing something it's O.K. But don't forget that's a Park over there. You don't want to get caught killing any deer once you're over the divide."

COLIN did not get out to Robbie's cabin again until fall. Robbie and Johnny Harris were waiting on the beach when he ran the canoe in and it seemed to Colin that their life together on the lake was suddenly back where it had been in the first years after he came in. The three of them walked slowly up to the cabin through the warm September sunshine and Robbie asked eager, almost boyish questions about Colin's trip.

"It's good country," Colin said. "I like it over there."

"It's a beautiful lake," Johnny said. "But I don't think it's got anything on this one. How's the trip through the Gap?"

"Fine, so long as the weather's good. It sure can blow up there, though, and it's tough in the wrong kind of snow."

"You're crazy to go up there when there's any snow at all," Robbie said.

"No," Colin said seriously. "I believe a person could make it through there in the winter any time the snow was solid."

They went into the cabin and Robbie began to cut meat for the meal. Johnny said: "What made you want to go through there? It's all Park over the divide. You can't get a trap-line in there."

"I don't know," Colin said. "Seems like a person wants to know what's in back of him. And that Park'll open up sometime. It might pay to know something about it."

Robbie threw several pieces of meat into the frying pan. "There's sense to that. There'll be tourists in there and you might be right in on the ground-floor." He reached towards the pepper-pot on a shelf behind the stove and noticed the letters leaning beside it. He took them and tossed them over to Colin. "Hell," he said. "There's some mail for you. Looks like a couple of government letters."

Colin took the letters. He ripped the envelopes open and studied the two similarly confusing interminglings of printing and typescript, then handed them to Robbie. "What the hell?" he said. "Looks like a call-up notice."

"That's what it is," Robbie told him.

"Call-up?" Johnny said. "Why don't I get one if Colin does?"

"Likely you will," Robbie said. He handed the letters back to Colin. "Looks like you're kind of late, but if you go in right away and tell them how it was you'll be O.K."

"You don't think I'm going through that phony set-up again, do you?" Colin said.

"Sure you are," Robbie said. "They'll come and get you quick enough if you don't."

"Don't be a nut, Colin," Johnny said. "Go on down and get it over with. They'll just throw you out like they did the first time."

"They won't get a chance," Colin said. "Let them come in and find me if it's so all-fired important to them."

IT was a very cold winter. There was only a foot or so of light snow down near the lake, but most of it had been on the ground since before Christmas, and now it was mid-January. All the way up the valley Colin had found powder snow so light that the least wind disturbed it; the side creeks were slowed to narrow trickles, Amabilis Creek itself ran softly and darkly between banks of ice, and there was ice along the edge of the big lake. But it was good weather for traveling and good weather for traps. For the first time since fall he found he could afford to stay over for an extra day at the beach cabin.

It was a brilliantly sunny morning, with only a light breeze that fanned down from the head of the valley. On the front steps of the cabin, sheltered from the moving air, Colin found the sun almost hot and he sat there to stretch and flesh his skins. He saw the canoe when it was still only a little way beyond Johnny's valley and watched it from time to time as it grew larger against the quiet surface of the lake. He recognized Robbie's little red Peterborough and saw that there were two figures in it. Robbie had seen the lights of his cabin, he supposed, and stopped in at Carlson's Creek to pick up Johnny. In a sweat about something, Colin thought; driving her with all they've got. Likely something bad about the war or another call-up notice or something. What do they do if you don't answer a call-up? They couldn't ever hurt a man out in this country if he didn't want to get caught. If he had some matches and a few shells and a blanket he could travel for months and never need to go hungry.

He looked at the canoe again and suddenly knew that the second figure was not Johnny. A moment later he recognized Clyde Munro. He made a sharp, instinctive movement towards the door of the cabin, checked it and looked back at the canoe again. "The old son of a bitch," he said aloud. "He didn't have to do that to me. He could of let Clyde find his own dirty way up here." He felt his heart beating strongly and a dryness in his throat. For a moment he thought of his rifle, standing against the wall inside the cabin. He wanted it in his hands, wanted to be up the valley with it, traveling hard towards the Gully, towards the snow slopes above the Gully. Then flight seemed suddenly pointless. From a friend, he thought, from my own brother-in-law. He walked slowly down the beach to meet the canoe as it headed in towards the narrow shelf of ice. Robbie was standing in the bow, a pole ready in his hands to break the ice. Colin saw that his face was set and serious.

"Thank God you're still out here," Robbie said.

Colin caught the bow of the canoe and eased it on to the ice. "Why?" he asked. "What's the trouble?"

"Johnny's lost somewhere up the valley. Been gone since day before yesterday." Robbie stepped out of the canoe and Clyde came stiffly forward from the stern.

"You looked for him yet?" Colin asked.

Robbie shook his head. "Just half a day. Then I went out and fetched Clyde. There was no light up here and I couldn't see smoke through the glasses."

"There's coffee on the stove," Colin said. "Go help yourselves and I'll throw some stuff together. Where did he go? What makes you think he's lost?"

"He went to hunt goat," Robbie told him. "Said he'd be out to my place night before last, but he never showed up."

"Robbie followed his track for a way up the east side of the valley," Clyde said, "then lost it where the snow had blown away from the rock."

Colin looked up from strapping blankets to his packboard. "Goats? What would he want with goats this time of year?"

"It was a notion he got." Robbie set down his empty coffee cup. "Said he wanted to get up in the hills in the clear weather. Said a change of meat ought to go good."

For the first time Colin felt real concern. He remembered now that Johnny said he was going to learn his way about the mountains of his valley, discover them as Colin had the mountains of Amabilis Valley. He remembered, too, how Johnny was in the mountains, hesitant and cautious, always a little afraid, clumsy in a way that he never was on flat ground. Johnny knew nothing of the treachery of snow on steep slopes, nothing of the deceptively easy ways that can lead a man to a blind end of climb or drop with only a hard way back to safety.

"No chance he's in one of his shelter cabins?" he asked Robbie.

"Hardly, unless he's hurt or sick. Even then he'd make it out to the beach easier."

"Robbie fired a bunch of shots up the valley," Clyde said. "And there wasn't any answer. But he might be down in some place where he couldn't hear."

"You set to spend a night out?" Colin asked him. "Likely we'll have to if we get up in those hills this afternoon."

"I've got everything," Clyde said.

2 8

COLIN sat up in his blankets. The stars were still bright in the west, but there was a faint light in the sky behind the tall peaks to the east of the valley. The mountain over the hidden lake was clear and huge against the light, a broken, formidable silhouette, closely joined to the peaks on either side.

They were camped on a little flat place under a slab of rock that leaned like the roof of a shelter and had made a good reflector for the heat of their fire the previous evening. Colin slipped the blankets away from him and began to rebuild the fire. He set water to boil and saw that the light behind the hills was stronger, though the whole valley was still in darkness.

Clyde was still asleep in the warmth of his sleeping bag, but it was bitterly cold even close beside the fire; it seemed to Colin that cold gleamed through the darkness against the ice-sheeted rock and that the stillness all around him creaked and strained with it. He tried to hope for Johnny. Robbie had gone up the valley to the shelter cabins. If he found him he would signal, with rifle shots and smoke. But Johnny's track had led them up from the valley, out of the sheltering timber on to these slopes and terraces of ice-sheeted rock. It was a safe time, Colin thought; too safe. The powder snow had blown away from the rock almost as it fell. The few inches that had somehow clung to the rough surface had long ago melted in the sun of cloudless afternoons and frozen into ice almost as hard as the rock itself. Yet Colin's boot-nails had gripped it well as he and Clyde climbed through the previous afternoon and Johnny's sharp caulks had gripped even more securely. Too securely, Colin thought again, too safely. Johnny would have thought it easy and gone on to learn his mountains; he had gone on, at least this far, because Colin had been able to find occasionally the scars of his passing on the ice, occasionally the clear imprint of the spiked boots on sheltered snow patches in the gullies he and Clyde had crossed.

He heard Clyde move and looked around. There was strong light behind the mountains now and all across the sky, paling the stars, reflecting faintly down into the valley. Clyde asked him: "Have you been up long?" and at once crawled out of his bag and began pulling on his boots.

"There's no hurry," Colin said. "We can't move until there's light enough to see what tracks he's left."

Clyde came up and crouched with Colin beside the fire. Colin made coffee while they watched the light grow slowly on the snow-covered peaks across the valley.

Clyde asked: "Was Johnny a good woodsman?"

"Yes, sure. But he was no good in the mountains. He hardly ever went above timber."

Clyde watched the pink flush of dawn as it spread down from

the peaks across the snow slopes. "I've never been around mountains much myself," he said. "Some of those places we crossed yesterday had me scared stiff. But it sure can be beautiful."

"You didn't act scared," Colin said. "I've seen Johnny scared, though. That's why I'm worried about him now."

"What made him come up hunting goats this time of year if he's scared of mountains?"

"He's been restless ever since they turned him down for the army. I don't figure he was really hunting goats at all or he wouldn't have come along this way."

"I've been thinking that all along," Clyde said. "Seems like he was just walking, not hunting."

Colin nodded. "That's right. I guess it felt kind of good in the sun with all this open rock to travel and the mountains to look at."

They were silent for a while. Colin turned the bannock he was baking and Clyde reached behind him for his sleeping bag, dragged it up and wrapped it round himself.

"It's goddamned cold," he said. "I don't see how you stand it."

Colin cut the bannock and poured more coffee. The light was quite strong all through the valley when they had finished eating, so they made up their small packs and started out again.

It was easy traveling at first, over almost level rock, but Colin could feel that the ice had hardened again during the night and knew that his boot-nails were not gripping as they had the previous afternoon. Carlson's Valley was a strange place. It had a wide, timbered floor, almost flat, ending abruptly in savage bluffs of gray rock that reared with scarcely a break for two thousand feet or more, then rounded into the bench along which they had followed Johnny. The bench was broken again and again by deep, snow-filled gullies cutting back to the steepness of the high mountains that rose everywhere above it. It sloped always outward, towards the sheer drop to the valley floor, sometimes gently as at the place where they had camped, sometimes steeply. Looking ahead, Colin could see that the pattern carried on out of sight ahead of them, gully and sloping bench, gully and sloping bench, clear to the long smooth line of the glacier that fed the creek above the lake.

They came to a gully whose face was a snow-slide so steep that it seemed to Colin the snow must have frozen as it fell to stay there at all. Johnny had crossed it, somehow kicking steps that had held him.

"He could have died right there," Colin said. "He must have done that in the afternoon, when the sun had softened it." He thought of Johnny as he had seen him in the mountains, hesitating to cross a bad place, always cautious and on guard. What changed you, Johnny? What made you go on like this? Why couldn't I have known? We could have been together then.

Clyde was looking down at the long white slide of snow below Johnny's steps.

"I thought you said he was scared."

"Not that time he wasn't," Colin said. "Not scared enough." He started across the slope, kicking at Johnny's steps to test them. They were deep and the night had frozen them rock-hard. Clyde followed behind him and they came on to the new slope. It was steeper than most of those they had crossed, but Colin felt his way for the first few steps, found himself secure and began to travel fast. He hesitated only when he had missed Johnny's track for several hundred yards. Clyde came up to him and Colin looked into his face and saw that it was strained and pale and sweating.

"Don't mind me," Clyde said. "I told you I got scared."

"I'm sorry," Colin said soberly. "There wasn't any sense to flying at it like that. I could have stopped to tell you it was safe."

"That's O.K. I figured it was, but I just couldn't convince myself. You tell me next time and I'll believe you."

"I've missed his track somewhere," Colin said. "But I'd have seen if he slipped." He looked around him, first along the slope, then out to the gap that marked the valley; then he turned slowly and looked along the slope of the mountains above them. "It's bad," he said. "If a man could only know what he was thinking. He couldn't have come this far and figured to get back to the beach the same night."

"We ought to see his track where it crosses the next draw."

Colin nodded. "You want to wait here while I look?"

"Hell, no. It's my job, not yours."

Johnny had found an easy way across the draw and his track was plain. Colin found it again on the new slope, cut deeply into the ice and frozen there. He knew then that Johnny had not turned back, that he had meant to go on and find a way down by the glacier to his cabin at the lake.

The sun was high now, above the peaks, lighting the valley, giving them warmth. A drift of wind came up the valley so suddenly that Colin stopped and looked around. There were clouds over the lake, the nearest of them already reaching to the peaks at the foot of the valley.

"We've had the breaks," he said. "From here in she gets tough."

"Looks like a southeaster," Clyde said.

Colin nodded. "Means we've got a couple of hours. After that we can start to worry about us, not Johnny."

He glanced ahead again along the slope, his eyes searching the monotonous alternations of dark steps and white terraces for the way Johnny might have followed. Then, as his body balanced to step forward again, he saw the glint of sunlight sharply reflected from something a little way ahead along the slope. He looked towards the mountains and knew that the broken ice could not have fallen away from them. He began to travel again, almost at a run. He could feel the ice hard and solid on the rock, but his foot slipped once as the slope grew steeper and he forced himself back to caution. The slope was very steep now and he wondered how Johnny had dared to cross it, then remembered that the ice had been softer for Johnny's crossing and his spikes would have bitten deeply into it. He thought of Clyde and turned to see him coming slowly and steadily, kicking at the ice to roughen it under each step. He came up and Colin saw that his face was strained and wet with sweat again. But Clyde asked him steadily: "What did you see?"

Colin pointed silently to the broken ice a little way ahead and they went on until they came to it. A six or eight foot width of the sloping rock was stripped of ice and below that a jagged mass of ice had been torn away from the main sheet, leaving the rock bare and black right out to the edge of the sharp step that dropped

242

to the next slope. Johnny's caulk marks were frozen solidly into the ice one short step from the break.

"You think he slipped there?" Clyde asked.

"The ice slipped with him. Broke away above him. He didn't have a chance." He crossed the narrow path of the little slide and examined the ice on the far side. There was no mark anywhere on it. Colin looked back and saw that clouds had already closed in the foot of the valley, though the sunlight was warm and strong where they stood.

"He's down there," Colin said and walked the hundred feet or so of open rock to the edge of the step. Clyde followed and they stood looking down at a steeper slope of ice and snow running clear out to the bluffs that dropped away to the valley floor. Broken ice was scattered over the slope. Clyde dropped over the step ahead of Colin and worked cautiously out on to the slope in the path of the slide.

"Looks like he was dragging his rifle butt to try and save himself."

Colin nodded. "An axe would likely have done it." He let himself down over the step, then stood looking back again at the clouds. They were across the sun now and across the peaks, thin swift clouds, and it was suddenly cold. A few hard, dry pellets of snow fell around them.

"What do we do now?" he asked Clyde.

Clyde was watching the clouds. "Could he be alive?"

Colin knew what he meant. "He could be," he said, and pointed to where the slope disappeared from sight. "Depends what's over there."

"Can we get down to look?"

"I think I could. I can use the axe to cut steps. I've done it before." He meant Clyde to understand that the place was not for him.

"It's my job," Clyde said again.

"We'll both go," Colin slipped the packboard from his shoulders and took the coil of light rope he had slung over the top of it.

By the time they had tied the rope to themselves the wind was blowing in strong gusts, and squalls of snow were sweeping along the valley towards them. It was not necessary to cut steps at first, but they moved only one at a time over the steep and slippery slope. Colin watched Clyde's awkward, cautious movements impatiently. Now that he knew what had happened to Johnny he felt a fierce anxiety. He tried to tell himself that Johnny was dead, that the cold of the past two nights would have killed him if the fall had not. But he couldn't believe Johnny dead. The warmth of his own blood, the strength of his own hands, seemed to deny it in some way he could not understand. He knew that he had to climb down to the edge of the slope and see whatever lay below. And he began to know that Clyde would go with him, without slipping or failing or yielding in any fraction to the strain just short of panic that showed so clearly in his face.

The clouds had closed in the head of the valley and the afternoon was dark gray everywhere. The edge of the slope was only a few feet away now, but it was hard to see through the driving snow. Colin felt the wind cold through his clothes and the snow like needles against his face; he was glad because it meant that the old snow and ice would remain solid. He came to the edge of the slope and saw not a break but only a further steepening of the old slope. The drop-off lay somewhere ahead, hidden in the snow. Clyde came down to him, slowly and painfully, in the cramped awkwardness of fear, but without fear's hesitation. From now on, Colin knew, there would have to be steps.

He told Clyde: "I don't know where in hell I'm taking you," and pointed into the gray scud of the snow.

"We can't go back till we find out," Clyde said; and Colin knew he understood that the going back might not be easy.

He lifted the clumsy wood axe and drove it into the icy snow below him. It bit deeply and the step split out to his second stroke. From then on he was conscious only of cutting, testing, stepping, cutting, testing, stepping until he saw the sharp break of the slope's end. He stopped there, signaled to Clyde and watched him come down. Once a sudden gust of wind tore at Clyde's body, twisting his balance so sharply that Colin threw himself forward against the haft of his axe, buried deep in the ice, and waited for the rush of his fall and the shock on the rope. But Clyde recovered and came on down until they could speak. Colin pointed to the break.

"I've got to go out there," he said. "Get a good hold with your axe and keep the rope short."

Clyde nodded and buried his axe. He seemed confident now and Colin trusted him. He went down four or five steps, then drove his own axe savagely against the snow, testing for an overhang. The snow was solid and he came out on it to the edge and looked down. There was only whirling snow below him. He cut away a piece of ice, saw it go down and disappear under the cliff before the snow hid it, and he knew he was not far enough. He cut two more steps, drove his axe above him and stood straight in the second one. From it he could see the ledge, a good broad ledge, deeply snow-drifted and supporting trees, not more than thirty feet below him. He signaled to Clyde again.

Fifteen or twenty minutes later they were standing on the ledge together. The afternoon light was almost gone.

"He should be up this way," Clyde said.

They found him almost at once. Johnny sleeping, Colin thought, not worrying, not afraid, wrapped in his blanket, asleep. Clyde was kneeling beside Johnny, one big hand on his wrist, the other fumbling at his chest.

"He's alive," Clyde said.

Colin looked at the blackened embers of a fire near Johnny's feet, pushed his hand into them, felt warmth. For the next hour they worked steadily, rubbing life back into his feet and legs and hands and arms, and at the end of it Johnny was conscious. The ledge was sheltered from the worst of the storm, but Colin had been able to cut enough boughs to make more shelter and build a big fire. They poured tea and rum into Johnny and wrapped him in Clyde's sleeping bag. Then they made their own meal.

Eating it, looking out into the darkness beyond the falling snow, Colin felt a tremendous elation. It was not merely that they had found Johnny, that he was alive and almost certainly would live. Those things were in it, but over them and beyond them was the strength he had felt in Clyde. He felt it again now, in Clyde's calmness, his matter-of-fact acceptance of the night and the storm and the position they were in. He is stronger than his body, Colin thought, stronger than his mind, stronger than any total of his strength. He was afraid back there on the ice-slopes, yet he never paid any attention to being afraid. He was played right out before we even started down here, yet he came and he hasn't stopped for one moment since we found Johnny. While we were traveling he followed me, yet he made most of the decisions. Here on the ledge I'm following him.

Clyde's quiet voice said beside him: "We've got to splint that leg before we start out with him."

Colin nodded. "Is it a bad break?"

"Bad enough. More than one place. I'm scared for the foot too. I'm going to rub it some more in a minute."

Colin threw wood on the fire, then reached for the pot and poured more tea into Clyde's cup. An eddying gust of wind tore at the jackpines on the ledge and drove snow against them. "I can cut some snow blocks and stop that," Colin said.

"Good. It's going to be a long night, and it'll take us all our time to get him up out of here tomorrow."

"Not up," Colin said. "Down. I think I know this place and if it's where I think it is we'll be able to get right down into the valley."

Clyde looked at him and smiled. "That's the best news I ever heard," he said. While they were talking he had opened the corner of the sleeping bag and was working on Johnny's frozen foot again. "I didn't want to say it, but I figured that getting him up on top might be just a little more than tough."

Because they had used both blankets and sleeping bag for Johnny neither of them slept longer than a few minutes at a time during the night. A little after midnight Colin noticed that the shriek and hum of the wind against the rocks above them had died away. Then the snow stopped. He watched the sky and after a long while saw a star high up across the valley, then another near it. He threw wood on the fire and Clyde woke and they made fresh tea. Colin showed him the stars.

"We've got her made now," he said. "That's the only break we needed and I figured it wasn't coming."

They rolled cigarettes and smoked. After a while, Clyde said: "I was supposed to come in and see you this month anyway."

"About those call-up notices?" Colin asked him.

246

"That's right. You'll be going down there pretty soon, won't you?"

"I don't see why I should. They threw me out once."

"The draft board doesn't know that. It's all routine with them."

Colin threw his cigarette butt into the fire. "Why can't they ever leave a man alone to do what's right?"

"There's too many," Clyde said quietly. "It's all routine and red tape, but they have to do it."

"Would you take me in if I didn't go?"

"I guess I'd have to."

"I suppose it's your job," Colin said bitterly.

"Let's not quarrel about it," Clyde said. "You're going down there. You know you are."

Colin rolled another cigarette and lit it. He saw that his hand was shaking. "I guess you cops are all the same," he said. "The job's everything. You don't care what dirty stuff it takes you into." When Clyde didn't answer, he said, "Did you ever beat up a prisoner?"

"Not once I had him locked up. Maybe I'll have to sometime but I never have yet."

"Why would you have to?"

Clyde shrugged. "Ever tried to sleep with a couple of drunks raising hell in the cells? Ever watched your wife listening to their filth and trying to sleep? It can be plenty hard to take."

At the other side of the fire Johnny moved and murmured in his sleep. Clyde went to him at once, felt his face, reached into the sleeping bag and felt his hands. He nodded to Colin. "O.K.," he said and came back. He stirred the fire and poured more tea, then looked at his watch.

"Five more hours," he said. "And it ought to be light enough to start out."

Colin felt his strength again as he had felt it after they found Johnny.

"I'm sorry I shot my face off like that," he said. "There wasn't any sense in it."

"That's O.K.," Clyde said. "How long is it going to take us to get out tomorrow?"

Colin thought for a moment. "We ought to make it down into

247

the valley before noon. Then we can fix up some kind of sled and take him right down the trail."

2 9

COLIN waited behind the ruined wall and tried to keep warm. The wall wasn't protection, but it felt like protection and at least it blocked the cold wind that was blowing from across the river. There were no stars tonight and he supposed there would be more snow. Terry Murphy said there would be and Terry was usually right about the weather; he was usually right about food and rest and leave and mortar fire and canals and rivers and most of the other things that the war seemed to be made of. Terry was a lot like Curly Blake that way, Colin thought, but Curly was dead, had been dead for over a year, somewhere down in Italy with the Seaforths.

There was some firing across the river, and half-a-dozen light explosions that sounded like hand grenades. Colin moved, but Murphy's voice said beside him: "Too far away to bother us."

"Think she'll stay quiet all night?" Colin asked.

"No," Murphy said. "This here's a lousy place, in between two creeks. We ain't got no business being here." He spat into the darkness. "This Holland," he said. "This Nijmegen. Seems like we been in wrong ever since we come near the place."

Colin laughed. "We've had it worse. Want to go back to Caen?"

"We was young then," Murphy said. "And the climate was good. Anyways, they kept the snow up where it belongs."

They were comfortable enough, except for the cold, and even that didn't seem as bad as it should have. They had waited in so many places, hurried through so many places, gone out together so often in the seven months since D-day, that nothing seemed really bad any more. They were the last of the unit's original stretcher-bearers and at that Terry had been out for over a month with a leg wound.

It was always a canal or a creek or a river that stopped them now, Colin thought. Broken bridges, twisted iron, shattered masonry; planks, doors, girders, anything and everything wedged and zigzagged so that they could walk across. This time there was the rubber boat. They used it to get the casualties across the stream behind, between them and the dressing station, weaving it in and out among the wreckage on the creek bed, continually worried that the current would drift it against something sharp and tear a hole through the canvas.

It was hard to think back beyond the army, harder to think that there would ever be anything but the army. In some ways it wasn't so bad here as it had been in England or back in Canada. It made more sense. You did something and it was done. Back there you were always getting ready to do something that would probably never be done. Training, training and more training, someone driving or nagging or checking, morning, noon and night. "You won't last long if you don't learn . . ." "You better smarten up or . . ." "That stuff won't go when you get overseas." And the other one: "Kill the enemy."

There was enemy mortar fire somewhere over on the right and Colin heard Terry move beside him in the darkness.

"If they start that on us we'll have to get out of here," Terry said.

Colin knew he was thinking of the wall. It was queer how they both preferred it to the slit-trench they had dug nearby. There was something very comforting about the wall, even when you knew it was probably more dangerous than open ground—at least it was standard human shelter. In the slitty you were safe as you could be anywhere, but safe like a rat in a sewer. Some kind of animal, anyway. Fox-holes the Yanks called them, so somebody else must have felt the same way.

"We could just as well be back the other side of that goddamned creek," Terry said. "Don't take but five minutes longer to get up from there. Better yet, they could rig some way to get the jeeps over and save all the packing."

"If this stall keeps up much longer they're liable to pull us out into rest," Colin said.

"Sure, sure," Terry said. "And the zombies are coming up for reinforcements and that'll be the end of the war and we can all go home."

"Well," Colin said. "It ought to make some difference." Canada's two armies, he thought, the quick and the dead. Why did they have to pull that one on us? Call us up and then tell us we didn't have to go overseas unless we volunteered for it. Because of Quebec, people say, but there's whole units over here from Quebec. They either needed us or they didn't need us. And they did need us, that's sure; the unit's never been up to strength since D-day and I guess all the others are the same.

He shifted his feet on the cold ground. "I was a zombie for a while," he said.

"Yeah?" Terry's voice was surprised. "Me too. For a couple of weeks. Until I got things doped out."

"I stayed that way right through basic and advanced," Colin said. "It made me sore the way they pushed us around trying to make us join active. Most of the guys had some reason for staying the way they were." Both of us zombies, he thought, and we never knew it. You'd think it would have come up before this, except for the way a person forgets almost everything that happens in the army.

Terry moved again and the stretcher he was lying on creaked under him. There was more rifle fire, closer to them now, and several bursts from a Bren gun with it. "Sure," Terry said. "They had reasons. I listened to reasons till I got dizzy and went active. Bastards. They hadn't got any more reasons than the guys that went. Just figured their skins was too precious to get holes in."

"I guess it depends more on how it hits a man than on what reasons he's got," Colin said. "The dirty part was the way they put the pressure on after you were in." But he remembered the everlasting barrack-room talk, complaint and defense and explanation, some of it sincere, some the pale echo of other men's sincerity, much of it simply words that covered nothing, not even fear. The sum was not cowardice, nor quite selfishness, nor quite ignorance, but something smaller and meaner and more depress-

250

ing than any of these, a failure rather than a fault. We weren't generous, Colin thought; we hadn't any generosity in us.

Colin heard the break of frozen snow under footsteps and sat up to listen. A voice said quietly and clearly: "Stretcher-bearers."

"I figured that last bit was too close," Terry said.

They stood up and Colin folded the stretcher and shouldered it. The runner had come up and Colin recognized his voice when he spoke again. "One platoon. Over in the farmhouse."

"Can we handle it?" Colin asked.

"Sure. There's only one hurt bad. Some silly son of a bitch fumbled a grenade in the kitchen."

They walked down towards the farmhouse. They were in dead ground behind the high bank of the river and there was no firing now, but their boots were noisy on the crisp snow and the light of the stars was a shadowy brightness. Colin had the feeling of nakedness that often came to him when he was going forward. He was not afraid. To his own surprise he had seldom been afraid since the landing. In training, fear had been with him often, fear of his own clumsiness and foolishness, fear of the blind, driving urgency and hostility that seemed to build in the men around him. Here it was different. Fear was remote and invisible; the men one could see were working together, in friendship. Death was a bullet in the heart, swift, painless, far less likely to come than when he had wished for it years ago in the alder flat. Looking on death and suffering in many forms, he had tried to warn himself, had even tried to find fear. But the burnt and shattered bodies he had tended so often would give no warning, only work that pushed fear yet farther away.

They were near the farmhouse now and Terry said: "I hate this son of a bitching place. It's a hoodoo. I wish we'd get the hell out, forward or back. Don't matter which."

The words were spoken violently, without the easy humor that was an essential part of almost everything Terry said.

"Christ," the runner said. "This ain't near as bad as some places we been at. Like that christly canal for instance."

"It's a hoodoo, I tell you," Terry said. "Two nights ago them poor bastards getting burned like that in the tank. And now they've gone to spilling live grenades all over the kitchen floor."

They were passing the shadowy bulk of the burned-out tank as Terry was speaking and Colin remembered how it had been; the burned rags of clothing on the living bodies, the smell of burning flesh, the men in pain, strange, terrifying pain that shock did not restrain as it restrained the pain of most wounds. And the shocked pity in Terry's voice, so unlike his usual cynical yet kindly acceptance of wounds and death as an unwarranted visitation of labor upon him. "The poor bastards," he repeated over and over again as he worked. "The poor bastards. This goddamned, dirty war."

The runner took them into the farmhouse. The kitchen was at the back, a practically undamaged room, and there was a light behind blacked-out windows. The platoon sergeant was the only man badly hurt and Colin went to him at once. From the moment he began to work on him he was absorbed, utterly unconscious of the room and the other men in it. His hands were sure and strong, the bandages and dressings were familiar tools, and he had the sense of understanding that always came when he was working with wounded men; it was as though the injured body were his own, yet he was detached from it, knowing the channels of pain and the intensity of shock, and knowing also the true degree of damage in the wound and its relationship to the body's life. The work had meaning for him because many times, as now, he had seen pain draw away under his hands. The same power was in his voice and gestures, even in the red Geneva cross he wore on his breast and back. Now he was old in the fighting and most of the men he tended were new; because of this his assurance was stronger, his absorption yet more complete.

"Ready?" Terry was standing beside him. Together they lifted the sergeant on to the stretcher.

"The knee's bad," Colin said quietly. "He'll have to go back right away. What about the others?"

"Walking," Terry said. "Band-aid scratches. Them mortars is starting again."

Colin listened. "It's light," he said. "Same as they started up the other night."

The sergeant was a big man, but they were a good team, used to each other's stride and pace, and they crossed the hard snow easily, past the tank, past the ruined wall and down to the rubber boat on the near bank of the creek. The nearest of the mortar fire was over a hundred yards to the left of them and they paid no attention to it.

Fifteen minutes later they were back at the wall, but Terry said: "We better get down in the dirt. We're due for a pasting before morning, sure as this ain't Portage and Main."

The slit-trench was more ambitious than most of the dozens they had scraped out since D-day. The ground was dry and digging had been easy once they were through the frost, so Terry had cleaned out the overhang until there was room for a man to lie down under it on the stretcher. He set the stretcher down there now, fumbled for a moment and came up with a lighted cigarette between his lips. "What time is it?" he asked.

"It was around three-thirty when we came back from the creek," Colin said.

"Christ, it's a long bloody night. So goddamned cold a man doesn't even feel like going to sleep. You want to try to take a spell?"

Usually they slept in turns on a quiet night. But Colin only said: "What's the trouble, Terry?"

"Hell, I don't know," the cigarette glowed and faded in the dark. "Must be getting me down, I guess. Used to be I didn't ever think ahead. But now I want us to get moving and finish the damn thing. I want to get the hell home before it's too late."

"Can't last much longer," Colin said. "Not with what's piling into them all the time."

"What's the hold-up then?" Terry wedged his back more firmly against the end of the slit-trench. "Look at that poor bastard there tonight. If they'd wound her up yesterday or last month he'd be O.K. right now instead of crippled up for the rest of his life."

Colin knew what he was thinking. "They haven't got you and me tagged," he said. "We'd have had it before this if they had." An old thought came back to him: if you die in a war everybody thinks you had guts. They talk about you and put your name on a memorial. I guess it's a good thing they don't know how some of us die.

"I never seen you stirred up yet," Murphy said. "There's times

I think you like this goddamned war. Don't you ever want to get the hell home?"

"Sure," Colin said. "I'm going to get me a nice quiet farm and raise dairy cattle."

Terry laughed. "What about them mountains and trap-lines you're always talking about?"

"No," Colin said seriously. "If a man wants to raise a family he's got to forget that stuff. My dad's got a place where I could make out farming." There or the Underhill place. Better Underhill's, maybe, now the old man's got himself married again. Except it'd be tough to start up at Underhill's and it would have to be beef, not milk up there.

"You going to marry the girl that writes the letters?" Terry asked. "I thought you said she was your schoolteacher."

Colin felt his face flush in the darkness. "That's right," he said. "She is. But she's only a couple of years older than me."

"You don't want to marry one older than you. They wear out too quick."

"Like as not she won't have me," Colin said.

"Then what? You got others?"

Colin laughed. "Maybe I could find one. Most guys get married in the end."

"I ain't seen the one I'd marry yet. But I'm sure going to look around once I get the store going good." Terry had worked in a hardware store before he was called up and he planned to have a store of his own after the war. "Hardware's good clean stuff," he had told Colin. "And real interesting. And there's a big spread. A guy can make a clean-up if he knows his way around."

They were silent for a little while and it was very silent everywhere about them. For a moment it seemed that the war had gone on and left them.

"Christ, it's quiet," Terry said. "Something's going to happen, surer than hell. Them tanks'll be moving again, weather like this." He kicked at the snow in the bottom of the trench. "Go on talking," he said. "How come you stayed a zombie so long?"

"I told you," Colin said. "I got sore." He remembered the impersonal routine of the recruiting center, the sudden realization that he was through the medical board, in the army. The shamed resentment, the sense of having been trapped into something he had once accepted willingly. "They turned me down back in '39," he said. "Then called me up and said I was O.K."

"I've heard of that happening. It happened to a lot of guys. But it don't make much sense. If a guy wanted to go one time, why wouldn't he want to go the next?"

"I guess I didn't want to go the first time."

"Jesus, you're a hard guy to figure out. I never did get it straight how you came to switch over from a sniper into a stretcher-bearer. It don't add up when a guy's supposed to be the best shot in the unit."

"I'm yellow," Colin said.

He had spoken without emphasis or emotion, in simple explanation. Terry started, shocked by the word, then laughed. "Sure," he said with heavy sarcasm. "I seen that all along."

"That's right," Colin said quietly. "I'm not kidding. I can't fight. I couldn't kill a man. I thought maybe I could for a while, if it was going on all around. Then I found out I couldn't."

"So you transferred over?"

"They got wise and kicked me out. I got so I couldn't do a damn thing right in training. That Major Allison was a good officer. He figured I'd maybe make out where I didn't have to fight."

"That ain't being yellow," Terry said. "I'm not yellow, but there's been plenty times on this job when I was scared and you wasn't. I never seen you scared yet."

"I guess I'm not scared of dying," Colin said slowly. "That happens to you and it's quick. I'm scared when I have to do something. That's why this job's O.K. We've just got work to do. We might get killed, sure, but nobody's aiming to kill us." He shifted his feet in the snow and sat forward a little. "I used to work on a bridge-crew. A man can fall off a trestle and get killed or something can drop on him and kill him. There's sense to that because a man has to take some chances to do anything at all. But there's no sense to men hating each other and trying to force each other to do things they don't want to." He hesitated a moment, then he said: "A man could die in the mountains, like my partner nearly did once and it would be peaceful, almost like a part of living; nobody would have been hurt by it, not really hurt, because there was no hate in it."

Terry shook his head in the darkness. "That's too deep for me," he said. "If a man gets hurt or killed he suffers just the same whether some other guy means it or it's an accident."

"It's a hard thing to explain," Colin said. "Even to yourself. I guess I'm not scared of being hurt or killed so much as I am of people wanting to hurt each other. It used to scare me even to see my old man get mad."

"Christ Almighty, that ain't being yellow. You said you was yellow."

"Yes it is. When the world's made up of that kind of stuff a man ought to be able to stand up and take his part in it, not run away and hide every time."

"Most men feel safer packing a rifle than they do packing a stretcher."

Colin moved a hand impatiently. "I know that too. I'm not talking only about the war. It's the whole of life. A man's got to be able to go out into it and do the things he's afraid of doing just as though he wasn't afraid. I can't."

"Everybody's different from everybody else. You do too much deep thinking, that's all. Like me earlier on tonight when we went up to the farm. I couldn't seem to leave off thinking about them guys being burned in the tank, then that crazy son of a bitch had to go and drop a grenade in a kitchen of all goddamned places. Seemed to me like the set-up was hoodooed." He looked up at the sky. "Not more than an hour to daylight," he said. "I'm going to get me some sleep."

He was asleep almost at once, and Colin sat on in the trench listening to his calm, even breathing. Suddenly he felt very tired and very lonely. He had Terry's feeling that this thing would never end, that they would go on and on, from river to canal to river again, always seeing death and smelling death and hearing the fierce heavy sound of death all about them. And if it did end, what would be left? Robbie and Johnny and Wind Lake all seemed very small and far away.

Clyde and Margaret had their own children, their own joined life to live. Even Mildred was far away, though she wrote so regularly and so fully; reasonable, wise, strengthening letters, cool and orderly, with only a reflected light of the powerful love that had grown between them before Martha's death. He still did not know what it was that Martha's death had done to them, only that it had brought a sense of shame to him that all Margaret's reproaches had never stirred. It was not shame for his love of Mildred, nor even for the way of it, but rather because it had come between himself and Martha; and it was made suddenly strong because there was no longer the possibility of giving back to Martha whatever had been taken from her. If she could have known all of it, Colin thought, she would have understood and would not have minded. Wherever she is now she must know and understand.

And that must change something with the other, he thought. Mildred will know, Mildred will know. So much time has passed now, so many things have happened that it can't be still between us, whatever it is. Surely nothing can be between us if I live through this and if she still loves me. Then he remembered the letters, cool and controlled, lovely as a glacier's blue-green ice, remote from what he wanted of her as the unclimbed peak of Amabilis Mountain. As the first faint gray light grew in the east and the mortars started up again, he knew he was still lonely and it seemed there was little to hope for.

The mortar fire was heavy, patterned, accurate and there was artillery fire with it and behind it, all along the river. Terry woke at once and moved closer to Colin in the narrow trench.

"Means business," he said. "They're going to try and shift us the hell out of here."

Very soon they were working. There were casualties in all three platoons on the island between the two rivers and they were the only stretcher party. There was no time to carry back to the rubber boat, but they moved two men in from the open ground to the shelter of the ruined wall. "It'll take a direct hit to knock it over," Terry said. "And at least it stops the bits and pieces." Terry was calm and happy, Colin knew, and his big hands were gentle with the wounded men.

An hour after dawn a new company came on to the island and passed through to the high bank along the river. There were more stretcher parties now and Colin recognized the figure of the M.O. wading towards them through the ground mist. He checked the two wounded men, then stood for a moment with Colin, looking forward from the shelter of the broken wall.

"The R.A.P.'s moving up to the farmhouse," he told Colin. "And we ought to have the jeeps across the river any time now. These men'll be O.K. here. Any others you get, bring 'em to the farmhouse." He looked back at the wounded men again. "And watch the bleeding, corporal. These goddamned mortar fragments are bad."

Colin nodded. The M.O. was new with the unit, but he was a calm man and Colin liked him. Terry said: "We going to get moving again?"

"You can bet your life on that," the M.O. said. "There's enough Canadian armor on both sides of us to shift everything between here and Berlin." He turned to Colin again. "Better get on up to the farmhouse," he said. "They'll be looking for you there from now on."

They moved up through a strange quiet and saw that more and more troops were coming on to the island. Swirls and wisps of mist shifted with unreal slowness everywhere over the low ground and Colin had a sudden sense that he was a part of something gigantic and powerful, something welded into greatness beyond itself and full of purpose. The feeling passed and left him only with the certainty that he was very hungry and very short of sleep, but he found an echo of it again in the elation of Terry's face when they came to the farmhouse.

"This is it," Terry said. "We're on our way. Look at those babies moving up." He pointed behind them and Colin turned and saw tanks riding the mist and more men behind them. Then the mortar fire started again, intense and deadly, all along the bank of the river. They were called forward into it, brought back a wounded man, went out again. As they started back the second time Colin saw that the mortar fire was bursting over the bank, all across the flat ground between them and the R.A.P.

"Give it five minutes," he told Terry. "They'll shift again, likely."

The man on the stretcher had been unconscious when they loaded him, but he moved his head and spoke to Colin.

"Where's the damage, chum?" he asked.

"Left leg and thigh," Colin said. "You'll make out."

"You ain't kidding no one. It's the back, ain't it? There ain't any part of me moves except my head."

"They'll fix it," Colin said. "They can fix anything."

"Throw me off and take another one. One they can do some good for."

"You'll make out," Colin said again.

The mortar fire had shifted, so they picked up the stretcher and started out again. The steep bank was awkward on the slippery snow, but the flat ground was easy and good and they moved swiftly over it. The wounded man spoke from the stretcher again.

"You'd better of taken somebody else," he said.

Colin looked ahead to the farmhouse, saw Terry stumble, felt the ground heave under his feet. His knees bent to the shock, the stretcher wrenched sideways out of his grasp, then the heaving ground seemed to hit him in the face. He heard no sound and saw no flash, but he knew that he was blinded, on his hands and knees in the snow. Then he could see again, not clearly but enough. He crawled to his right, searching for the stretcher and the wounded man. But there was no man and no stretcher. Blood dripped from his face, into the snow and on to his right hand. He shook it away angrily, crawled forward and found Terry. Terry was face down in the snow and quite still and Colin thought at first he was dead. Then he remembered Johnny Harris in the snow. He reached out the hand with the blood on it and pushed on Terry's shoulder, trying to roll him over. It was too hard for him, so he moved again and used both hands and made it. Terry was dead.

T H E   H I G H E S T   H I L L

3 0

COLIN walked slowly along the road from Blenkinstown towards the Ensley farm. It was late August and very hot. He was still in uniform, carrying a kit-bag over his shoulder, but he knew he was finished with the army. He had to report back to the hospital in thirty days, but they had told him it would be for discharge.

He had thought at first, when he stepped off the boat, that the town was little changed. Mark Dufler, the wharfinger, had recognized him and spoken the proper welcoming words. As he walked off the wharf Jim Hurley had stepped out of the telegraph office and held out his hand. "Welcome back, Colin," he had said. "Clyde and Margaret are away right now, so I sent the message out to your dad. I guess he couldn't make it down to the boat, but he's home." Colin hadn't expected to be met, but he remembered now that they sent telegrams. Next of kin: Mrs. Margaret Munro, Blenkinstown, B. C. It had seemed more logical to put down Margaret's name than the old man's. He had wondered at the time if the army might not find out about the old man and tell him to change it. The thought made him smile a little now. After four years the army no longer seemed all-seeing and all knowing.

As he walked through the village he had begun to realize that it was changed. There were new stores on the main street, stucco-fronted and with the colored tubes of neon signs flaunting out from them. There were many people on the street, few of whom he recognized. And as he went on, past the school and on to the gravel surface of the old road, he saw that there were many new houses in little clearings in the bush. They were unambitious houses, most of them only half-finished, with tar-paper tacked to the outside walls; but they were in places where it had never occurred to him that houses would be built. There was even one beside the creek where he had cleaned up after the fight with Tod Phalling.

The new houses and the people moving in them and near them stirred a vague resentment in him. It was hard to believe that these ordinary things had been going on during the years he had been away, that people had had time for them or heart for them. He remembered the warnings they had been given in England before the hospital ship had brought them over: "You fellows needn't expect to find the flags out and the hero's welcome. People haven't any time for that. Life has been going on over there while you've been away. You'll find changes, but mostly you'll find things going on just the way they always were, your friends having a good time, making good money, getting ahead. Remember, that's the way you wanted it. That's what you fought for . . ."

It had seemed that they were wrong, until now. All the way across the continent the flags had been out and often enough the welcome had been there, waiting for them at every station as the train pulled in. The tall Canadian trains with the high-wheeled locomotives. Talk of Canadian places: "Think Timmins is a pretty good place to live, Bob?" "I'll be through to Winnipeg by Saturday." "Down to Windsor." "Calgary—Edmonton I go to really." Montreal, Toronto, Saint John, Toronto. Vancouver, Ottawa, Saskatoon, Regina, Quebec, Victoria, Lethbridge, Toronto, Montreal. "They're in a hurry to get the Westerners back home so they won't be cluttering up Canada too long." And proudly, chalked on the coaches of a troop train around a colored drawing of the unit insignia: "N. Africa—Sicily—Italy—France—Belgium—Holland—Germany—VANCOUVER. No thanks to you, zombies." More gently, the English names: "Soho, Piccadilly, Tottenham Court Road, Aldershot, Borden, Witley, Farnham. Sold out. No more bitter." There had been a lift to coming back, a shared triumph of escape, survival, hope. Shattered in the moment that the trains stopped for the last time, its little pieces scattered with the men who turned to their families and the busses, trains, boats, taxis that took them on to the street numbers and whistle stops, the farm and logging and fishing hamlets, the places where life had gone on.

Of course life had gone on. People had had a good time, high wages, plenty of work, essential work that kept them safe from the call-up. It only seemed strange that they should have been expanding, building up, changing familiar things that had seemed unchangeable. But that also followed naturally. There had been a deepsea ship loading lumber from a big new dock at Blenkin's mill. And Phalling's mill was much bigger than it had been, with a new refuse burner carrying a bold lettered sign on the seaward side. The town had gone ahead. Colin remembered someone had told him that down in Vancouver, or was it in England, someone in the hospital? The town had gone ahead, so people had come in and had built houses for themselves where it had seemed there would never be houses.

He had turned in at the familiar gate by the familiar mail-box before he saw what had happened to the Ensley farm. There were half-a-dozen new houses along the roadway in the barn field—houses like the others he had seen, unambitious, half-finished. Farther back in the field were some piles of lumber, the foundations of another house, two or three automobile trailers. Close by the house was a cluster of small cabins. Colin stopped in amazement, then turned slowly around and looked for the big maples by the gate. They were there. He looked again at the house and knew it was the house, knew that the barn was the place where he had milked Martha's cows. For a moment he wanted more than anything to turn and go away, go anywhere but into the house where he would find his father and the woman his father had married.

Then he saw Mrs. Gibberd in the doorway, waiting for him. She had seen him and waved to him, and he went forward to meet her. Mrs. Gibberd, he thought, Mrs. Ensley now. She must have made him do this, he'd never have thought it up by himself.

But he went on and she smiled as he came near and said: "Welcome home, Colin. Mr. Ensley's right inside washing up. We didn't expect you this soon." He saw her eyes on his face, assessing the scar of his wound and he thought: there isn't so much to see there, the medicals did a good job. She touched his arm and tried to take the kit-bag from him. "You shouldn't have carried that all the way out here when you've just got out of hospital," she said. "We could have had them bring it up later. Come on in and sit down."

His father's bulk was behind her in the doorway then. Colin saw an old man, stoop-shouldered, gray-bearded, the head bowed forward a little between the stooped shoulders, the broad, bold face heavily lined, tired, shrunken away from its boldness. He slipped the bag from his shoulder and stepped forward into the kitchen. "Hello, Father," he said.

The old man looked up at him and held out a thick, still powerful hand. "You look tired, son," he said, and the gentleness of his voice touched Colin so that he felt tears close to his eyes. "Come in and sit down."

Colin passed into the kitchen and sat down. The room had been painted, he saw, and there was a new stove and a new sink and new chairs. Mrs. Gibberd had gone to the stove and was cooking a meal for him. Will Ensley sat opposite him, watching his face with the same gentleness that had been in his voice.

"You'll find the place changed a lot, Colin," he said at last, and there was anxiety in the voice that had once been so resonant and over-powering.

"Yes," Colin said. "It's changed." You've changed it, he thought, you've dirtied it and killed it for me. And why shouldn't you? It's yours, not mine. Not yours really, hers. But she's dead or she'd never have let you do it. Don't crawl to me and tell me why you did it. I'm no part of this any more, no part of this house, no part of this place.

"I made your father do it," Mrs. Gibberd said from the stove. "He's not strong enough to work any more the way he used to and we had to make something out of the place."

Colin looked out of the window at the houses along the road. "I know," he said. "I could see there were changes all the way along. A lot of new houses going up. It's the same everywhere, I guess."

"The Mayhews and the Hunts and the Meldrums wouldn't sell any land," she said. "So they came on out to us. We had put the cabins up before that." She came over with a great plate of food and set it in front of him, then went back to the stove for the coffee. "Go right ahead and eat, don't mind us. We had ours an hour ago."

Will was looking at Colin's uniform and the ribbons over his left breast. "Have you got to go back?" he asked. "I thought it was all finished."

"To the hospital," Colin said. "They check you pretty close."

"We heard you were wounded. They sent word to Margaret. Is it likely to trouble you?"

Colin touched the scar on his face lightly, then raised his arm to show the free movement of the shoulder that had been injured. "No," he said. "I'm O.K." He could see they were genuinely worried about him, afraid for him and afraid of him, and his resentment faded. "How's Margaret?" he asked. "And Clyde? And all my nieces and nephews?"

"You'll be proud of them when you see them," Mrs. Gibberd said. "Little Clyde's just like Margaret. And the girls are like Clyde. I'm not sure about the baby."

COLIN knew Mildred would not be back until school started in

September; she had written from California and the letter had been waiting for him in Vancouver, forwarded from the hospital in England. She had not known he was coming home and it was an anxious letter: "I do hope they will send you home soon. You say you weren't badly hurt, but it's worrying to think how long they have kept you in hospital. I want to see you and *know* you are all right. And I want to hear you talk. We've had only letters for so long. They're not enough." For so long, he thought, and now this much longer. And what shall we be to each other when she does come? I used to be so sure she would know, but will she? Perhaps I'm the one that should know.

He used the first few days of his leave in going to see the Meldrums and the Mayhews and in re-exploring the alder flat, finding the old cattle trails grown over and the drinking places along the creek unused except by deer. Once he tried to climb the mountain, following the route he and Margaret had used years before. At first it went well for him; his legs were strong and his lungs were good and he felt all the old happiness of being alone in country that he loved and understood. Then, as the climbing became more difficult, he found that his injured shoulder would not do the work he asked of it. He went on, hoping that the stiffness and weakness would wear away with use. But weakness became pain, mild at first, then fierce and persistent, and his whole arm was useless to him. So he turned back at last and went down to the valley again.

He stayed at home the next day, moving carefully to keep Will and Mrs. Gibberd from knowing what had happened. On the day after his shoulder was better and he went out along the road to find his old trail to the forestry camp at Strathmore Falls. As he came to Mike Varchuk's house he saw that someone was living in it; the window frames had been painted, there was a new roof and faint blue smoke rose from a new brick chimney. A small, stooped man was working in the garden and Colin saw as he came closer that it was Varchuk himself. He thought for a moment of turning off the road and cutting round through the brush to his trail, but something in the way the old man was working there, alone in the garden of his lonely little house, something remembered of Will Ensley's disapproval of Varchuk, made him hesitate.

At least he's an old-timer, Colin thought. And walked on along the road.

Varchuk did not hear him until he leaned his arms on the gate and said: "Hello." Then the little man straightened up and peered towards him, the wrinkles of his brown face strongly shadowed under the brim of his hat.

"Young Ensley," he said. "Will's boy." He came to the gate and held out his hand, still peering as though his eyes were weak. "It is a long time, but I know the tallness and the shoulders."

Colin laughed and opened the gate. "I've seen taller than me," he said.

"Come into the house," Mike said. "There is beer, good beer, just ready for drinking. You are finished with the army?"

They went into the house and Mike got out his beer; he filled two glasses and set them on the table, then put two more full bottles beside them. "Drink up," he said. "There's plenty more."

It was cool in the little room after the hot sun outside and the beer was good, dark and heavy-bodied like the dark brown ale they had occasionally found in England. It seemed strange to be there in Varchuk's house after all the things he had heard said of him, after the mystery of his disappearance and the house's long emptiness. And Varchuk's quick acceptance of him seemed strange too.

"You are tired, son," Varchuk said suddenly. "War is a hard thing on the people."

"I'm O.K.," Colin said and touched the thin scar on his cheek. "This makes a line that isn't really there."

Varchuk nodded. "I saw it at the gate. You were wounded. One shoulder moves stiff, too." He took an opener and pried the caps off the two bottles of beer on the table. "We needed to have more in Spain. Then your war would not have happened."

Colin remembered that one story of Varchuk's disappearance had been that he had gone to fight in Spain with the McKenzie-Papineau battalion. "Were you there?" he said.

Mike bent forward and pulled up one trouser leg, then turned to show the ugly, infolded scar that ran along his shrunken thigh, from the knee up out of sight towards the hip. "We were the first front," he said proudly.

Colin understood the little man's quick hospitality. That's why he looks old, he thought, and why he speaks clearer English than he did.

He drank from the full glass, remembering the Spanish veterans he had known in the army; Stavic, who had refused to go overseas and been a powerful influence among the zombies; and Kroez of the sniper platoon, wise, dangerous, savage, killed near Caen. Intense, bitter and difficult men both of them, yet each as different from the other as they were sharply different from Varchuk.

"What you do, now you've come back?" Mike asked suddenly. "Go to work in the woods like your dad?"

"I thought I'd go farming," Colin said. "I'm not sure now. Everything's changed so much. I guess a person has to get used to it, then look around."

"There is no farm where you live, even if Will did not sell the land. It is not producing land and there is not enough."

Colin nodded. "I had thought maybe a man could run beef cattle over on the flats at the mouth of Wind River, the way Underhill tried."

"And now there is the new logging company there at the mouth of the river, and they talk of the pulp mill also." Varchuk laughed. "They have been busy while you were away."

Colin smiled. "I guess there's always the trap-line," he said.

"Furs, for the backs of rich women. No. There is more for you than that."

Varchuk opened two more bottles and filled the glasses again. Colin watched him curiously, trying to guess what might be behind his interest. It seemed closer and stronger than anything that would develop simply from the shared experience of war.

Varchuk sat down again and lifted his glass. "They say you are clever with the axe, like Will. It is good work for a man."

Colin moved his arm to indicate the injured shoulder. "I'd have to get this straightened out first."

"You are young and strong. It will get better. The iron is still in there?"

"I guess so. They said in England they might have to operate again." There's sense in what the little guy says, he thought.

There are worse jobs, and a man would have a better chance to look around for likely farm land than he would back on a trapline.

"You are lucky," Varchuk said. "We fought too soon. We must be our own doctors."

Colin glanced at him in quick surprise. Nobody called you out on that one, he thought; it was all your own idea. Watching his face, Varchuk smiled. "It is not important," he said gently, touching his wound. "It is important that those who fought against fascism should not quarrel. The fight against fascism is everywhere and all the time."

Colin stood up and turned restlessly towards the window of the little room.

"Who wants to be fighting all the time?" he asked. "Why can't a man just live his life and work at his job?"

"He must fight too," Varchuk said. "The worker must always fight, even to keep what he has." He poured more beer into the glasses on the table. "The union is strong now," he said. "Not like when you went away. But it will need the strength of the men who come back from the war."

Colin turned back from the window. He did not like Varchuk's gentle intensity and still did not understand its purpose. "We'll join, I guess. Why shouldn't we?"

"There may be some who think that those who did not go to war have gained more than is right. It is a danger. And there are always those who try to divide the workers."

Colin nodded. "They had the best end of it. But I guess that's their business. I'm not griping."

"Some will. They must be guided."

Colin laughed. "Don't ask me to guide them," he said. "They've got a right to the way they think same as I have. You picked on the wrong guy, Mike."

Varchuk looked at him, smiling faintly. "Perhaps," he said. "Perhaps. But you will help. Even Will helped us."

MILDRED arrived home a few days before Colin's leave ended. He went to the cottage as soon as he knew she was home and she met him in the doorway; she held out both hands to him and drew him inside.

"Colin," she said. "Colin, Colin, Colin."

He followed her into the small living room and for a moment they stood looking at each other, as though by looking they could wear away the years of separation.

Colin said at last: "You haven't changed. Everything else has, but you haven't." He wanted to tell her she was more beautiful than ever, richer and more deeply appealing even than he remembered her. But the words would not come easily to him and for the moment this other, that she was unchanged while everything else was changed, seemed the more important.

She laughed quietly, happily, still open to him. "I'm older," she said. "We both are. Five long years older." She raised her hand and touched the scar on his face. "Is that it?"

Colin nodded. "Does it look awful?"

She shook her head vigorously. "No. It's almost hard to find, except it changes your face somehow." She moved away from him. "Sit down," she said. "Tell me everything there is. About that. And the shoulder. And are you home for good? Everything."

Colin laughed. "I think you're younger and I'm older. Everything, all at once?"

"The shoulder first."

"It's O.K.," he said. "I have to have more treatments. But it's going to be O.K."

"How soon?"

"I have to be back at the hospital next Monday."

They talked on, quietly and easily, feeling the gaps in their knowledge of each other, still searching for change; and in the ease of their talking the time they had been waiting for passed from them, unused.

Mildred sensed its passing long before Colin. It seemed to her she had known it almost from the first. He had come to her freely, for the first time in his life. That alone was enough and she had accepted it, had offered him everything in the enchanted repetition of his name. But the time had passed and now they were talking calmly, without impatience or tension, as close friends, friends of a long time, no more than that. Yet it is there, she thought, in him as well as in me, and the shadow of Martha holds it quiet.

After he had gone she turned back to the job of unpacking. In a little while she was crying. The years, she thought, and the letters. And now this. Yet this may be right. The other would be so difficult, so dangerous for both of us, unless we needed it beyond everything else. And we don't or Martha would not still be there between us. Perhaps we don't know yet, perhaps the years are between us as well as Martha; and the letters and all the times we have turned away from each other and everything that has happened since that first day when he wrote about mountains and touched my shoulder. Now he will go back to his mountains.

She gave up what she was doing, went into the living room and sat down as though to recapture the feeling of his being there. If he needed me, she thought, and not the mountains, would I be ready for him? I was today, but would I be again, would I know? What would a woman do, not a schoolteacher but a real woman? I've always been his schoolteacher, even when we were closest and I tried hardest not to be. He will come to me again, as surely as he will go back to the mountains again. Let me be ready then, let me be free of littleness, just for that once.

COLIN spent most of that fall and winter in hospital, but they operated on his shoulder for the last time before Christmas, and by January the wound was healed. The doctor told him: "It'll be weak at first, but there's no permanent damage there. Get it working, easy for a while, then pile it on."

"Is using an axe O.K.?" Colin asked.

"Nothing better. Just watch it till the muscles build back, then give her hell. You'll never know we did a thing to it."

He was back in Blenkinstown by the end of January, staying with Clyde and Margaret, but going out to his father's place each day to cut cordwood. Within a month much of the strength had built back into his arm and shoulder and he hired out with the Blenkin Lumber Company. Gordon Holman was still superintendent and welcomed him warmly.

"Glad to have you back, Ensley," he said. "You didn't leave us to join, but there's always a job here for a returned man. Where do you want to work?"

"I'd be best scoring for a while, I guess," Colin said. "But I'll be able to handle the big axe again soon enough."

Holman nodded. "We heard you'd had trouble with your arm. Just say the word when it's in shape again. There's plenty of work for another broad-axe man. I wish we had your dad back on the job."

Why did you kill the strength out of him, then, with your blacklists? Colin thought. Why did you take his pride and make him an old man? He looked Holman in the eyes, searching for some sign of regret or apology. There was none. Only smiling, good-natured assurance.

Holman's hand touched Colin's shoulder in an easy, friendly gesture. "Glad to have you around again," he repeated. "I'd like to see you grow into the company the way your dad did."

"I might not stay with it as long as he did," Colin said and turned away. Grow into the company, he thought. You don't even remember what you did to him, you self-satisfied son of a bitch. It wasn't any more important to you than rolling a cigarette or going to the can.

Colin stayed on with Clyde and Margaret when he went to work in the camp. He liked them and liked their three children, and it kept him within reach of Mildred. It was evident that Margaret had never renewed her friendship with Mildred and she spoke of her very seldom. But when she did so it was without bitterness; and she made no effort to influence Colin.

Colin went up to the cottage frequently, sometimes for a meal, sometimes for an hour or two in the evening. Occasionally he and Mildred walked along the beach road on a fine afternoon or visited a farm to buy fresh fruit. Once he took her back through the alder flat and showed her the start of the climb to the mountain, but generally he kept well away from the road that led out to the Ensley farm.

During this time they held to the relationship that had grown out of that first meeting after his return. They were friends, with a closer intimacy for having been lovers, yet with a rigid restraint of passion that would not have been necessary between friends. As time went on this tension of unfulfilled love strained at them both more and more powerfully. Mildred felt it and in her wisdom was afraid; but the very faith that held her back from Colin would not let her deny him friendship. Colin felt it and wanted to use it to break away what stood between them; but for a long while he believed it was in himself alone and he dared not use it. Mildred had become again all that she had been during his schooldays—cool and unattainable, infinitely desirable, yet set beyond any reach of desire by the qualities that made her so desirable.

Mildred still probed and searched to bring out the things that were shut deepest in him, but her searching was gentler than it had ever been and the more effective for that. Now war had given him experience far beyond her knowledge and she made him describe and explain it to her until it took on clearer values for himself.

"You didn't hate the army," she told him once.

"Why do you say that?"

"You say it. You were very happy sometimes—often when the fighting was going on and you were with your friend Terry Murphy or one of the others."

"I suppose that's true," Colin said slowly. "If being happy is being too busy to be miserable."

"No," she insisted. "It's more than that, much more. It's being able to forget yourself. And you only do that when there's something so big, so tremendously important to be done that it takes every part of you to do it."

"I didn't like it. I hated seeing men hurt and knowing they couldn't get right again. I didn't like thinking about them afterwards, or remembering how they were before they got hit or burned, strong and laughing and full of life."

"It isn't a question of liking something," she said. "But you did like it. You didn't wound them or burn them, you helped them. You knew they trusted you and depended on you, you could see the pain go quiet in their faces when you worked on them. You must have known lots of times that you had done something that kept a man from dying before he got back to the dressing station. You hadn't time to think about yourself then, you hadn't time to be afraid even. There were much more important things."

As he watched her speaking it seemed to Colin that she was more beautiful than she had ever been. All the beauty she had had ten years ago was still there, the glinting lights of her pale hair, the smooth stretch of the milky skin over her strong cheekbones, the clear blue of her eyes, the rich and gentle fullness of her mouth. She will never grow old, he thought, only more alive and more beautiful. He felt his love for her grow in him until his face was hot with it and his eyes could hardly see her face. His throat was dry with wanting her and he could feel the little quiver of stirred muscles all through his body. When he answered her it seemed to him that his voice came from somewhere outside himself.

"That was how it was," he said. "And it was like that because everybody was helping everybody else. Even in training nearly everybody tried to help the other guy, except a few that wanted to look extra good. And once we were on the continent it seemed like everyone was your friend except some guys you couldn't even see." He felt calmer now and pulled out his tobacco pouch and papers to steady his hands. "Back here you get to feeling that everybody's suspicious, everybody's trying to get ahead of the other guy, everybody's sore about something."

"You sound like one of the real old soldiers—the kind that spend their lives saying nothing will ever be so good as it was in the army."

He smiled at her. "You started it. You said I liked it in the army and made me admit it."

"Well," she said. "What's so bad about us all back here? This strike you're going to have?"

"No," Colin said. "We've got to have the strike—unless they give us what we want without it." He frowned and leaned forward in his chair with his elbows on his knees. "But the strike seems to bring it out more than anything else. Most of the boys think it's got to come, but they don't want it. They're scared of it and they're scared of each other. There's a lot of bulldozing going on and a lot of tough talk. Maybe I'm crazy, but it seems to me men ought to be able to get together without that sort of stuff if they really believe in something."

"There have to be leaders," Mildred said.

"I know, but not this way."

"You take it all too seriously," she said. "Come in the kitchen while I make coffee." He watched the firm, strong movement of her body as he followed her. He wanted to touch her, make her stop and turn to him, but he believed she had not restored his right to and he dared not. In the kitchen she did turn to him, abruptly, her face happy and young. "Are we going somewhere again next Sunday?"

"Yes," he said instantly.

"To see that Underhill place at Wind River?"

"If there's anything left of it," he said.

CLYDE also talked to Colin about the strike. He was a corporal now, in charge of the four-man detachment at Blenkinstown and several smaller detachments farther up the coast. He told Colin once: "I'd sooner face a Jap landing, the way we figured for a while it might come here during the war, than these labor troubles."

"I don't think there'll be trouble this time," Colin said. "Not the kind you'd come into."

"No strike has to mean trouble. But it's a time when trouble is very easily made. That's why it's always a policeman's headache."

Colin remembered the talk in the crummy on the way to work the previous day. John Halsborg's big voice saying: "Ask Ensley here. His brother-in-law's a cop."

"What about it?" Colin had asked in the expectant silence.

"They bringing extra cops in for the strike?"

"How would I know?"

Halsborg's laugh, bitter and hostile. "Here's a guy can't forget he was wearing a uniform himself a few months ago." Men near Halsborg trying to quiet him. Earl Mayhew's voice beside Colin: "Let it go, Colin. He's trying to get you sore. These goddamned power-saw fallers think they own the union since they started making big money."

Clyde crossed the room and stood looking out of the window. "Marge is late," he said. Then he turned back to Colin. "Maybe I shouldn't have said all that. I don't think there's going to be any trouble this time. But I hate strike duty or anything to do with labor troubles. Every policeman does. It's the only thing in this job that could ever make me want to take off my uniform for good—and I'd do it before I'd do some of the things that could come up."

"I don't see why a strike should be police business at all," Colin said.

"It isn't police business," Clyde said sharply. "Not unless things get out of control and there's property damage or people hurt. It's our business then and so it should be. The only trouble with that is we have to go against whoever's been doing the damage and that's always the strikers. The bosses may have pulled every lowdown trick in the book to make the boys step out of line, but that's not our business. All we're supposed to ask is who did the damage. Mind you," he added, "strike leaders can go out of their way to make trouble, too, if it suits them."

"Have you got extra men coming up?" Colin asked.

"Laid on ahead of time? Lord, no. They wouldn't send them if I asked for them and I sure as hell wouldn't ask. It's not that. I don't expect any trouble." He paced across to the window again. "I guess I'm beefing to you to get it off my chest, the way any man does when he's up against some part of his job he doesn't like."

Colin stood up. "I'll be glad when it's over," he said. "Seems like there's been nothing but strike talk and union talk ever since I got out of the army. If a strike will clear the air and put things back to normal, I'm all for it."

T H E strike, when it came, was quiet and orderly except for an incident at the Phalling mill on the second or third day. Tod Phalling had inherited the mill on his father's death, shortly after he was discharged from the army. He made a half-hearted attempt to operate the mill with a few non-union men. But the picketing was effective and Clyde Munro warned that there would be no police support, so the men would not go through a second time.

Colin was picketing at the Blenkin mill for a few days, but there were no more incidents and the pickets were reduced to one or two men. It became quite evident that there would be no further attempts at strike-breaking and there was little to be done except wait; but there was still a great deal of activity around union headquarters and the more aggressive leaders worked hard to keep the men together. After a few days Colin went up to his father's place to cut some cordwood, but Ray Kreutzer and Joe Davidson, two members of the strike committee, came up and told him to stop.

"Hell," Colin said. "It's just to give the old man a hand."

"He pays you, don't he?" Davidson asked.

"I never asked him to yet," Colin said.

"It might be O.K. then," Davidson said. "You could take it up with the committee."

"No," Kreutzer said. "If the old man don't pay him he'd have to pay someone else. Besides, he eats his meals free up at the house."

"Let it go," Colin said. "Skip the whole goddamned thing." He turned and flung his axe away from him so that it made half-a-dozen whirring circles in the air and buried itself solidly in the smooth gray trunk of an alder thirty or forty feet away. He looked at it with satisfaction, seeing the handle straight with the trunk of the tree, the unburied blade bright in the sunlight. "You guys make me tired," he said. "Let the son of a bitch stay there."

He stopped in at Earl Mayhew's on his way home and found

Johnny Meldrum there with him in the yard in front of the house. Joan Mayhew came to the door of the house. "If you boys want to come inside I'll make you a cup of tea," she said.

"It's more of a day for beer," Earl told her. "There's some in the ice-box. What do you say, Colin?"

"Sure," Colin said and they all sat on the steps and drank beer.

"Those guys make you quit?" Meldrum asked Colin. "We saw them going up the road."

Colin nodded.

"That's a lot of bull," Earl said. "You could go down and ask the committee and you'd be O.K."

"I wouldn't ask them for a damn thing," Colin said. "I'm going up to Wind Lake and work on my cabins till this mess is over. They can stand it."

"You still got that trap-line?" Meldrum asked.

"Sure have," Colin said. "I'll be using it again, too, the way things look to me right now."

"They're liable to stop you going up there if they know about it."

Earl shook his head. "I don't think they'd bother him. It's not like doing something where he'd be earning wages."

"There's some of the boys want to go fishing," Meldrum said. "They'd have been quitting to go anyway if the strike hadn't come along. They've been told they can't go."

"It makes some sense," Earl said. "They want everybody to be in it together. Makes it stronger that way than if some of them go off to other jobs."

"Doesn't make sense to me," his wife told him. "If you had a boat and went off fishing around this time every year I'd see you went, strike or no strike." She cupped her strong chin in her hand and looked affectionately at Earl. "I'm glad you haven't got one, though."

Colin said slowly: "Seems like the union's God Almighty all of a sudden. I guess it's a good thing—at least it's stopped blacklisting and that other phony stuff they used to pull when the company was God Almighty. But it's kind of hard to take sometimes."

Meldrum laughed. "Shake off one set of shackles and hook on another," he said. "Next thing you know there'll be closed shop

277

around here and you'll be blacklisted if you don't join the union."

"That's a rough way to put it, John," Earl told him. "Closed shop would be our own business. We'd have some say in keeping it fair."

"Not with guys like Halsborg and Kreutzer and Davidson at the head of it. They're in the driver's seat, but good. There's not more than a dozen of them and a few stooges run the whole local. The ordinary plug is scared to get up and say a couple of words at a meeting—if he goes."

"We can change all that," Earl said quietly. "It's just a question of getting in there and working at it, the way they do."

Colin stood up impatiently. "Isn't there any way a man can be free to work at a job and mind his own business?" he asked.

"No," Earl told him gently. "Not any more there isn't. I guess maybe there never was."

Colin felt a sudden sense of desperation. He struggled to find some violent word or phrase that would express it, then shrugged his shoulders hopelessly. "I better get moving," he said.

"Stay to supper," Joan Mayhew asked him. "I can have it ready in a few minutes."

"Thanks a lot," Colin said. "But I better get moving if I want to start up the lake tomorrow. Thanks just the same." He looked at Earl. "And if anybody tries to stop me I believe I'll take a poke at him."

Earl smiled. "They won't," he said. "Don't let it get you down. We'll all be working again inside of a month."

COLIN stayed up at the lake for a little over a month. It was the second time he had been there since his discharge; but the big camp at the mouth of the river, the logging railroad and the heavy operation in the flat valley depressed him as it had the first time, even though the machines were all silent. He saw that the railroad was through to the foot of the lake now and they had been rigging a loading boom when the strike came up. There was a big raft near the dock with a donkey engine already on it.

He had stopped for a couple of days with Robbie and Johnny on the way up, then had gone on to Amabilis Creek. Robbie had seemed depressed and suddenly much older. "They're putting an

A-frame on the lake to log some of the good pockets while the market's high," he told Colin. "Andy Grant was right. They'll have a railroad up my valley first thing I know."

Johnny was more cheerful. "I kind of like to look down there and see the lights at night when the camp's working. And it feels good to have some place nearer than Blenkinstown where you can go to get grub and tobacco. They been real good about bringing freight through for us on the railroad."

Up in his own valley Colin forgot everything in the joys of rediscovery. All his cabins except one were in good shape. The exception was a shelter cabin that had collapsed under a heavy fall of snow. He rebuilt it into a far better cabin than it had been before, then went on to the cabin in the Gully. The snow had already gone from the meadow and the young grass was growing steadily. The deer had moved up from their winter haunts in the valley and the bears were working the swampy places for roots. There seemed to be game everywhere and Colin watched it and moved amongst it with a sense of possession, almost of fellowship.

There was still snow on the mountain slopes, but he climbed through it to Windstorm Gap, traveling warily and resting through the middle of the day while snow and ice, thawed by the hot sun, avalanched everywhere about him. He camped one night near the gap, then swung back over the known way to the narrow corridor that led through to the hidden lake. He made his way through to the break-off, where he could look down and see the little lake again. The snow was deep and wet and rotten under him, but he worked forward on it, trying to look down at the small broken ledge that made the platform for the jump to the start of the ledge trail. Somewhere just in front of him, almost under his feet, he heard a creak, then the sighing plunge of a great mass of snow down the face of the mountain. He threw himself sharply backwards into the corridor and did not try again.

Back at the beach cabin, Colin worked steadily on his traps and snowshoes and other gear for nearly two weeks. It was satisfying to feel the old, used things, rusted and rotten with disuse, come back to life under his hands. It was satisfying to know that the musty smell had gone from the cabin as the breezes from the lake poured through the long-closed doors and windows again, to feel the dampness draw out of the log walls, to see the arrest of decay and hear its creeping silence end. He thought again of Mildred, of her love of the mountains, of her deep pleasure in the short trips they had made during recent week ends. She could come here, he thought, she would be happy here. But only for a little while. It's no life for a woman. And if it's no life for a woman it can't be life for a man. Once the strike is over it will be easier and simpler outside. A man will be able to live his life there quietly and sensibly, work at his job, save money, find a farm somewhere. That doesn't seem so very much to ask.

When there was nothing more to be done at the beach cabin, he went up the valley again. But this time, instead of following Amabilis Creek up to the lake and on to the Gully, he swung aside to follow the little tributary stream that drained the hidden lake. It was bad country, a narrow little valley, steep-walled so that the sun scarcely found a way into it, damp and moss-grown. It had held good timber once, but a freak wind had swept it, piling windfall fifteen and twenty feet high; on the slopes the second-growth conifers were so thick that it was difficult to force a way between them; near the creek salmonberry and devils' club, alder and salal strove together in fantastic competition. Colin knew all this and was glad of it. For a while he worked along the creek, ducking and weaving and twisting a way through the brush. Then the valley drew in to a narrow, high-walled canyon and he climbed through windfall and second-growth almost to the ridge. He was on wet, moss-covered rock now, bare of brush and sparsely timbered. Occasionally he had to climb steep places, but he made good time and in a little while he was looking up at the first fall that drained the hidden lake. It was a handsome fall, wide and sharply white against the gleaming black rock on either side, dwarfed by the height of the sheer, bare walls that climbed straight above it for two or three hundred feet.

The place was very familiar to Colin. He had been to it only twice before, but he had thought of it a hundred times. Waiting for sleep or hewing bridge timbers, waiting for casualties, lying in hospital, through deadened miles of marching, he had forced it into his mind and held it there, searching always for some weakness, some easy way up. He saw now that he had remembered it well. The way was there, for fifty or sixty feet through the single flaw in the smooth face. Twice he had climbed that, to be stopped without further foothold or handhold ten feet below and twenty feet over from a flat lip that overhung the curve of the falls. From below it still seemed impossible. But from above it would be almost simple. A man could drive a stake into the rock, then work down and across from it on a rope, driving more stakes until he reached the head of the flaw. Once the stakes were driven and the rope fixed the way would be there, a way that would be open in any weather and at any season.

3 3

FOR more than a week after Colin came out from the lake the strike still dragged on. The men were restless in it, weary of the quibbling, technical nature of negotiations they no longer attempted to understand. When the settlement came they accepted it gladly and went gladly back to work; they had a good wage increase and better hours. These things were clear and concrete.

Colin slipped back into the painless routine almost without effort. He found it easy to sit near Earl Mayhew and John Meldrum through the long rides out to work, silently for the most part, shutting his mind in thought. It was a cool but pleasant summer, with rain somewhere in almost every week, and they were building a trestle across a long, swampy hollow in standing timber. He was using the broad-axe again now and his shoulder was strong enough to drive it steadily through the longest day without tiring.

He realized only slowly that the outcome of the strike had done little to ease the tension and anxiety among the men he worked with, and still more slowly that he himself was a part of the conflict. It was not by chance that he sat with Earl Mayhew and John Meldrum on the way to work. Halsborg and Davidson and several others of the more active union men rode the same crummy and there was a silent hostility between the two groups.

Earl Mayhew explained it when Colin asked him. "We wouldn't string along with some of the stuff we thought they were pulling," he said. "So they make it tough for us to have any say at all now."

"You mean it will go on then?"

"Sure it will. Until the rest of the boys see what the score is and throw them out. The way things are going now that's liable to be a long time. Most of them don't care who's doing the leading so long as nobody bothers them. And the ones that do care are scared to say much."

"What is there to be scared of?" Colin asked. But he remembered Halsborg's big voice challenging him about Clyde, remembered Kreutzer and Davidson during the strike.

Earl shrugged his shoulders. "Mostly the boys are scared of being made to look foolish. At a meeting especially—that's why they stay away. But there's more than that. Those guys can make it pretty uncomfortable out on the job for anybody who doesn't think their way."

"What do they want?" Colin said.. "What's the matter with them?"

"Politics," Earl said shortly. "They like the little piece of power they've got now and they think they'll have a whole lot more when the big day comes."

"Mike Varchuk's a commie. Always has been. But he's not in there with them."

"Oh, Mike's pretty close. They're a little too crude, even for him, but he plays along with them."

"Mike's not looking for power," Colin said.

"No, Mike's sincere. Some of them are. Mark Swetzer gave away his share in a power-saw when someone told him he was owning the means of production. You've got to respect a man like that."

Colin nodded. "Mike'd do that, too," he said. He felt the old sense of helplessness and discouragement that had come to him so often. "But what's the use of it?" he asked Earl. "Where's it going to end?"

"It'll end the same way as it's ended before," Earl said. "In a split union. Then we'll have it all to do over."

After he had talked with Earl, Colin tried to settle back into the routine of the working days; but the thing seemed everywhere about him, threatening and insistent. It rode with John Halsborg and Joe Davidson in the crummy, rode again when they boarded the train to go out into the woods. It was in the beer parlors over the week ends, in the stores and restaurants and he knew that men took it with them into their homes. The men on the bridge-crew all belonged to the union and talked of what was happening almost daily, jokingly yet bitterly, during the lunch hours. Colin listened to them. They were easier, less afraid than most of the men he knew, less afraid than Earl Mayhew and far less intense, less afraid than Halsborg and Davidson and the other men who blustered, less afraid than the simple men who clustered near Halsborg and listened to him so often in strained silence. But it seemed to Colin that even these men, the quiet, warm men he had known so long, like Sam Boulder and John Meldrum and old John Smith were touched by fear, that fear and anxiety spoke through the bitterness of their jokes. He listened and he heard the stuff of violence all about him, fear, bitterness, hate and violence. A violence darker and more fearful, because it was between men who had the same lives, the same needs, the same dangers to face.

In the end he met the violence and made his answer to it. It was early in September, a few days after school had opened up and Mildred had come back from her summer holidays. Colin had been to see her at the cottage and had arranged to meet her on Sunday to go up to Strathmore Falls. As he walked back towards Clyde's house he met Earl Mayhew and Sam Boulder and John Meldrum and went with them into one of Blenkinstown's three beer parlors. Some men they knew were at a table near the door and they sat down with them.

It was a Friday evening and the place was crowded and noisy. John Meldrum said to Colin: "Don't see you in here very often."

"You can't blame him for that," Sam Boulder said. "These beer joints don't look much when you're used to English pubs."

"There's a difference, all right," Colin said.

"You're darn right there is," Sam said. "They let you act like a human being over there. Walk around if you want or play a game of darts or have a bite to eat. Here all you can do is sit and stare at a table full of beer glasses."

"They've been at it longer than we have," Colin said and for a while they all went over the old arguments about the province's liquor laws.

John Meldrum said suddenly: "Look over there, would you?" He jerked his thumb towards a table across the room. Colin followed the movement and saw Halsborg and Kreutzer sitting at a table with several other men. Halsborg was talking excitedly.

"The goon squad at work," Meldrum said.

Earl Mayhew sat around and picked up his beer glass. "Be fair, Johnny," he said. "Somebody's got to work up membership."

"That kind of a way?" Meldrum asked. "Ganging up on some poor dumb son of a bitch, calling him names, scaring the hell out of him? What kind of a union are you going to get that way?"

Colin looked at Halsborg's table again and saw that one of the men was sitting in sullen silence with his chair pushed back a little. Colin recognized him as a new man on the steel gang, a tense, dark man, part Negro. His hands were moving nervously at the edge of the table and his eyes watched Halsborg defensively.

Earl was answering Meldrum: "It'll work out, Johnny. They won't stand that forever. You can't bulldoze men in a free country and not have them turn around and throw you out sooner or later."

"Who is Halsborg, anyway?" Colin asked.

"There's lots like him," Earl said. "Started working in the woods during the war, to keep away from the draft. Found he was making big money with a power-saw, so he stayed with it." He glanced towards Halsborg's table again. Two men had moved away, but the steel-man was talking excitedly and angrily. "He wasn't a bad sort of guy until he got to be vice-president of the local a while back. Then they went to work on him. Now he's straight political. Thinks they'll make him a commissar or something when the revolution comes."

"He's big enough," Sam said. "Looks right for the strong-arm stuff."

John Meldrum snorted. "Beats his wife around some. That's as far as it goes. I seen him back down from a guy half his size in here one night."

Earl laughed. "He was alone that time. With the rest of the goons he can be quite a guy. Kick anybody's teeth in if somebody knocks the poor bastard down first."

About half an hour later Colin left them. He went out by the side door, into a narrow passageway that led to the street. Halsborg, Kreutzer and another man were in the passage. Halsborg had his hands at his sides, but he was pushing forward against the third man, forcing him against the wall. Colin heard him say: "Better think it over. Might be good for your health." Then he heard Colin and turned towards him. Colin walked on, came up to him, tried to get past. Halsborg blocked his way. Colin lowered his right shoulder a little, then drove it against Halsborg's chest. Halsborg staggered and crashed back against the wall. Behind him Colin heard Kreutzer say: "What was that for?" But he walked on out of the passageway without turning to look back.

On the street he stood for a moment under the bright lights in front of the beer parlor. Cars were moving and people were passing. His body was shaking and his heart was beating fast; his mind was dulled by a helpless anger that he hated. He knew that someone was standing beside him, not Halsborg because this was a small man. Then he heard Mike Varchuk's voice.

"They are fools," Varchuk said. "They cannot force the workers. They have not the strength. Later there will be no need."

Colin looked down at him. "Are you in this, too?"

"All men are in it, all men everywhere."

Colin felt the anger slowing in him a little and he wanted to laugh. "Bull," he said. "Men don't want all that stuff you guys preach. They want a chance to live and do things, build houses, sleep with wives, raise kids. They don't want to be afraid all the time and hate each other and beat each other up. Why can't you leave us alone?"

Mike smiled gently. "You will understand it better one day," he said.

"Like hell I will," Colin said.

COLIN watched the swing of Mildred's skirt as she went ahead of him down the long flight of steps towards the falls and thought he had never seen her so happy. The day was brilliant with sun that had the full warmth of summer, and the light westerly breeze was warm about them.

At the foot of the steps she stopped to lean against the railing and look up at the wide thin veil of water that poured over the slanting rock. Then, as Colin came up to her, she turned and faced him.

"I came here often while you were away," she said.

"You did? Why?"

She looked up at the long graceful flow of the steps behind him, weathered now and blending smoothly into the timbered hillside. "Because I knew you had worked here. And I could tell which work was yours."

He moved beside her and looked back at the steps. "We had fun building those," he said. "But it all broke up later on."

She nodded. "I remember." Then she said: "What is it that's broken up this time, Colin?"

He glanced at her quickly. "Nothing. Why?"

"Yes it has. You're going away again."

"Who told you?"

"No one. I just know. I know you so well, darling. You forget how well I know you."

"No I don't. It's the only thing I have—that and the valley. I'm going back there again." He knew suddenly that everything was changed for them, that the barrier was drawn away.

"What about that farm?" she asked.

He noticed that she was smiling, not concerned or angry as he had thought she might be. "I've got to think about it," he said. "Down here I haven't got any place looking for it. Up there there's time to think. I might think of something that would work for me."

They had begun walking along the wide foot-trail that led on past the falls. There was no one else in the Park in spite of the fine Sunday, and Colin was suddenly glad that the river was low and quiet in the summer heat.

"I'm not running away," he said. "That's my place up there, the only place I fit. A farm could be all right too, I guess. But it's not so easy to find one as I thought it would be."

"I've never been able to think of you as a farmer," she said seriously. "I've tried, but it doesn't work."

"A bush farm. Like the Underhills had."

"Perhaps," she said doubtfully. "Something would have to change in you first. I'm not sure I want it to change any more."

They had turned on to a side trail which led them up along a little creek that tumbled down the side-hill in an endless succession of tiny falls. They came to a bridge across the creek and she stopped again and asked him: "You built this too, didn't you?"

"Yes," he said. "It's outside the Park here, but I wanted to and they let me."

Beyond the bridge they left the trail and climbed through two or three hundred feet over the gray rock that bordered the creek. The climb brought them to a wide flat bench in which the creek was a deep narrow pool.

"I didn't know about this," she said. "It's beautiful."

"There are a hundred places like this in the mountains." Colin heard his voice suddenly harsh against the softness of hers. "I could take you to them if you'd come."

She turned away from the creek, towards him. "I'm going to come," she said. "That's why I'm so happy today. Couldn't you tell?"

He stood looking at her in unbelief, then she moved a little and he took her in his arms.

"When?" he asked. "How soon can you come?"

The smile went away from her eyes and he saw the beginnings of fear there, and pleading. "It's harder than you think, darling. It won't be right away. Can you wait a little?"

He laughed then and kissed her, kissed the serious mouth and the unsmiling eyes and felt her part of him as she had not been for years.

"Wait?" he said. "We should have learned by now to wait for each other."

She drew away from him at last, very gently, then led him over to the shade of the timber. She lay down on the soft, sloping ground under the trees and he saw that fear had gone away from her.

"It's not even ready for you up there," he said. "But I wish you could come right away. Just to see what it's like. You could, couldn't you?"

"Not and go on teaching school in Blenkinstown, darling. They're not sure about me now, but they'd be quite sure then. And it's worse than it ever was, with the camp there."

He knelt beside her and she put out her hands and he took them. "I know all that. I've thought about it often. You could come in the other way, by Menzies Lake, and I could meet you in there."

She shook her head. "Let me have a year, darling," she said. "One whole last year to finish it all out cleanly. I know it's awful to ask that, but I've planned it and arranged it and now it's the only way that seems right. You see, I hadn't meant to tell you so soon."

"Why does it have to be so long?"

She drew her hands away from his and lay back on the mossy bank. "Because I'm a schoolteacher, I suppose, with a little fussy mind that has to do everything a certain way." She looked up at him. "But we do have to think this time, darling. So far we've always let things happen and they haven't happened very well for us."

"I know," he said. "I'm the one that should be thinking and I haven't let myself. I should find the farm and have it ready for you before I ask you to come at all."

"No," she said. "We can find the farm together, later, if we want to. I'll come to you in the mountains, in the fall. You said that once—remember? Fall will come, you said."

Colin watched the brightness of the sunlight on her neck for a moment, then bent forward and kissed it. She raised her head and he kissed her mouth again, then held her away a little and she read the question in his eyes.

"Of course," she said. "My love." She moved towards him, hard against him, and she said: "Oh, darling Colin, why do I always wait until you are going away? Why can't I be generous, the way other women are when they love someone?"

"You are," he said. "You're the only generous person in the world."

She laughed, a little, deep-throated, satisfied laugh. "That isn't true," she said. She buried her face in his chest and he felt her strong body quiver against him. "You're the generous one, to let me come my own silly way. You've always been the one that gave and waited. That's why I love you so." She raised her face to his and he saw that the happiness was still in it, brilliant yet without strife, deeply calm yet with all the intensity of ultimate decision. "Love me, darling, please," she said.

Colin held her to him and felt the world draw away. Into the depths, his mind said, into the dark, enfolding depths. It is such a little way, yet one can go down and down into them forever. Even death is not so deep.

3 4

COLIN came down Amabilis Valley to his cabin at the lake through the storm of an early November day. It was a savage storm, violent with a gale of wind that broke limbs from trees and drove scattering sheets of ice-cold rain and snow through the protection of the timber. Long before he reached the cabin his thick woolen clothing was heavy with rain and his body was touched by a more exhausting cold than any he had known from snow and ice and the freezing winds of the high hills. He remembered this cold, this draining of all warmth, from low-altitude storms of other years. It made him think of death, a comfortless, strength-sapped, lonely death, unlike the swift mercy of a bullet or the peace of dry snow in the high places. The word "perish" was in this death, the word "exposure," the word "exhaustion." He felt his body powerful and resistant to them all, guarding its heat against the persistent, intense attack, secure in its reserve of strength. But he was glad when he came to the cabin and went into its close shelter.

Inside, his movements were habit. A twist of his shoulders freed the sodden packsack and dropped it to the floor; he set the rifle in its corner, took three steps from there and began to lay the fire in the stove—shavings, pitchwood, kindling; he lit the shavings and, with the same match, his first lamp. Then he was free to strip off his wet clothes.

The familiarity of the routine made it swift and automatic, almost unfelt. Yet this, like everything else in his valley, had new meaning for him now; over everything and through everything was the thought that she would come, not tomorrow, not even soon, but soon enough and surely. So surely that often in the hills he felt her with him already; so surely that thought must recognize the changes her coming would make in even this simple, changeless routine of return.

Through the evening, as the storm lessened, she was with him. She read beside him in the lamplight, stood beside him outside the door as he watched the few stars in the clearing sky and heard the dying wind still strong in the treetops, the dying swell still heavy on the beach, and she was beside him again as he slept.

He was up early the next morning, to a gray and windless day of gentle rain. As he cooked breakfast he decided to go down the lake to see Robbie; there would have been little movement of game during the hours of storm and it might be some while before he had another chance to go down on a calm lake.

He had cleaned up the cabin and was almost ready to start out when he heard the distant sound of the motor. Both Robbie and Johnny had outboards for their canoes now and he thought at first it might be one or other of them; but he saw as soon as he looked down the lake that it was a boat, not a canoe, that was coming. He turned sharply from the window and for a moment he felt something like panic. He glanced quickly at his mackinaw and empty packsack, gauging the time it would take him to get together the stuff he needed and start up the valley. Then he realized, with a sharp sense of astonishment, what he was doing. He said aloud, "What's the matter with me? Can't some guy come up the lake without me hitting for the bush?"

He went to the door, opened it and stood watching the boat. It was close enough now for him to see that there was only one man in it. From the logging outfit, likely, he thought; chances are he's going on to the head of the lake, won't even stop in here. But as he watched, the bow of the boat swung a little and he saw that it was heading directly for the cabin.

He stood in the doorway without moving while the little boat ran in to the beach and the man stepped out. He still did not move but watched while the man walked up towards the cabin— a big man, heavily built, with a round, cheerful face.

"Mr. Ensley?" the man asked as he came to the foot of the steps.

"That's right," Colin said and watched his eyes.

The man held out his hand. "Arnold's my name," he said. "Jeff Arnold. Mind if I come in for a few minutes?"

Colin took the offered hand and led the way into the cabin. He pushed a chair forward for Arnold, then looked into the kettle on the stove.

"I'll make coffee soon as she boils," he said.

"Thanks," Arnold said. He looked appraisingly around the cabin. "Pretty nice place you have here. Build it yourself?"

"Sure," Colin said.

Arnold nodded approvingly. "You certainly know how to go about it. Well, we won't disturb you much."

Colin turned sharply towards him. He knew this was what he had been afraid of. "You won't what?" he asked.

"We'll try not to bother you any more than we have to. When we start logging."

"You mean you're going to log the valley?"

"Sure," Arnold said. "It's a great stand of balsam and the price'll never be better. An easy truck show, too. We ought to be able to move the fallers in right after the new year unless there's a lot of snow."

Colin listened to the easy, casual words and felt anger and

291

despair grow in him until he could hardly speak. He said at last: "It's my valley. You can't log it."

Arnold laughed sympathetically. "I know how you feel. But you don't have to worry. We'll see your cabin doesn't get hurt. We'll take care of you—give you a job if you like. We could use you fine."

Colin watched him through narrowed, dangerous eyes. "*You'll* take care of me," he said. "*You'll* give me a job. Didn't you ever stop to think maybe there's people in the world don't want to be taken care of? People that don't want anything more than to be left alone?"

Arnold shrugged his big shoulders. He had dealt with difficult people before and had no intention of losing his temper. "We're just trying to make it as easy as we can for you. The timber's got to be logged."

"Why?"

"Because the market's right," Arnold said patiently. "Because the owners figure . . ."

"Owners!" Colin put a violence into the word that made Arnold stand up and face him. "What did they ever do to own it? They never even saw it. How can anybody own something he never saw?"

"Look," Arnold said. "I just work for them. Don't take it out on me. We're trying to make things as easy as we can for you. Hell, we'll be all through inside a couple of years." He turned and walked to the door. At the door he stopped and turned back: "Look," he said again, "trouble's the last thing we want. But don't ever think we can't handle it. We've run into your kind before."

"Get out," Colin said. He watched Arnold start down the beach, then suddenly crossed the cabin and picked up his rifle. He worked the lever swiftly, flicked the butt to his shoulder and held it with the sights lined steadily on the back of Arnold's neck. Then anger left him and he felt only helplessness. He lowered the rifle, walked to the bunk and threw it down on the blankets. He sat down on the edge of the bunk and a great weight pressing through his whole body made him rest his forearms on his knees and lower his head to his hands. He began to tremble uncontrollably. "The bastards," he said. "The bastards."

DURING the week after Arnold had come to the beach cabin Colin moved nearly everything he owned up to the cabin in the Gully. He worked intently and secretly. Several times he saw boats coming up the lake and always moved away before he could be seen. Once he watched from the bush while Arnold and another man came up to the cabin, knocked, opened the door and looked in, then went away. He knew a small tent camp had been pitched in the bay just over on the other side of the creek and that men were working on a line up the valley.

He took up the traps from the lower part of his lines and ran them out again within easier reach of the Gully. Once that was done he felt calmer, but he was not satisfied. He waited for a spell of fine, cold weather, then loaded a heavy pack and made the climb to Windstorm Gap. He had brought with him a small tent, which he pitched carefully in a level, sheltered place near the Gap. Then he went on over the divide into the Milk River valley, traveling steadily and swiftly until he was down to the timber line again. Just below timber he built a rough shelter and camped for the night.

During the next three days he prospected the valley for signs of fur and built another shelter within two or three miles of Menzies Lake. Then he climbed to the Gap again, spent a night in his tent and dropped down next day to the cabin in the Gully.

The intense, straining activity of these days occupied him fully and even gave him an exultant happiness. But as he traveled his trap-lines near Amabilis Lake and in the lower parts of the valley, anger and desperation returned to him. He traveled through to the beach and saw that a good-sized campsite was being cleared near the mouth of the creek. He followed the newly staked survey lines, trying to judge the scope and scale of the logging operation from them. Sometimes he spent hours watching the survey crew at work, himself unseen on a slope above them, behind a log or a root or a tree. At first he had played with his rifle, sighting it on the men as they worked, fingering the trigger. It seemed as though it should be within the power of a bullet to stop them at this early stage of things. A bullet fired high, to scare them out; perhaps several bullets, fired at unpredictable intervals over days of time, cutting into the ground near them or smashing in the transit as they worked, passing close overhead as they walked to and from work, crashing into the ridge-pole of a tent as they slept. But he knew in his heart that this would not turn them away. Perhaps a single shot, fired to wound or kill. But he could not find the strength of anger in himself, nor the cold desperation, to fire such a shot. These were not the men. And all too soon, watching them, he got to know them: Jake, the axeman and Slim, the head chainman, bold, cheerful men and close friends; quiet, frail, gray-haired Sandy, who ran the transit; Sam Carey, the plump and perpetually exasperated little man who always managed to fall over the least obstruction—log or root or brush or rock. Once they became individual men to him, Colin found himself watching them with tolerance, even with amusement. He left them and went back to his traps.

During the next spell of good weather he crossed Windstorm Gap again and ran out two short lines of traps from his shelter in the other valley. By the time he got back to the Gully again it was within a day or two of Christmas. He decided to go down and see Robbie and Johnny.

He found Johnny at his cabin and went on with him to Robbie's. Robbie welcomed them, as always, with a cheerful friendship that was almost fatherly. He poured them rum and made hot coffee and they began to talk. Robbie asked almost at once about the camp at Amabilis Creek.

"What are they doing up there? There's a pile of stuff gone up in the last month—everything from wash tubs to bulldozers."

"They're going to log," Colin said. "You know that."

Robbie nodded. "Arnold stopped by. Said you was kind of hard to do business with."

"That's too bloody bad," Colin said. "So will you be when they start to log your valley."

"I hope I don't live to see it," Robbie said. "But it's no use to fight it. A man may as well play along with them."

"It's hard to take," Johnny said. "I guess I'll feel about the same as Colin if they come to Carlson's Creek."

"Seems like there's no place left where a man can keep to himself and act like a man," Colin said. "Me least of all. Why in

294

hell's name would they have to pick on Amabilis Valley first out of this whole goddamned lake?"

"Pulp," Robbie told him. "It's all pulp now. You and Grant helped them pick on that valley, first time you was ever in here."

The next day was Christmas and they made a big meal off two geese Johnny had killed, and drank a lot of rum. Afterwards Robbie went to sleep on his bunk. Johnny and Colin talked quietly with the rum bottle on the table between them.

"It's sure as hell good to have you back here," Johnny said. "I thought for a while you might be going to stay outside."

"No need of that," Colin said. "The way the outside is moving in with us."

"It won't be so bad as it seems now. They won't get up as high as your best marten country and Robbie says they'll likely be through in a couple of years."

Colin looked over at Robbie on the bunk and saw that he was sleeping soundly. "Look, Johnny," he said. "I wouldn't want Robbie to know this, but I'm moving over the divide. Into Milk River. I've got traps out there already and next spring I'm going to build me a cabin."

"Jesus," Johnny said. "You can't do that. That's park country. The whole goddamned works is game reserve."

"I'm doing it. They'll never know the difference so long as I go in from this side."

Johnny got up from the table, walked over to the window and stood looking out at the lake. "They'll catch up with you sooner or later," he said slowly. "Bound to. If the mountains don't make it first. You can't travel that Gap all the time and get by with it."

Colin laughed. "Look, Johnny. Remember the time we found you up the valley? You weren't suffering any, were you? There wasn't a damn thing hurt you till we began to bring you out of it."

"That's right. But I'm sure as hell glad you did bring me out."

"That's the difference," Colin said. "I don't believe I'd give a damn. That's why I won't ever die in the mountains."

Johnny came back to the table and poured himself another drink. "I still can't see it," he said. "Taking all those chances just because there's a few loggers come into the valley."

295

"I was figuring to work over that way before I knew they were coming."

"There's no more fur over there than there is on this side. Your line's been rested for years."

"I know," Colin said. "It wasn't fur I was thinking of. I like that country. If it's park country they've got to leave it alone, the way it is, haven't they? They can't log in there or bitch it up any way."

"I guess not," Johnny said slowly. "But I still don't get it. If you want some place that's not disturbed you've still got the Gully and the mountains."

"You can't make a living up there, or find meat after the first big snow." He suddenly leaned forward across the table. "Can't you see, Johnny? A man's got to do something sooner or later. He can't let himself be pushed around and pushed around forever. Every place I've been so far, all my life, I've let them run me out Now I've let them run me out of the valley. I hadn't even got the guts to stop and fight for that."

Johnny shook his head slowly. "It don't sound like you talking at all. You couldn't stop them any more than you could stop a rock-slide. It's their timber."

Colin reached for the bottle and poured himself another drink. "Don't pay any attention to me," he said. "I guess I'm tight." He looked across at Robbie and saw that the old man was still asleep. "You know, Johnny, sometimes I think I'm going crazy. Maybe I've always been crazy and that's the whole trouble."

Johnny laughed. "You've had enough sense to put me straight a few times," he said. "Seems to me I remember you were always pretty bright in school."

"You don't have to be dumb to go crazy," Colin said. "All you have to do is think hard enough about something that matters a hell of a lot to you. The harder you think, the worse it gets until you feel like you're backed into a corner and everybody's throwing things at you. You've got to either fight or get out some way. If you fight, you're crazy, like the rest of them. If you run away, you're yellow."

"That sort of a set-up only lasts for a spell. Sooner or later things work out right and you get a break."

Colin thought of Mildred. "I know," he said. "That's one reason I've got to work down in towards Menzies Lake."

"What's that got to do with it?"

"I'll tell you sometime," Colin said.

Robbie stirred on the bunk, opened his eyes and sat up. Johnny glanced anxiously at Colin, started to say something and checked himself. "Hell," Robbie said. "It's a good job I came to while there's still something in the bottle."

3 5

THROUGH the early spring months, whenever the wind drew up the valley, Colin could hear the sounds of the logging operation. The high walls of the valley seemed to echo and emphasize the irritating, intermittent rattle of the power-saws and he grew to hate them. The other sounds were familiar—the heavy roar of the donkey engine down at the beach, the rattle of the caterpillars on the slopes, the occasional rending crash of a great tree falling; but the power-saws were new and their nagging persistence strained at him in constant reminder that change and violence could reach back even into the hills.

About a week after the end of the season, when he had taken up his traps and stored them away, he tried to work through Windstorm Gap and go down the other valley. But it was an early season after a winter of heavy snowfall, and the tons of snow and ice that broke away from Amabilis Mountain during every hour of the day made the Gap impassable. He went back to the cabin in the Gully, made up a new pack and started out before daylight the next morning for the pass to the hidden lake. The slopes below the pass were dangerous with thaw and slides, but the danger fitted his mood and he traveled recklessly, finding pleasure in the thunder of avalanching snow and ice. He found his mind and body working smoothly together to calculate risk and evade death; often he crossed slopes while the glinting flecks of snow particles from the last slide still hung over them, knowing that another slide might follow at any time; once a great mass of snow broke away under him and he saved himself only by falling forward and driving the butt of his rifle deeply into a bank of snow that held; once he found himself trapped while fragments and boulders of ice rolled and bounced past on both sides of him, but he moved on amongst them and was not touched. He felt triumph in his safety and a restoration of his old faith in the hills that the sound of the power-saws had almost destroyed.

He had expected to find an overhang of snow where the corridor opened to the platform ledge and had made up his mind to try to break it away. But he found it had already fallen and he dropped to the platform and made the jump to the start of the ledge trail without serious difficulty. The trail itself was dangerous, but he traveled it late in the evening, when the air had begun to cool, and came safely through to the open water of the lake.

For a few days he was happy in the hidden valley. He built a rough shelter and hewed out the foundation logs for a cabin. No sound reached him from outside the valley. At nights he lay in his blankets, listening to the quiet murmur of falls not yet fully freed from ice, finding silence in the stars that filled the circle of dark sky overhead and outlined the peaks. Through the warm days the mountains shed snow and ice in an almost continuous roar of sound that held no jarring note for him. But he felt restlessness grow on him again and traveled to the foot of the lake, then climbed the lip above the falls to check the difficult route he had examined from below. The sounds of the logging reached him again there and he turned back from them. The valley seemed suddenly narrow and confining. Moisture was everywhere in it, pressing in on him from the wet and heavy snow piled on the lower slopes of the mountains, rising from the still surface of the lake, hanging in the motionless limbs of the trees. A man could live here, he thought, but it would press him down and destroy him in the end; not in summer or fall, perhaps, but in the hard winter silence and through the heaviness of spring. She could not come here and if she could come it is not a place for her. She is not here now, these are not her mountains, this is not her place. A man could live here but he would be a dying man, old and dying, without hope.

Colin stayed in the valley for almost a week longer, but made no further effort to test the way out by the falls and made little progress on the cabin. He built a raft and fished for trout and explored the lake more thoroughly than he ever had before. But the weather became cold and stormy and clouds blotted out the peaks and new snow fell. He broke his camp on a morning of storm and climbed the ledge trail gladly, into the snow and clouds of the pass.

He had intended to start out at once to attempt Windstorm Gap again, but the weather was still bad and his restlessness took him instead down the valley, towards the logging. He found that the road had been pushed right through to Amabilis Lake and split there to pass on either side, clear around the lake. No one was working there so he went down and walked along it for a mile or more to feel the strangeness of the clear and easy way through the country he knew. In the end it oppressed him and he turned back into the timber, following high along the east side of the valley until he was directly above where the fallers were working. From there he dropped down the hillside and moved unseen until he was within a few feet of two men who were working with a power-saw. He watched them drop a tree and slipped away, still unseen, to watch a caterpillar yarding out logs to the road.

The next day he traveled the other side of the valley clear down to the lake. They had left his cabin unharmed and there were a few wind-stunted trees still standing near the edge of the lake. The rest, the whole floor of the valley on both sides of the creek, was a tangle of limbs and stumps and broken tops and shattered saplings. The brutal destruction of logging was a familiar thing to Colin; he had grown up with it and long ago accepted it as a part of the life that men lived. But seeing it here, in the closely familiar place that had seemed unchanging, he felt rage pour like a red flood through his body and burst into his mind. He felt choked with it and half-blinded by it and his right hand gripped the stock of his rifle until the blood was held back from his fingers

299

and they grew numb. "The bastards," he said. "They didn't have to do it like that."

He traveled swiftly back up the valley and angry thoughts surged like fire in his brain. He thought of how close he had been to the power-saw men and thought again how easy it would be to kill —to kill and slip away to the hills, then come down and kill again and again until they took the warning and went away. Better, he thought, a terror that did not kill. A crumbling of the mountains around the valley, a succession of rock- and snow-slides, always threatening, killing impersonally if at all, but making a certainty of danger that would turn them away.

He heard the power-saws on the opposite side of the valley and heard the deep-throated clatter of a diesel truck on the road and anger flared in him again. It held with him and drove his body until he was beyond Amabilis Lake, climbing through the scattered, slide-broken timber of the entrance to the Gully. Then the rhythm of climbing calmed him and he recognized the wildness of his thoughts. They were only men down there in the valley, tiny against the valley in spite of the noise and power of their machines. Men like Earl Mayhew and Sam Boulder, like John Halsborg and Ray Kreutzer; ordinary men who would pass on to work elsewhere and leave the valley to grow back to itself again. Anger against them could mean nothing and achieve nothing. The old sense of helplessness and failure came back on him until his body felt weighted under it and his step slowed.

He was coming into the meadow now. There were still great islands and peninsulas of snow on it, but he could walk near the stream without touching snow. The windows of his cabin shone clear pale gold in the westerly sun and he felt hope again. There is this, he thought; she can come here and see this. And there is the other valley, where she said she would come and from where she can come to this.

The next morning he loaded a heavy pack and started on the trip through Windstorm Gap to Milk River.

COLIN built the cabin in the Milk valley during the summer months. He had chosen a place about two miles up from Menzies Lake and five or six hundred feet above the level of the river, where a strong creek from the mountainside fed a small lake. There was good timber all around the lake, most of it small but clear and clean, with a few great cedars in the swampy places. Colin placed his cabin at the head of the lake, a few hundred feet along the lakeshore from the creek, just above a wide beach of gray gravel. Looking down the lake, a great snow mountain across the main valley was framed between the sloping walls of the draw. Behind the cabin the timber ended abruptly and the mountainside climbed steeply and roughly to the broad, sloping ledges that led to Windstorm Gap.

Colin built slowly and carefully, yet with a sense of purpose and urgency. Mildred was closely with him in everything he did now. He built for her as deliberately as he had avoided building his other cabins for her. Now he thought only of what would please her, of how to make her like the place, of how best to show the valley to her.

Very often, in spite of the urgency he felt, he left the work for days at a time to climb through the valley and learn it for her as closely as he knew Amabilis Valley. It became necessary now to find the safe and easy ways, yet still to reach the high places. Because of this it began to seem more and more often that she was actually with him, climbing beside him, standing beside him to look out over the sweep of the valley and the lake below from some high place, stopping to exclaim over the loveliness of a creeping, blossom-covered plant or the tortured beauty of a wind-stunted fir. Occasionally, yet more and more frequently as time went on, he talked aloud as though she were with him and even heard her voice in answer. He would wake abruptly from such moods, check himself in something approaching irritation and turn always to some exacting physical endeavor. Yet they held an intensity of pleasure and a depth of peace beyond anything he had known, and he returned to them.

Throughout the summer he saw no one in the valley except a party of climbers who passed through to climb the big mountain on the far side. But he often watched the boats of campers and fishermen passing on Menzies Lake and he knew that they sometimes came in and camped near the mouth of Milk River; one party of fishermen stayed there for over a week and one of them went up the river each day, wading deliberately and carefully, and working his fly skilfully over the swift water. Colin watched him with interest that grew almost to unspoken friendship, but he remained unseen and unheard.

Several times Colin crossed Windstorm Gap to his cabin in the Gully and twice he went down Wind Lake to pick up mail and supplies. Robbie was away in the hills each time and had left notes to say where he would be; but Colin felt no inclination to find him and simply scribbled a few words to say he had picked up his stuff, then went on his way. Each time he crossed northward through the Gap and came to the new valley again he felt a sense of freedom and relief.

Fall came early that year, with heavy frosts in September and a quick intensity of color through the valley. Colin was happy. It seemed to.him his senses had never been so keen, nor the run of blood through his body so strong, nor hope so clear in his mind. Snow had already fallen on the high rock slopes, but the first October days were very warm and on one of them he followed the creek behind the cabin up to the first bench. There was a pool here, round and deep and very clear and a ten-foot fall entered at the head of it. A little belt of trees had found foothold on the rocky bench and grown strongly enough to make shade for moss and vine-maple and other small deciduous growth. Colin had found the pool when he was still searching the valley for the best place to build his cabin and it had reminded him of the pool on the creek above Strathmore Falls, so he had returned there often.

It was a windless day and the sun had warmed the rocks. Beside the pool heat and sunlight seemed trapped by the trees and intensified by the clear air. Colin stripped off his clothes and slipped into the pool, as he had many times before. He swam to the falls, dove under them and let the turbulent water roll his body and force it back down the pool. He came out then and lay on the warm rocks while the sun drew the water's chill from his body. For a while he watched a pair of bald eagles riding the air currents above the valley; then, as they drifted out of sight, his eyes and mind seemed filled and satisfied by the heavy green of the treetops against the pale, distant blue of the cloudless sky. He knew that he would bring Mildred here and that she would recognize it as he had. She would see it first in winter, with the falls half-frozen and ice at the edge of the pool and it would be strange to her. Then she would come to it again in summer and would know it. She had written from California, calmly, confidently, happily. "I have been so stupid, darling, but I don't think I need be any more. I understand myself now and I think I understand everything that has happened to us. I shall come in November. It will be a good time to start, with storms in your mountains and ordinary people everywhere close in their homes."

It would have been better now, he thought, better still in early summer. Yet she's wise to come in winter, then all the rest will be still ahead. I need so much of her, more than I can ever have of her, to be always with her, to be lost in her, cooled by her, borne up by her. She is strength and I am weakness; yet I am not all weakness and with her the strength that I have can find itself.

He began to dress, slowly, watching the light through the trees on the horizontal branches of the vine maples and their scarlet foliage. He hated to leave the pool, but there was work still to be done on the cabin and it was almost time to think of the traps again. As he climbed down the broken slope below the pool he heard a blue jay scolding somewhere along the lake. It scolded again, more fiercely and close by as he came to the cabin and he wondered idly what would be traveling the woods to disturb it now. Then he saw the man.

The man came forward through the trees quite slowly, looking about him as though surprised by what he saw. His eyes met Colin's and he nodded, but looked away again at the cabin and seemed to shake his head. He came up and stood beside Colin, still looking at the cabin.

"Comfortable little place you have here," he said. "Real pretty location."

"It's O.K.," Colin said. What is it to you, he thought. Then he realized the man's clothes were vaguely like a uniform and that he had a rifle in his hands.

"Your name would be Ensley, I guess?" the man asked. Colin nodded. "Thought so," the man said. "I'm Ches Burdick. In charge of the Park here."

"You better come in and eat," Colin said. "I was just going to cook up a meal."

"Thanks," Burdick said. "I guess I'd better take a look around first."

He walked to the front of the cabin and stood with his back to the lake, his feet apart, hands deep in his pockets. For nearly a minute he studied the front of the cabin and seemed to approve. He passed on, around to the other side, and stopped at the lean-to shed that Colin used to store wood. Colin knew he must have seen the hindquarters of the deer and the traps hanging there, but he said nothing and continued on his circuit of the cabin. When they came back to the beach again he stood looking at the lake for a moment. Then he said: "Mind if I take a look inside?"

"Go ahead," Colin said. "I asked you to come in and eat."

Burdick looked at him. "I'm afraid I'm going to have to take you out," he said. "I wouldn't want to eat without you knowing that."

Colin nodded. "I know," he said. "It's O.K."

Starting the fire, moving about the stove as the meal cooked, Colin was amazed at the calmness of his body and the steadiness of his voice. It was over now, he knew that; she could never come in here now. He watched Burdick, a quiet, slow man, sitting at the table looking out at the lake. Burdick's rifle was out on the porch, leaning against the wall just beside the door. Burdick waited quietly, asking only occasional questions until Colin set a plate in front of him. As Colin sat down, Burdick said: "Seems too bad. You picked yourself a swell place."

"What'll they do?" Colin asked.

Burdick shrugged his shoulders. "I wouldn't know. Never had it happen before. You've got a trap-line some place on Wind Lake, haven't you?"

"That's right," Colin said.

"You're liable to lose out on that for a spell. They'll likely cancel your license."

They ate in silence after that and cleaned up in silence. Then Burdick said: "You better throw your stuff together. We've got quite a piece to go." He walked out of the cabin and down on to the beach and stood looking at the lake again. Colin watched him, then turned back into the cabin, picked up his own rifle and came silently to the door. Standing there, beside Burdick's rifle, he worked the lever and threw a shell into the breach.

Burdick turned swiftly to the sound and saw Colin with the steady rifle at his hip. He raised his hands a little, holding the palms towards Colin, but stood where he was. "Don't try it, son," he said quietly. "It won't do you any good."

"I'm not coming out," Colin said.

"They'll send a bunch in to fetch you out," Burdick said. "You may as well come along now and get it over with. We can forget about this part."

"I'm not coming out," Colin repeated. "You get started back for the lake before something happens."

Burdick shrugged his shoulders again. "You're the doctor," he said. "But that don't make you anything except crazy."

"Get going," Colin said. "I'll be right behind you all the way down there."

Burdick started to walk along the edge of the lake, his shoulders square, his hands thrust into his pockets again. After a few steps he stopped and looked back over his shoulder. "What about the rifle?"

"You'll find it," Colin said. "When you come back."

3 6

COLIN watched Burdick's boat until it was a tiny speck far down towards the foot of Menzies Lake, then traveled swiftly back to his cabin.

The afternoon sun was still bright on the surface of the little lake, the air was calm, the cabin stood as squarely set in the timber as it ever had, light and pleasant, its door wide open and Burdick's rifle standing where he had left it. Colin picked up the rifle, ejected the shells and threw them one by one into the lake. Then he took the rifle inside the cabin and set it carefully on the table.

For a moment he stood quite still, looking at the pleasant room, at the sunlight streaming in through windows and door, at the strong, closely-fitted furniture, the matched and patterned wood of walls and ceiling and cupboards. It didn't work out, he thought, after all. It never does. Perhaps it was wrong, the way everything else has been wrong, ever since the beginning.

He went out to the lean-to, took down the remains of the deer meat, cut away a few pieces, then took the rest down to his raft at the edge of the lake. He pushed the raft out until it was over deep water, then dropped the meat overboard. He came back, took all his traps from the lean-to into the cabin and began to make up a pack.

By late evening he was in Windstorm Gap. The still air was very cold and there were clouds high in the sky, far above the mountain tops, for the first time in many days. Colin slept the night in his tent near the Gap and started out again in the dim gray light of the next morning, against the first whisper of the storm.

He had meant to get down to the cabin in the Gully before noon, spend only an hour or two there, then start for Hidden Valley. The fierce drive of the storm and the fresh snow everywhere held him back and there was little daylight left when he came on to the flat white surface of the meadow from the last slope of rock. He approached the cabin cautiously, checking it from every side before he went up to it. But there was no one there. Inside, he lit a fire, stripped off his wet clothes and made the first meal he had eaten since the one with Burdick the day before. The effort of climbing from the little lake to the Gap, the still greater effort of forcing his way down against the storm, had used him physically and mentally and he had had little time to think of his position. He had made his decision while Burdick was examining the cabin and thus far he had followed it through. For the moment, because it was utterly unlikely that anyone would attempt to travel through the storm at night, he felt himself safe; and he began to think again.

Sitting here, in the familiar cabin, he tried to find again the triumph he had felt in disarming Burdick and turning him away. He could not find it. He remembered only the bitter, hopeless calm that had come upon him when he first understood Burdick's mission and realized that everything he had planned and worked towards was lost, taken from him by this quiet, impersonal man who spoke for some vague and distant authority. It had seemed wrong that this authority could reach out so far, to this place where no one came in year after year, to set a sudden blight upon it, to limit freedom, deny possession.

So he had turned Burdick away, disarmed his authority. He had done it calmly and defiantly, secure in the thought of the hills, in the certainty that he could travel beyond reach of the authority that supported Burdick. It had seemed triumph then, and as triumph and elation had carried his swift, efficient journey through the Gap and down to the cabin in the Gully. It must carry him further, into Hidden Valley, and on through the difficult things he would have to do to live there without being found. But it was triumph and elation no longer, only a great burden of loss and destruction. She could never come now, there could be no place for her to come to, no part for her in what had to be done. Defiance of Burdick had been a trivial, ineffective defiance because his authority was remote and impervious. Burdick himself had not resisted, he had been quiet and impersonal, not an enemy. Even when he was facing the rifle he had been without hostility. There was no triumph, only loss.

Colin sat on at the table in the little cabin long after his meal was finished. He was unconscious of time or the storm outside or his body's fatigue, he was little conscious of his hurt mind's long and tortuous search for understanding of all the things that had happened. Hours later he slept, still at the table, his head on his outstretched arms, the oil lamp burning quietly beside him. He still had not made the choice between Hidden Valley and the journey out by Menzies Lake to find Burdick and give himself up.

THREE days after Colin had turned him away, Burdick came back up the lake with a policeman named Delker. They landed at the mouth of Milk River and Delker stood for a moment looking uneasily at the timbered slope of hillside above them. Then he reached to his belt and opened the flap of his holster. "I don't like it a darn bit," he said. "He could be watching us from up there right now."

Burdick shook his head. "He's lit out for the high mountains. Good as told me he was going to. They say he knows them like the back of his hand." He bent down to tighten a boot lace, then straightened and switched the rifle he was carrying over into the bend of his left arm. "Come on. I want to get it over with."

They walked for a mile or more in silence, then Delker asked: "Do you figure the guy's nuts?"

Burdick shrugged his shoulders without turning. "Could be," he said. "I wouldn't know. Seemed a nice enough kid."

"He's Clyde Munro's brother-in-law. Nothing wrong with the sister, but they say Ensley's always been kind of queer."

"He wasn't too queer for the army. He was three or four years overseas."

"That was enough to turn some of them queer," Delker said. "I never did go for this chasing after crazy guys."

"Didn't look to me like he was the dangerous kind."

Delker laughed. "You didn't stop to argue any."

"Nobody's paying me to argue with a gun," Burdick said.

They came to the foot of the lake and Burdick pointed out the cabin.

"Seems a goddamned shame to burn it down," Delker said. "What's the idea?"

Burdick shrugged his shoulders. "Once you call a place a Park you've got to keep it that way."

"A neat little place like that don't hurt it any."

"The boss says he's got no right to build there in the first place. If you let one get by he says they'll all be doing it."

COLIN watched the two men come up to the cabin and go inside. He had been on his way down the valley when he first heard them, to go out and find Burdick. Hearing them, he had swung back along the ridges to come out on the broken slope behind the cabin. It was a gray day, heavy with unfallen snow and very cold. But he lay in close hiding among a mass of broken boulders and did not feel the cold. Burdick had come to him, Burdick or someone who would do as well. He wished now he had gone closer to them, to make sure that one was Burdick. They were both dressed in ordinary woods clothes, both slow-moving men. Only one carried a rifle.

Colin saw them come out of the cabin. The man with the rifle was carrying Burdick's rifle as well as his own and he walked across and leaned both rifles against a tree a little way from the cabin. The other had gone into the lean-to behind the cabin, but he came back at once with an armload of wood. Colin watched as they both worked for several minutes over something at the back of the cabin. One man straightened and stepped back. The other still knelt. Then, so suddenly that it was a jar of intense pain through his mind, he knew what they were doing. He felt the soft, comforting jolt of the rifle against his cheek, saw the kneeling man sway and fall forward over the fire he had laid. The second man whirled and stood motionless for a moment, looking towards the sound of the shot. Then he turned again and disappeared behind a tree. Colin waited and watched without moving, the rifle still at his shoulder, another shell ready in the breech. The man he had shot did not move. But he saw the second man crawl to the rifles and take one, then crawl back to the cabin and along the edge to where his friend was lying. He moved the body, evidently searching for some sign of life. He stood up at last, shook his fist towards the slope where Colin was lying, then turned and went away along the edge of the lake. Colin watched him out of sight and still did not move.

Much later, when it was almost dark, Colin stood up and climbed stiffly down the slope to the cabin. Only when he stood over the body and saw that it was Burdick did he realize fully that he had killed a man. He knelt beside him, touched the quiet face and the great wound where the bullet had broken out of his chest. "I'm sorry," he said and knew that he was crying. He lifted the body carefully, carried it into the cabin and laid it on the big bunk.

COLIN spent two nights and a day in the cabin with Burdick's dead body. Much of the time he prayed, searching his mind for

309

prayers, remembering his father's texts and his own earliest beliefs. For a long time he would not be fully convinced that Burdick was dead. It seemed to him that the calm eyes would open and the slow voice would speak again, carelessly and easily, discounting the bullet's awful wound. He remembered the shot, the slight pressure of his finger, the slight, familiar jar against his cheek, the tiny, distant body falling forward and lying still. Death seemed nowhere in any of this. But it was here now, in Burdick's stiffened body, in the silence of the cabin that should have been burned, in the stillness of the lake's surface under the storm-filled, waiting clouds.

He accepted it at last, knew that Burdick would not speak or move again. Accepting it, he was lonely; and the cabin, like Burdick, was dead to him. Early on the second morning he made up a small pack, took his rifle and his axe and went outside. For a little while he stood looking at the cabin and the lake, watching the first slow, small flakes of snow come down as though squeezed from the clouds. Then he walked forward and knelt beside the wood and kindling Burdick had piled against the cabin. He lit a match and watched the cedar shavings sputter and catch in its flame. Then pitch caught somewhere, then larger pieces of kindling, then the wood. Flame reached out under the cabin. Colin took his axe and chopped with sure and powerful strokes at the lowest log until the flames could reach through to the inside of the cabin. Then he went to the lean-to and brought more wood and threw it on to the spreading fire.

"That was what you wanted," he said, and began to climb the rock slope towards the hills.

THE morning Colin left the cabin a party of ten men landed from three boats at the mouth of Milk River. Clyde Munro was in charge of it. Delker was there, two other policemen, and a game warden. The others were Blenkinstown civilians, and one of them was Tod Phalling. They all carried rifles and they were a tense group. Clyde knew this and tried to ease them as they stood around near the boats.

"The first thing we've got to do," he said, "is find Ches Burdick. When we've done that we start looking for Ensley."

"Suppose he's out looking for us?" someone asked.

"He won't be," Clyde said. "That doesn't mean we don't have to keep our eyes open all the way, but he won't be. Something else. If we do come up with him, don't shoot unless he does. I've got a strong hunch he won't."

"He shot Ches Burdick quick enough," Phalling said.

Clyde looked at him. "O.K.," he said. "And he can shoot quicker and straighter than any man of us here. So the best chance we've got is to take him without shooting. Understand?"

Phalling grinned. "You're the boss," he said. "If it was me I'd say shoot first."

Clyde turned away from him. "I'm going ahead with Jim Delker and the game warden," he said. "The rest of you come on in two groups, one minute apart, one minute behind us. A policeman with each group. O.K.?"

"O.K., Clyde," one of the policemen said. "We'll move up fast if we hear any shooting."

The group broke up and the men made new groups, talking among themselves. They were easier now that they felt a plan and pattern in what they had to do. Clyde slung his rifle and started out with Delker and the game warden.

AS Colin climbed away from the burning cabin he felt an immense loneliness. There was nothing now, there never could be anything again except himself. He passed the little pool in the rock below the falls and thought of Mildred. She would hear about it, somewhere down in California, and know that she was freed from her promise. His last claim on her was burning in the flames that would soon destroy the cabin, had been killed with the bullet that killed Burdick. Not lonely, Colin thought, but alone. And it was not oppressive, nor terrifying, nor even sad to be alone. There was regret in it, regret for Burdick and all the destroyed things. But there was also pride in it and a clean strength and a purpose. To find death alone, away from confusion and fear and contempt and hatred. Not to seek it, not to aid it in any way. But to find it.

He climbed out on to the last broad ledge before the valley began to narrow to the Gap and knew that he was looking into death. It crept slowly towards him across the face of the mountains, blotting out draws and ridges and pinnacles as it came, gray white and silent. He looked behind him then, back down the still unsheeted valley, and saw at once the dark figures of men climbing far below him against the snow. He turned and went on and the front of the blizzard swept past him, hiding the climbing figures, closing everything into silence that waited for the first fierce sound of the wind.

There was death in the blizzard, Colin knew, but still a chance of life. He believed he could still pass safely through the Gap. After that there would be the full force of the wind on the open slopes at the head of Amabilis Valley. Walking, a man might keep himself alive. In the dark, he would not be able to walk. So there was only the tent. If no one had found it from the other side, and if they did not follow from this side.

The thought stopped him. He remembered what Andrew Grant had said of Tom Hughes' death in Windstorm Gap: "If you're ever in a spot like that, make them go back. Never mind the talk and kidding. Make them go back."

He stood for a moment longer, feeling the storm against him, hearing the high hard sound of the strengthening wind. Then he turned back. He picked his place well, a narrow place where the ledge sharply turned a ridge of the mountain. There was a short steep drop from it down to the wide main ledge they must follow if they were still coming against the storm.

Colin waited. He waited without fear, without hope for himself, yet without reluctance. He knew that the storm had almost certainly turned them back already, knew that time was closing in on him, that in an hour or two at the most it would be too dark to travel through the Gap. But he knew also that he had drawn them there and that if there was to be death again it must be for himself, not them. So he waited.

He saw them easily, more easily than he had expected, when they were still two hundred yards away. Six men, climbing grimly against the storm, following the dim outline of his track under the newly fallen snow. He fired once, over their heads, and watched them scatter into cover. Even then he could have killed some of them, because there was little good cover on the ledge. He wondered if they knew it, if they were afraid, and he did not want to fire again though he knew he would have to if he hoped to hold them there.

He saw a man crawling towards better cover and fired near him. There was an answering shot and the bullet sang away from the ridge above him. There was a long wait. Then Colin saw another man crawling forward. He fired once more, but the man did not stop; instead he stood up and began to walk slowly forward across the open ledge. Colin felt panic touch him. He heard himself shout wildly: "Go back," and he brought the sights of his rifle squarely on the center of the man's chest. Then he knew it was Clyde and saw that there was no rifle in his hands.

For a moment Colin hesitated. Then he stood up, his rifle held down at full arm's length across his thighs. He saw Clyde wave, then felt the shock of the bullet solid and heavy against his left shoulder. It threw him back, half-turning his body, and he fell to his knees. He looked back over the ledge and saw that Clyde had dropped down into cover. He fired near a man who moved, waited a moment and fired a second shot towards the other side of the ledge. Then he slipped away behind the ridge and began to climb the next ledge at a run.

He turned two more ridges, still running, then dropped back to his smooth, effortless mountaineer's walk. He was afraid only of Clyde. Clyde had known he would not shoot to kill. And Clyde would follow. It was Clyde who had brought those others up in the face of the storm and it was Clyde who would stand up and walk forward again, to find blood in the snow where Colin had made his stand and know that he was wounded.

Colin climbed on. He had wedged clothing between coat and the wound and it seemed to him the bleeding had stopped. There was little pain except when he tried to raise his left arm and he could detect no weakening of his body through shock or blood loss. He was still in shelter from the main drive of the storm, but the way turned out now, along the last jutting ridge that marked the entrance to the Gap. As he started towards the point of the ridge he knew he would be exposed to anyone traveling the ledges behind him, but he did not look round. If they're that close, he thought, let them shoot. But let them do it right this time, let them find the heart. At least I did that for Ches Burdick. It could have been the heart for me. A little lower, a little farther over; likely the guy shot for it, held high and pulled off a little. I always thought it would be the heart, I used to think it when I was a kid, used to think it overseas, a bullet in the heart, quickly.

Suddenly he knew he did not want to die. He was almost at the point of the ridge now and he stopped and looked back. He could see the ledge, white and empty around the long curve behind him, empty again through the next curve to where the falling snow shut it from sight. They were slow or they had turned back. It might be either. He climbed over the point of the ridge and met the full, howling violence of the storm. It tore at his face and hands, found openings in his clothing, held his body and battered it with the strength and weight of moving water. He put his head down and faced into it, not hurrying, not straining, yet using his body's strength to make speed from sure and measured movement. There was light still, a dim gray light that would not lessen much for an hour yet.

There were sloping ledges in the gap and rock that had to be climbed and slides that had to be crossed. He slipped once in climbing, because his left arm was not there to help him, but recovered. Once the new snow began to move under him, very slowly, but he crossed to safety and turned back to see the slide check itself and hold for lack of weight. He passed the narrow place where Tom Hughes had slipped, and reached the broad ledge beyond. The snow was thigh deep now, dragging at his legs while the wind resisted his body. Once he stumbled and fell and lay for a moment feeling the warmth and shelter of the deep snow. He knew it would be easy and peaceful to die that way, but his mind turned from death and he got up and went on.

He came to the tiny draw that sheltered the tent and turned into it without caution. He had plowed a dozen paces through the deeper snow of the sheltered place before he saw that someone had gone in before him. He stopped then, but it was too late. The tent flaps opened and he saw a man there. The numbed fingers of his single good hand fumbled with his rifle, dropped it and he stood there, disarmed and helpless. Then he saw that the man was Johnny Harris.

"Colin," Johnny said. "Jesus, I thought you'd never come." He stumbled forward through the snow and touched Colin. "You're hurt," he said.

"How in hell did you get up here?" Colin asked him.

They went into the tent and Colin slid the light pack away from his right shoulder. "I haven't got much time," he said. "They're liable to be coming still."

Johnny looked out at the storm. "Through that? Nobody would come through against that tonight."

"Only Clyde. Clyde would and he's with them."

"They're down at your cabin too," Johnny said. He was heating a can of soup over a spirit stove. "That's what I came up here to tell you."

"Thanks," Colin said. His mind searched for something more, but he knew only that he was afraid for Johnny. "You got blankets?" he asked.

"Sleeping bag," Johnny said. "I'm O.K. Here, drink this." He handed Colin the soup.

While Colin was drinking Johnny came round to look at his wounded shoulder. "Leave it," Colin said. "You'll only start the bleeding again."

"You've got to take your coat off sometime."

Colin shook his head. "I'm pulling out soon as I've drunk this. Think you can get back down O.K.?"

"You can't go any place tonight," Johnny said. "You've got to stay here."

"And let them walk in on me when I'm asleep?" Colin shook his head again. "I've made it this far and I can make it to where they'll never find me."

"You didn't kill that guy, did you? Not like they say you did?"

"I killed him," Colin said slowly. "Jesus, Johnny, you don't know how easy a man dies until you've done it. You do a little thing, just moving your finger. And after that the biggest thing you can ever do won't change it."

"He must have done something to you first," Johnny said.

Colin shifted his body sharply and sat staring at the little flame of the spirit stove for a long while before he answered. "Yes," he said slowly. "He did something. He tried to burn the cabin. It wasn't my cabin, Johnny. It was hers." He looked at Johnny. "You and Robbie knew about her, didn't you? I know Robbie did."

Johnny moved his feet and looked down at them. "Sort of," he said slowly. "You wrote letters all the time."

"Burdick had no business doing that. She never did anything to him." Colin stared gloomily into the flame again. "Don't ever kill a man, Johnny," he said. "Nothing's big enough for that. They're so empty when they're dead." He reached forward and pushed back the tent flap. "I've got to get moving before I stiffen up." His voice was suddenly urgent. "They'll be coming close now."

"They'll never come tonight," Johnny said. "You could sleep. I'd wake you at first daylight."

Colin took his rifle and his pack and stood up outside the tent. "Help me on with it, Johnny," he said.

"You've got no place to go," Johnny pointed out at the storm. "You can't live a night out in that." But he held the pack while Colin slipped his right arm through and settled the tump line.

Colin held out his hand. "Don't worry, Johnny. I've got a place to go to. Tell Robbie I had a place to go to."

They shook hands and Colin went out of shelter into the storm again. It was almost dark now and his body had stiffened during the short rest; but he had taken the spare snowshoes he kept in the tent and traveling was less difficult. For a little way he followed the trail towards the Gully, squarely into the face of the storm. Then he turned off at right angles and began to climb the sharp ridge that led to the face of Amabilis Mountain. He felt fear then, a clear, penetrating, physical fear of death and loneliness, of the growing darkness and the storm and the dangerous way ahead of him. He wanted to turn back to Johnny in the tent, to go in and lie down and sleep until Clyde came to wake him. But his body loosened as he climbed and he felt its strength again and found strength in the sound of the storm about him. Fear died and he felt freedom.

The ridge grew suddenly steeper and there was little snow on it. He kicked his snowshoes off, slung them on his pack and went on again, climbing faster than before. It was almost dark and he could see only a few feet in front of him, but he knew where he was and he turned from the ridge across the steeply sloping face of the mountain. He stepped carefully now, counting his steps, and so found the tiny sheltered crevice he was looking for.

It was scarcely more than a crack, cut deeply into the face of the mountain, protected at the lower end by a sharp turn that killed the winds drawing up it, shut off abruptly thirty or forty feet from the turn by a straight bold face of rock. He had spent a night there once before, many years ago, an uncomfortable night with a single blanket and no fire. The next morning he had gone out and cut half-a-dozen little stunted trees and piled them at the lower end of the crevice. He found them now, dry and brittle under the fresh snow, and lit a small fire. Then he took the blankets from his pack, rolled into them and was quickly asleep.

He woke suddenly and thought he had slept until daylight. But he saw the embers of his fire still red and knew it could not be daylight. He looked up and found stars in the clear sky above the crevice. His wounded shoulder sent a wave of pain through his body as he sat up, but his mind felt intensely clear. He took more wood and stirred his fire to fresh life and felt the warmth of it against his face and body. He ate a meal from the food in his pack, then folded his blankets away, picked up his rifle and climbed out of the crevice.

The wind met his body like a singing sheet of ice. It poured in swift and sweeping steadiness across the open face of the mountain and drove against the peaks until they gave back a great body of deep sound in vibrations that quivered against the sky. Colin felt the snow strongly crusted underfoot, saw the full moon high and brilliant in the sky, looked down and saw an infinite swirling whiteness of wind-driven clouds over everything below him. He began to walk, boldly upright, striding like a giant, across the steep face of the mountain.

As he walked, pain left him and fear drew far beyond reach or recall. For a little while Burdick walked with him, a quiet calm Burdick who shrugged his shoulders and found death as small a thing as life. Then Martha was with him and Curly Blake and Terry Murphy and laughter was with them all, loud and free on the clean sweep of the storm under the mighty vibration of the peaks. Colin strode across the face of Amabilis Mountain until dawn showed light beyond the clouds in the east and the moon began to pale in the west.

He had used up the mountain then, had traversed the whole head of the valley. But he crossed to the mountains of the west side and followed them down towards the pass to Hidden Valley. New clouds came high on the wind and snow swept under them, blurring the sun as it rose, then burying it behind fold upon fold of sweeping whiteness. Colin came to the narrow corridor and turned along its level floor. All through the night he had sought for Mildred among the others who had come to be with him on the face of the mountain. She came to him now in the snow, in the quiet of the narrow place between the mountains. Her voice was with him and the feel of her and the strength of her. He came to the end of the corridor, looked down into the snow that whirled and drifted over Hidden Valley, and knew surely that she was there also.

He dropped from the corridor into the deep snow of the little platform above the ledge trail. For a minute or two he stood there, kicking the snow away, clearing space for his jump. Blocks of snow dropped away from the movements of his feet, broke, broke again and disappeared among the flakes of falling snow. He tested himself, feeling his arm for pain, and there was no pain. Cold was no longer cold and the sounds of the storm had become silence. There was brownness where whiteness should have been on the falling snow. Colin knew that he was tired, that he must jump to the ledge trail and follow it down to her while there was still a little strength left to him. He moved his feet again, to clear away a last lump of snow, then felt the platform heave under him. He jumped wildly and with all the strength of his body. For a moment he was crawling on his hands and knees, reaching blindly for the stretcher that had been torn away from him and the wounded man it had borne. Then he knew that his body was falling, that it would find the death his soul had neither sought nor feared.